SWORD OF

A Novel by

Green Hill Publishers, Inc.

THE NORTH

Richard White

Pegma Books   *Ottawa, Illinois*

10 9 8 7 6 5 4 3 2 1

Printed in the United States of America

Copies of this book may be purchased from the distributor for $13.95. All inquiries and catalog requests should be addressed to Pegma Books, Box 738, Ottawa, Illinois 61350.(815) 434-7905.

Published by Pegma Books/ Green Hill Publishers, Inc.

ISBN: 0-89803-122-2

to
STEPHEN AND DIANE McCUE
"I was a stranger, and ye took me in."

Matthew 25:35

Acknowledgments

My debts are legion. For information, for introductions, for hospitality, for an encouraging word, my thanks are due to Lord Pentland (Henry Sinclair); Viscount Thurso; Sir Iain Moncreiffe of that ilk; Mr. Robin Prentice, deputy director, National Trust for Scotland; Mrs. T. C. (Muffy) Lethbridge; Mrs. Mary Catherine Sinclair; Messrs. Alan and Peter McBean; Mr. Wallace Jones, president, St. Andrew's Society of the State of New York; the staff of the National Library at Edinburgh; the staff of the Carnegie Library at Wick, in Scotland, and those of the county library at Kirkwall, Orkney. For typing and proofreading, thanks go to Jean Fanelli and to Frances Ewers, true friends to the craft.

To the late Frank Glynn of Clinton, Connecticut, and the late Tom Lethbridge, director of excavations for the Cambridge Antiquarian Society and for the University Museum of Archaeology and Ethnology, my gratitude is as deep as it is tardy. It was Glynn who found the final link in the long chain of evidence confirming Sinclair's visit to Massachusetts, and it was Lethbridge whose brilliant detective work confirmed Glynn's find. It is on their work that this novel rests.

Finally, and most especially, my thanks go to Frederick Pohl. His tireless labors in the Sinclair cause are a monument to scholarship and determination. His book, *Prince Henry Sinclair*, is the definitive account of the life and voyages of that great Scot. His kindness to me, a stranger, will be long remembered.

PART I

1

Dead. *My father is dead.*

Young Harry Sinclair remembered again the clatter of hoofbeats in the starlit courtyard beneath his window, the horse snorting and blowing, the courier's quick steps over the flags, the candlelight summons to his mother's chamber, the mingling of her tears with his as she held him close, seeking to give what she could not find—comfort and consolation.

Harry lay full length on the tender grass under the great oak that had flourished there at Rosslyn Castle even before his great-grandfather, Sir William, sheriff of Edinburgh and chief of the Sinclairs, had been granted the barony.

The oak was already of a great age when the boy's grandfather, Sir Henry, rode out from Rosslyn to fight for the noble Bruce at Bannockburn. And it was under this same oak that he had said farewell to his father, Sir William, bound away with the Douglas on Crusade against the Saracens in Andalusia. The tree still lived.

Harry fought back his tears, remembering, remembering . . .

"It is God's work we do," his father had said. "Should I fall in the fight, I think I could not find a better death."

Then he kissed the boy's mother, Lady Isabel, and swung up into the saddle. "Remember your duty to your mother, boy," he said, "and to Rosslyn and your own good name. God keep you in His care."

God, dear God, what a brave show his father had made, riding out

3

at the head of his troop, the sunlight glinting on armor and arms, the soft breeze bearing back the clink of steel, the creak of saddle leather. Harry, then but twelve, had clambered up into the arms of the oak for a last glimpse of his hero father faring off to glory and the grave.

Had his father known fear at the last? the boy wondered. Had he suffered greatly in his dying? Harry had heard of the Saracen ways, how they fought like hell's own minions, giving no quarter and asking none; and how they sometimes burned good Christian knights alive in their armor.

"God damn them," the boy whispered. Then he crossed himself as if he would erase the sin.

How would he die? Would he, like his father, fall in battle? Would he wet his sword with heathen blood? Would his own blood drench some piece of pagan earth, his bones to molder in alien dust?

So be it. He would not flinch, but stand to the foe and —

"Harry! Ho, Harry! Show yourself, lad!"

Young Sinclair started up, blotting his cheeks on his sleeve. "Over here!" he cried, forcing strength into his voice. He spied his cousin Ingram Gunn on a fat pony trotting toward him across the broad expanse of lawn. Behind Gunn, similarly mounted but moving much more slowly, came fair Janet Halyburton and Harry's cousin Malise Sparre.

"Good day, coz," cried Ingram, leaping down from his mount. "What are you doing off here by yourself this fair morning?"

"A question for a question, coz. Why does that great toad dally along with Janet so?"

Ingram, a freckled fair-haired boy of nearly the same age as Harry, shrugged. "Why, coz, as he hath scant skill in arms, he will try his luck at *amor,* I suppose. But come, come, coz, unknit thy brows and leave off scowling. You do not think that Janet could be taken by such poor bait as that?"

Harry Sinclair's gray eyes squinted as he watched the slow progress of Janet and Malise over the lawn. "Toad!" he muttered. "My father's requiem was sung five days ago. Why does he tarry here at Rosslyn?"

"Why, coz, I do suppose our uncle is not so foolish fond of the fellow's face that he would bid him hasten home. But smile, lad, lest you frighten the ponies." Ingram waved his arm and called, "Here's Harry! Come along, come along!"

"Good morrow, kinsman," said Malise Sparre as he reined up. "I trust we do not intrude upon your solitary musing."

"Not on my musing, kinsman," returned Harry, favoring his hulking cousin with a sour look. Then he turned to the girl and said, "I am glad to see you, Janet."

"And I you, Harry." Janet, her honey-colored hair shining in the sun, smiled down at him. "I trust you are well."

"Not so well as I have sometimes been, but I am fast improving, thank you. What brings you to Rosslyn this day?"

"My pony, good sir, brought me here. But 'twas to see you I bade him bring me."

"Why then it is a most worthy and deserving beast," said Harry, smiling now. "I am in his debt."

Janet laughed. "A sugar lump would square accounts, I think."

Young Sinclair bowed to the pony. "Gentle beast," he said, "when you make up your daybook, set me down for a lump—nay, a loaf of sugar, due and payable come Michaelmas."

Just then the pony took to nodding his head, and Harry clapped hands and cried, "A bargain, a bargain!"

"Well, now," drawled Malise Sparre, "'tis wonderful to see how my kinsman can converse with beasts."

"Why, as to that, kinsman," retorted young Sinclair, "you have seen me do so ere this."

"Did I?" Sparre's brows arched up. "Tell me when this was, for I do confess it hath escaped me."

"Why, sir, not a quarter hour gone I stood upon this very spot and exchanged good morrows with a toad."

Sparre's pale face flushed crimson. "Push me not, Harry Sinclair, I warn you. In mourning or out of mourning, you'll earn yourself a drubbing with your mouth."

"To me, sir!" cried Harry. "Come! And we shall see who drubs and who is drubbed before you are an hour older."

Ingram stepped in between Harry and Sparre's pony. "*Pax*! For shame. Be not so wroth and hot. The day's too fine for wrangles."

Janet Halyburton tossed her head. "Aye," she said, with a haughty sniff. "I have not come these twenty miles from Dirleton to witness brawling."

"Your pardon," said Sparre, doffing his cap and bowing low in the saddle. "'Tis only that the old sow at home has eat her farrow, and is in consequence so lonely that I thought to persuade good cousin Harry to come bide with me awhile and restore the old sow's spirit with his talk."

At that, even young Sinclair had to grin. "'Twas well thought of, kinsman," he said. "Your tender heart must be the fame of sty and wallow."

Sparre laughed in his turn, but there was that in either's eyes that prompted Ingram to play the placater. "Come," he said. "The sun is near the midpoint of his journey. Shall we lose this blessed day? I tell you, Harry, we were bound to take Malise to see Meg o' the Glen ere he sets out for home. Will ye no come wi' us?"

"What? To the witch woman? I think the parson would not like it."

"Oh, peace to the parson. Aye, and to the pope, too. 'S no harm in it, coz. She'll tell you your fortune and call up a bogle, or a goblin, maybe to tell us the latest news from hell."

"Humph. As to my fortune, I know right enough I shall be baron here at Rosslyn and shall ride against the Saracen to avenge my noble father. But to see a bogle, well, that's worth the parson's wrath and then some. Wait here. I'll fetch my pony."

Through brake and briar the young folk rode, the ponies picking their way with care as they fared deeper and deeper into the darkling forest. For though the sun was at his noontime height, so thick were the branches interlaced above their heads that the young riders moved in a twilight world. No game stirred. The woods were still. There was only the distant chortle of the rushing river as it hurried on its way to the falls—that, and the soft faint riffling of the breeze at play among the greening leaves.

"Is it much farther?" asked Malise, grimacing as he waved away the gnats that swarmed about his ears.

"Only a bit," replied Ingram cheerily. "We'll see her kennel from the top o' yonder rise."

The ponies plodded up the wooded slope; and Ingram, leading, reined in. "Down there," he said, pointing.

Deep in the glen below, amid the dark tangle of ancient trees, a plume of smoke lazed skyward. The young people could just distinguish the sagging roofline of the witch woman's hovel. A dank, drear prospect it showed, that cloudless day. From the fair lawns of Rosslyn to this benighted spot was a journey of but a league and a little more. Yet the difference was that of May and November. There were all flowers and birdsong; here, rank weeds and bramble, the haunt of crow and owl.

"A rare spot for a murder," muttered young Sinclair. He turned to Janet. "How would you like to bide here all All-Hallow's Eve, hey? You'd see summat to tell the grandchildren, I warrant ye."

Janet's great eyes flashed left and right, and she shivered for all it was so hot and close under the dome of mingled branches. "I'd not bide here even on Christmas Eve for all the gold in England."

"No harmful thing can rise and walk on Christmas Eve."

"Even so," murmured the girl. "Even so."

"Well, for gold," volunteered Malise Sparre, "for gold I might hazard the venture."

"On All-Hallow's Eve?" Harry's laugh raised an angry red to his kinsman's cheek.

"Would you, high-and-mighty Harry Sinclair?" Sparre flashed back.

"Not I," retorted Harry shamelessly. And he laughed again. "I hope I would stand up to a Southron or a Saracen, but I'll not look for quarrels with things a body cannot shoot or skewer."

"Nor I," chimed in Ingram Gunn. "But are we going to sit here wagging our chins, or—Hist! Listen."

The young people froze. Rising in the hot stillness like the smoke from her chimney, the witch woman's voice was heard:

Bones, bones, bones.
The huntsman's sweetheart moans.
He rode away at break o' day;
His horse returned alone.

"Jesu," breathed Malise. "There's a tune to dance to."

"Afeared, kinsman?" taunted Harry, who was himself feeling a chill that centered in the region of his liver.

"I am," Janet said.

"And I," said Ingram, laughing. "But there's the fun in it, to be afeared and go ahead. Come on."

Harry Sinclair grinned at his impetuous cousin. "Lead on, then."

The four urged their mounts forward, skittering down the ferny slope and pattering up to the dooryard of old Meg's crazy hut.

There was Meg, clad in castoff rags, her lank gray hair hanging down over her face as she muttered and mumbled over the stuff simmering in her great iron kettle. She did not look up nor look around, but kept stirring away and crooning her weird refrain, "Bones, bones, bones."

"Whose bones, old woman?" demanded Malise Sparre, looking to Janet for approval.

Old Meg straightened her bent back and turned to look at her visitors. With knotty fingers she brushed back her unkempt hair and revealed a face like a wizened apple, a face as old as time, as brown as earth, as seamed and wrinkled as a raisin. Meg had but one eye, and that a cat's eye, cold and green, unblinking. Her nose arched out like a plowshare, and the chin beneath the toothless mouth turned up and all but touched the nose. Rheum ran from her closed and useless eye, and a great wart bulged on her cheekbone like a nut in a gray squirrel's pouch.

Her head swung from side to side on her ropy neck as, snakelike, she eyed her callers. "Who asks about my bones?" demanded Meg, her voice rusty as any raven's

The bold Malise did not reply.

"They are my bones!" the crone cried. "Mine! You will do well to keep your own."

"Please, Mistress Meg," said Janet, her voice quaking, "we've only come to hear our fortunes."

"Fortunes is it, my pretty one?" Meg nodded. "Yes, old Meg can tell fortunes. She has the sight. Yes, yes."

"Would you tell us ours, then?"

Meg suddenly cocked her eye at Janet and snapped, "Pennies?"

"Y-yes," Janet said, "we have pennies."

"Marry me off to a princess and I'll give ye a florin," said Sparre, who had by this time got some of his courage back.

"The girl first," said the crone. "Come, dearie. Do."

With a doubtful backward glance, Janet followed the witch woman into the hut. In the space of ten minutes, the girl emerged, cheeks pink, eyes shining, a smile playing over her mouth.

"Was it a good fortune, Janet?" asked Harry.

"Aye"

"Well, out with it. You look like the cat that got the cream. Are you to be the queen of Scots, then?"

"Something like. But do you go in, Harry—"

"I'll go," said Sparre, and he strode off into the witch's den.

"A very forward fellow, my kinsman," muttered Sinclair, gnawing at his lip. Then he said, "But tell us, Janet, what's to become of you?"

"Why, I'm to be married, of course, and I'll have six children, and a great nobleman for to be my husband."

"The baron of Rosslyn, I'll wager," cracked Ingram, laughing.

Harry Sinclair felt his face go hot, but Janet said, "I do not know. She said something about—about a kingdom in the sea."

"Sounds drear and damp to me, Janet," Ingram said. "Better marry old Harry here and stay in Scotland and keep your feet dry. Ha-ha!"

"Pah!" said Harry. "'Tis nonsense anyway."

"And who was it came trotting to see a bogle?"

"Well, but—"

"Hush. Here's Malise coming."

Sparre, his face dark as a thundercloud, came stumping up. "Daft old scarecrow," he growled.

"What ails thee, kinsman? Did she prophesy the gallows for ye?"

"Scoff away, Cousin Harry. Go in and waste your coppers if you like. See what kind of future she serves up for you."

"Ingram?"

"After you, Harry."

Harry ducked his head and stepped into the hut. It was but a single room, lighted by a few sticks snapping on the hearth. The boy could discern but little—a table missing one leg, a low bench by the hearth, a heap of dirty straw in the corner that served as Meg's bedchamber. Meg herself was seated at the table, a few coins at her elbow, a tallow candle burning on a saucer directly before her.

"Come, my pretty knave," crooned Meg. "Come closer. We shall see what the future holds for thee."

Meg fumbled in her rags and drew out a little pouch. From it she took a pinch of a fine powder and sprinkled it on the candle flame. A sweet odor filled the hut, and to Harry's eyes the candle flame seemed to grow taller and wider, spreading outward, outward, like the ripples made by a stone cast into a glassy pool.

"Put your money in my hand, lad, and Meg will tell you what the candle shows. Ah, good. Good." The old woman began to rock back and forth, her one eye fixed on the flame. "You will wander far, young sir, far, far from Scotland's shore. I see sails, many sails. And men-at-arms I see, their swords flashing in the sun. And there's a king, surely; but not a king, a woman on a king's throne, a king's scepter in her fair white hand. Now a storm rages. I see men drowning in a wild and raging sea; ships breaking up and sinking under the waves."

"Am I to drown, then?"

"Nay, nay. Hush. Be still. I see you, a man grown, walking the deck of a ship. West, west, west. A fair wind is at your back. Before you I see a wild and rugged coast, all grown over with great stands of trees.

"Men. Strange men, clad in the skins of beasts, their faces like earth and dead leaves, surround you. Above you a great bird circles and soars, circles and soars with a sheaf of arrows in his claws."

"But—but what means this bird?" Harry stammered. "Is it some ill omen? The arrows—?"

"Shh, shhh, shh," the old woman hissed. "No more. No more. It fades, it fades, it fades. A life of battle, a life of blood, a long wayfaring that leads to a soldier's grave. Steel, steel, steel. A hard way and a long way. No rest, no rest, but in the earth. A sword goes before you, shining, shining, and you must follow, follow, follow . . ."

The witch woman's drone trailed away; her chin sank lower and lower; the candle guttered and flared. All was still in the close and reeky room. A great oppressive weight seemed to settle on the boy's heart. He wanted to go, to run out into the air, but his legs seemed leaden; he had no power to stand.

Suddenly, Meg raised her head and fixed him with her cold cat's eye. "Knight and more than knight; baron and more than baron; liegeman of a pair of crowns, the sword shall lead you; the sword shall serve you; the sword shall cleave you and hollow out thy grave."

Young Sinclair found his legs, got to his feet, and, his face pale, his eyes shining, said, "So be it, dame. I follow the sword."

And he groped his way out into the timeless twilight of the glen.

There was little conversation as the young people rode slowly homeward under the dark old trees. Janet, dreaming dreams of her noble husband, was far away in future time. Malise Sparre, slumped and sullen, rocked along with the easy gait of his mount. Young Sinclair, head high, seemed to be gazing out at some distant prospect, with purpose plain in the set of his jaw, with a dream of glory in his eyes.

But Ingram, the irrepressible, could not forbear caroling as he jogged along.

At length, Malise remarked crossly, "You are merry, cousin Gunn. Did the old hag promise you an heiress for your portion?"

Ingram laughed. "Not so much, kinsman. Yet I am to inherit land sufficient to my need. But tell us first your own doom, and I will gladly tell you mine."

Sparre's thin lips twisted and he spat in the dust of the forest floor. "The daft old bitch said I'd reach for more than I can hold and lose my hold, my hope, my life in the space of a single day."

"Sad," replied Ingram, "sad, sad. I am distressed to hear it, kinsman. But if you can keep your hands to yourself, mayhap you can avoid this sorry end."

"Pah!" Sparre spat again. "Crazy old crow. But what of this inheritance of yours? Where lies this grand estate?"

"Why, kinsman, 'tis not so grand, but it is enough. It lies, unless the old dame lies, full half the world away. And if she lies not, I shall lie there, and the land itself lie on me while the worms work in my bones."

"Humph. If I can mine truth from all this lying, the old crone spoke of grave matters."

"Grave enough, Malise," agreed Gunn, nodding. "I shall lord it in a narrow mansion, while most ungrateful vassals consume my person wi' my portion. God 'a mercy."

"And yet you sing?"

"Should I greet, then, and blubber like a bairn that wants its mammy? A short life or a long one must end at last. 'Tis something I learned while still in dresses. What life I have I mean to live. I will not spend it weeping."

And Ingram Gunn took up his song again, and he sang them many a merry tune along the way to Rosslyn.

2

Master Harry, thy mother would see you in her chamber."

"Directly, Duncan." Harry Sinclair smiled at the old serving man. "Let me but brush the dust from my tunic and wet down these rusty locks o' mine, for I would not go shabbily to my lady mother."

"Aye, but if you water your locks they will but rust the more."

"Bring the candle closer, Duncan. Look. My beard is coming."

The old servant squinted and made a great business of scanning his young master's face. "God bless me," he said, "there is something. A shadow? No, 'tis not a shadow; 'tis—'tis—"

"Yes?"

"'Tis snot, by God! Yer nose wants wipin'. Hee-hee! Hey! No! Put down thy cudgel, Master Harry. Ye would not beat an old body."

"Beat it and break it and bury it," growled young Sinclair. "You sniggering, shiftless, shambling old scut!"

He advanced menacingly on the old man, then burst out laughing. "Duncan, Duncan, when will you ever give over thy crack-brained jokes and show a fit respect for thy betters? How my father endured you I will never know."

"Ah, sir, that was because thy father knew I could not help being an honest man."

"You, honest?" Harry laughed again.

"Aye, as this world goes. You will not find an honester."

"Angels and saints defend me from all such honest men. Why, when thou wast chief herdsman, did not my father beat thee for watering the milk?"

"Aye."

"And when thou wert but a stripling, wast thou not brought up before the magistrate for poaching?"

",Aye."

"And did not three separate serving wenches charge thee with lechery?"

"Aye, aye, and aye to all of it, Master Harry."

"And yet you call yourself an honest fellow."

"As this world goes, sir, I am in truth honest."

"Why, when you are in truth you are indeed honest, I grant you. But when in all your long and idle life were you found to be in truth?"

"Why, sir, whenever I was catched in a fault, I never did deny it."

"When you were 'catched.'"

"Aye."

"And you call that honest."

"As this world goes."

"Then God help you in the next world, Duncan, for 'tis plain you have helped yourself to much in this one."

The old man grinned a toothless grin. "St. Nicholas be my patron, sir."

"'Tis some other Nick, I do believe, and that a horned one," retorted the boy. "Now hand me my belt and be off with you. My mother awaits me."

"Aye, I never kept a lady waiting in my life."

"But left not a few in waiting, I'll be bound." Young Sinclair fastened his belt and quit the room, with old Duncan's cracked-voiced laughter following him down the stone stair that led to his mother's chamber.

Lady Isabel looked up from her needlework at the sound of her son's footfall. A smile lent warmth to the remote blue eyes and the sculpted cold perfection of the lady's face. Her pale hair, neatly arranged in filleted silver curls, caught the rushlights' gleam, and the flicker of their beacons lent a hint of color to her flawless waxen skin.

"My duty to you, madam," Harry said, coming forward to kiss his mother's hand. "You are looking well."

"I am well, my son; God be thanked. Come sit you down upon this stool and tell me all of your day's doings."

Harry seated himself at his mother's feet and said, "'Twill not be long in the telling, Mother, for 'tis an idle tale."

"You were idle, then?"

"Aye, and for no good reason. But when I'd done my exercises in the knightly arts, I felt on a sudden so low and muddleheaded that I did not even go to see the new colt, but only wandered off alone and dreamed away the morning altogether."

"Ah, well, the blood runs thick at this season. I shall ask the leech monk to make you up a purge."

"Nay, Mother, I do not want it," protested the boy. "'Twas but a passing mood that brought me low. The holy brother's medicine would bring me lower still. Besides, my cousin Gunn came riding up at noon with Janet Halyburton and Malise Sparre. I could not long be dull with Ingram there."

Lady Isabel eyed her son shrewdly. "'Twas Ingram, then, that saved the day?"

Harry flushed, but he spoke out boldly. "I was very glad to see Janet, too."

"I warrant ye," his mother murmured. "And not so glad to see your kinsman Sparre."

"I cannot help that, Mother, for all his kinship. My cousin Gunn's as dear to me as any brother could be; he's more friend to me than kinsman. But as to Sparre," the boy shook his head, "not all the bonds of blood could make me sad to see him gone from Rosslyn."

"And yet," replied his mother, "I wish you could contrive to dissemble somewhat in this. Family is no light matter, and who can say when you may have need of a kinsman's boon?"

"I think my father would not have counseled so."

Lady Isabel's pale eyes widened. "Would he not, then? Thy father was a proud man, Harry. And his greatest pride was in his family. He never tired of telling how these very walls sheltered Wallace in the rising against Edward. And he could and would relate every noble deed of every Sinclair before or since that time. I never knew him to disown a kinsman merely because he did not like him."

"I would in all things be like my father, madam. Therefore, though I'll not dissemble, yet will I be ever civil to my cousin Sparre."

"Civility can be cold fare, Harry."

"I cannot serve a warmer and be honest, Mother."

"You are young to hold to so stern a standard, Harry. I have sometimes wondered why it is you do not laugh more, or romp, or caper like other boys your age."

"I do laugh, Mother, when there is laughing matter."

"With Ingram, yes, or with thy brothers, or with old Duncan even; but not with me, Harry. Never with me. It used to go to my heart to hear you rollicking with your father, laughing even when he played with you too roughly." Lady Isabel, her fair brow puckered in a frown, fixed her pale eyes on her sturdy son. "Why are you ever stiff and formal with me?"

"I did not know I was, Mother," said Harry Sinclair, dissembling now. For what could he say to this cold white beauty? She was indeed his mother; yet he could not, never could talk easily with her. She was to him like the virgin in the chapel, an image to honor, revere even, but never to embrace.

"You do love me, my son?"

"Aye, Mother."

"'Aye, Mother.'" Pain flickered across her lovely face. "Oh, Harry, Harry."

An awkward silence lay between them. The boy, damning himself for his inability to say whatever would give comfort to his mother, shifted his weight on the low stool. "I—I had an adventure today, Mother," he said.

"Then you were not idle all the day."

"No. My cousin Gunn would have us all ride over to see the witch woman and have our futures told."

An amused smile smoothed Lady Isabel's face. "And did she foretell fair things for thee?"

"Aye, very fair." The boy paused a moment to collect his thoughts. "She said I was to be 'knight and more than knight, baron and more than baron, and liegeman of a pair of crowns.' "

Lady Isabel sat bolt upright in her chair. "Said she so?"

"Mother? What's the matter? Why—?"

"Go on, pray. Go on. What more did she tell you?"

"'Tis hard to remember all of it," said young Sinclair slowly. "There was something about a lady king and a great storm. It seems I am to be a sailor and a soldier. My life—she said my life was to be a long wayfaring, that a sword goes shining before me."

"A sword, you say?"

"Aye. She said I must follow the sword." The boy stared wondering at his mother. Lady Isabel hunched forward, a flush staining her cheek.

"Can you recall aught else she said?"

Harry shrugged. "She spoke of a distant land and men dressed in the skins of beasts. And there was something about a great bird with a sheaf of arrows in his claws. I could make nothing of it."

"But there was a sword?"

"Aye."

"And a pair of crowns?"

"So I remember."

"Jesu, Mary!" breathed Lady Isabel. She rose on a sudden and said, "Come with me, Harry. I've something to show thee."

The boy followed his mother down a torchlit corridor and up a flight of stairs to a small chamber in the northeast tower.

"Fetch a torch, Harry," Lady Isabel said. "'Tis dark as the grave in here."

Dark it was, and churchyard chill in the bare room. By torchlight, the boy could see only a narrow bed, an oaken *prie-dieu*, and a little low chair squatting in the far corner like some ancient and contemplative frog.

"Whose room was this, Mother?"

"Why, no one's really. I daresay few have slept here since the castle was built, save for a mendicant friar or some pilgrim bound for St. Katherine's well. But I have sometimes made of it a keeping place for things too poor for show and too dear for discarding." Lady Isabel looked about her in the circle of torchlight, then said, "I know. It's under the bed, for the old midwife put it there when the lady pilgrim came to her time in this very room three years ago last August. Poor soul. She was but little helped by it, I fear.

"But do you rummage under the cot, Harry, and bring forth what you find there."

The boy dropped to all fours and groped about under the bed. His hand touched metal. "Here's something," he said, and with some effort he drew forth a great and ancient sword. "By Peter, that's heavy! Whose was it, Mother? Some giant's?"

Lady Isabel smiled. "You find it hard to heft, my son?"

"Aye. 'Twould be no child's play to wield that blade. It makes my father's look like some mere misericorde to dangle at some perfumed courtier's side."

Lady Isabel seated herself in the low chair. "Bring it here, my son, and place it on my knees. There now. This sword, Harry," said she, stroking the pitted blade and gazing earnestly at her handsome son, "this sword belonged to thy great Norse forebear, Sigurd, who fell at Clontarf more than three hundred years ago."

Harry Sinclair, his eyes round with wonder, took up the sword in both his hands. "He must have been a mighty man," he said.

"The men of the North were mighty, Harry. And their blood flows in your veins. You are, I know, proud of thy father's Norman strain, and justly so. But from thy mother thou hast received a royal heritage. For my line descends from very kings—Eystein, Halfdan, Ingiald, names little known in Scotland, true, but names of mark in Norway."

The boy smiled. "Then I am very near a prince."

"Nearer than you suppose." Lady Isabel's tone was so earnest that the smile faded from young Sinclair's lips.

"What mean you, Mother?"

"Just this. My father was earl of Orkney. At his death, the title was bequeathed to me for my male heir. But because I was his second daughter by his second wife, the legacy has been a matter of hot dispute among my kinsmen. My sister's son—she being daughter to my father's first wife—claims the earldom on grounds of seniority, and this in spite of thy grandsire's stated wish."

"That is my cousin Alexander de Ard?"

"Aye. He is, through his guardians, the chief obstacle to your inheritance."

"But I knew nothing of this, Mother, Indeed, I am not certain I could locate the Orkneys on a chart. I knew thy father, Earl Malise, was lord of those isles, but I did not know I was his heir."

Lady Isabel frowned and smoothed away a wrinkle in the fold of her green silk gown. "I said nothing of it because I was loath to stir your hopes, my son. And thy father, God give him peace, did not encourage me in contesting my right. He—he spoke but lightly of the earldom. His wish and fondest hope for you were that you would reside here always, and bring honor and fame to Rosslyn.

"'For why should Harry fret himself over a scattering of windswept islands peopled by beggarly folk in thrall to Norway?' That was his word on it."

Harry smiled. "I can almost hear him saying that."

"He was a goodly husband, Harry, and a most excellent father. But he would not look beyond the Pentland Hills. His heart was here."

"As is mine, madam. And yet—"

Young Sinclair looked down at Sigurd's sword, and on a sudden his eyes were filled with dreams. His mother studied him, curious, remarking that the boyish roundness had all but left his face, that his strong jaw and his aquiline nose endowed him with an appearance of stern purpose and strength beyond his years. He had grown much since his father had said his last farewell. The sturdy limbs, the deep chest, the erect and easy carriage bespoke the man that would be—skilled in arms, hardy, fit to endure without murmur the rigors of active knighthood.

Lady Isabel had seen her son tilting at the quintain; she knew of his vigorous exercises with the poises, those heavy weights calculated to strengthen the sinews of his arm; and she had listened with scarce-concealed pride to his master's accounts of the boy's skill with sword and lance. He was, she knew, a superb horseman and a disciplined athlete. Surely, if the man redeemed the promise in the boy, Harry Sinclair could claim and defend his legacy.

It was much to hope—for her son to be both baron of Rosslyn and also earl of Orkney, premier noble of Norway. Still, there was the witch woman's prophecy. And there was Harry himself, with his keen intelligence, his character, his strength. Might it not be so?

The boy's voice broke the silence in the little room. "If the earldom's mine by right," he said, "I mean to have it."

He turned and faced his mother, but her approving smile brought from him no smile in return. He was, it seemed, cool and composed; not mere ambition but resolution prompted him. "Madam," he said, "I swear by St. Katherine, patroness of the Sinclairs, to claim and to keep that which thy father willed me."

Lady Isabel thrilled to her son's words, but her feelings showed only in the brightness of her eyes. "'Twill not be easy, Harry," she said. "King Magnus of Norway is determined to have his revenues from the earldom. My youngest sister's son, himself a Swede, had for a time control of the isles; indeed, Magnus even granted him the title, and I despaired of fulfilling my father's wish.

"But my brother-in-law proved at once arrogant and incompetent to rule, and so Magnus sequestrated his estates in Norway and declared his title forfeit."

"And none is now earl of Orkney?"

"No one. But thy cousin's friends are surely pressing his cause on Magnus. And he may well give ear to them, for he is displeased with the presence of so many Scots in Orkney now and fears that Scotland may look to the isles with lustful eyes.

"You, my son, for all thy Norse blood, are a Scot and, indeed, kin to the high steward. All this will Magnus reckon with, and all this will weigh against thy cause."

Young Sinclair nodded. "Even so, Mother, I am sworn to claim my inheritance. And I will. This sword I should like hung in the great hall so that it may serve as a constant reminder, a goad to my spirit even at our feasts and revels, so that I shall never be tempted to forget even for a day what it is I am to be."

"It shall be done, Harry. I'll have the armorer burnish the blade."

Harry Sinclair looked at the warrior's sword, flecked as it was with rust, and scarred and pitted with age and use. And he shook his head and said, "No, Mother. We will hang it just as it is. I like it better so."

3

The tilt yard lay like a green tile in the early afternoon sunlight, so squared and trim and meticulously kept it was. For the tilt yard was the special care of Oliver Knox, master armorer at Rosslyn, an old campaigner and a demanding taskmaster. It was Knox who was charged with training Henry Sinclair against the day when he would receive the golden spur of knighthood.

The old soldier was pleased, very pleased, with his young pupil this day, although he gave no hint of that by word or look. That was not the way of Oliver Knox. Harry had been some time in learning that a grunt from Knox was equivalent to an accolade from any other. And should Knox unbend so far as to say, "That was not so bad," then Harry's cup indeed brimmed over.

Knox looked down the length of the yard to where Harry was preparing for another run at the quintain. "God's wounds," said Knox to himself. "He's the spit of his father, even to the way he sits his horse."

Harry, couching his lance loosely in his gauntleted right hand, shifted easily in his saddle and called, "Ready, Knox."

Knox squinted in the light glancing off Harry's helmet. Unlike some other masters, the old veteran preferred to have his charge practice in armor. It was well enough in the early days to let the lad ride unencumbered, for God knows it is quite enough to manage horse, lance, and shield without the added weight of helmet and mail. But now, given the boy's mastery of his horse, it seemed to Knox unwarrantable pampering to allow his pupil the relatively easy run *sans* armor.

As for Harry, it was a pure and deep delight to have his little page, John Clarke, play squire and, on tiptoe, hand up shield and lance. For little Clarke, who looked on Harry with a spaniel's devotion, it was heaven. He would never be himself a knight, he knew; but a squire he could be. And were he to be squire to Harry Sinclair, he would count himself a made man.

"Gi' it a good thrust, Master Harry," piped the page, as he stepped back to watch the run.

At the signal from Knox, Harry swung his lance athwart and gave heels to horse. The stout black mare leaped forward into a smooth canter that carried her rider over the turf with the speed of eagles. Harry, all his thought focused on his task, stayed loose in the saddle, his eyes fixed on the target depending from the crossarm of the quintain. He did not see the riders approaching to the left; he heard nothing save the pounding of his own mount's hooves. It was not his intent ever again to feel the thwack of the sandbag that was only too ready to swing round and hammer the unfortunate whose thrust was off the mark.

The target loomed up large. Harry swung his lance into line and clamped the butt of it with his elbow. He sat his mount firmly, heels down, knees pressed tight against the mare's sides. Then—

A shrill whistle sounded off to the left. The mare, ordinarily the most imperturbable of beasts, went off stride; the point of Sinclair's lance hit off center; and, like the dispassionate judgment of doom, the arm of the quintain swung round, and the sandbag smote Harry between the shoulders with such force as nearly to unhorse him.

Pain, shame, and white-hot anger coursed through the boy's frame. Tears welled in his eyes, and he could taste blood from his lip where his teeth had torn it. Deliberately, he rode on a little way—to gain time, to let his head clear, to compose himself under his burden of humiliation. Then he turned his animal's head and trotted back.

His quick glance took in the two mounted figures on his right, Ingram Gunn and Malise Sparre.

"So!" Harry's mouth tightened and his face grew pale. While old Knox and little John Clarke looked on, young Sinclair guided his horse over to where his kinsmen sat astride their own mounts. He halted directly in front of Ingram Gunn and looked him full in the face. "Was it you, cousin, distracted my horse?"

Gunn looked aggrieved. "Can you think so?"

Harry did not answer. Instead, he turned to Malise Sparre and said, "Was it you, then?"

Sparre reddened, but the smirk had not quite faded from his face. "'Twas meant for sport," he muttered, his eyes avoiding Sinclair's.

"If it is sport you want," retorted Sinclair, "I will right readily oblige you." And he tore off his gauntlet and flung it on the ground.

"What's this? What's this?" cried old Knox, drawing up at Harry's stirrup, with little Clarke at his heels.

"Why, Knox," replied Harry, "my kinsman here is looking for some sport, and I have offered to joust with him."

"I—I have no arms," said Sparre.

"Do you but take up the gauntlet there and we shall find you arms and armor, too," said young Sinclair. "We know how to oblige our guests at Rosslyn."

Sparre was caught and he knew it. Yet he hung fire. He had been guilty of an odious breach of courtesy, and he knew that his slighter, younger kinsman had right on his side. He knew, too, that to refuse to take up the glove would cover him with shame. He looked to the master armorer in hopes that the old soldier would play peacemaker. But there was no help there. Conflicting feelings warred in Knox's soul. He had no wish to see anybody hurt, but his old warrior's heart craved justice—that, and the chance to see his prize pupil in combat, for Knox was human too.

"What say you, Knox? Can we not outfit this fellow?"

"Aye, Master Henry. I've no doubt we can."

"Well, then?" Sinclair's eyes bored into Sparre's.

Seeing no out, Sparre leaned out of the saddle and retrieved the gauntlet. "Very well, then," he blustered. "If you insist on playing the fool, I'll accommodate you."

In the space of a half-hour Sparre was armed and ready. Knox directed him to one end of the tilt yard, Harry Sinclair to the other.

"Now then, young sirs, let us have fair play, and God defend the right!" Knox raised his arm, then let it fall and the combatants charged.

Sparre, having scant skill at the tilt, determined to use the lowly strategy of maintaining his lance athwart in hopes of sweeping Sinclair clean out of the saddle. But Harry, scorning such tactics, would thrust straight like a proper champion.

On the horses came, their hoofs drumming on the sun-drenched sward. Shield to shield the riders sped. As they closed, Harry swung his lance over his mount's arching neck and, well ahead of Sparre's intended sweep, caught him fairly and high in the chest, just above the heart, and sent him crashing to the ground.

Harry wheeled his horse around, dismounted, and called for swords. Little Clarke trotted out and handed over a weapon, then went to where Sparre lay groaning. "Here's a blade for thee, Master Sparre," said the page, pert as any jay. "Take it and welcome, if thou hast the stomach to use it."

Sparre got to one knee, glaring at the little fellow. "Give it me," he growled, "and I'll flail your arse with it."

Clarke prudently lay the sword on the grass. "When you have finished the business at hand," he said, "'twill be time enough to abuse so small a thing as I."

"Remember, young sirs," called Knox, "the flat only. No blooding, or the match is forfeit."

Harry Sinclair, his feet planted firmly, his shield held high, cried, "Look to yourself, kinsman!"

Sparre made no reply, but seized his weapon and lunged forward, swinging wildly. Harry backed step by step under the onslaught, catching the blows adroitly on his shield. Then, as Sparre's arm wearied, young Sinclair took the offensive, driving Sparre relentlessly back under a veritable rain of blows. His anger under control now, Harry contented himself with administering a humiliating drubbing. He beat about Sparre's helmet with calculated mischief, intent on making the fellow's head ring.

Sparre, his brief surge of vigor spent, was unable to defend himself. He retreated, his shield ineffectual on his weak left arm, almost to the wall of the tilt yard. Then, in a last despairing effort to avoid the ultimate shame of being back to the wall, Sparre summoned up his last reserves of strength and deliberately thrust at his cousin with the point of his blade.

"Forfeit, forfeit!" shrilled little John Clarke.

But before Knox could intervene, Sinclair had turned the thrust aside and proceeded to belabor his opponent with such force as to bring him to his knees.

"*Pax! Pax!*" cried Sparre, dropping his shield and flinging his sword aside.

Sinclair stood over him, his nostrils pinched and white, his chest heaving. His blood was up, and wrath boiled in his veins. Only his knightly training kept him from giving way and utterly wasting the cowering fellow at his feet. But he was a Sinclair; he would not disgrace the name.

"*Pax* it is then," he muttered, and he turned on his heel and stalked off the field.

Later, as little John Clarke helped him out of his armor and tended him at his bath, Sinclair found his anger had fled and he smiled as the brightly clad page prattled on about the day's great victory.

"You were magnificent, Master Henry," declared the little fellow. "You whacked him and whacked him till he could no more stand up to you than to a tempest."

"Hand me yon towel, lad, and leave off prating." Sinclair rubbed himself till his skin glowed, then pulled on his hose and slipped into a fresh clean tunic. "Where're my shoes?"

"Here, Master Harry. Let me help."

Harry seated himself and allowed the page to slip the soft leather shoes over his toes. He grinned at the boy and said, "You're a blood-thirsty fellow, John Clarke."

"Aye, Master Harry. I cannot help it." John Clarke stood and straightened his own parti-colored hose and tugged at the skirt of his short jacket. "The Clarkes was ever a fierce and warlike people."

Harry laughed. "I'll have to watch myself around you then. I'd not want to stir the tiger in your blood."

"I'd never fly at you, Master Harry," said the little page, gravely. "I swear I would not."

"Hist! No swearing. You must set a good example for the younger lads. But, by the mass, I am glad to hear I've nothing to fear at your hands. I saw how you looked at Malise Sparre. I'd not give a groat for his chances if you were ever to set upon him."

"Oh, I would rend him, Master Harry. I would smite him and smash him and—"

"Holloa. Art dressed, Master Henry?" Honest Knox's broad face appeared in the doorway.

"Aye, Knox. I was just listening to Clarke here telling me the most harrowing, bloodcurdling things he'd do if ever he were to face an unworthy foe."

Knox nearly smiled. Then he said, "May I talk wi' ye for a bit, Master Henry? Alone?"

"Aye. Go along, John Clarke, and frighten the kitchen maids with your tales o' gore. Mayhap they'll spare you a tart or two in return."

With a bob of his yellow curls, little Clarke made his manners and scampered off.

"Now then, Knox, my good teacher, sit down on yonder bench and say what is in your mind."

The old soldier did smile now. 'Tis always thus, he mused to himself. They are boys till the first taste of victory, and then something inside 'em changes. They are man and master grown between the thrust and the fall.

Then to Harry he said, "Tell me, in your own honest estimate, how do you think you handled yourself today?"

Harry eyed the master armorer curiously for a moment, then said, "I was pleased, Knox. I believe I did very well."

"You know it?"

"I know it."

"Good, then." Knox nodded his graying head. "That is what I had to find out. For 'tis no use to be adept at anything if you do not know that you are so. And it is worse still to be fooled into thinking that your skill is greater than it is. I would be sore troubled in my mind, aye, and disappointed too, if I learnt you were wide of the mark in your estimate of your own powers."

"I have had an excellent teacher, Knox."

"Aye. I know that. For look you, Master Henry, I do not underestimate my own worth either. I do believe that we were well met and well matched, master and pupil. And I am very glad, very, very glad, that you neither mince about wi' false modesty nor blow and brag wi' fool's bluster when it comes to your gifts. For they are gifts, Master Henry, make no mistake. I can teach the elements and the refinements, but only God Himself can gi' a man the eye and the arm and the nerve that make a champion.

"You have the gifts as much as, and maybe even more than, did your father, God ha' mercy on him. The thing is, lad, you have a duty that goes with 'em. You'll be knighted in a few years' time, and you will have the care and keepin' o' this place and o' your goodly name. I believe you are bound to bring honor to both, but I must caution you to beware anger, Master Henry. Beware of it. I watched you close on the field this day, an' I know what a contest was goin' on inside ye—a harder contest than that which you won on the field. Ye nearly lost it, did ye not?"

Harry Sinclair reddened. "Aye."

The old soldier placed a hand on the boy's knee and looked earnestly at him. "Lad, lad, before I would have ye use my teaching in the heat o' anger, I had rather your good right hand be withered. No! Let me say this out.

"Master Henry, I am getting an old man. I have spent my life under arms. And I have seen too many good men die because a passion seized them and clouded their brains and undermined all the mastery o' their weapons. I'll have no pupil o' mine made crows' meat by a moment's rage. I care too much and I work too hard to have my time and teaching wasted over a fool's quarrel and a fool's wrath.

"Ye must promise me—nay, promise your own self—that never, never, never will ye let the heat of anger cook your brains and turn your breast into a naked target for any cooler hand to pierce."

The old man's voice was charged with such feeling that Harry stared at him in wonder. "Why, Knox," he said, "I do believe you love me."

The master armorer stood up. "Aye," he said, gruffly. "I do. And I loved your father before ye. So I ask you to promise you'll no make a by-Our-Lady fool of yourself and get your skull cracked over damned nonsense."

Young Sinclair stood and embraced the old soldier. "Knox, Knox," he said, "and I thought you a dour and tough old carcass with a lump o' flint where your heart should be."

"But do ye promise?"

Sinclair laughed aloud. "Stubborn, tenacious, single-minded Knox! Yes, yes, I promise. I'll make a vow on it when I take the sacrament tomorrow."

Old Knox sighed. "Good, then. Now, I do think ye were a little slow in the swordplay today. So when we take the field a-Monday, I want you to use the weighted blade. We have got to build up that arm of yours a bit more if we're to make a first-rate swordsman of ye."

Harry Sinclair could feel his eyes smarting, and he had to look away. "Good, Knox. We'll work on that, then."

"Aye. And I think ye'll have to work on your mother a bit, too."

"Oh?"

"Your worthy kinsman got to her with a tale of this day's doings, and I think you and I have had a fall from grace. She thinks me a bad and bloody man, I fear. And what she thinks o' you, well, that you will discover anon."

"Ha-ha!" Young Sinclair shook his head. "Poor Mother, Well, never mind. I'll square accounts with her directly. But what of my cousin? How fares he?"

"Why, sir, the fellow's been put to bed, and the leech monk's sent for. He will recover to go on to a long life of villainy, I fear. But his manners will be the better for this day's lesson.

"Oh, and t'other one, young Ingram Gunn, he's wanting to talk wi' ye. Ye'll find him at the stable, I warrant ye. He's a great lover o' horses, that one."

"Aye, and a great friend too. I'll go to him now, Knox. Fret not about my mother. I'll set things right with her." Harry turned to go, then he turned back and held out his hand. "Thank you, Knox."

The master armorer took the boy's hand in his and nodded. He knew wherefore the thanks were offered.

"I've had my thanks," he murmured, as he watched young Sinclair walk away. "God's nails, what a body'd give could Sir William see this son o' his."

It was dark in the stable, and warm, and ripe with horsy stinks, the scent of hay, the essence of old leather. As Harry's eyes adjusted to the changing light, he saw his cousin proffering a fistful of clover to the mighty black destrier that had been his father's favorite.

"Ingram?"

"Oh, Harry." Gunn looked up and smiled. "I was just telling Gobelin here what a fine joust I've seen this day."

"Knox said you wanted to see me."

"Aye. I've a message for you—from a lady that dwells not far from here."

"Janet?"

"Who else?" Ingram sighed and rolled mischievous eyes to heaven. "Aye, me! That I should be a mere go-between in this. You'd think a girl o' Janet's breeding would look higher. But there, she is perhaps put off by my dazzling beauty and my courtly airs."

"I may put you off your feet and on your back, an you don't leave off your nonsense," growled Harry. "What's the message?"

Ingram handed him a folded sheet of paper. "Here, coz, you must read it for yourself. She did not tell me the burden of her news."

Harry took the note and stepped to the stable door to catch the light. "Damnation!"

"What's the matter?"

"She's going away."

"Janet?"

"Aye. Her people are packing her off to the nuns at Perth to finish her schooling. She leaves a-Tuesday."

"This is hard news, coz," said Ingram, coming over and laying a hand on Harry's arm. "I am sorry. Let us hope the holy dames cannot persuade our Janet to take the veil and vows o' barren spinsterhood."

Young Sinclair's eyes flashed fire. "No fear," he said. "I'd storm the nunnery before I'd see that day."

Ingram took a sudden interest in the beams overhead and whistled himself a soft bar or two.

"You think I would not?" demanded Harry.

"Hm? Would not what?"

"Storm the nunnery."

"Harry, Harry, d'ye think I'd ever doubt it?" Ingram grinned. "Come, cheer up. 'Tis early days to be fretting yourself over the lasses. You've your spurs to win and wars to fight and a wide world to wander through before you think o' weddin'."

"Aye, but Janet—" Harry bit his lip and broke off. "Well, then, I shall send her letters."

"Ah, letters. I had a letter once."

"From a sweetheart?"

"No such thing. 'Twas from my father, who had gone a pilgrim to Canterbury Town in England, bidding me to say my prayers and mind my mother. Still, it was a letter. It made me feel quite, quite grown up, as I remember. I carried it about with me for weeks, till it quite wore out wi' handling.

"I say, Harry—?"

"Aye?"

"Tell me," said Ingram, taking up a scrap of leather and toying with it, "on the field today, why did you ask me if I had caused your horse to stumble? You surely did not think that I had done it."

Harry shook his head. "No coz, I did not. But I was that wroth I could not trust myself to speak to Sparre at first."

"And if I had done it, Harry. What then?"

Young Harry Sinclair turned unsmiling eyes on this, his best-loved friend and kinsman. "I should have served you as I served him."

Ingram nodded. "It's what I thought," he said.

4

Sinclair took shelter in a niche in the castle wall and from his pouch drew forth a precious bit of paper. He smoothed it out flat on his knee and read again:

"Dear Harry,

"In some ways it seems I have been here all my life. And yet the days and weeks fly by. My French is much improved by daily conversation, and I have become quite a competent needlewoman. But, alas, I fear I shall never acquire the gift of music. Dame Eleanor told me yesterday that I am no more tuneful than a rock. But I can play some several pretty tunes upon the harp, and if I cannot sing I can yet make music.

"There was much excitement here last week, for the Joiners' Guild presented a play about Goodman Noah. We were given leave to go, it being a moral and acceptable entertainment.

"Dame Eleanor scolded me for laughing when Noah beat his wife, but I could not help it. She was such a shrew—Noah's wife, I mean; we will not speak of Dame Eleanor, and poor Noah such a longsuffering man, that it did my heart good to see him thump her. Plainly, it was just what she needed, for she was mild as milk and sweet as honey thereafter.

"I am often lonely here, for all that my days are so full. I do have some one or two particular friends, but the best has gone off to be married to a rich old knight her family's found for her. She cried so at leaving that it near to broke my heart.

"Many a girl here envied her, but not I. For while I would be glad to quit this place, I would not wed an old knight for all the gold in England. Not, sir, that I have any objection to knights, but only to old ones...."

Harry Sinclair grinned. It would be three mortal years before he would be knighted, but even then he would not be old. So long as Janet could tolerate a young knight, all would be well.

He drew his cloak more snugly about him, for it was chill, even cold, in the sunny courtyard. The wind was in the east and blowing strong. There had been a hard frost the night before, and ice skimmed the puddles outside the stable door. Still, it was good to be out in the air after the forenoon's drudging over lessons with Brother Michael. Lord! Would he never have done with schooling? Days like this called to his blood and urged him to horse and away.

But it was, he knew, important that he be able to reckon his accounts, to write a fair hand, to converse easily in Latin and in French. And if Boethius made his head ache, still it was fine to read the *Chanson de Roland*. (He wished he could have crossed swords with the treacherous Ganelon!) A book's a bonny thing, he thought, especially when it tells of jousts and wars and high adventure. But better the thing itself than read about it, even as he would liefer see Janet than read her letter.

Well, he would see her at Christmas, *Deo volente*. Last Yuletide he had danced with her and stolen—nay, not stolen, for it was gladly given—his first kiss. And she had given him the lock of hair that lay curled in its silver housing against his breast.

But what a weary time it was since he had seen her! Would she find him changed, he wondered, for he was now near fully grown and daily plied the razor over his cheeks. Old Knox accounted him a thorough master of sword and lance, and held that he was ready now to enter the lists against knights full grown. That would be a great day, when he could joust in earnest with the champions of the land. No question whose favor would be streaming from his helm.

A cloud crossed 'twixt earth and sun, and Harry shivered despite the comfort of his fur-line cloak and cote hardie. He stowed Janet's letter in the leathern pouch that dangled at his belt; and, not quite willing to go indoors again, he stepped along quickly toward the stables. He'd not gone far, however, when little John Clarke—whom the years could not seem to lengthen—hailed him.

Harry turned, grinning to see the page scurrying along before the wind like a parti-colored leaf blown from the branches of some strange tree. "Dig in your heels, man," Harry cried. "Dig in, or ye'll be wafted clear to Norway."

"Aye," puffed the little fellow, as he drew near. "I emptied my purse in almsgiving, and there's naught but my own great bulk to hold me down."

"What's called you from the fireside, young jackanapes? 'Tis unlike you to venture forth in such rough weather."

Little Clarke blew on his fingers and hopped from foot to foot. "Nay, by Peter, I do not like it. But I have news that will not keep, and you shall have it so soon as we take shelter from this most un-Christian weather."

"I was on my way to the stable."

"So far?"

Harry laughed. "Let us nip into the armory then, for I would not have your news spoiled by long keeping. Come; in here."

"Phew! God bless me," cried the page, dropping down on a bench and huddling deeper into his crimson cloak. "I think the parsons have it all wrong about hell, for 'twould be to me a heaven to be forever warm."

"Why, then, go to hell, an it pleases you; but not before you tell your news."

Little Clarke wiped his nose on his fingers. "To hell it is, then, and I suppose I shall have to run and fetch for you there as ever I did here."

Sinclair chuckled. "You young rogue! So I'm to burn with you, hey?"

"Surely you'd not leave me there alone with all those English?"

"Ha-ha! Well said, John Clarke! Satan himself's a Southron, I do not doubt it; and many a Plantagenet's a-roastin' there below to keep him fed wi' English beef and mutton."

"But not this present Edward's father, I think, for he had his share of hell on earth, if all the tales I've heard o' him are true."

"A Plantagenet's a Plantagenet, and an Edward's an Edward. Grandfer, father and son, they may lie and smoke in hell till their hands are cleansed of Scottish blood, and then we'll talk o' pardon.

"But come, lad, what's the news?

"Why," said the page, drawing his knees up under his chin, "'tis only that there'll soon be one less bachelor at Rosslyn."

"How now, what's this? That old fool Duncan's no been snared again?"

"Nay, nay. 'Tis a younger man by far."

"Not you?" Sinclair looked incredulous.

"Ha-ha-ha! God's wounds, Master Harry. Ha-ha! No, 'tis not I. I could not bear to make one lass happy at the expense of so many others. 'Twould be too cruel."

"Well, then?"

"Well, 'tis this way. I was passing by thy mother's chamber and heard her deep in talk with Friar Donal."

"And you stopped to listen."

"God forbid, Master Harry! You think me a common spy?"

"Nay, not common." Sinclair's smile was tinged with irony. "But as you were only passing by, what is it that you chanced all unwillingly to hear?"

"Why, only your mother saying, 'She is the wife for my son, Friar Donal. 'Twould be a perfect union.'"

"No more?"

"No more. For just then Kit, the dairyman's daughter thy mother's got so fond of, came tripping down the hall, and I could not linger wi'out seeming to be listening. Which, of course, I was not."

"Of course." Sinclair smiled. "So they talk of wedding, hey? Ha-ha! Well, Janet will have a merrier time of it this Christmas than either of us thought likely.

"Here, Johnny, here's a florin for ye. I think I will go in now; my mother looks for me, most like, and I would be found right readily." And Henry Sinclair strode off whistling merrily.

Little John Clarke spun his cold coin in the air and caught it neatly. "Now God bless all masters when they be blithe and lightsome," said he. "And God send me good news to carry every day."

Lady Isabel, her Psalter in her lap, looked up as Harry entered her chamber. With her fair hair loose and flowing, her lovely white throat set off by the rich deep blue of her gown, she looked scarce old enough to be a mother, let alone mother to so tall and stalwart a son.

"God be wi' you, Harry. Your coming here is timely. I was about to send for you."

"Indeed? Then I am doubly glad to be here."

"There is a matter I would discuss with you, touching your future prospects. Stay but a moment whilst I send for Friar Donal." Lady Isabel summoned the pert and buxom Kit, but lately chosen to be her tire-woman, and dispatched her to fetch the friar. That reverend person was prompt to respond, and came huffing in on sandaled feet with many a salutation to his lady.

"Friar Donal, you are welcome," said Lady Isabel. "Pray, be seated and impart to my son here the matter we spoke of earlier this day."

The priest, his great belly a monument to many a hearty nooning, plumped his bulk into a cushioned chair, adjusted the folds of his coarse brown robe, and leaned back with a heavy sigh. He fixed Harry Sinclair with his shrewd little eyes and, lacing his fat fingers over his paunch, said, "Do you, young sir, know well the church's view of the married state?"

"Aye, I think I do, Reverend Sir."

"You know, then," said the friar, his voice rumbling up from deep in his chest, "that our Blessed Lord Himself accorded such dignity to holy wedlock that no Christian dare enter into it lightly."

"Aye."

"For God in His wisdom hath ordained that man and woman shall cleave to one another and beget offspring to be raised up to His glory. And though some folk are called to live apart from this world and forgo the pleasures of the flesh to better serve our Savior, the greater part of mankind are spared the rigors of the cloister and allowed to gratify the lower passions that the race may be continued unto the last day."

"Aye." Harry passed his hand over his face to hide a smile at the evident envy Friar Donal felt for 'the greater part of mankind.'

"You, young sir, I thought to have the makings of a fine monk."

Young Sinclair's eyes widened at this. But the stout friar went on undeterred. "You have an aptness for learning and a good understanding. I have no doubt that you would have risen high in the church. But you have responsibilities to the name you bear and to the titles that will be yours. And these cannot be lightly put by. We deem it expedient, therefore, that you should marry and beget sons to carry on your line."

"So I would think," murmured the youth.

"As your Lady Mother's confidant, I am acquainted with her views in this, and I assure you they quite correspond with my own."

"Quite," said Lady Isabel, smiling.

"And so," said Friar Donal, shifting his great hams in quest of a more comfortable position, "your mother and I have discoursed at length concerning your future station in life. We have concluded that it would be well for you to marry, and to marry as becomes your station, with all its heavy cares and grave obligations.

"With great folk it may not be as with the commons. 'Tis well enough for Tom the ploughman or Gib the butcher to be ruled by appetite in choosing Jenny or Jane. It matters little, so long as they enter into a lawful union and keep their vows.

"But for people of rank, it matters a very great deal; for the blood must not be sullied, nor estates risked, nor fortunes marred by imprudent, careless marrying. This is the consideration that must be ever in the forefront when we weigh the pairings of the great.

"You, young sir, have this to consider. The blood of kings flows in your veins. The lands and titles that were your father's are soon to be your own. And, so your Lady Mother tells me, there is yet another title, and that a lofty one, within your grasp."

Harry glanced at his mother, but her eyes were on the friar's lips as if all truth and wisdom thence flowed.

"It is with these weighty considerations before us, that your noble mother and I have been these several weeks deliberating. Nor have we failed to refer our judgment to God in humble prayer."

"It seems you have been diligent, Reverend Father," murmured Harry.

"I am glad to hear you say so, young sir. It has been with me a most serious matter, and 'tis good to know my care and thought do not go unremarked."

"And yet," said Harry, rising from his stool and stretching cat-fashion, "and yet I could wish that I had been consulted in a matter that touches me so nearly."

"Ah, but my dear young sir, that is why we are here at this hour. We grayer, wiser heads have given much time and thought to your own good interests, and we mean now to impart to you the happy outcome of our long deliberation. I think you will not be displeased."

"As to that, Sir Priest," said Harry, folding his arms across his broad chest, "I can assure you that it pleases me mightily to think of marrying, and I am pleased to know that you and my mother find your own thoughts tending thither."

"Good!" cried the friar, smiting his knee with a fat palm. "Then you will be glad to know that this very morning letters have gone forth from here to Denmark to—"

"To Denmark?"

"Aye, young sir, to Denmark, to negotiate a nuptial contract between yourself and the Princess Florentia."

"The Princess Florentia!" Harry Sinclair's voice crackled like heat lightning. "What—Mother! D'you hear this? Do you agree in this—this brokering? Yes, yes, I see that you do. You were party to it.

"Well, by God, I will have none of it! Me? To be let out for bid like any Southron princeling? No, madam, I assure you. I am no haunch of beef to be sold off on Market Day. I am Henry Sinclair, a freeborn Scot, by heaven! I'll not be bartered and bid for like some poor bond slave."

"The Princess Florentia! I'll have none of her, were she twenty times a princess. I had rather be an anchorite and live on roots and berries than be a titled booby chained against my will to some pampered royal milksop. Great God Almighty! An I heard this not with my own two ears, I—"

"*Pax, pax!*" cried the priest, starting up from his chair, his face flaming to the color of his bulbous nose.

"A pox on you, thou great gross ale-and-roast-meat friar! Thou breaker of fasts and swiller of wine! I'll no be marketed by the like o' thee. No, I thank you. Get thy great guts gone out from this, thou mealsack, thou pudding, thou—thou lump!"

Young Sinclair made as if to offer assistance with his foot, but Friar Donal, surprisingly nimble for one of his girth, scuttled clear. "My lady," he yelped. "You will not let me be used so! 'Tis mortal sin to strike a cleric. Ward off thy son; his soul's in peril."

Lady Isabel, her pale face paler still, her voice charged with scorn, cried out, "Enough! You, Harry, remain. And you, Friar Donal, had best get thee to the chapel and compose thyself. This unseemly bellowing hath made my head ache. Go, friar, and leave this intemperate and unruly boy to me."

Right gladly, the portly son of St. Francis quit the room. And Harry Sinclair, small knots of anger working at the corners of his jaws, turned to his mother and said, "I am no boy, madam. I pray you, do not apply that word to me."

"Why, sir, when you act the boy what else shall I call you?" Then Lady Isabel's voice softened. "Come, Harry, sit you down and hear me out. You know your interest lies nearest my heart. Be still now and let me lay all before you; then judge as becomes your father's son, with reason and in cool blood."

"I will hear you, madam."

"So stiff and cold, my son? Ah, well. If this is how my love and care are to be repaid, so be it." Lady Isabel seated herself opposite her son. "If we cannot parley as loving son and loving mother, let us then treat of this like allies in a common cause, two generals who, to achieve a higher good, can lay aside their lesser differences and come to such terms as will assure the accomplishing of the desired end."

"Which is?"

"That you be chosen earl of Orkney." Lady Isabel eyed her son shrewdly. "You do desire that, do you not?"

"Aye."

"Well, then, consider. Magnus of Norway is most anxious to secure his isles and have his revenues from them. But he hath small reason to entrust their keeping to a Scot. The Orkneys lie nearer Scotland than to Norway, and even as the Hebrides fell from Norway's grasp into Scottish hands, so could it befall with these.

"Magnus is not ignorant of your high-placed Scottish ties, and these he may well consider a grave impediment to your claim. Were you to ally yourself with Denmark—peace! Let me finish.

"Were you to contract marriage with this royal infant, then might King Magnus look kindly on your claim. It is that simple.

"Do but consider, I beg you, what is at stake here. As earl of Orkney, thou shalt be a very prince, entitled to wear a coronet, to have a sword borne before you in ceremony. In Norway thou shalt be accounted first among men of rank, and shalt yet retain thy lands and honors here in Scotland.

"Think, Harry, what a prize to be had at so small a cost—a prize not only for thine own keeping, but for thine heirs and their own in perpetuity. Think of the luster added to thy father's name! The glory of it, Harry; the pride and the power! Think on it."

Young Sinclair rose and paced the room. "In truth, madam, I have thought on little else since first you told me Orkney could be mine. But, God help me, I cannot forswear the love I bear toward Janet Halyburton; not for crowns nor coronets nor all the wealth of Norway's store."

Lady Isabel rose and went to her son. "Look at me, Harry," she said, taking his strong hands in hers. "That you love Janet is no news to me. And for all your youth, I would not make light of it. You think me a cold and ruthless woman. No! Do not deny it. You do, and that I cannot help. But, my son, surely you realize that with the privileges of rank there go also heavy burdens. Kings, princes, nobles, these are by God's ordinance given power to rule and govern the conduct of lesser folk, to maintain order, to keep the peace, to ensure the security of the realm.

"For this, they are richly recompensed. But for this also they are most seriously charged to put duty ahead of self—such duties as that of preserving the purity of the blood, of continuing the line, and of securing in safekeeping all titles, lands, and honors due them and their posterity."

Harry sighed. "I know all that, and have no quarrel with it. Indeed, I am quite willing to wed, to get children, and to secure what's mine and theirs. Janet's blood—"

"Is Scots. And Magnus cannot risk losing the isles to Scotland."

"God's blood!" The word escaped in a whisper.

"Are you to be more privileged than kings, Harry? D'you think they marry according to the desire of the heart?"

"Nay, good mother. And that is why there be such a deal of whoring in all the courts of Christendom. Would you have me a whoremaster? Would you make of Janet a common doxy?"

"I would have you do your duty."

"At whatever cost to me?"

"Duty, Harry, is all that separates great folk from the rabble. It is the only test of greatness. It is the one foundation of all precedence, all subordination, all order under heaven. Make no mistake about it. Once great folk in any number put pleasure before duty, disorder will become general, and chaos will complete the ruin of all things lawful and good.

"Why even from England we hear reports of insubordination and unrest among the common people. You yourself remember the monk that tarried here last Lady Day and talked of the wicked writings of some country parson—Lackland or Langland or some such name, it was—who stirs the folk to rebellion against the established order. 'Tis an omen, Harry; I fear it."

Harry Sinclair uttered a mirthless laugh. "As to that, 'twould give me small sorrow to see all England in revolt."

"Could it be contained in England, perhaps. But mark me well. Such words and notions as this ungodly parson spreads have power to travel. You are young to remember the years of the Black Death, but you have heard many speak of it, how it coursed through all nations like a torrent, sweeping all before it as it ran. So, just as I would tremble to learn of plague in England, so do I tremble now to know that the seeds of insubordination find congenial soil there. Believe me, Harry, let one state fall, and another will follow; and another and another, until every noble house is pulled down, and any renegade priest or smock-clad churl may set himself up as Lord of Misrule.

"If we who are great will not carry out the duties that to greatness fall, then shall we fall ourselves, and all decency and all order fall with us." Lady Isabel's splendid eyes flashed fire. "Duty, Harry, is everything. You cannot shunt it aside and still account yourself a worthy son of William Sinclair."

Harry's face clouded. His eyes looked strangely old, and his fine frame, usually so erect, seemed bent now as with a great burden. For a long moment he seemed to be seeking something lost amid the rushes on the floor. Then he raised his eyes to his mother's own and said, "Madam, I will think on what you have said."

"And think on this, too, my son. I have told you of your cousin de Ard's much pressed claim upon the earldom. What I have not told you, and for good reason, is that another claimant hath come forward."

Sinclair's brows shot up. "Who now?"

"Thy cousin, Malise Sparre."

"What?"

"Even so. I knew so long ago as when you so sorely beat him on the tilt yard, but feared to occasion worse for him by telling you."

"Jesu, Mary," muttered Sinclair, rubbing his forehead, "but that sits ill with me. Malise Sparre to wear my coronet?"

"It need not be, my son, if you seize this opportunity that Friar Donal and I have put before you."

Sinclair shook his head. "Madam, I will think on it. I pray you will excuse me now, for I am weary and much troubled in my thoughts."

"Adieu, then, my son. God give you rest. Only think well where your duty lies, and all will be well."

But he only said again, "I'll think on it." And he retired from his mother's chamber.

5

"Christ, Janet, ye cannot think I want to wed that child."

Janet Halyburton, her lovely face framed in a fur-trimmed hood against the Christmas cold, inwardly damned the tears that filled her hazel eyes. But she lifted her round little chin and spoke forthrightly. "I know nothing of what you want, sir. I think you know no more than I. But then, what can I know of the ways of earls and princelings? Or of princesses, for that matter."

"Janet, dear—"

"Not dear enough, it seems. Not so dear as thy mother's ambition; not so dear as a coronet, or a puling sickly royal poppet; not so dear—"

"As dear's my life," rasped Harry Sinclair, clasping her in his arms.

Janet pushed against his chest with her small hands. "No, sir. No more of clipping and kissing and false vows. I'll not be toyed with."

Sinclair let go his hold, and as Janet retreated a pace, he said, "You know right well I love you."

"Love? Yes, you did speak of it as I remember. Aye, and write of it, too, whilst I pined away in the company of those cold virgins. Well, I have kept your letters, and do gladly now return them to you to serve as models for correspondence with your betrothed."

"I do not want them."

"Nor do I." Janet tossed her head, causing her hood to fall back and reveal the sheen of her hair in the torchlight that filtered through the narrow windows to dance on the cold battlements of Dirleton Castle. How lovely the girl had grown! She was a girl no longer, and none was more conscious of that than Sinclair. And yet, this festive night, he was losing her; he could physically feel her withdrawal from him, from his life, and there was nothing he could do or say that would bind her to him.

"The dancing has started. I must go in."

"Janet!"

The girl paused in midflight, poised like a young deer, ready to bound away at the first snap of a twig. Sinclair dared approach no nearer. All his hope trembled in the balance; and yet, he knew, there was no hope. Still, he said again, "Can you deny you love me?"

"In time, sir, I will be able to deny it. Until then, I will deny you further access to this house and to me."

"No!"

"You are plighted to another. There can be no honorable intercourse between us now. And if I loved you an hundred times more than I did once, I would not debase my honor or my father's name to play the whore. Not even for you. I wish you well of your princess, sir, and of your high ambition. Between them, they may contrive to warm you on nights like this."

"And what of you, Janet? What will you do?"

"Why, I thank you for your interest, sir. What will I do? Tonight I will dance my legs off, and tomorrow I will go back to my nunnery to become a novice and wear out my knees and my life in prayer."

Sinclair's face went white. "For God's sake, Janet!"

"For God's sake, Harry." And she went in to join the dance.

Sinclair did not follow. He could not, would not beg. There was nothing more to say. Janet was right. He could offer her nothing but an unlawful love—that, and all the attendant heartbreak and shame. He who had so often expressed his contempt for the mannered adulterers of the courts had found himself only too ready to take up the game himself. Bitter stuff rose in his throat; his head hurt; he felt hot and flushed despite the ice-edged wind whipping in from the sea. The sounds of revelry within jarred like the din of Satan's forge. Not clarion, viol, and tabor, not laughter and song, but the discord of a score of gibbering imps shaping swords and daggers on hell's own anvils he seemed to hear.

Sick and faint, he leaned his sweating forehead against the cold stones. God! Why had he listened, why had he yielded to his mother's counsel? What good, what use was an earldom to him without love, without joy, without Janet?

A sudden roar of laughter and shouts of "Wassail!" assaulted his ears. Christ's wounds! He must get out of this. He jerked his hood up over his head and sped down the treacherous stairs to the courtyard below.

There was no one about. Servant and master alike were making merry that night. Even the littlest scullion and turnspit were for this night at liberty to share in the general joy of Christmas.

Sinclair ran to the stable and himself saddled Ragamouffin, his gray gelding. He vaulted astride and, with a cruel yank of the rein, urged his steed out into the murky dark. Once clear of the courtyard, Sinclair applied his spurs, and the great horse sprang forward into a reckless gallop that quickly left Dirleton and the sounds of revelry behind.

In the great hall of Dirleton, the dancers capered and swirled in the torchlight while their elders sat long and drank deep. From his chosen coign of vantage in the shadows at the far end of the hall opposite the sweating musicians, Ingram Gunn lounged against the wall, his arms folded across his chest, watching with amused detachment the antics of the guests. A smile, not unkind, played about his mouth. He did not scorn these people and their play; he only preferred to stand aside and find his pleasure in observing theirs. For Ingram had changed. He was still gay, still quick with a song or a jest, but he had, in growing older, developed a knack for keeping a little distance between himself and others. Not that he was cold; never that. But he was blessed, or cursed, with a monkish gift for standing aside and auditing even those scenes in which he played a part.

Still, when he saw Janet Halyburton attempting to steal away unnoticed from the noisy throng, he was not so uninterested that he could forbear to intercept her. He had seen her leave with Sinclair; he saw her now alone and painfully distressed. And because he cared, he drifted quietly out into the corridor and called softly, "Janet!"

The girl turned, startled, then relieved to see the strong good-natured face of a friend. "Ingram, I am glad to see you."

Gunn smiled. "I have seen you looking gladder."

"I suppose my eyes are all red."

"Aye."

Janet bit her lip and lowered her gaze. Ingram said nothing, only waited. From the hall they could hear a gleeman singing a carol to the infant King. The voice rose high and sweet, its joyful burden all the more poignant for the contrast it made with the misery in Janet's breast.

The girl lifted her face to Gunn. "You knew, of course."

"Aye. He told me of it."

"Oh, Ingram, why?"

Gunn cocked a quizzical eyebrow. "Better men have been bigger fools ere now," he said. "Though, as this world goes, 'twould not be counted folly to trade off so much and more for such a prize."

"Would you do so?"

Ingram's lips twitched in a wry smile. "I have no such fair goods to trade with, lady."

"But if you did?"

"I could not conceive of wanting more." He shook his head in wonderment. "It fair amazes me, I do confess it. I have known and loved my kinsman since we were tiny boys together. Always I held him in such high esteem that where he would lead, there would I follow. Nor did I count it any less in me to acknowledge always his chieftainship in games or lessons or exercise of knightly arts."

"He is, I know, thy dearest friend."

"Aye, and that constantly. I think we never quarreled till now, and I am—"

"Quarreled? You and Harry?"

Ingram rubbed his crown with the flat of his hand. "Well, let us say that we commenced a passage of words. Or I did. But you know my cousin. He hath gained such a hold on his temper that now, where other men wax hot and wroth, he turns to ice; and words fall on him with less effect than sunlight falls on stones. I came away frostbitten."

"Was he so unyielding?"

"Aye. And when I faced him with his honorable duty to you, he reached down a ghastly Norseman's blade of ancient make, a grisly thing all chased with rust and greenish mold—indeed, I wondered if he meant to use it to put a period to my meddling. He held the horrid thing in both his hands and, with a look of granite purpose in his face, he said, 'I have sworn upon this sword to claim my earldom. And nothing in heaven or on earth will turn me from my purpose.'"

A tear slipped down Janet's cheek; and Ingram, his careful heart unguarded for the time, yearned over the glistening drop like a miser lusting for a brilliant. He stepped to her and, with his thumb, gently wiped the tear away.

Janet, quite, quite broken, leaned her lovely head upon his breast. "Oh, Ingram, I love him so. God help me."

"Aye," muttered Gunn, stroking her soft silken hair, "God help us all."

Sinclair scarcely felt the bite of the wind; indeed, he was but half aware of the pounding hoofs and the rippling stride of his mount. He rode as in a dream, or through one. There was no moon. The great oaks and slender birches that lined his route, lifting their naked arms to the heedless sky, loomed like giants on either hand. The rutted road was hardly visible at arm's length, so overcast was the bleak night sky.

Two miles, five miles, gray Ragamouffin flew. His blood was up, and the great horse began to sweat for all that it was so bitter cold. He tossed his head and blew the foam from his lips, then stretched his neck and charged along the familiar road to Rosslyn. Sinclair, loose in his seat, was a veritable centaur; horse and rider were as one. They knew each other well, these two, and had ranged far together. Sinclair trusted his steed, even as the horse in its own brute way had come to trust its master. And it would be no new thing for the pair of them to make twenty miles through even so black a night as this.

But then, even as Sinclair was about to pull Ragamouffin back into a walk, a coney fleeing the talons of a hunting owl burst from the roadside brush and leaped zigzag across their path.

The gelding shied, reared, then bolted headlong down the road as if hell's legions followed.

Sinclair, his cloak streaming in the wind, fought for control. A grin stretched the corners of his mouth, and his blood sang with the sheer excitement of it. "Curse you," he shouted, but half in anger, "will ye have us killed, then?"

He strove mightily to turn the animal's head, but Ragamouffin was having none of it; he thundered on like an avalanche; all that Sinclair could do was ride. And ride he did, laughing, cursing, the tears stinging his eyes, his cheeks nipped by the biting wind. A very goblin horseman he must have seemed, had any been there to see the flame-haired rider astride the mad and lathered demon steed.

On they came, careering wildly all down the dark roadway till the path veered away to the left. Here, Sinclair tried again to turn his horse's head, and here Ragamouffin went down like a felled ox, breaking his knees and flinging his rider clear.

The gray gelding screamed in pain, tried to rise, and could not. The beast lay over on its side to wait the mercy of the gathering cold.

A scant three yards off lay Henry Sinclair, face down on the frozen earth; he did not move at all. There was no sound save the rushing of the winds through naked boughs. Above the scudding clouds the constellations wheeled; earth's clock advanced an hour, two, three. The cold deepened; the iron frost tightened its hold upon the shriveled land.

6

Pain lay in wait like a feral thing, crouched, slavering, claws unsheathed, ready to lunge, to rend, and tear its prey.

Sinclair moaned, stirred, woke, and pain struck, raking every nerve and sinew with talons fell and keen. "God!"

"Easy, easy, young sir." A clear firm voice penetrated the sickly fog that clouded Sinclair's brain. A hand, dry and cool, rested for a moment on his burning brow. "You are fevered and much hurt. Drink this; come, I'll raise you gently up. I'd not undo my handiwork by having you strangle."

Henry Sinclair blinked and squinted against the yellow light. A figure, a blur of gray, loomed at his elbow. A strong arm cradled his neck and raised his head so that his mouth could meet the lip of a brimming cup. Cool and faintly tart, a soothing potion flowed over his parched tongue, and the welcome wetting made him for a grateful moment forgetful of his pain.

"There now. You will find your hurt lessened somewhat by this; but 'twill return, I fear, in a few hours. I will try to anticipate the time and bring you another cup ere then."

"You—you are the leech monk, Brother Ambrose."

"Aye, young sir." The nut-brown face crinkled in a smile. "You did not know me yesterday, nor yet the day before, but did rate me roundly for a clumsy, fumble-fingered muttonhead. 'Muttonhead' was your word, I think. There were some others that will not bear repeating."

"I—I cannot remember. If I gave offense—"

The leech monk chuckled. "Who could offend so poor a thing as this I call my self? Think no more of it, my friend. I have called my self by harder names ere this."

"I am home, then?"

"Aye. A carter happened on you and your poor beast at dawn of Stephen's Day. You he recognized and brought home for me to mend. Your horse, alas, was all but dead, and the good churl sped him out of this world with a stroke of his ax."

"My poor Ragamouffin," murmured Sinclair.

"Lie back now and rest," urged the monk. "You have some bad hours and days ahead of you. You must not tax yourself unduly."

"I am not—crippled?"

"No, no. Though God He knows you are lucky to be living at all, let alone likely to be a whole man again. Thy shoulder's broke, and thy left arm, too. Thy fingers and toes were so near to frozen that I feared for a time you would lose some part of them. But beyond that and three or four cracked ribs, why, you have no great matters to contend with.

"There is the swelling in your right ankle, to be sure, and the great lump above the left temple. But if the lungs stay clear and no mortification afflicts the flesh, there is every reason to hope that you will be up and stirring by Candlemas."

"I shall live if I don't die, hey?" Sinclair started to laugh, but a stab of pain cut him short.

"Enough now," admonished the monk. "I'd a deal of work to set your bones. I'll not have my labors undone by idle talking. Rest. Sleep if you can. And I will come back in a little while to see what you can do with a little gruel."

Brother Ambrose padded softly from the sickroom, his spare frame fading wraithlike from Sinclair's blurred vision. Down a long dim passage the monk hurried, coming at length to Lady Isabel's chamber. Her door was ajar; Ambrose scratched lightly and stepped in.

At her *prie-dieu*, Lady Isabel knelt in prayer. She did not hear the leech monk's soft footfall. Ambrose hesitated a moment, then he said, "My lady?"

She looked up then, and the good man's tender heart was moved by the traces of grief on the proud pale face. "Henry?" she said, and all her care was in her voice.

"He was sensible; he knew me. I gave him a draught of the sleepy potion, for he was in grave pain. But I am greatly heartened by this turn. In a few hours' time I will go to him again and try if I can get him to take a little nourishment."

Lady Isabel crossed herself and got to her feet. "You think he will recover, then?"

Brother Ambrose nodded. "Very likely. He is young and strong. The hurts he hath sustained are no light matter, but I make no doubt that he will rally now and soon be mending."

"God be thanked."

"Amen."

"May I go to him?"

"Soon. Do you but wait till I have seen him again and tended to his needs. Then shall you have a few minutes with him."

"Brother, we are in your debt."

"Not mine, but Christ's. He is the physician; I am only His instrument. But pray you, lady, leave off grieving now and rest yourself, lest I should find myself with yet another patient on my hands. I think you have scarcely slept or tasted meat these three days together."

Lady Isabel favored the monk with a wan and piteous smile. "In truth, I could do neither while Henry lay so sorely stricken. He is nearest my heart in all things, Brother Ambrose. I think I could not live did he not also."

Brother Ambrose eyed the woman curiously. "You love him so much?"

"He is my firstborn." Lady Isabel held her head a bit higher. "I would sacrifice anything for my son's good."

"Including your son?"

"What?" The self-satisfied expression drained from the lady's face. "What did you say?"

Brother Ambrose slipped his hands into his wide sleeves as if he would get a grip upon himself. "Lady," he said, with a gentle smile, "I have no authority to preach; I speak only as a friend to this house. And as your friend and brother in Christ, I must caution you against excess in love."

"What? For my own son?"

"Most especially. There is that in him which promises a man of most uncommon abilities and worth. But he must be allowed, even helped to the fullness of a man's estate, or—"

"And who is of more help than I?"

Brother Ambrose sighed. "Alas, lady, how often it happens that when we seek most to help, we manage only to make matters worse. I have myself, when I was very young, trusted too little to God and nature, too much to herbs and unguents. There are some ailments which, if left alone, will soon or late correct themselves. Too diligent purging, too much application of medicines can sometimes speed a soul to judgment before its time. I mind me of a poor woodcutter that once I treated for an ague. He—"

"Good brother, I fear you have lost me." Impatience danced in Lady Isabel's bright eyes and a slight flush tinted her cheek. "What has all this to do with me? Or my son?"

Ambrose unsheathed his long brown hands and set to rubbing them briskly. "Well," he said, taking a turn about the chamber, then pausing and looking directly at Lady Isabel. "Well, sometimes the long way round is shortest, but let my try to be more pointed.

"I have spent these past two nights and three days in your son's company. And I have heard things—words, muttering, cries such as any physician is auditor of over years of attending the sick. Ordinarily, we pay scant heed to any of it, knowing that bodily hurts can cause a very saint to rant and curse and speak things unseemly. But your son," Ambrose shook his tonsured head, "your son pierced my heart with his unhappy raving. I began to fear some sickness of the mind would make vain all my care about his broken body."

"What? Is he mad?"

"Nay. For when I spoke with him just now, 'twas plain enough he is not afflicted in that way. But, lady, I fear he is not happy."

"Happy? Who is happy? What is happiness but a theme for bards and gleemen?" Lady Isabel sniffed haughtily. "Make my son well, brother, and we shall leave happiness to fend for itself."

"God wants us happy."

"Then let us trust to God to make us so."

The leech monk nodded. "'Tis fairly spoken, my lady. Yet, when we contrive to set our will against another's happiness, do we then not go against God's will? Your son—"

"Is my chief concern, good brother. I would not have you think me ungrateful, but it would be best if you were to tend to his hurts and leave his happiness to me."

"And Lady Janet's?"

"Who spoke of her?"

"Why," said Ambrose, mildly, "your son did."

"In his ravings, perhaps. His mind was straying."

"I spoke also to his young kinsman, that loyal fellow who hath haunted the castle corridors since your poor lad was brought in by that carter."

"Ingram Gunn? You spoke with him of this?"

Ambrose nodded. "Aye, lady."

"Wherefore?"

"Because I knew him for your son's friend, and I thought to learn from him something of the matter that troubles your son's mind and keeps him from repose."

"And what said he of this?"

"Why, lady, he told me an old story, one familiar to me since I was but a boy in my father's house. A lad loves a lass; she loves him. But something, or someone, thwarts their love, breeds misunderstanding, and blights all hope of happiness. It is an old, old tale, one I had all but forgot; but if I remember right, the lovers at last are reunited and all ends happily and well."

"In stories, it may be so."

"Never in life?"

"It may be. I do not concern myself with moonshine."

"Not now, perhaps; but surely once when—"

"Brother Ambrose," Lady Isabel's tone was brittle, "I think we have quite talked the topic out. There is nothing—"

"My lady!" A fresh young voice called from the doorway.

Little John Clarke entered the chamber. "I have letters, my lady, brought here by a sailorman but lately come from Denmark."

"Bring them to me, Clarke. No, you need not wait. Nor you, brother. My son must not be left unattended. Look well to his needs, I pray you. God be with you."

"And with you, lady." Brother Ambrose inclined his head in a slight bow, then followed little Clarke into the corridor outside.

"How does my master?" Clarke asked, as he paced in step with Ambrose, his bright garb a rainbow beside the soft gray of the leech monk's robe.

Ambrose smiled down on the stout little page. "He has much pain and a dull time ahead of him. But I think we may look for him to be quite himself again ere long."

"I am glad to hear it, brother," said Clarke, his black eyes snapping. " 'Twould be a sad loss to me were he to be dead or maimed."

"Would it so?"

"Aye." Clarke nodded his curly head emphatically. "When he is knighted, I mean to ride with him against the Saracens. We will kill them by the cartload, and I shall return to Scotland a made man."

Brother Ambrose chuckled. "What a martial spirit's here! You, my young friend, are a terrible man."

"Aye," returned Clarke, proudly. "War's the sport for any man o' mettle."

"Ah, and what if a man of mettle should find himself skewered on a Saracen's blade?"

" 'Twill not happen. Master Henry, he'll be Sir Henry then, he would not let harm come to me. I am too valuable to him."

Brother Ambrose placed a kindly hand on the page's shoulder. "I believe you are right, John Clarke," he said. "And now, you must excuse me while I go and tend to our suffering friend."

Ambrose entered the sickroom and found Sinclair sleeping. Asleep also in the chair beside the bed was Ingram Gunn, his chin sunk on his breast, his lute lying on the floor beside him. The leech monk frowned; then, the physician in him giving way to the saint, he smiled and traced the sign of the cross over the sleeping comrades.

Ingram, just at that moment, opened one eye. A slow smile lighted his freckle-peppered face. He yawned, stretched, and rose quietly from his chair. Ambrose, a finger to his lips, motioned Ingram out to the corridor.

"Good day, Brother Ambrose," said Gunn, stifling another yawn. "Wuff! Pardon me. I am but half awake."

The leech monk's eyes twinkled. "And if 'twas my heavy step that waked you, I ask your pardon."

"Nay, good brother. For I heard nothing. 'Twas as if I felt someone was in my room, and the little sentry in my brain called me to wake and arm against intruders."

"You, young sir, were the intruder, and that against my strict order that none should venture into thy cousin's chamber. But never mind. Your claim of love and kinship takes precedence over mere physic. I freely grant it."

"I meant no harm."

"And did none, I am sure of it. Your cousin will welcome any pleasant distraction over the weary weeks ahead. I am heartily glad that you are here; I ask only that you do or say nothing that might distress him. And I know you will not wittingly."

"I cannot vouch for my wits this morning. But a little rest will set me to rights, and then I think you may rely on me for anything needful for my cousin's health."

"There is one thing I would caution you against," said the leech monk, halting and facing the sleepy-eyed Gunn. "Let your discourse with him be ever so wide-ranging; do not, I pray you, introduce the matter of Janet Halyburton. I fear—"

"Hist!"

"What? The Lady Isabel! Madam, what's the matter?"

The lady, her face drawn and paler even than its wonted hue, favored Ingram with not so much as a glance. "Brother Ambrose," she said, her voice but a harsh whisper, her eyes brimming with tears, "I would speak with you alone."

Gunn bowed. "God be wi' you, lady. I'll to my chamber."

"Now, then, lady," said Brother Ambrose, his mild eyes full of sympathy and concern, "what is it gives you such distress?"

"These, these!" cried Lady Isabel, waving some several sheets of paper almost in the leech monk's face. "We are undone, Brother Ambrose. Our hopes, our plans—"

"Pray, lady, do not weep. There's naught so bad as can't be mended." The good monk grieved to see that countenance crumple, the set mouth quiver, the cornflower eyes red-rimmed and wet. "Those are the advices from Denmark?"

Lady Isabel swallowed hard and nodded. "Even so. And curse the bark that brought them, and the news they bear. The Princess Florentia is dead, dead of a bloody flux, and all our hope of Orkney goes with her to the grave."

Brother Ambrose blessed himself. "The child's with God," he murmured. "May she have everlasting joy and peace."

"Better she had lived to find joy in Henry's bed," retorted Lady Isabel. "Dead! And gone to God, you say? And where's all Henry's hope now? His dreams? His future?"

"Lady, these too are with God, surely."

"God, indeed! Really, Brother Ambrose, I wonder you do not abandon all simples, balms, and possets, and leave your labors altogether to God's doing."

"So have I sometimes thought myself," replied the leech monk, sadly. "God He knows how little my scant skill avails. But 'tis our portion, nonetheless, to do what we can with what we have, trusting to God always to supply our many lacks."

"Oh!" Lady Isabel stamped her little foot on the rush-strewn stones. "You put me out of all patience. Find Friar Donal and send him straightway to me. We'll see if we cannot get more sense from him—more of sense and less of God, I truly hope."

She turned away abruptly and, with regal haste, retreated to the cold and hallowed precincts of her chamber. Brother Ambrose stood for a time, following her retreat with mournful eyes. "Would that God would grant me the power to heal you, lady," he murmured.

Then he went off about his errand.

7

There is a young gentleman to see you, Janet."

Janet Halyburton looked up from her embroidery. "A gentleman, Dame Alison?"

"Aye. The prioress is with him in her parlor." Curiosity sparked in Dame Alison's periwinkle eyes. She had taken the veil at sixteen, and knew but little of the ways of the world. Yet she had read romances, heard the ballads, and seen many a secular maiden leave the shelter of the convent to marry some shrewdly chosen husband who, if he was not blessed with a handsome person, had at least a handsome patrimony. That she herself would live out her life a virgin did nothing to diminish the plump little nun's interest in affairs of the heart. And the gentleman waiting was a very well set-up gentleman to be sure. Or so Dame Alison thought, and such was the thought she added to her announcement.

Janet affected indifference. "I cannot imagine who it is," she said, her voice cool in contrast to the warm pink mantling her cheek. "In a little time, I shall profess my vows, and I think I might more profitably spend my time at prayer than in conversation with young gentlemen of whatever degree."

"You were not praying just now," Dame Alison pointed out.

"I should have been shortly," retorted Janet. "I really think, Dame Alison, that I had better not grant this interview. Do you go tell Reverend Mother that I am obliged to be at chapel to keep a vow I made."

"What vow is that?"

"Oh, just a vow."

"And made just this instant, too, I'll warrant. Can you not keep your vow in half an hour?"

"Really," said Janet, smoothing a wrinkle from the skirt of her novice's habit, "if you like, Dame Alison, you may go in my stead."

"What, to chapel?"

"To the parlor. As you find the caller so—so interesting, perhaps you should visit with him in my place. I am sure Reverend Mother would not object."

Dame Alison giggled and blushed a fiery red.

"You are a ninny," remarked Janet, not unkindly.

"And you are a greater if you keep the gentleman—and Reverend Mother—waiting."

"Humph. Obedience to Reverend Mother is my duty, of course."

"Of course," agreed Dame Alison, bursting into giggles once more.

"Dame Alison," said Janet, slowly and with precise articulation, "you are a goose."

The merry little nun was still bubbling as Janet descended the stone stairway to the prioress's parlor. But Janet could hear little else but the thumping of her own heart as she approached the parlor door. She gave a tentative little scratch on the oak panel and then, at the summons from Mother Genevieve, entered the dim, stuffy little room, guarding her eyes and keeping her fair hands folded under the scapular of her robe.

Even with eyes downcast, Janet could make out the pair of goblets on the table, the spare figure of Mother Genevieve seated before the single window, and, to Reverend Mother's right, just the impression—the shadow, as it were—of a broad-shouldered figure in azure and scarlet.

"You sent for me, Reverend Mother?"

"Yes, child." Mother Genevieve's voice, although softened by the accents of her native France, was dry and brittle as old bones. "This gentleman has come a long and weary way to see you, and although it goes contrary to my general rule, I have agreed to let him speak some few moments with you."

"How are you, Janet?" The sound of a male voice in these sacred environs rang harsh and strange.

"It—it's you?"

"Aye." Ingram Gunn rose from his hard chair.

"Pray," Mother Genevieve interposed, "be seated, sir. And you, child, take the chair to my left."

Janet, a little dazed, and more than a little disappointed, groped her way to her seat. For a little time, all sat like figures in a *tableau vivant*, silent and still. Then the brave Ingram cleared his throat and tried again. "How are you, Janet?"

"Why, I—I am well, thank you. Well and content."

"You look well."

"Thank you." Janet stared at the hands in her lap as if they were other than her own. Then, raising her eyes only slightly, she said, "Are you well?"

"Very fit, thank you. Aye."

"And—and everyone at home?"

"All quite well. My—my cousin, whom you may remember—he that had such a dreadful fall from his horse at Christmas—?"

"I do remember hearing something of it."

"Aye. Well, he grows daily stronger and has left his bed at last, although his—"

A brisk scratching on the parlor door cut short this involuted parley.

"Come," demanded Mother Genevieve.

Dame Alison's wimpled face appeared in the doorway. "Reverend Mother," she cried, "I beg you pardon me, but the cook and the gardener are promising to murder each other."

"*Ave Maria!*" cried the prioress. "Can there be no peace in this house? Dame Alison, stay here. I will attend to this."

Away went Reverend Mother, her black robe flapping militantly about her ankles. Dame Alison curtsied to Ingram and, alas, winked at Janet, then closed the parlor door and stood guard—outside.

"Janet—"

"Oh, Ingram, is—did he—?"

"He does not know that I have come."

The light went out of Janet's face. "Then—why are you here?"

Ingram crossed to her and knelt beside her chair. "Janet, listen to me, for God's sake. We haven't much time."

"Time? For what?"

"Janet, just listen, please. Harry needs you. He—"

Janet jerked her hand away from Ingram's urgent grasp. "I will not hear it, Ingram. Talk of it no more."

"Girl, you must hear it. He loves you and you love him. I'll no stand idly by and let two stiff-necked fools destroy their hope of happiness through senseless pride." He took her hands in his and said, "Janet, you do love him, do you not?"

Great tears formed on the girl's long lashes. "Ingram, please—"

"You know you do. And you know that his mother's ambition is all that came between you."

"Not quite all."

"Very well. 'Twas his ambition, too, and his folly in ever allowing Lady Isabel to rule him in this. But that's all changed now."

"Why? Because his infant betrothed is dead?" Janet shook her head. "I confess to you, Ingram, that when I had word of it I did hope your cousin might have the—courage to write to me and—and—"

"Janet, he could not."

"Was he so ill?"

"No; yes. Yes, in spirit he was gravely sick. Even as you are now."

"What, I? I do not understand."

"Pride, Janet, pride; the evil canker that works within your breast—and his—to both your detriment. D'ye not see? 'Tis as hard for him, harder even, to humble himself as 'tis for you to bend your pretty neck and yield to your own heart's prompting.

"Look you, Janet," Ingram said, pressing her hand, "what's one tiny gesture as measured against a lifetime? Could you not bring yourself to pen him a line or two to— No! Now, don't shake your head. Listen to me! Just to write a very little note, to wish him swift recovery from his hurts, what is that? Pooh! So small a thing I count it that 'tis scarce worth talking of. To spill a little ink—"

"Ingram, no! I cannot do it."

"What, then? Will ye wear out your life here in fasts and vigils? Will ye give your love to statues of cold stone?"

"Do not mock me, Ingram, pray. I am promised here. My father has paid a handsome dowry to—"

"Thy father would gladly have ye back and let the dowry go. You know it broke his heart to bring you here. And you know he loves you so that he would indulge your leaving at least as readily as he did your coming. And Harry—"

"Is a faithless, proud, self-serving wretch."

"Then write and tell him so! Give him an opening, Janet. Give him that much."

"I cannot. 'Twould be immodest."

"Immodest? Jesu!" Ingram got to his feet and ran a hand roughly through his dark brown curls. "Janet, you make me mad. Immodest! You prate like a mewling greensick girl, some paste-daubed Southron poppet, all airs and laces. You—"

The parlor door swung in and Dame Alison hissed, "She comes!"

In confused haste the players took up their former posts just as the prioress returned.

"Young sir," said that worthy woman, all huffed and flustered, "young sir, you have overstayed your time. I must bid you good day and a safe journey. Janet! Come, child. You must not tarry longer."

Ingram, his eyes desperate, rose and said, "For this courtesy, much thanks, Reverend Mother. Janet, think on what I have told you. I—I can say no more. Farewell."

Janet, with difficulty, found her voice. "Fare you well, Ingram, my—my good friend."

"Good day, sir, good day," said the prioress, briskly. And Ingram, without quite knowing how, found himself passing through the door and out into the brief bright midwinter's day.

As he flung himself into the saddle for the long ride home, the unhappy Gunn roundly cursed himself for being seven times a fool. Then he cursed women in general, Lady Isabel in particular, and, glancingly, Janet and Dame Genevieve. By the time he made the outskirts of Edinburgh he'd got as far down the list as Henry Sinclair; and him, kinsman and friend though he was, he excoriated with imagination and pith.

At Holyrood, he'd got to earldoms and aspirations thereto. Pungent animadversions on crowns and coronets sustained him to Blackford Hill, and it was not until he was in sight of Rosslyn Castle that he got to the headings of rough rides, rough roads, and rough weather. All these he dispatched with a thundering blue oath that all but impoverished his profane store.

He prodded his jaded horse into some semblance of a trot that carried him into the courtyard. There he dismounted, flung the reins at the shivering stableboy, and took the stairs at a dead run. Down the long cold corridor he flew, frost-nipped, mud-caked, saddle-weary as he was, brushing by serving wenches and castle minions like a blast of northern air, narrowly missing a collision with fat Friar Donal, and on up the torchlit stairs to his cousin's chamber.

He burst into the room without so much as a by-your-leave, and flung himself, chest heaving and cheeks aflame, into the nearest chair.

Henry Sinclair, wrapped in a shawl, sat next the hearth toasting the aches from his mending bones. He looked up from his book and, with a certain coolness designed to mask the start this brusque invasion had given him, said, "Enter, coz, and welcome, I'm sure. I would have opened to you, but I fear I did not hear you knock."

"Knock, is it?" wheezed Gunn, hunching forward in his chair. "I tell you, Harry, I'd like to knock some heads this day. And were you not sitting there a shawled and bandaged invalid, I'd choose your skull to start on."

Sinclair dropped his book. "I will be damned," he said.

"Aye. Most likely. For did not the parson say o' Sunday that pride's the chiefest sin? Oh, Harry, Harry, you mulish, stupid stubborn clotpoll! Get well, heal up, and meet me in the tilt yard that I may tickle a tune from your ribs with a good oak cudgel."

Sinclair could not help it; he threw back his head and laughed. "Why, you lunatic! What ails thee, boy, to come roaring in here like some pot-valiant noddy? The day that thou couldst best me in any feat of arms has never dawned and never will. Try me at draughts or else backgammon; there you might have some semblance of—"

"God damn you, Harry!" Ingram sprang to his feet. "You sit there braying like an ass, and every hour that passes brings you that much nearer to losing your one best hope of joy and comfort in this world."

"Ingram!" Sinclair's voice cracked like a whip. "Sit down, sir, and give over ranting. Now!"

Ingram, his fists clenching and unclenching, fought back his words and resumed his seat. In the brief silence that ensued, Sinclair studied his kinsman's face almost as if he were seeing it for the first time. Ingram returned his gaze unflinching.

"Well, now, coz," said Sinclair, calmly, "'tis plain enough you are sore distressed and not a little wroth with me. Did I doubt your love for me or mine for you, I think I could not with honor sit here and suffer myself to be thus rated, like some poor scullion that's spilt the milk or left the loaf to burn.

"But you are my childhood friend, and dearer to me than any man living. For that, I will put honor by and hear you out." Here Sinclair raised a forestalling hand. "But mildly, coz, I pray. Go mildly."

Ingram took several deep breaths, struggling for composure. He was thoroughly tired from his long ride; he was uncomfortably conscious of having, in his own view, behaved like an idiot; and he was decidedly surfeited with the pride and folly of his friends. Still, he would try.

"The thing is, Harry, the thing is this. You know right well that you have behaved unseemly toward Janet Halyburton, and—No, sir, let me finish if it cost me your friendship!

"You love her; you know ye do. And yet ye lift not a finger to mend this breach between you, a breach of your own making. I know I risk much in speaking thus to you, but, damn it, I do love ye both, and I'll no sit by and watch whilst the pair o' you let love slip away.

"You are the offender in this, Harry. And ye know it. Ye put ambition ahead of a heart that you yourself had studied and strove to win. And having won it, ye seemingly valued the prize so little that you could put it by for a chance—a mere chance, mind—of acquiring another title and dominion over some scattered windswept bits of earth."

Ingram rose and circled his chair, paused behind it and braced his hands on its carved oak frame. "I do not know ye, Harry. I thought I did, but I do not. Christ, man! You were to me the very paragon of honor; destined, I thought, to be the nonpareil of knighthood, aye, and of manhood, too."

"And now?" Sinclair's tone was dry, neutral, controlled.

Ingram rumpled his hair, then let his hand fall in a gesture of hopeless puzzlement. "Now I do not know," he said, shaking his head. "I have been these several weeks at endless war between what I see and what I thought was true. Harry, for God's sake, must ye be so utterly unbending?"

Sinclair got to his feet, cradling his damaged left arm with his right hand. "Ingram," he said, "d'ye mind the time we talked in the hall below, and I told ye of the oath I swore on Sigurd's sword?"

"Aye, I do remember."

"I mean to keep my oath. Believe me, coz, 'tis not ambition merely, but honor and justice that urge me on. I do not mean to cool my heels in Rosslyn while some usurper lords it over my domain.

"That I love Janet, or that she loves me, does not signify. What matters is that I come into my own, that I claim and keep that which is mine by right, that I am recognized as earl of Orkney and premier noble of Norway."

"Damn Norway!" cried Gunn.

"It may be damned for all o' me," replied Sinclair. "But the isles are mine. And I mean to have them."

"But look you, Harry, that contrived marriage between you and the little Dane is by death itself annulled. What boots it now to wrap yourself in pride and leave poor Janet, whom you say you love, to pine away in perpetual virginity? Your hope of Orkney is in Norway's hands. Either you shall have it, or you shall not. But this making of politic marriages can avail you nothing if Norway's otherwise disposed.

"Consider. What if you were to marry this or that royal piece of goods and yet lose your Orkney hope to some more favored claimant? Where are you then? Tied for life to some blue-veined ninny, of love and lands deprived, doomed to grow old in a cold and loveless union, with naught to show for it but your own monumental obstinacy and pride.

"Jesu, Harry! You are better than that, are you not?"

Sinclair's eyes were turned on some distant prospect that they alone could see. "Time and events will determine that," he said, slowly. "But marry whomsoever I may, I will have my lands even I must take them by force of arms."

"Then marry Janet, for God's sake, and make war if you must."

Sinclair smiled. "'Tis well said, coz, but you are forgetting that she is now promised to Another."

"Not so! Not yet. She has made no profession. If you but climb down out of your towering pride and go to her—"

Sinclair placed his hand on his kinsman's shoulder. "You love her, too," he said. "No, do not trouble to gainsay it. Do not say anything. We will leave that here, never to be spoken of again.

"Well, then, by heaven, I'll hazard the thing. Find Clarke for me, my gentle coz, and bid him bring me pen and ink. We'll see what words can do to mend that which pride hath broken."

Ingram, his eyes fever bright, his cheeks flaming, seized Sinclair's good hand. "God prosper ye, Harry, in this and in all things."

That same evening, far away in Perth, the cook's boy stole out of the convent yard, a contraband letter tucked snugly under his smock, a letter polite, formal, yet not altogether cold, sent from a fair hand to Henry Sinclair, away to the south at Rosslyn.

8

Old Walter Halyburton, Lord Dirleton, was neither wiser nor less wise than most fathers. Certainly he was no fool. And when a note from Janet, asking if she might come home, was followed immediately by a message from the Reverend Mother Genevieve suggesting that, as Janet had behaved contrary to the spirit and the letter of convent rule, it would perhaps be best for all if the girl were to be called home, old Halyburton's first thought was, Who is the fellow?

He would be more than glad to have his child home with him; but, God smite him, he hoped she hadn't gone and yielded up her maidenhead to some scented poxy whoreson knave, all ribbons and ruffles and courtly airs, with no brain and no spine to him. Well, he would smoke her out, but softly. Softly. He remembered his own days of folly and, as he was a just man, he could not well reproach his child for treading paths that he himself had trod. "'Tis in the blood," the old lord reckoned. He shook his head. "God ha' mercy, but I was a wicked fellow in those days. Hee-hee! Many's the jolly romp I had, God ha' mercy. 'Od's wounds, I hope the girl don't turn up wi' a big belly."

But Janet, to her father's considerable relief, was still her slender self when she arrived at Dirleton. And the old man, grateful for small blessings postponed, made her most heartily welcome. In truth, he doted on this daughter, and had only reluctantly packed her off to school at the urging of his late wife's meddlesome old crow of a sister.

When, at Yuletide, Janet had told him she would take the veil, he had roundly rated her aunt for having put the child in the way of this folly. But, indulgent parent that he was, he paid over her dowry and let his daughter go, telling himself that at least her prayers would shorten his stay in purgatory. Though, as to that, he'd liefer roast a little longer and have his Janet happily wedded and bedded and well looked after by some worthy knight.

Well, he had forfeited the dowry, but he had his Janet home again, and the halls of Dirleton were brighter for her being there. And so glad was old Halyburton to have her home that he allowed some days to slide by before taking up the theme of her having renounced the veil.

"So, dearie," he began, after some clumsy circling about the subject, "ye'd no calling to be a holy sister after all?"

Janet looked up from her book with a smile and said, "I fear not, Father. 'Twas but the fancy of a green girl, most like. But I am most heartily sorry for the loss of the dowry. That was—"

"Pish!" Old Halyburton waved away the apology. "'Tis worth ten times that to have my lassie home wi' me. But o' course I'd not come between you and God's calling. I hope it's no sin for me to be so glad ye did not take your vows."

"If it is, then we are a pair of sinners, Father. For I am myself so very glad to be home again."

"Hem! Well, that's good. But, tell me, child, what was it got Mother Genevieve so wroth wi' ye? That is, if ye've a mind to talk of it."

Blushes painted Janet's lovely face, but she did not look away. "'Twas letters, Father."

"Ah, letters." The old man shook his head knowingly. "Letters can be a deal o' trouble. I wonder that any man, or woman either, takes the trouble to learn to write at all. There have been more harms wrought by letters than by all the swords and shafts o' Christendom. Aye, aye! When a man sits down to write a letter he holds a dagger to 's own throat."

"Do you never write letters, Father?" Janet's clear eyes twinkled with mirth.

"No more. Once, mind you, I did commit my thoughts to a plaguey letter, but I was young then, and knew no better. There was a lady of no very high degree for whom I'd formed a boyish fancy. And I did write to her in such a vein as to excite her expectations beyond my own intent."

Janet clapped her hands in glee. "And what did you do then?"

"Why, I did what any man of spirit would do in that situation. I went on Crusade, and was seen no more in Scotland for three long mortal years."

Janet shook her head. "I fear you were a wicked fellow."

"Aye," said Lord Dirleton complacently. "I cut a wide swath in those times, child."

"And what became of the lady?"

"Why, in God's own good time she became enamored of a worthy miller, and he took her to wife and lived quite cheerfully with her for up'ards of thirty year, at which time, being quite ground down wi' his labors, death sacked him in the flour of his good old age."

"Go to, go to!" cried Janet, laughing. "This chaffing goes against the grain."

Old Halyburton, delighted at this word play, could not forbear remarking that his daughter was in a "rye humor" and that it ill became her to jest at this harvest of his wild oats. Then he said, "But these letters of yours, are you willing I should know the receiver and the subject of them?"

"Why, my lord," replied Janet, rising and crossing to him, "their subject is an old story, such as hath been told since first the world began."

"'The way of a man with a maid,' is it?"

"Something like," acknowledged Janet, her smile radiant and proud.

"Name the man, child," said old Halyburton, embracing his heart's darling. And Janet whispered Sinclair's name.

"Ha-ha!" cried the old man, hugging her tighter. "Yon Harry, is it? Afore God, child, I could not be gladder."

"Oh, Father, d'you mean it?"

"Mean it? Why, girl, I love the fellow as I loved his father before him. And did I not drag these old bones full twenty miles in the dead o' winter to see young Harry knighted. And did I not wi' my own hands present him with a handsome purse in honor o' the occasion? Oh, he's a bonny, bonny man, is Harry. Not one o' your mincing, idle, paltry coxcombs as hang about the court and spend their days in currying favor wi' other men's ladies. He's a true knight and no mere by-Our-Lady lute-playing loll-about. God bless me, Janet, I guessed none o' this, but I am that glad of it that I—"

"Tell me, does he mean marriage?"

Janet burst out laughing. "Surely you did not think I meant to be his doxy?"

"When, child? When's it to be?"

Janet shook her head. "All things in proper order, Father. Harry means to ride this way so soon as he comes back over the border, where even now he is no doubt making things warm for Edward's minions."

"Off raiding, is he?"

"Aye, my lord. King David hath dispatched him to harry the border outposts, now that Edward's once more at war with France."

"The Southrons will be well Harry-ed, then," said the old man, chuckling, "for Harry's a fellow as loves a fight."

Janet's face grew sober. "Sometimes I think he loves too well the business of war, Father. He hath three times since his knighting crossed over the border, and hath most recklessly rolled dice with death for the taking of some little fort or some scurvy town not worth one drop of his dear blood, let alone his precious life. I fear for him, Father, and that terribly."

Old Halyburton slipped a comforting arm around his daughter's shoulders. " 'Tis the Sinclair way, child. I mind my father telling me how your lad's grandsire rode so rash against the Saracens. He ran so far ahead of his own troops that he got himself surrounded. The Douglas—God! What a mighty man he was!—went riding to his rescue, and both were slain."

The old man felt a shudder course through Janet's frame. "Tush, tush," he said. "Harry's a shrewder man than his grandfer was. He hath all the old man's mettle but a longer head. He's not the lad to get himself killed, not while he's a lass the like o' you to come home to. Ah, don't be afeared, child. Let the young blood have its course. A man must try his powers and test his worth. 'Twas ever so.

"I was myself a most eager chaser after glory in my salad days, and many's the time I looked death full in the face. Yet, here you see me, a doddering old body full of years, content to hug the hearth and take my comfort in a good dinner and a soft bed.

"No doubt 'twill be so wi' Harry, and he'll end up a gray-haired old veteran, content to nod by the fireside and hold your hand and talk o' these times, and laugh wi' you at all your girlish fears."

"Oh, Father, I hope so. I pray so. I want him safely home."

And so it came to pass. For in the space of a fortnight and a little more, a lone rider crossed the drawbridge at Dirleton, tossed his reins to the waiting groom, and fairly flew up the winding stair to receive a hero's welcome.

"Oh, dearest, dearest Harry," said Janet, with a happy sigh, "I am so glad you are here and whole and well."

"I should have come sooner, my own love, but I had first to pass some days at court. The king is grievously ill, and for some time I could not see him to give an account of our doings over the border."

"And was David pleased?"

"So pleased that he seemed to rally, which quite confounded the physicians—and quite disconcerted his nephew, who can scarce sleep nights for thinking of the crown. Indeed, dear heart, the poor old king was so pleased that he hath named me lord chief justice of Scotland, and hath bestowed on me lands and a not inconsiderable purse."

"Oh, dear." Janet looked dismayed.

"Why, what's the matter?"

"Oh, sir, I fear you are grown so great that you must needs look higher for a wife suitable to your station. I cannot think—"

"Nor can I, when you prate so," growled Sinclair, crushing her to him and ending her teasing with a kiss. "Indeed, I cannot think at all, my head's so muddled with just being near you. Janet, God, how I do love you."

"And I love you, my—oh, Father!"

Old Halyburton appeared in the doorway. "Well, well, so it's you, Sir Harry? Got home in one piece, did you? I trust you taught the Southron dogs their manners."

Sinclair clasped hands with the older man. "Lord Dirleton, it is good to see you."

The old man's gaze shifted from Harry to Janet and back again. "Yes," he said, dryly, "I expect it is. I am intruding. You must excuse—"

"No, no. Not at all," protested Sinclair. "'Tis I who intrude. I ought not to presume upon your hospitality."

"Presume? Hell, ye're a Sinclair, ain't ye? Sinclairs are welcome here whenever they've a mind to call. But sit down, sit down, sir. Tell me, how was the campaign?"

Sinclair's eyes flashed and his smile softened his stern features. "We had good sport, my lord. My cousin Jamie and I ranged over Northumberland like a pair of soaring merlins, spying out our prey and striking here and there almost at will."

"Ye don't say?" The old warrior's eyes gleamed with interest.

"Aye. One fair morning we came upon a garrison of Southrons taking their ease all unprepared and unsuspecting. Jamie and his men—"

Poor Janet rolled her lovely eyes to heaven in mock despair, gave up, and quit the room to give orders for their supper. She stayed away the rest of the afternoon.

"And the old king's ailing, ye say?" said old Halyburton, when Sinclair had come at last to the end of his narrative.

"He is dying."

"Ah, well, God be good to him. He was not a happy man, sir. And he's not had a happy reign. His time in captivity did him no good. No good at all. He was never the same man afterward, for all that he went on to live a long, long life." Lord Dirleton shook his head. "It will be the Stewart now, poor David having no son to succeed him. I hope he has better luck than his uncle."

"Well, sir, with Edward so busy between the French and his mistress, the Stewart has a most excellent opportunity to strengthen our borders and secure us against future threat to our independence."

"If he can rely on lads like you Sinclairs to maintain him, his throne will be secure enough. Aye, and Scotland, too."

There was a long silence as each man fell into his private reverie; Lord Dirleton thinking on past deeds of valor, Sir Henry dreaming on glories yet to be.

At length, the old man broke the spell. "Harrumph! My daughter, sir, tells me there is some purpose to your visit."

Sinclair sat up with a start. "Hey? Oh. Aye! Hem!" He got up on his lou out on a certain matter."

"Did intend?" The old man cocked a quizzical eye at his young guest.

"—er, do intend. Do. And shall." Sinclair made a stand before the great stone hearth and faced his interrogator. "My lord, Janet and I have been—friends for some years now."

"Friends?"

"Aye. And, well, she hath given me reason to believe that she finds me not—not altogether odious."

"Odious? I should hope not, sir. No, no. Not odious."

"Well," said Sinclair, waxing desperate, "what I mean is, she hath given me reason to think that I might be welcome as a suitor."

"Has she so?"

"With all due modesty, of course, my lord. She is very modest."

"Of course."

"But, well, a man can tell—I mean, a man senses when a lady might willingly give ear to—to honorable proffers of marriage."

"Proffers? Pooh!" Lord Dirleton wrinkled his long nose. "D'ye mean to have the girl?"

"I do, my lord, if she be willing, and you do not oppose it."

Old Halyburton wagged his head. "Dear, dear, dear. I tell you, Sir Harry—as a friend, mind you—that if you conduct your campaigns against the Southrons in this fashion, Scotland will soon be overrun. Boldness, sir, boldness carries the day! This shambling shill-I, shall-I stuff don't serve. No, sir. It don't serve a-tall. Proffers! What kind of talk is that for a Sinclair?"

"Sir—?"

"Nah, nah, lad. An you were the stuff o' your forebears, ye'd not stand about and talk o' proffers! You'd just ride in and carry the baggage off and marry her at your leisure. And then, if you were of a mind to, you might come tell me the news, or you might not. Or maybe you'd wait and send a full-grown grandson to me to bring me word o' the weddin'." The old man's eyes sparkled with mischief. "Ye damn well would not stand about shuffling your shoes and talking proffers."

Sinclair, a broad grin spreading over his face, stepped forward and clasped the old man's hand.

"What are ye holding hands wi' me for? Go to her, lad. Make your silly proffers and see what ye let yourself in for. You've had your last peaceful day, you young lunatic. Mark my words. You are takin' on troubles ye never dreamed of."

"I'll risk it if she'll have me."

"If? If she—? Why, man, she's had her nets spread for ye since ye were a runny-nosed bit of a boy. And now, God help ye, ye've flown into the trap, and no power on earth can loose ye." The old man poked Sinclair in the ribs with his thumb. "Well, go on. Go ahead, an you're determined to put yourself under petticoat rule. I've no doubt she's hanging about nearby, all eager to seal your doom. Go on. Don't keep her waiting."

Sinclair wrung the old man's hand and started off.

"Oh, and Harry—"

"Aye?"

"I'd take it kindly if ye'd let the parson have his say afore ye start up a grandson for me."

The old man's ribald laughter followed Sinclair out of the room and down the hall, as he flew to the waiting arms of his love.

9

And nothing can change your mind?"

"No, madam." Henry Sinclair gazed directly into his mother's eyes. "Janet has consented to be my wife, and nothing—not even the knowledge that I do not deserve that honor—can keep me from accepting it."

"Not even the loss of Orkney?"

"Is it lost?"

Lady Isabel rose from her chair. "This marriage could lose it for you. Think, Henry. With Robert on the throne of Scotland, your great-aunt Euphemia is now queen. Add marriage with a Scottish girl to ties of blood to Scotland's throne, and what choice has Norway's Magnus then?"

Sinclair shrugged. "He still must choose a man equal to the task. Alex de Ard—"

"Yes, yes," his mother broke in. "De Ard's a weak, vacillating creature. We know that. But what of Malise Sparre?"

"Mother, you know you seek to gall me." Sinclair smiled and shook his head. "It would curdle my blood to see Sparre crowned earl of Orkney, but I will play no more with Janet's love. 'Tis no small thing, Mother, to be loved. I have that. I nearly lost it once; I will not hazard it a second time."

"Of course not, my son." Lady Isabel laid a white hand on Sinclair's sleeve. "But can you not see the wisdom of delaying for a little time, that you might press your claim unencumbered?"

"Unencumbered?"

"By a Scottish wife. Oh, Harry, don't you see? Magnus would surely choose you over your cousins. But given your kinship to the king of Scots and your marriage to Lord Dirleton's daughter, he would have such doubts as to your allegiance as to make the choice impossible."

"Aye, Mother. And if I delay more in keeping my pledge to Janet, she may herself have such doubts of my allegiance as to prevent her choosing me." Sinclair held up a forestalling hand. "No, Mother, no. I listened to your counsel in this, and nearly lost my hope of happiness. By right, I should have lost it. And I shall be a long time in coming to peace with myself on that score."

"You did what you thought was right."

"No, Mother. I did what others thought was right. That is not the same thing. But, come, give me your blessing, for I am bound to marry Janet, and I would have our life begin in peace and with your favor."

"You are Sir Henry Sinclair. You need neither my favor nor my blessing. Indeed, I can only hope you will allow me to remain here at Rosslyn to live out my days on your bounty."

Sinclair looked long at his mother. She seemed to him no older than when she used to hear his prayers o' nights before he slept. And yet it was true that, on his coming into his majority, she had become his dependent, trusting to his grace and goodwill to keep her here in the only home she had known since her marriage to his father. And here was this proud woman acknowledging so much. He guessed something of what it cost her.

"Mother," he said, taking her hand in his, "Rosslyn is your home. And be I Sir Henry or Earl Henry or King Henry, you have a claim here and on my heart that none can abrogate."

Lady Isabel's eyes brimmed with unshed tears. "I have always—always sought your good, Harry."

Sinclair bent and kissed his mother's cheek. "I have never doubted it," he said. "We are a strange pair, you and I. I wonder how it is we manage to hurt so much those to whom we owe such debts of loyalty and love. But never mind, Mother. You shall dance at my wedding, and you shall bide here at Rosslyn as my most welcome honored guest. It is your home and shall be so long as you shall live."

The tears came now. And Lady Isabel, here eyes streaming, reached up and took her son's strong face in both her hands and, kissing him, said, "God bless you, Harry. God bless you and Janet both, and give you joy and long life."

"You will welcome Janet, then?"

"As the daughter I always wanted but never had, I promise you."

"You know," said Sinclair, smiling and patting his mother's cheek, "you are a handsome woman."

Lady Isabel brightened. "Do you think so, sir?"

"I do indeed. Why, if you put your mind to it, I have no doubt that you could snare for yourself a titled gentleman in time to make the one ceremony serve two marryings."

Lady Isabel smiled. "Would it surprise you to know that I have received proposals of marriage, Harry?"

"Nay, madam, not in the least. There's many a man would seek your hand, and not only for your fortune."

"That will I take for a compliment."

"So was it meant to be."

Lady Isabel turned and walked to the window to look out on new green lawns of April's making. "When I married your father, I knew then that I could never love another. And when he died, I thought I should die also.

"You have, I know, thought me cold sometimes, and hard, and even cruel—yes, yes. You must have." She turned to face him. "But, dearest Harry, you must know that all my care has been that you and your brothers should prosper. It seemed to me that to die when your father died would have been too easy, too—weak. And so I resolved to live, for my sons. Perhaps I have cared too much, tried too hard, struggled too recklessly to make events conform to my ambitions for you. I do not know. But, my dear, when you are older and wiser even than you are today, I hope you will judge tenderly of me. And teach John and David to do likewise. Say, when I am gone, 'She meant for the best.' Say that at least, my son, and I will have nothing to complain of t'other side the grave."

Henry laughed, but his laughter was somewhat forced. "Mother, Mother, what mood is this? 'When I am gone,' indeed! You will outlive the lot of us, I warrant. Or me, at any rate, and will linger on to tell thy beads for me beside a soldier's grave."

"Jesu!" Lady Isabel's voice rose in a piercing cry.

Sinclair sprang to his mother's side. "Mother, what is it?"

"Harry, never say it. Never say that again. I pray God and His holy mother that I should be taken now, this very minute, rather than be spared to such a day."

"Mother, forgive my clumsy jest. 'Twas but a way of teasing you out of this funereal mood." He put his arm around her waist. "Come, no more of this. 'Tis time to talk of wedding feasts and celebrations. I think you might do well to get you to your chamber and set to writing letters and making lists and planning all the thousand things needful to make a proper marriage. God He knows I'd rather have the care of planning the invasion of England or the coronation of a pope than a simple wedding. Although I do confess I never understood how there came to be so much ado over so slight a thing."

"Slight?"

"Why, madam, men and maids have been at marrying since Adam

woke in Eden to find the lady Eve new minted from his side. And yet no man may go simply and easily to the bridal bed. Oh, no. There must be a thousand guests, an hundred pomps, and pipers, priests and plates of meat, deep drinking and low jests and infinite delays, so that when the poor fellow at last reels up the stairs to bliss he can neither see nor hear nor think what he's about. I wonder, truly, that men endure it."

"Men endure it? Good sir, if you had even the faintest notion of what careful thought, what diligent preparation, what a welter of—"

"Aye, aye. 'Tis what I said. And damned nonsense, too." Sinclair grinned and took his mother by the elbow and guided her to the door. "But you will have it so, and I am not so foolhardy as to try to prevail against the petticoat army. So get you to your chamber, woman, and weave your plots. As for me, I'll walk about the courtyard and study how to meet my doom as becomes an honest knight."

"Doom, indeed! I think my first business should be to draft a letter to Janet to warn her off."

"Will you write to her, Mother?"

"Of course." Lady Isabel smiled. "She is a beauty, Harry, and a sweet child. Perhaps her charm can accomplish what all my stratagems could not. I think you should take her on a journey to Norway. Let old Magnus but see her, and he'll make you earl of Orkney if only to win from Janet the favor of her smile."

"Oh, Orkney!" Sinclair rolled his eyes to heaven. "Mother, I count myself fortunate to be baron of Rosslyn and more than fortunate to be wed to Janet. Let Magnus keep cold court in frosty Norway and leave the isles to be ruled by wind and wave. If I am meant to have 'em, I shall have 'em. If not, well, I shall have to do without 'em."

"But, Harry, you did swear—"

"Aye, so I did." Sinclair nodded, his face sober now. "And, God help me, I do want it. I do, Mother, truly. But, damn it, I cannot go this politic course of contrived marriages, or equally contrived postponements. What's the good in being Orkney if I be no longer Henry Sinclair. Magnus will have me, or he will not. But it is me, my true self, that he must choose or reject, and not some shadow self that walks about in my flesh.

"I swore that I would have my inheritance. But if I cannot be myself and Orkney both, then I had better never set foot outside Scotland."

Lady Isabel pressed his hand. "I will trouble you no more with this. You are a man, my son. And you must do as heart and conscience bid. I confess I do not understand all that you have said, nor do I agree with all that I do understand. But I know this. You are your own man, Henry Sinclair. And I am proud to be mother of such a son."

"Why, God bless you, Mother; that is very good to hear."

"God bless you, Harry." Lady Isabel smiled radiantly up at him. Then she said, "I leave you now to go and plan the execution of your doom."

Sinclair watched his mother leave, then turned and ran lightly down the winding stair that led to the courtyard below. Shading his eyes with his hand, he stepped out into the bright midmorning air and looked away to the Pentland Hills, those timeless guardians that soon would wear mantles of heather to shield their heavy shoulders against the summer's dew.

God, what a morning! What a time to be alive and young and in love! Sinclair smiled at the thought. His whole being seemed awake and on tiptoe. He thought that if he could but be still enough, he would hear his own rich blood singing in his veins.

He was indeed blessed in his youth, his titles, and his lands. Soon he would bring to this fair plot and these stout walls a new mistress of Rosslyn, one who would learn to love as he did every stone his noble forebears had caused to be placed here, to keep the Sinclairs safely in, to keep all danger out. He would be a builder, too, he thought. The work is never finished. And there will be a need for room when the children come, as come they surely would.

A father! Sinclair grinned at that. Of course he would be a father. There must be more Sinclairs to get more Sinclairs on down the years, to enlarge the estates, to add luster to the name.

"And if I give them no more than this that has come down to me, they'll have nothing to complain of." Sinclair nodded to himself. Still, if he could add the realm of Orkney—he shook his head and tried to tell himself it did not signify. But he knew that always in some corner of his mind there would lurk the thought, the hope, the desire to claim the islands for his own.

He clapped his hands as if he would drive the gnawing thought away. Damn. He wished Ingram were here. But Ingram had pleaded his own affairs away to the north in Caithness, and had long since departed Rosslyn with a promise to return "when you least expect me."

God bless Ingram. He shall stand godfather to the first child. He should find himself a girl like Janet. I wonder if—

"Good morrow, Harry!"

"What, Johnny?" Sinclair smiled to see his fair-haired younger brother, his helmet in the crook of his arm, come limping over the flags. "What ails your leg, boy? You haven't gone and hurt yourself?"

John Sinclair wiped his nose on his sleeve and shook his head. " 'Tis nothing, Harry. Old Knox had me at the quintain so long that I grew careless and got myself unhorsed. A hot soaking will set me to rights, I expect."

"Good man. Knox has been pushing you hard, hey?"

"Aye. He means to cripple me, I think."

Henry Sinclair laughed. "I know what you are going through, Johnny. But trust Knox. He is a dour old soldier, but he means to see that you do not get yourself crippled—or worse—when you ride out against a real foe."

"D'you suppose I ever will, Harry?"

"We Sinclairs have ever been a soldier breed, Johnny. You'll get your share of it, no fear."

The boy sighed happily. "I'd like best to ride against the Saracens. Or maybe the Southrons. The Saracens, I guess, because they killed our father."

Sinclair put an arm about the lad's shoulders. "D'you remember him, Johnny?"

"Aye. He was a grand man, wasn't he, Harry? I was only eight years old when he went off that last time, but I remember him. I don't think Davey does, not really. But I remember how he used to throw his head back when he laughed. And I remember how brave he looked on horseback. D'you mind the time he gave me my first pony?"

"And didn't know I had already taught you how to sit a horse?"

"Aye. He nearly died o' fright when I went trotting off before he'd got the lead rein fastened."

Sinclair chuckled. "He had a word for me that day, I well recall it. But he was pleased all the same. I heard him later boasting to our mother about the way you leaped the river where it winds below the wall. Ah, God, John, I miss him still."

"Old Duncan told me that our towers flamed when our father died. Is it so, d'ye think?"

"They say it happens, Johnny. I have heard that when our grandsire was slain with the Douglas in far-off Spain these towers gave forth a light that flickered and flared like some coastal beacon. They say 'twas seen as far away as Holyrood."

"Old Duncan says that whenever a chief of the Sinclairs is about to die the towers of Rosslyn will appear to be on fire."

"Well, old Duncan talks a deal of crazy stuff, but it may be so, young Johnny. It may be so. We may have been sleeping, you and I, when the towers burned for father. But I do recall there was much talk of it at the time, so let us not discredit Duncan altogether."

"You like old Duncan, don't you Harry?"

Sinclair laughed. "Like him, aye, and love him, too, the rascal. He is part o' Rosslyn."

Johnny nodded. "It is a very special place."

"It's our home, Johnny, and was our home even a hundred years before our great-grandsire won for the Bruce his splendid victory against Edward Longshanks."

"I love that story, Harry. Our grandsire had but 8,000 men to Longshanks' 30,000, and yet he beat 'em and drove 'em back over the border to England."

"He was a mighty man, lad. And a hasty one. He'd had no Oliver Knox to teach him mastery of tongue and temper. But, as to that, I suppose we'd have no such estates today had our father's father been more temperate."

"Why so, Harry?"

"The royal hunt, remember? The Bruce had been long chasing a white deer that ranged those same hills and that moor of Pentland, and he never could come up to it."

"Aye, and our grandfer wagered his head he could bring it down."

Sinclair laughed. "He was a rash, rash man, I fear, Johnny. He could no more back away from a wager than he could from a fight. And so he got his hounds—"

"Help and Hold."

"Aye, the very ones, and he prayed to Christ, the Virgin, and St. Katherine, and let loose the dogs."

"And they brought down the white deer."

"So they did. and our reckless grandsire vowed then and there to build the church of St. Katherine in the Hopes."

"I remember father telling how a monk was sent for from Holyrood to bring the holy oil to consecrate grandfather's church, and he fell asleep along the way and spilled the oil and lost it all. And grandfather ordered men to dig on the spot, and water bubbled up all mixed with oil."

"St. Katherine's Well." Sinclair nodded. "'Twas a miracle, Johnny, I do not doubt it. And still the pious pilgrims visit there in hopes of healing through holy Katherine's power."

"It was a miracle," echoed John Sinclair.

His brother laughed. "The real miracle is that our grandsire did not lose his head, and instead gained for us the Pentland moors. But come along in, boy, and we'll order a hot bath for you. We cannot have you pull up lame on us."

Together, the brothers headed toward the castle. "D'ye think the Bruce would have taken grandfather's head, Harry?"

"I wonder, Johnny. The men of Scotland were resolute in those days. If a Scot said he would do a thing, he did it. And not even friendship would stand in his way."

"Well, 'tis a great thing to hold to your purpose, surely, But I am very glad St. Katherine came to our grandsire's aid."

Harry Sinclair glanced up at the northeast tower shining in the warm rays of the April sun. "So am I, Johnny," he said, roughing his younger brother's flaxen hair. "So am I."

10

Old Duncan, turned out in a new smock in honor of the occasion, lolled in the chimney corner, a flagon of brown ale clutched fast in his gnarled and knotty fist. With head and foot he kept time to the fiddlers, and his bright eye roved the hall taking it all in.

There was Robert himself, the king of Scots, that morose and worried-looking man, come here no doubt to please his wife and to acknowledge Scotland's debt to the Sinclairs of old. The queen, at least, seemed to be enjoying herself.

There was Walter Halyburton, Lord Dirleton, a hale rosy old man, here to give the bride away, standing apart and deep in conversation with Lady Isabel. Old Duncan shook his head. 'Fore God, she's a handsome woman to be so long a widder. It seemed to him a shameful waste.

And there, resplendent in scarlet and black, dancing with Gilly Percy, was Malise Sparre. Lord of Skuldane he calls himself now, the pasty-faced Swede. He'd eyes for Sir Harry's lass himself, the puffed-up popinjay! Old Duncan took a long pull at his ale.

"Having a good time, old tosspot?" chirped a merry voice beside him.

"Eh? Oh, 'tis you, John Clarke. That's a very pretty doublet you are wearin'. New, is it?"

"Aye," replied the diminutive squire, drawing himself up proudly. 'Twas a gift from Sir Henry. And a purse o' money, too."

Old Duncan wiped his mouth on his sleeve. "He's too good to you altogether."

"He treats me well because I serve him well," retorted Clarke, haughtily.

"Hee-hee! An he knowed how you served the kitchen maids, he'd not be givin' you no money purses. Look at Molly there, wallin' her eyes at you like a calf that has got the bellyache. A great strappin' wench like that! What she wants of a toy man like you is more'n I can fathom."

"You are a horrible old man," said Clarke, matter-of-factly.

"Aye, that's the truth of it. 'Tis what Sir Harry allus says of me. And his father before him." Old Duncan nodded. "'Duncan,' he used to say, 'if you escape the gallows 'twill be a scandal and a shame to the nation.' Hee-hee! Sir William was a merry man, God-a-mercy on 'im.

"Ain't the music gay? I've a mind to shake a leg myself, if only I were not so plagued with the rheumaticks. Look at young Sir Ingram there, a-footin' it wi' the Douglas girl. Now there's a fellow as knows dancin'."

And, indeed, Ingram Gunn, groomsman to his cousin, cut a handsome graceful figure as he led his dainty partner lightly over the crowded floor. Others besides Duncan noticed. At the center of the high table, over the wine, Janet Halyburton remarked to her husband, "'Tis good to see Ingram so lightsome and so glad."

"Aye. For all he's such a happy-hearted fellow, 'tis not often ye'll see him join in a frolic."

"Then why today, d'you think?"

Sinclair smiled and pressed his bride's hand. "For us, my dear love; he is that happy for us."

Janet smiled. "This day is very much his doing."

"And I am forever in his debt. Why, had he not braved my surly temper and all but forced me to write you that first letter—"

"But 'twas he made me write you!"

Bride and groom burst into laughter, laughter that drew knowing looks from those nearby.

"Ah, Janet, Janet, I was a fool." Sinclair leaned over and kissed his bride. "I tremble to think what I almost lost through my own—"

"Shh!" Soft fingers pressed against his lips. "Talk of it no more, husband. 'Tis past and will be soon forgot."

"Will it? I wonder. But never mind. We have our life before us, and I am so happy that I could almost go down and shake hands with Malise Sparre."

"He looks quite handsome today, don't you think so, Harry?"

"What, him? I don't—ho-ho! So that's your game, is it? Trying to make me jealous even on our wedding day. Just for that—"

But whatever ominous threat Sinclair was about to make was interrupted by the appearance of his mother. He rose to greet her.

"Harry, you and Janet are sent for. King Robert would like to speak to you."

"At once, Mother. Come, dearest." He took Janet's hand in his and led her through the parting throng to where the king sat beside his queen on the dais at the far end of the hall.

Bride and groom were the cynosure of all eyes as they passed, he in sable and silver, she all in white with a wreath of early summer flowers crowning her shining hair. Together, they knelt before their majesties.

"Come, come," puffed Robert. "Stand and let us have a look at you. That's better. Well, Rosslyn, this is a happy day for us. We are old friends of this house, and the Sinclairs hold a most secure and special place in our affections, the moreso as we are kinsmen, you and we. We knew your father and loved him much. He was a rare man, loyal and brave, unswerving in his fealty to the late king, my uncle, and altogether worthy of his knighthood."

"He would be proud to hear you say so, my lord."

"Yes, yes. A most worthy man. And you yourself have already, young as you are, won Scotland's favor. My uncle spoke most highly of your courage and your enterprise." Robert gnawed at his nether lip. "Tell me, Sir Henry Sinclair, baron of Rosslyn, may we look to you for that same loyalty and devotion?"

For answer, Sinclair bowed and kissed King Robert's trembling hands.

"Hah! That's well, that's well, You shall not find our service unrewarding." The king looked at Janet. "And you, lady, wilt thou release your husband to us at Scotland's need?"

Janet smiled. "My lord, if he come not, I will come myself."

King Robert croaked and wheezed with laughter. "You are your father's daughter. God smite me, but I doubt not you would do it. What say you to that, wife, eh? The lass will come riding to us if her husband will not."

Queen Euphemia extended both bejeweled hands to Janet. "Here's a kiss for thee, my pretty."

Janet suffered herself to be bussed, and a cheer went up from the guests as she did so. Queen Euphemia, damp-eyed as much from wine as from emotion, smiled fatuously and waved and nodded to the crowd.

"Well, now, young people, here is a wedding gift from your king," said Robert. And he signaled a little page in scarlet and gold, who came forward and, on bended knees, held up before the king a velvet cushion on which there rested two rings of gleaming gold.

"Gi' us your hand, child," said Robert, and Janet held forth her hand while the king slipped the smaller circlet on her forefinger.

"And now you, Sir Henry." The band would not slip down over the first joint; Sinclair quickly offered his smallest finger but Robert, vexed, merely placed the ring in his palm. "Let these rings be a symbol of your loyalty to us, just as your wedding rings are symbols of your loyalty to each other."

"Thank you, my lord."

Robert squeezed Sinclair's stout wrist. "We will have need of your sinew and your courage, Sir Henry."

"You have but to send for me, sire."

Robert nodded. "Now go and make merry. And you, lass—"

Janet paused, expectant.

"See you get strong sons of this knight, champions mind you, who will bring honor to Scotland and to the Sinclair name."

Janet curtsied low. "You may rely on me to do my part, my lord."

"Ha-ha!" cried the king, clapping his frail hands. "You hear that, Rosslyn? God bless us! 'Tis a good match you have made this day. I warrant our bold baron has his work cut out for him."

The stout queen clapped her hands at this glancing bit of ribaldry. "Oh, he's the man for it, I make no doubt, my lord. We shall be quite overrun with little Sinclairs in this part of the world."

"Well, well, Scotland has need of 'em," said Robert. "Now be off, the pair of you, and God gi' ye joy and long life."

"We are honored by your presence here, my lord," said Sinclair, bowing. "God prosper you and your most gracious lady."

As bride and groom withdrew from the royal presence, fat Friar Donal sidled up to Lady Isabel. "Your son stands well with King Robert, I see. That bodes well."

"Would that he stood so well with King Magnus," replied the lady.

"What? You mind is still turning on that point?"

Lady Isabel favored the priest with a glacial smile. "You do not know me, Friar Donal, if you think my hopes are so lightly laid by."

"But this marriage, my lady, surely works against those hopes."

"Indeed it does, but while any hope survives I will not resign my Henry's claim to Orkney. 'Tis all very well that he find favor with Robert, but I have watched poor Scotland's fortunes rise and fall like the ocean tides. And who can say when English eyes shall look this way again with lustful purpose, or for how long this sad and troubled man can keep his throne?

"Rosslyn lies too far to the south for comfort, my friend. This present Edward has neither forgot nor forgiven his father's humiliation at Bannockburn. And though his creature Balliol could not deliver Scotland into England's keeping, the present Edward may try where his father failed."

"He is a most bloody and warlike prince, i' faith," said the friar. "But I think he spent himself so prodigally in making war in France that he can scarce have treasure sufficient to mount an assault on Scotland."

"Friar Donal, I sometimes think that Scotland exists as a diversion for English princes when fortune fails them in France. Mark you, Edward has achieved something like a peace with the French, but this Charles is not a man to accept meekly the English presence on French soil. Should war break out again, and I think it likely, England may find in

Charles a foe to reckon with. I cannot doubt that Edward would launch an adventure into Scotland should matters go awry in France. And where is Henry then? And Rosslyn?"

"My lady, you do anticipate too much," rumbled the priest. "And, as to that, even were your son to secure the realm of Orkney, I warrant you he would yet ride at Robert's call."

Lady Isabel sighed. "You are no doubt right in that, Friar Donal. He is his father's son. But still, if all else went amiss, were Scotland to fall and England to force a union, my son would have the isles."

"As a refuge?"

"That, and as a virtual principality. For, look you, whoever hath Orkney is as much a king as Robert is. Magnus is not like to meddle so long as he has his revenues."

"Well, I know little of such matters, for I am but a simple priest," said Friar Donal, not remarking the smile that played about Lady Isabel's mouth. "But I will keep your intention in my prayers, lady, and will do what I can to serve you in this and in all things."

"Do pray, Friar Donal, by all means. I think it will require God's intervention now. But, soft, here comes the bride.

"Janet, my dear, how lovely you look! And here is my son, the happy rogue. Kiss me, my children, and receive a mother's blessing."

"Bless you, Mother," said Henry, his eyes shining with wine and love. "Janet and I are hoping to steal away now unnoticed if we can. My faithful Ingram hath promised to create a diversion by calling on old Duncan for one of his bawdy songs."

"Ah, Ingram. He never fails you, does he, Harry?"

"Never, Mother," Sinclair said, refusing to take up the gauntlet. "And now, with your blessing, we'll slip away and hope for an hour's peace before the more sportive of our guests set up the customary caterwauling beneath our window. Good night, Mother. Reverend Father, good night. Janet?"

Hand in hand, the newly married pair tripped lightly up the narrow winding stair. Sinclair led the way to the bridal chamber, bedecked with heather and sprigs of yew all intersticed with bluebells, daisies, and sweet wild roses. Costly candles of pure beeswax cast the lovers' shadows on the wall.

"How lovely it all is," whispered Janet. "Oh, Harry, how lovely."

"And how much lovelier you are, my love. Ah, Janet, Janet, let down your bonny hair."

PART II

11

Sir Henry Sinclair stood alone in the great hall of Rosslyn Castle, staring up at the grim sword of Sigurd where it hung above the mantel. On the hearth, flames crackled and leaped, while outside an east wind beat about the castle walls, sobbing like a penitent before the throne of grace. The countryside lay bleak and bare, ravished of its last leaf, open and vulnerable to the onslaught of winter's vanguard.

Sinclair's thoughts were somber as the season. Janet's time had come. After a most trying pregnancy, a pregnancy so much desired and so joyously welcomed—and so pitifully endured at such a cost to that tender body and that sweet nature—Janet lay in labor now, struggling to bring a new Sinclair into being.

She had had excellent care. Brother Ambrose was virtually resident in the castle these last months, tending to Janet with all the skill and wisdom at his command. Now it was all in the hands of the midwife—and of God. Sinclair never felt more useless in his life. Nor more afraid.

HIs love for Janet had, if anything, increased in their nearly two years together. With her he could be easy, even gay. War, ambition, the affairs of state seemed trifling and remote when he walked with her about the grounds or when she rode beside him over the open fields. He had not, save for a brief foray in the service of King Robert, been away from her a single day since first she had come here as his bride. If she were to die—Sinclair shook his head like a dog come in out of the wet. He would not allow the thought to take hold.

Brother Ambrose, for all he looked so grave, had done his best to foster hope. Purges and leeches he had applied to good effect and, as he said, Janet had always enjoyed an uncommon degree of good health.

"She is strong," the gentle brother had said. "Every tooth is sound; the skin clear as a babe's. She neither overeats nor fasts unwisely, takes exercise in moderation and, in short, lives prudently and well. Unless the infant be in some way malformed or—"

Sinclair shook his head again. Jesu! That he could not bear to think on. He had, God knew, seen his share of suffering—in the field and among the miserable hovels of the poor. And he could look on it, deal with it, find answer for it in his philosophy. But the hurts of children were another matter. Children born hurt, no; he could not make his peace with that. Once, and once only, long ago, he had sounded out Friar Donal on the matter. The fat friar had talked such stuff as to set Sinclair's teeth on edge and make him long to kick the fellow down the stairs.

If his child came imperfect into the world, what then? The thought circled again and again, strive as he might to drive it away. And so he faced it, and so he came at last to answer: "I shall but love it more."

Sinclair took to striding up and down. God! What a time this was taking! Poor Janet. If she should die—Sinclair smote the surface of the long oak table with the flat of his hand, a hard stinging blow, and the sound and the sting brought him some relief. He wanted to leave, to run out into the wind and wet, to saddle a horse and ride breakneck over the moor, to outrace thought, to feel strong and sure and whole again, to have control over something, if only a mettlesome steed.

Away in the tower chamber, Janet, the beads of sweat standing out on her forehead, writhed in agony.

"There's my love, there's my love," crooned the apple-cheeked midwife, her plump fingers all but crushed in Janet's fierce grip.

Lady Isabel, her own face white almost as Janet's, took a linen cloth and wiped the girl's face. Her own childbearing, as well as she could remember it now, had been nothing to this. Her sons had all but leaped into the world, as if eager to take up life and be off on the pilgrimage, however long or short it might prove to be. But this child seemed loath to leave its mother's womb and brave the late November chill. For ten hours now, Janet had struggled and wept, trying so hard not to cry out, not to give way and scream, rage, curse, anything to vent the mounting anguish.

Others had wept. Kit, the tiring woman, had had to be dismissed and sent to the chapel with others of the household to pray God and His Blessed Mother to come to Janet's succor. Molly, that carefree, blooming, seeming scatterbrain had gone quite green at first, but she had rallied, caught hold, gulped back her tears, and made herself useful.

Lady Isabel beckoned to Molly now, and the girl came forward with the basin of rosewater. With her own fair hands, Lady Isabel dipped the cloth, squeezed out the excess water, and bathed the sufferer's face. Across the bed, Lady Isabel's gaze met that of the midwife. The latter shook her head. "We can only pray, my lady."

The three women knelt, Molly and Lady Isabel on one side of the bed, the stout midwife on the other. But for the stifled groans of the tortured Janet, all was still. Then Lady Isabel took the girl's hand in hers and said, "Scream, Janet. Let go. It's all right, child. Let go."

And as if this permission were all that had been wanting, a loud, piercing cry seemed to well up out of the girl's innermost being. It tore from her parched throat like the shriek of a soul in hell. Again and again the cries came, searing the hearts of the waiting women.

"Harry! Jesu! Mercy!"

Outside, the wind rose, circling the tower, trying the narrow window as if it would come inside. Rain beat down, and darkness spread over the sodden land. Night settled over the Pentland Hills.

In the hall below, Sinclair kept his vigil still. He tried to pray, and could not, could only pace, pace, pace, and let his mind run on. A thousand thoughts swirled and capered in his weary brain, but one thought stood in the midst and loomed like some dark and direful clawed and scaly thing, rising from the mist-shrouded depths of the midnight regions of the man's own mind. To be alone, to go on—living? Without Janet, without all the wonder, the hope, the joy?

"Sir Henry?"

Sinclair wheeled about. "Oh, Clarke. 'Tis you."

Little John Clarke, his round cherubic face quite sober, executed a stiff bow. "I am heartily sorry to disturb you, my lord, but there is a gentleman come from Norway."

"From Norway?"

"Aye, my lord. I have shown him to the antechamber and ordered hot wine for him. He is even now toasting before the fire." There was an awkward pause. Then Clarke added, "He would see you, Sir Henry, at your convenience. I—I did explain, sir, that the house is in some disarray, and that you—"

"Thank you, John Clarke. Whatever betides, this house will not fail in hospitality. I will go to him directly. Do you take my post here, and run straightway to me should—should any word come down concerning Lady Janet."

"Aye, my lord."

Sinclair strode off to the antechamber. As he entered, he beheld a tall, well-built man dressed in serviceable high boots and a leather jerkin warming his hands before the fire. A drenched and dripping cloak lay over the back of an oaken chair, and a pair of leather gauntlets, soaked to a deep dark brown, lay with the stranger's sword and belt atop a small round table.

"You are welcome to this house," said Sinclair, advancing to greet his guest.

The tall man turned, the strong face under the crop of ash-blond hair mirroring sympathy and regret. "You are Baron Sinclair?" he asked, in heavily accented English.

"I am, sir."

"My lord, I do apologize for having come at such a time. I could not know how matters stood here. I am sorry."

Sinclair nodded. "You are welcome all the same. But who are you, sir, and why have you come?"

"Forgive me." The tall man offered his hand. "I am called Leif Jansson. I am a gentleman in the service of Sigurd Hafthorsson, a nobleman of some consequence in my own country."

"And your errand?"

"Is to inform you, as I have already informed your King Robert, of the death of our King Magnus."

"Requiescat in pace," murmured Sinclair. "I am sorry to learn of it, Leif Jansson. I never knew your king, but I have heard that he was a goodly ruler, wise and strong, yet compassionate withal. You may tell your lord that we share his grief and will order masses sung for the soul of your late sovereign."

Jansson bowed. "I shall so inform Lord Sigurd and our new king, Haakon."

"Long life to him," said Sinclair.

"May God grant it. But, sir, I must not keep you from your own concerns. My lord made special point of my stopping here, for his father was a great friend to your mother's father, and Lord Sigurd is aware of your interest in the isles. He bade me tell you that, although you and he have never met, he bears a fellow feeling for this house and would, with your consent, be willing to advance your cause with Haakon."

Sinclair's eyes widened. "Why, that is kindly thought of, sir. Although I do confess I cannot fathom why your lord would rally to a Scot."

"But half a Scot," replied Jansson, smiling. "But, as to that, I think I may venture to say that Lord Sigurd hath not so high a regard for your rivals. Them he has met and does know."

"And did he know me he might have cause to alter his judgment of them, my grandfather notwithstanding."

"Sir, you have some reputation as a bold man. Oh, yes, we have heard of your services to the Scottish throne. And my lord is most ambitious to secure for Norway its just revenues from the isles. Of the three claimants, it is you he deems most likely to fatten Haakon's coffers with the monies due."

"He is commendably loyal to his king's interest."

Jansson smiled. "He hath interests of his own, sir. For he hath large holdings in Hjaltland—Shetland, you call it—and 'twould please him mightily to have the isles well governed and in good order."

Sinclair rubbed his chin thoughtfully. "Has your lord much influence at court?"

"Some. But Haakon is not Magnus, and there are many skilled intriguers vying for his ear. We are sure of this much: Haakon will not be for long content to let the governance of the isles stand vacant. He is a man of purpose, strong willed and impatient of delay. I think he will move quickly in the matter, and will exert himself in resolving this long contested issue. He wants the isles secure; he needs the revenue. And he will not long postpone action to achieve those ends."

"My compliments to Lord Sigurd," said Sinclair. "You may tell him we are grateful for his support in this. Tell him too that, whatever Haakon may decide, I hope for an opportunity to meet your lord and thank him for this courtesy."

Jansson bowed. "I will tell him. And now, my lord, I will intrude no longer. If you will but send your servant to fetch my horse—"

"Indeed not, sir. I will not hear of it. 'Tis true you come at a troubled hour, but our hospitality is no sometime thing. I pray you will avail yourself of such accommodation as we can offer in this circumstance, and wait out this rough weather ere resuming your long journey."

"I am obliged to you, baron; but a guest—"

"Will ever find a welcome here at Rosslyn. Think no more about it. My squire will provide for your comfort and—"

"My lord! My lord!" John Clarke, all out of breath, came sprinting into the room.

"Softly, Clarke, softly. What's amiss?"

"Upstairs, my lord. You are sent for."

Sinclair crossed himself. "You must excuse me, sir. My wife—"

Jansson nodded. "Stand not on ceremony, Baron Sinclair. God be with you."

"Clarke, see to this gentleman's needs. Stint nothing. Anon, sir. We will talk more of this matter presently." And Sinclair sped away.

Jansson smiled at little John Clarke. "Your master is an uncommonly gracious man to worry after a stranger's comfort at such a time."

"Why, sir, he is the grandest knight in Christendom."

Jansson's smile widened. "I confess I am much taken with him. His fame is not unknown in Norway, but I had not thought to find so much civility in so bold a fighter."

"Oh, he is a fierce man in the fray, I promise you," replied Clarke. "But he is surely the most openhanded and courteous of lords."

"So I find him. But, alas, I wish I had not come at such a time. I hope with all my heart that all will be well."

"So hope we all, sir. But come, I'll lead you to your chamber."

Sinclair took the stairs by twos and arrived scarcely panting at the door of the tower room. Lady Isabel met him, her face strained, her eyes bright with tears.

"Well, Mother?"

"God is good, my son. You have a sturdy boy to carry on the line."

"But Janet, how—"

"She is sleeping now. Brother Ambrose hath given her a posset. Poor child, she hath had a sorry time of it, but Brother Ambrose assures us that she will soon be well."

"Thank God," Sinclair all but sobbed. "Thank God."

Lady Isabel ached to embrace this strong man, her son, to hold him to her heart and comfort him. But she said only, "Would you not like to see your son?"

Sinclair blinked and brushed roughly at his cheek with the back of his hand. "I think I cannot like the fellow for all this grief he gave his mother. But, as he hath seen fit to join us at last, I suppose I must bid him welcome."

Lady Isabel rested her hand on Sinclair's sinewy forearm. "Oh, he is a bonny, bonny boy, Harry. Wait here a moment and you shall see."

In no time at all, a smiling tearful Molly came into the hallway, bearing in her plump and sweetly rounded arms the heir of Rosslyn. Sinclair looked down in wonder at the little face, the crown of white-gold hair. Tentatively, he touched a finger to the infant's cheek. The babe yawned, and Sinclair laughed softly.

"Ye've given us a deal o' trouble, laddie. The least ye could do is show some little interest and concern." Sinclair looked to his mother. "He is very small, isn't he?"

"Nonsense, Harry. He is a stout strapping fellow and will grow to be a most doughty champion."

"He—he is altogether sound, then?"

"Perfect, Harry. He is completely perfect."

Sinclair smiled down at his son and said, "God be thanked."

12

Little Henry Sinclair was duly christened, with Ingram Gunn come all the way from Caithness to stand by as godfather and to "renounce Satan and all his works and all his pomps" in behalf of this diminutive heir to the kingdom of heaven and the barony of Rosslyn. King Robert and Queen Euphemia sent a silver cup, and from Norway came a silken purse crammed with gold pieces and accompanied by a most courteous greeting from Sigurd Hafthorsson.

Leif Jansson, who tarried at Rosslyn for the christening, and was then persuaded to stay on till Yule, presented the child with a pair of golden spurs against that distant day when he would be Sir Henry. Oliver Knox made a gift of his own sword and vowed to withstand the encroaching years so as to have the training of this new Sinclair. Old Duncan, with trembling hands, offered a toy horse he had carved with great labor and much love.

The youthful uncles, John and David Sinclair, emptied their purses to buy a fat pony that would one day carry their rosy nephew about the grounds—and would one day disgrace himself by depositing his young rider plumb in the muck after too generous a taste of the whip. Little John Clarke gave the child a silver brooch, and old Lord Dirleton came through handsomely with a chalice and six gold candlesticks, which he presented to the monks at Holyrood in thanksgiving for his daughter's safe delivery and the arrival of a grandson.

From folk great and small the messages and gifts came pouring in, and Sinclair grumbled that he'd have to build a new wing on the castle "just to store the plunder." But none took his grumbling seriously, for all could see that his heart was light and his spirit merry.

Janet made a quick recovery, and her rapture in the beauty of her child effaced all memory of those anguished hours of labor. All her thought now was to regain her strength and to revel in the mothering of the babe. She had rejected out of hand the suggestion of a wet nurse, and would suffer no interference in the weighty affairs of mothering.

Sinclair himself was alternately annoyed and amused by his wife's ardent devotion to their child. He confided to his kinsman Gunn his doubt that "even holy Mary did not so dote on the wee Lord Jesus as to leave goodman Joseph so utterly out in the wet."

But, in time, the life of the castle returned to something like routine. Christmas came and went. Ingram returned to Caithness, and Leif Jansson to Hafthorsson's hall in Shetland. The flow of guests and gifts subsided, and Rosslyn folk learned to accommodate themselves to the presence of the infant Henry Sinclair.

In time, too, the child's father regained his rightful place in Janet's bed and, by All Hallow's, Janet found herself again with child.

Whether it was because Janet had found at last her true calling, or that the arrival of small Henry had somehow conditioned her slight body to the task, she carried this second child with little discomfort; and after a very brief struggle, William Sinclair came into the world.

Again there was joy at Rosslyn, but nothing on the scale that followed Henry's birth. Sir Henry remarked that it was a good thing Willie knew nothing of the celebration for his brother, for "'tis a poor enough fate to come second; no need to know just how poor from the start."

But Willie was not without an ally. John Sinclair, himself a second son, not only stood godfather to the boy, but developed a deep and special fondness for him that stood Willie in good stead well into manhood and beyond.

Now did Sinclair count himself blessed. He delighted in his children, adored his wife, and had at Rosslyn all the comfort and security any reasonable man could want. Yet there were times when, passing through the great hall, his eye would light on that Viking blade and his thoughts turn on old ambitions and an old vow, and for all his deep content he could not help wondering at the silence in Norway.

He did not speak of it to anyone, not even to Janet. But there were nights when sleep would not come readily, when he would lie in his bed staring up into the dark and wonder if this was all—to bide here at Rosslyn, to manage his estates, to watch his sons grow up, to feel himself grow old.

Soon he would be thirty. What then? Slide down to forty, fifty, doddering old age, with nothing done, nothing of note accomplished? Nothing added to the family holdings? No new honors? No more campaigns? No adventures worthy of his sinew, nerve, and brain?

Things were dull in Scotland. Robert was proving a lethargic, uninspired king. Oh, he was a good enough old man, Sinclair allowed, but he could not help wishing him possessed of greater vigor, hotter blood, and something like the daring of the Douglas or the Bruce. There was work for the man of spirit in those days, by heaven! None of this lolling about and waxing fat while swords rusted and harness grew green mold.

England's Edward's dead and gone. The boy, Richard, is but lately crowned and is not so securely seated on his throne but what a bold invasion of hardy Scots might throw his kingdom into such turmoil that it might not recover in our lifetime. But Robert sits and sits, and slips daily deeper into his dotage while I am stifling here for want of soldierly employment.

Slowly the seeds of discontent took hold in Sinclair's soul, put down their roots, and began to grow.

Then, shortly before the birth of his third child and first daughter, word came from Norway. Haakon had decreed that Alexander de Ard should govern the isles. He did not go so far as to create de Ard earl; for, as Sigurd Hafthorsson was to explain in a belated letter, Haakon was too shrewd a man to leave himself no option should de Ard prove incompetent.

But Sinclair, when he heard of de Ard's preferment, took no comfort in the withholding of the coronet. The storm, long gathering in his brain, broke now and raged, its thunder reverberating even to the very core of his being.

Sinclair had cared, had wanted, more than he himself had suspected. In Orkney lay his last best hope of adventure and a cause. And when that hope was dashed, he grew first wrathful, then morose, and finally almost sullen. In his heart, he damned Haakon, damned de Ard, damned Hafthorsson for having held out encouragement, and damned himself for his too eager embracing of it.

Janet tried to comfort him, but he only smiled wanly and bade her think no more of it, that this was surely God's way of admonishing him for his too keen ambition. In her love and concern, Janet sought out Lady Isabel, but that availed her nothing and worse.

"I knew it must come to this," Lady Isabel declared, not troubling to conceal her own bitter disappointment. "He is too much the Scot for Haakon's liking.

"For, look you, he is allied by ties of blood to Scotland's throne. And, indeed, I told him when David, the king that was, named him lord chief justice that it would hurt his cause at Norway. What could he expect?

"But then he never heeded my counsel in this, even when he was young. Now he must bear the outcome as best he can. No, Janet, I do not grieve so very much for Henry; he would go his own course, and he has done so. It is for your children that I do most sorely lament. They could have had so much, so very much more, had only their father been more politic, more shrewd, more amenable to the advice of older heads than his."

"Aye, madam," retorted Janet, with some spirit. "And had he heeded you, these children would not be."

"Janet, I never meant—"

"You never meant for Harry and me to wed." Janet's round little chin began to tremble and her voice to quake. "Indeed, I think you have never reconciled yourself to his marrying me, and do only just manage to endure me for the children's sake."

Lady Isabel, not well accustomed to such plain speech, took refuge in hauteur. "I can see no profit in continuing this—this conversation. 'Tis plain to me now how you have dissembled your true feeling toward me all this long while."

"I assure you, madam, I dissembled nothing."

"Oh, but you have. And I am glad all's out in the open now. For I would not remain here another day on false footing. You are mistress here; I acknowledge it. And if you find my presence here odious, you have but to say the word, and I shall make shift to find accommodation elsewhere."

"Madam, I have no wish—"

"Oh, but you do. And I could the more respect you did you but express that wish without equivocation. This house is yours. I do not intend to stay on an intruder. I shall make arrangements to quit Rosslyn and seek hospitality at a nunnery."

"I ask only—" here Lady Isabel was obliged to dab at her eyes—"I ask only that I might sometimes be allowed to see the children."

"You talk like a fool!" The words were no sooner past her lips when Janet clapped her hand to her mouth in round-eyed horror.

Lady Isabel's face flushed a deep crimson, then paled to chalky white. She drew herself up in a most regal mien and, gathering her skirts in her beautiful hands, swept grandly out of the room.

The upshot of this skirmish was Sir Henry Sinclair's discovery that, be he baron or swineherd, no mere husband can ever hope to impose a peace in quarters where two women vie. In due course, and by those same laws of inevitability that govern the cosmos, Sinclair was entertained with tearful and detailed accounts of grievances on both sides. And, almost as inevitably, being only a man under the weight of all his titles, he tried logic, persuasion, diplomacy, and guile, singly and in combination, to restore tranquility under his roof. 'Twas all in vain.

The chill deepened, the rift widened, factions formed, and all the household took to talking in whispers and going about on tiptoe. Lady Isabel did not in fact fly to a nunnery, but neither did she move so much as one step in the direction of reconciliation. Rather, she kept herself aloof and apart, so far as circumstance permitted. The sole company she sought was that of her grandchildren, on whose tender and unsuspecting heads she poured such copious vials of honeyed love as would soon surfeit and sicken any more discriminating victim.

This was all gall and wormwood to Janet, who, for her part, moped about red-eyed, silent, and aggrieved. She more than made up for her diurnal reticence, however, by nightly unburdenings in Sinclair's abused and weary ear.

So matters stood that soft April afternoon when Ingram Gunn quite unexpectedly turned up to avail himself of his kinsman's hospitality. Sinclair was glad, nay, overjoyed, to see his friend.

"By God, Ingram, it does my heart good to have you here," he said.

"Why, coz, 'tis very good to be here. I have thought of you often this long while, and at last I gave way to the lure of milder weather and to my own desire to be sojourner again at Rosslyn."

"I am heartily glad you did."

Glad, too, were others of the household. For the presence of the merry Gunn tempered the bleak domestic clime. Even Lady Isabel was seen to smile, albeit with a restraint becoming to her martyred state. And Janet so far forgot herself as actually to laugh aloud. But the tension was there, and Ingram would need to have been made of duller stuff not to remark it.

On the evening of the third day of his visit, he and Sinclair sat late over their wine. The servants had been dismissed; the family were all abed. It was a quiet time, a time for talk, a time for open dealing.

"Tell me, Harry," said Gunn, carefully choosing his words and, with equal care, keeping his gaze focused directly into his cup, "is all well between you and Janet?"

Sinclair drained his own cup and refilled it before replying. "I believe so, coz. Why? Did she speak something to the contrary?"

"No, no," Ingram hastened to assure him. "It's just that—well, there is this feeling I have of something being amiss."

"Here?"

"Here. Tell me, I have not come at an awkward time, have I? For if I have—"

"Nonsense." Sinclair took another mouthful of sack. "There is no awkward time where you are concerned, Ingram. You should know that. Fill your cup?"

"Thank you, no." Ingram shifted uncomfortably in his chair. "Um, I—uh, I would certainly be the last one to meddle—"

"The very last," agreed Sinclair, splashing more wine into his cup. "I'd fight the man who said otherwise."

"Aye, well—" Ingram eyed his cousin curiously.

"You may rely on it, Ingram. I would not stand idly by and let any whoreson slanderer speak so of you." Sinclair nodded emphatically. "I'd gi' him the lie to his teeth."

"Thank you, Harry," murmured Ingram, biting back a smile.

"'S nothing." Sinclair reached for the silver flagon. "Lemme help you to s'more sack, coz."

Ingram slid his cup over and watched as Sinclair, with knit-browed concentration, contrived to get nearly as much wine into the cup as puddled onto the oaken table.

"Happy days," echoed Ingram softly. "There! Le's drink to happy days."

"Well, there have not been many happy days here, I can tell you," declared Sir Henry, slumping back in his seat. "Damn women. Never a peaceful day when they're about. Nothing but carp and complain, carp and complain until they drive a man mad with their nattering."

"As bad as that?"

"Worse." Sinclair blinked owlishly across at his cousin. "Never marry a woman, Ingram. What're you grinning at? 'S as good counsels ye'll ever get in this world, my lad. See you heed it."

Ingram made his face sober. "I will, Harry. Thank you."

Sinclair dismissed the thanks with a wave of his hand. "Take me, now. What d'ye see? I will tell you. Ye see a shadow of myself. A shadow. A ghost that glides about in the semblance of the man I was.

"I ever tell you about the raid I led into Northumberland? Hey?"

Ingram shook his head.

"Well," declared Sinclair, smiting his chest, "this was no shadow then, I can tell you."

"I believe you."

Sinclair gulped down the dregs of his wine, then got unsteadily to his feet. "We rode right up to their walls, man, and caught them breaking fast. I rode my horse right into their dining hall. Ha-ha! By God, I wish you could've seen their faces!

"They dove this way and that," cried Sinclair, weaving wildly and sending his chair crashing to the floor. "They ran like rats, scurrying hither and yon, trying to gather up their courage with their arms.

"One young fellow—by God, I give him his due. He picked up a tankard—" here Sinclair suited action to his words and caught up his own cup, while Ingram stared in goggle-eyed fascination—"and he flung it straight at my head."

Sinclair's cup banged off the mantel and ricocheted halfway across the room. Gunn only blinked and leaned forward, his chin cupped in his hands.

"Yessir, straight at my head. I dodged, but even so it glanced off my helmet with force enough to make my ears ring. I could have loved that fellow, was he anything but a Southron. But, well, I had my work to do. So did we all."

Sinclair took up a tall candlestick and began to wave it about before him in a vigorous reenactment of the martial scene. "We beat 'em, and hacked 'em, and carved 'em up like so many roasts to serve up at a state dinner in the court of death. But then the guard—roused no doubt by the din we were making—came pouring in at the doors to besiege us on all sides.

"I sprang up onto a table." Sinclair did just that, and was within an ace of breaking his neck when one foot came down on the plate of the wondering Ingram. But he maintained his footing and, with the candlestick clutched now in both hands, lay about him lustily, dispatching whole hordes of phantom foes. "One fellow's skull—ugh!—I split —ugh!—like a ripe melon. Another—ugh!—saw his hand and sword together go sailing—ugh!—the length of the hall. Ugh! And then—"

But whatever bloody deed it was went unrecounted, for Sinclair's capering had carried him perilously near the table's edge. A last graphic swipe of his candlestick sword sent him flying through the air to land with an awesome thud and lie like a corpse on the unyielding floor.

His propulsion forward sent the heavy table crashing backward, taking both Gunn and his chair with it in the fall. Gunn could not help himself. He sat there, pinned to the wall with the table in his lap, and he began to laugh.

First to arrive on the field was Janet, followed shortly by Lady Isabel, Johnny Sinclair, David, Molly, and Kit. As Ingram witnessed the horror register on each succeeding face, his laughter took on a maniacal pitch and volume quite appropriate to the scene of devastation that lay around him. He was still howling when Johnny and David relieved him of the table; indeed, he could scarcely stand. And although he tried to help carry his fallen kinsman off to bed, he was so racked and weakened with laughter as to be of no use at all.

Harry Sinclair was not on hand to break fast with the rest of the household that next morning. Gunn, to his credit, was. But he was most uncommonly subdued throughout the meal. Once, Davey Sinclair caught his eye, and that young wretch came near to choking on his own stifled snicker, and had to flee the room in purple-faced mortification. Gunn, however, had apparently exhausted his store of mirth, for he stayed the course and was still at table when all but the mistress of Rosslyn had gone their several ways.

For a long and painfully quiet interval, nothing was said. Then Janet, looking as severe and prim as she could manage, said: "Perhaps, Ingram, you can shed some light on the —the events of last night."

Ingram could feel the corners of his mouth twitch, but he steeled himself to look full solemnly at the young matron. "Why, my lady," he said, "I was in hopes you might enlighten me."

"I?" Janet's fair face mirrored perfect astonishment. "I assure you, sir, I do not take your meaning. Certainly I was no party to that—that brawl."

"Were you not, then? I wonder. It seemed to me that I looked last night on the direct and inevitable consequence of a household rife with discord, faction, and most un-Christian bickering. A man—hush! Let me finish. A man cannot go on for long playing the rope dancer between two camps under his own roof. Soon or late, something like that which happened last night must happen. Or worse."

"Worse?"

"Softly, softly, Janet, pray." Ingram rubbed his brow with a none too steady hand. "Look you, I know little of what's awry in this house. But that something is awry was plain the day I entered. And I would guess from some words Harry let fall last night that this state of affairs has gone on long enough.

"Janet, I know Harry. And I know he is not—like some of my noble Highland neighbors—a man given to drunken roistering. Indeed, I never saw him in his cups before last night. Have you?"

"N–no."

"Well, there you are, then. Something or someone had driven the dear man to this pitch. And I," here Ingram rose from his chair, "I will leave it to your conscience to supply the answer."

"My conscience! My—why, what makes you think my conscience holds the key? You cannot know what it has been like here, Ingram. You have no notion. It is Harry's mother, I tell you. She's the cause. She continues to bear me a grudge since the day Harry and I were wed. She blames me that he did not receive the coronet of Orkney. She meddles and fleers and turns my own children against me. She—she—" And Janet burst into tears.

Ingram could feel his soft heart grow softer still. But he would not yield. "Oh, yes, weep. By all means. There's the resort when nothing else stands between you and your blame."

"Blame?" Janet mopped at her cheeks with both tiny fists. "My blame?"

"Janet, dammit, you are Lady Sinclair. You are Harry's wife and mistress of Rosslyn. If you have not yet the wit and skill to exercise diplomacy in your relations with your high-born mother-in-law, then perhaps you had better return to Dirleton and play at being Janet Halyburton again. For you have not acted like Lady Sinclair here."

"Oh, Ingram," Janet wailed, "you don't know her. She is a—"

"A dreadful woman. I quite agree, Janet. She hath more than once cast an unfriendly eye on me. And, I do confess it, when I was a boy it did unsettle me somewhat.

"But I am not a boy any longer, Janet. And you are yourself a woman grown, with a husband and three lusty children. What is more, you are in the ascendant here. You have the man, the house, everything. Lady Isabel has only her memories and her disappointments—and the sure knowledge that she is growing old.

"Surely, Janet, given all that you have, you can afford to be—what? Generous in victory? Yes. That, I think, is what you must be."

"But with her?"

"Especially with her. For Harry's sake, if not for charity's. Come, Janet, make it up with the old woman. Make peace. You can afford to make the overture; you are young; you have so much. Let her have her pride

What can it matter so long as you and Harry have again that which brought you first together?"

Ingram crossed over and took Janet's hand in his. "Will ye do it, lass? For Harry?"

Janet, biting her lips and blinking back the tears, could only nod.

"Good girl! God bless you, Janet. Why not go now and have it over with? Then you can go with a light heart to give comfort to our stricken friend."

Janet looked up at Ingram and, with something like awe in her voice, said, "He was very drunk, wasn't he?"

"Lady, he was roaring."

So it was that peace returned to Rosslyn. Janet very prettily made a truce with Lady Isabel. And that noble dame went so far as to acknowledge that she too may have been in some measure at fault. On the common ground of their love for Henry Sinclair, wife and mother-in-law laid down their arms and embraced, not without reservations on both sides, but with a show, at least, of honorable intent.

Janet then slipped softly into Sinclair's darkened chamber. Tenderly, she kissed his wounded brow, told him of the armistice and confessed herself a fool. Sinclair judged that, among all fools then living, he stood in the front rank. But Janet would have none of it. Contrition, she discovered, is quite a pleasant state, and she was determined to have the worst and the best of it. There was very nearly a dispute as to whose folly was the greater, but that soon ended in the timeless fashion of such quarrels.

By the time Ingram set out on his homeward journey, there was a durable peace in the making. Lady Janet and Lady Isabel had established boundaries that were mutually respected, and Henry Sinclair began to know something like content.

A year, two years came and went, and life at Rosslyn beat to an even, gentle rhythm, in time with the passing seasons and the stately dancing of the stars.

13

Little John Clarke opened one eye, winced at the brightness of the early morning sun, and yanked the coverlet up over his head.

"Nah, nah, now none o' that, my wee laddie. Mornin's coom an' ye maun get out o' this afore folks is stirrin' about."

Clarke poked his tousled head out. "Ah, for the love o' God, Molly, gi' us a kiss and lie down again. 'Tis early yet."

For answer, Molly yanked the covers clean off the cot. "Will ye no hear me, man? 'Tis mortal late, and my lady'll be lookin' for me to tend the bairns. Willie's got a tooth comin' and he's that fretful that only I can quiet him. Little Master Henry's got to be given his porridge, and who's to do it if I don't?"

"God's nails!" growled little Clarke, easing his legs out and sitting on the edge of the cot. "This place is turned into a by-Our-Lady breeding farm."

"Mind yer mouth, John Clarke," retorted the buxom Molly, hustling into her shift. "My lady's wi' child again, and if Sir Henry heard—"

"Again!" Clarke groaned and smote his forehead. "Now God rot me if I do not think we'll all be drowned in piss and milk. If the man could make war as diligently as he makes babies, a fellow'd have a chance to rise in the world. How can I make my fortune biding here at Rosslyn wi' the nurses and the midwife?"

He reached for his hose and drew them on. "I tell ye, Molly, my lord's a disappointment to me. A great disappointment. D'ye know that yesterday I came upon him in 's chamber, and he was down on all fours wi' little Henry on his back a-waving a wooden sword and wearin' his father's helmet?"

Clarke stood up and pulled on his shirt. "I tell ye, Molly, this is no place for a man of action."

Molly tossed her head. "Ye seem to find action enough hereabout, my hero. An' when it coom to makin' babies, there be three or four little blessin's creepin' about the countryside as could call theirself Clarke if they'd a mind to."

"A man may get babies," retorted Clarke, "but he needn't give all his time to 'em. Where's my belt? Oh. I have it. Come, gi' us a kiss, Molly, and I'll be off to wait on Sir Henry. Belike he'll want me to play Bo-Peep wi' little Willie or take Mistress Betsy's doll baby for an airing."

Clarke stood on tiptoe and bussed the fair Molly right heartily. "There now," he said, with a tug at the skirt of his short jacket, "God gi' ye good day, lass. I'll look in on ye this even after prayers."

Molly could not forbear to smile after her little paramour. "You should be glad," she said, "aye, an' thankful too, that Sir Henry goes raidin' no more. Last time you crossed the border wi' him, you was nigh killed wi' fallin' off yer horse."

"Fallin'!" John Clarke wheeled about. "Fallin'! I was throwed, woman. Throwed. I never fell off a horse in my life."

Molly laughed. "Aye, ye're a bonny rider, I'll vouch for that. Now get along out o' this; I maun get dressed and see to mistress."

Little John Clarke slipped furtively out of Molly's below-stairs den and was tripping lightly up the stone steps leading to the great hall when a hearty voice put him off stride.

"Hey, John Clarke! The fox has been at the chickens again, I see."

Clarke executed a nimble step to save himself from breaking his shins on the stones. "Oh, 'tis you, Master Johnny," he said crossly. "Ye near caused me a tumble, speaking out o' the shadows like that."

"Why, I would be right sorry to do that," said John Sinclair, stepping out into the splash of sunlight spreading over the rush-strewn floor. "After the tumble ye had last night, any more would be dangerous to a man o' your slight stature."

"Never mind my stature," replied Clarke. "I give as good an account o' myself as the next man."

The younger Sinclair draped a friendly arm over Clarke's shoulders. "Now don't be cross wi' me, John. I've got good news, news that'll bring a smile to the dour mouth ye're wearing now."

"Nay, let me guess," said Clarke, glowering up at his master's brother. "Betsy's weaned and Willie's tooth's broke through."

John Sinclair threw back his head and roared with laughter. "Clarke, Clarke," he cried, enveloping the little squire in a bear hug, "had I a

sword as sharp's your tongue, I'd be the champion knight o' Christendom."

"Swords! Faugh! Don't talk o' swords to me. Why, there's not a bright
blade in the whole castle. Rust is England's ally here at Rosslyn."

John Sinclair loosed his hold and fell in step with Clarke. "'Tis true,"
he said, "we have been a long while idle here. My brother was so
heaped with honors after his last campaign that I wondered what more
Robert could give, short of his own crown. But now—well, this seeming
sloth hath greatly puzzled me, but my brother's not a man to be questioned, if you take my meaning."

"Aye," replied Clarke, his tone grim. "Once I tried to sound him out
on the why o' this—this lying about. Once was enough."

"And did he rate you?"

"Not he. He only stared at me wi' those cold blue eyes o' his till I
thought myself spitted on his gaze." Clarke shuddered. "I remembered
on a sudden that I had business elsewhere, and I retreated from the
field in disarray."

"Ha-ha! I can well believe it. I dote upon my brother, but I'd sooner
brave a pagan horde than ask him to explain his actions."

"What actions? Christ's wounds! Our shields are used for cradles
here, and our banners for bunting—or worse."

"Whew!" John Sinclair grinned and shook his head. "You talk like
King Herod i' the Bible. I shall have to warn my brother and Janet to
take the children and fly to Egypt."

"You'd make a proper angel, you would. But come, what's this news
you promised me?"

"Ingram's here."

"Your cousin Gunn?"

"Aye. He arrived late last night, whilst you were elsewhere occupied."

Clarke clapped his hands. "That is good news! If anyone can stir your
brother up out o' this—this baby farm, it is Sir Ingram. I mind the time
the pair o' them got roaring drunk on 's last visit. Oh, we were lively
then. Gi' me a jolly bachelor every time. We are the lads for a fight or
a frolic. Ho-ho! There be some great doings now, I'll wager. Sir Ingram's
our man, and no mistake."

"I trust ye are right, John Clarke. I have been aching for a chance to
prove myself. A border raid would suit me right down to the marrow."

Clarke skipped for joy. "By God, I feel my appetite returning! What
say you? Shall we break our fast together?"

"Right willingly. For myself, I think I could eat an ox, horns, hooves,
and all. But come, let's make a party. I'll go and call my brother and Sir
Ingram, and we shall all break fast together. Wait here."

"Be quick," Clarke called after him. "My belly's pressing on my back-
bone now."

Sinclair loped off, and as he skipped up the stairs he encountered his mother descending, with his nephews in tow. "Good morrow, Mother," he said. "Have you seen Harry this morning?"

Lady Isabel smiled. "What? No kiss for thy mother?"

John made haste to remedy the oversight. "Did you sleep well?"

"Passing well, my son. As I grow older, I find I am wakeful early. Friar Donal says an old body will not sleep so long as a young one. He says 'tis because the long sleep approaches, and our nature will have us hoard up all the sunlight we can ere we are shut up in the earth."

"Friar Donal is a foolish old woman," replied the youth. He stooped and caught up the smaller child. "Hallo, Willie, ye rascal. Get thy fingers out o' thy mouth and let us have a look. By Our Lady! I can see the top of a snow-white tusk coming through."

"I have my teeth, Uncle Johnny," declared Sir Henry's namesake.

"I should hope so, a great fellow like you! We shall have to be buying razors for you before ye know it."

The boy rubbed his blooming cheeks with his pudgy hands. "Does it hurt to get whits-kers?"

"Nay, lad. 'Whits-kers' gi' ye no trouble till ye go to scrape 'em off."

"Shan't do it, then," declared the little fellow.

"What? D'ye mean to go about like old Duncan with a great bush a-sproutin' from yer jaws?"

Henry nodded. "I think it's lovely."

"Ha-ha! Why none o' the girls would want to kiss ye."

"I saw Molly kiss old Duncan at Christmas. He caught her around—"

"Harrumph! Well, at Christmas maybe. But what'll ye do in battle? Ye cannot fight very well if ye have to keep worryin' about steppin' on yer whits-kers."

"I could tie 'em up with ribbon."

John Sinclair chucked the boy under the chin. "Do that," he said. "Ye may start a new fashion in the kingdom."

"I do believe that men were bolder when they went bearded," remarked Lady Isabel. "But then memory will play false with older folk and make all that was seem fairer than all that is."

"Now, Mother," said John, setting Willie down, "if you expect me to tell you that you are looking younger than ever, you must wait a long while. I'll no play that game with you. You know and I know that time has quite forgot you."

"I am a grandmother thrice over, Johnny."

"And a very pretty one, too. There, now you've made me say it, and I meant not to." John shook his head. "Ye're a scheming tricksy lady that will have her plate of flattery with every meal. I wonder how my father managed you at all."

"'Twas I managed him," replied Lady Isabel, smiling. "But I took care he never knew it."

"I can well believe it. But come, Mother, where is Harry to be found this morning?"

"Why, with his precious cousin, to be sure."

"And Ingram?"

"Is with Harry."

"Go to, go to!" cried Johnny, half vexed, half laughing. "'Tis most unmotherly in you to bait me. I would see my brother."

"I would see your brother, too. I swear I do not know what hath become of him. He was a bold man, a man of promise. Now—"

"Mother, pray. No more o' this."

Lady Isabel nodded. "I know. You never, even as a tiny boy, could bear to hear anyone speak less than well of him."

"Why, as to that, I do confess it. I think my brother the most upright and admirable of men. He hath, I think, done nothing—"

"He hath done nothing."

"Madam!" the good-natured face grew set and stern. "Was it for nothing Robert named him lord chief justice?"

Lady Isabel waved a languid white hand. "I grant that, but—"

"Please, madam, I pray you. No more. 'Tis not fit that we should debate my brother's merits before his children."

Lady Isabel looked down upon her fair-haired grandsons, a bemused expression crossing her still youthful face. Then she raised her eyes to her son. "It is for them that my concern is so great."

"Then show your concern by letting them keep their reverence for their father. Mother, I do not mean to overstep myself, but I must tell you that your unrelenting judgment of my brother is having an un-wholesome effect. I came near to striking Davey not a week ago when he began to echo thoughts that could only have come from you."

"You did not strike your brother!"

"Nay, Mother, but I was sore tempted. The little upstart! I heard him tell Oliver Knox that there was no need for him to master arms, that so long as Harry's master here there'd be no call for deeds of valor."

"Did Knox rebuke him?"

"He had no need to. I came upon them just at that point, and I seized the little puppy by the scruff o' the neck and lugged him off to the stable where I delivered myself of a most unclerical sermon. 'Twas all I could do to keep from boxing his ears."

"Does Harry know of this?"

John shook his head. "No. I would not trouble him with it. Davey saw the light and was, like St. Paul, fast converted. I yielded him up to Knox, to whom he did make a very pretty act of contrition, and I left him to his penance."

Lady Isabel frowned. "I do not like it that Knox should be spoken to with anything less than courtesy by any of this house."

"Then, Mother, for God's love, set a watch about thy tongue. Davey was sorely wrong in this, but he was not speaking his own thoughts. This disrespect is rooted in your own uncharitable speech. We must not let the contagion spread, or the whole house will become infected."

Tears glinted on Lady Isabel's fair lashes. "You would have made a most eloquent preacher, Johnny."

"But 'tis not meet that I should preach to you. And I confess that I am myself beset by doubts of Harry's purpose. Still," he reached out and touched his mother's cheek, "still, I think we must be wary, both in our speech and in our thoughts, lest disaffection spring up among the people."

"You are in the right on this," Lady Isabel replied, pressing his hand. "Go to thy brother, then. He is closeted with your cousin in the tower chamber. I'll take these two pretty fellows below."

"Adieu, Mother. And, if I have spoken more bluntly than I ought, I pray you, pardon me."

"Nay, my son. 'Tis I who am in need of pardon. For that, I pray you keep me in thy prayers."

John Sinclair watched his mother and the bairns descend; then he turned and made for the tower.

Ingram Gunn's face lighted up with a wide smile as Johnny entered. "By the mass!" he cried. "This is not our Johnny, surely? Why, Harry, he's a head taller than you."

"But not so tall that I cannot still bring him down when th' occasion warrants," drawled Sir Henry Sinclair, offering his hand to his brother. "Come in, Johnny. Take a chair. Our worthy cousin brings most interesting gossip from Caithness."

"That is news in itself. I never in my life have heard anything of interest from that corner of the kingdom."

"Mind your manners, boy," growled Ingram, trying to look fierce. "Great matters are afoot. Pray, maintain a respectful silence in the presence of your elders."

"I shall be mum's a mouse, old graybeard. What is stirring?"

"Why," said Sir Ingram, drawing his knees up under his chin, "'tis this: an embassy from Norway even now approaches. It tarried awhile in Caithness, for one of the party was taken ill aboard ship, and it was thought prudent to delay the errand till he recover."

"And did he?"

"Aye. The wholesome airs o' my native ground have wonderfully revived the fellow, and he feels now well enough to risk the fogs and damps of this low-lying fen."

"Fen!" The younger Sinclair was moved to protest. "Why, this place is to Caithness as—"

"*Pax*, Johnny," said his brother. "Let the slander go. We'll deal with that presently."

"As I was saying," went on Ingram, serenely, "the party will arrive here in a day or two. But I am privy to their errand, having, as you know, some skill in diplomacy—"

"Hah!"

"Some considerable skill in diplomacy," continued Gunn, ignoring the younger man's interruption. "And I was able, by many a shrewd and roundabout interrogation, to smoke out their purpose and intent."

"Which is what?"

Ingram looked to Henry to take up Johnny's question. "Well, John, it seems that our cousin Alexander de Ard is no longer governor of Orkney. King Haakon VI has relieved him of that burden and, apparently, the isles are up at auction once again."

"Jesu, Mary!" breathed the youth. "Then you might be—"

Henry Sinclair waved a careless hand. "Might be; might not be; might never be. Who can say? I think we must not make too much o' this."

"But look you, Harry," Ingram put in, "why else would these fellows come all this long way?"

Sinclair shrugged. "I confess I can think of no other business than the isles. Haakon is not so fond of Scots as to dispatch ambassadors for mere courtesy."

"He sends for you. Never doubt it."

"Well, now, coz," replied Sinclair, leaning back in his chair, "let us not be too previous. I charge you, and you, Johnny, say nothing of this outside this chamber. 'Twill not do to stir folks up on the strength o' windy rumor."

"You mean our lady mother," said Johnny.

"Her most especially." Henry nodded. "Let us keep our own counsel for this present time, and let us keep our hopes in check. I think we must not invest too great credence in what might be or what could be. We shall know soon enough where Haakon's thoughts are tending."

"And Janet? Will ye tell her?" Ingram asked.

Sinclair smiled. "'Tis plain you are a bachelor still, my friend. Come! Let us go down and break fast. We need something more substantial than rumor to chew on."

John Sinclair clapped a hand to his brow. "I had forgot John Clarke!"

"What of him, little brother?"

"He hath been waiting for us in the hall for near an hour. The man will be dead o' hunger."

"Why then," said the elder Sinclair, leading the way out, "we will but carry him to the table and pour porridge down him till he revive again."

The three came quickly down the stairs and turned in at the great hall. There, Johnny Sinclair halted abruptly and collapsed against the wall in helpless laughter. To Henry's and Ingram's puzzled frowns he could make no answer, but only point to where little John Clarke, the terror of the nursery and the scourge of infants, sat cross-legged on the floor playing at cat's cradle with wee Henry and Willie Sinclair.

14

Friar Donal, his face beaming like a great red moon, rubbed his padded paws in satisfaction. "God has heard your prayers, my lady," he huffed. "Sir Henry is a made man."

Lady Isabel looked up from her needlework. "'Tis early days yet, Reverend Father. We know only that Henry is sent for, along with Malise Sparre and de Ard. How Haakon will decide is anybody's guess, and guessing's a game for fools and children."

"But surely, lady, we can rule out de Ard. And if it is a choice between Sparre and Sir Henry, what can Haakon do but choose your son?"

"Your bias does you credit, Friar Donal," said Lady Isabel. "But it is Haakon, alas, and not you who'll do the choosing. I fear my son's too much the Scot for Haakon's liking. Still, we must take the long view. If not now, then one day surely my son or his son must have the isles."

"Had your son only—"

"Good morrow, Mother. And you, Friar Donal." Henry Sinclair strode into his mother's chamber. Spurred and cloaked, his helmet crooked in his arm, he advanced to his mother's seat and knelt before her. "We are off now, Mother. Will ye gi' us your blessing?"

"With all my heart." Lady Isabel laid aside her work and placed her small hands on her son's bowed head. "God and St. Katherine attend you, my dear son, and keep you safe always." Sinclair rose and kissed his mother. Then he turned to the stout priest. "And you, father, will you bless us also?"

Friar Donal sketched a hasty sign of the cross, and mumbled a benediction.

"Amen," said Sinclair, crossing himself. "And now, Mother, I must ask you to keep a kindly eye on Janet while I'm away. Her time draws near, and I would have her most tenderly looked after."

"You need fear nothing on her account. She shall have every comfort that this house affords."

"I shall take my leave with a lighter heart for that. My thanks, Mother, and fare you well. You shall have letters from me by the first boat from Norway."

"God keep you, my son." Lady Isabel embraced him. "And God grant your errand prosper."

Sinclair grinned. "'Tis a fool's errand, more than likely. But 'tis good to be riding out with Ingram again."

"Do you keep a watchful eye on Johnny, I pray you. He is scarcely more than a boy."

"What? That great lout? Why, Mother, I was relying on that brawny knight to keep an eye on me." Sinclair chuckled. "But I'll see to him and do my best to steer him clear o' mischief."

"Now, Mother, it really is farewell I would have a moment alone with Janet ere Molly brings the children down to see us off. God be with you."

"And with you, Harry." Lady Isabel's eyes were dim.

"Adieu, Friar Donal," said Sinclair, nodding to the priest. "Keep me in your prayers."

"Never fear, Sir Henry," rumbled the friar. "I shall lay siege to heaven in your cause."

"Whatever that may be, hey?" Sinclair winked and, with a last wave of his hand, departed.

"I do wish your son liked me," muttered the friar, when Sinclair had quit the room.

"Why, Friar Donal, I have sometimes myself felt the same wish," replied Lady Isabel, taking up her needlework once more. "But I have learned to content myself with having his love."

"And yet there is none who has given more thought and care to his well-being."

Lady Isabel's smile was rueful. "That, however, is not necessarily a warrant for being liked."

In another quarter of the castle, that same theme was under discussion: "I wish I could like your mother, dearest, but I cannot. I feel—" Janet frowned. "I feel that she still has not accepted our marriage."

"What? After three children?"

"Even so."

Sinclair took his wife into the circle of his arms. "She is not unkind to you?"

"No. Never unkind."

He kissed her lightly on the brow. "Well, then, it is enough that you and I accept our marriage, accept it, live it and rejoice in it all down the years. Let others make of it what they will."

"You are so strong, Harry. Give me some of your strength that I may endure this separation without tears."

"I think I would not like that," replied Sinclair, stroking her soft hair.

"You'd have me weep?"

"Sometimes. When evening comes on and I am far away, 'twould comfort me to know that you are longing to have me home and close to you."

"Oh, my dear love, you know that I shall be but half myself till you return and make me whole again."

"God bless you, Janet." Sinclair's voice was husky and low. "I wish I could be here when this child comes. Will it be a girl this time, d'you think?"

"Would you like that?"

"Aye." Sinclair's smile was warm, lighting even his clear eyes. "Betsy would be glad of a little sister, and I—well, I do confess I find it a joy to be father to a girl."

"How so?"

Sinclair shrugged. "I do not quite know myself. But when I think on little Henry or Willie, I think of their training and schooling and the responsibilities they must be strengthened for. With Betts, well, I just enjoy her."

"You think, sir, that we women have not our share of responsibility?"

Sinclair rolled his eyes in mock supplication to heaven. "Now, madam," he said, "let me not walk into that snare. I know right well 'tis no easy thing to be a woman. And, indeed, my fondest hope for Betsy is that she will be the woman her mother is. But it is pleasant to be in thrall to a tiny lass, to mend her doll babies, to walk out with her and see the world through her eyes, and not to be forever speculating on titles, wills, inheritances, and feats of war."

Janet reached up and touched her husband's cheek. "I know, Harry. And I do love to see you and Betsy deep in talk over the great matters nearest her heart. In truth, it is a happy wonder to me how good a father you are."

"I am glad you think me so, but where's the wonder of it?"

Janet turned thoughtfully away and walked to the cold hearth. "Even as a boy, Harry, you were—well, stern. I—I do not mean that as an indictment of your character." She smiled sweetly. "It is just that I thought of you always as all steel and sinew and stern purpose. It was as if you never were a child, really."

"But I was, I assure you, and robbed birds' nests and broke my toys and plundered orchards with the worst."

Janet giggled. "I am glad, for—shall I confess it?—I wondered once if you were not born wearing armor."

"Ha-ha-ha!" Sinclair threw back his head and roared. "God pity my poor mother!"

"Oh, Harry, you know what I mean. And yet, when I see you with the children, it—it makes my heart fairly skip with delight."

Sinclair crossed to her and, catching her by the wrist, he drew her to his breast. "And how fares your heart when we are alone like this?"

"Ah, then my heart like the young hart leaps, as if it would escape its bonds and lie next yours in warm security."

"Then would you be quite heartless."

"But if you give me yours for mine—"

"Why, lady, you have had mine in close custody since we were lad and lass at play."

"Dearest, hold me. Tighter. Tighter still."

"Love, I must go."

"Harry." Janet kissed him long and lovingly on the mouth. "Think of me while you're away."

"The whole time, I swear it."

Janet, the tears starting, gazed up into Sinclair's face. "I charge you, husband, let not your eye or mind or heart be prey to the glamours of Haakon's court. I would not—"

"Hush, hush." Sinclair sealed her lips with his. "My heart will be here at Rosslyn, my mind on you only, and my eye, so long accustomed to feasting on your form and face, can scarce be tempted by any foreign fare."

Janet nestled her head on Sinclair's broad chest. "Harry, do you want this prize so very much?"

"More than I have admitted even to myself. But I have schooled myself against wanting too keenly. It is not likely I shall have it, so—"

"But you do want it?"

"Very much. God He knows how much I have already. But, dearest, what a great thing it would be to rule at Orkney, to secure the isles and leave to our sons so rich a legacy. I think 'twould make me young again to be about the work of establishing my hold on that long disputed claim, to enrich our holdings, and to try my hand and brain at governing that watery domain.

"Aye, Janet, I want it. God help me. Time and again, even in these happy years with you, I have taken down my ancestor's great sword and, clutching it in this good right hand, have dreamed such dreams and seen such visions as make my blood to sing."

"But you have been happy?"

"Aye. I count myself among the favored of this earth. And yet, sweet-heart, a man needs some enterprise, some great work, some task that calls up from deep within him all the courage, strength, and skill that he can muster. That, to me, means more than the rank and trappings of the thing. I want the task, Janet, for its own sake. Can you understand that?"

Janet sighed. "I think so. And because you do want it, I'll pray Christ and St. Katherine that you may have it. But I fear it, Harry. I fear it may take you from me, and from the peace and joy that have been our portion here."

Sinclair took her hands in his and kissed her slim white fingers. "Love, let your mind be easy. I think I will not get the coronet. And if I should, I swear that nothing short of death shall ever sunder us.

"Now, lass, one more kiss and I must go. There. God keep you. I will be with you ere the last leaf falls. Farewell."

Sinclair turned abruptly and hurried away to the courtyard where his men were already mounted and waiting. His children, under the watchful eye of the handsome Molly, came forward each in turn for his father's kiss.

"Now, Henry, as you are eldest, I look to you to keep order here. Mind Molly, and help your mother all you can."

"I will, Father."

"And you Willie, I trust you will have your prayers by heart by the time I return."

"The Ave, too, Father?"

"Aye, the Ave, too. And you, Mistress Betsy," Sinclair said, taking his little daughter up in his arms, "you must not forget your father while he is away. Promise?"

"I promise, Father."

Sinclair kissed her heartily. "There's my love. Now, then, God be with you all and—ah, here's Master Davey come to see us off. Hallo, Davey. Gi' us your hand, lad, for we must haste away."

David Sinclair took his brother's hand. "I wish you would take me along wi' Johnny," he said, his handsome face marred by an expression of petulance.

"Well, Davey, do you but attend to good old Knox and learn your lessons, and I make no doubt we shall find employment for you ere you are grown much older." Sinclair gave his youngest brother's hand a hard squeeze, then he turned and, taking the reins from little John Clarke, swung lightly up into the saddle. He sat there, a handsome martial figure, erect and strong, the early August sunlight glancing off his burnished helm. His quick glance surveyed the upturned faces, the grounds, the towering gray walls of this his beloved Rosslyn. A movement at the tower window caught his eye. Janet. He raised his hand in half salute, and that slight motion seemed to his impatient steed the signal to off.

Caught by surprise, Ingram, John Sinclair, and the little company raised a shout and urged their own mounts forward. Away the band clattered over the drawbridge after Sinclair. Their long road lay north to Caithness, where Scotland's rugged coast confronts the timeless storm-tossed sea.

15

Sigurd Hafthorsson, a stocky, hale, hearty nobleman in the warrior mold, was among the very first to welcome Sinclair and his party to the court at Marstrand. His bluff good nature quickly penetrated Sinclair's native reserve, and soon the two were leagued together in soldierly fellowship.

"I tell you, baron," declared the older man, in an oddly lucid blend of Latin, Norse, French, and English, "this is a happy day for me. Leif Jansson spoke of you as a most able and likely knight. From the look of you, I judge he was on the mark. You are the man we need, I feel certain of it."

Sinclair smiled. "Now if Haakon can be persuaded to your view, Lord Sigurd, my journey will not be in vain."

"Ah, Haakon! He is no fool, my friend. Let him but get a look at you alongside that old woman de Ard and this fox Malise Sparre and he can have no choice but to name you Orkney's lord." Hafthorsson clapped Sinclair on the shoulder. "Jarl Henry Sinclair! It sounds good, yes?"

Sinclair could not help thinking that it sounded rather strange, but *jarl* or *earl*, 'twas all one to him. He allowed that it was indeed pleasant to think on, however he was called.

"What is Haakon like?" he asked.

"A good king and a good man." Hafthorsson nodded assent to his own words. "We have had our troubles here. Those pirates that style themselves the Victuallers Brotherhood continually threaten our coast, so trade is sluggish; there is, of course, unrest in the isles; and now we have the charming spectacle of the two popes, with half the world acknowledging Urban, and the other half supporting Clement's claim.

"We, by the way, are officially in Urban's camp."

"Aye, and Scotland hath come down on Clement's side. I suppose that Haakon will weigh that, too, in his deliberations."

Hafthorsson shrugged. "He may. But he will put the security of the isles ahead of church affairs. I would counsel you, my friend; do not raise the topic in your talks with Haakon. If it must come up, let him be the one to raise it. Then, if you are the wise man I take you for, you will pass over it so lightly that it will not signify—unless, of course, you have strong convictions in the matter."

"I assure you, Lord Sigurd, I do not care who is pope, so long as it is not I."

"Ha-ha!" Hafthorsson clapped his hands in glee. "A heretic! I smell a heretic!"

"Not so, my lord," replied Sinclair, gravely. "For though I hold no love for politic pope or priest, I count myself a true son of holy church, and do acknowledge her authority in all things touching salvation."

"Well spoken, my friend. But what, I wonder, will you make of William of Orkney?"

"What is he?"

"An ecclesiastical knave, a mitered rogue, and long a thorn in the side of Norway. He is bishop at Kirkwall, and so far is he from being a good shepherd that all his care seems to be to keep the people in foment and disorder.

"You will have in him a powerful enemy when you are at last installed as jarl. He is a jealous, scheming, wily old man, no friend to Scots and no use to Norway. He maintains a veritable army at his castle there, hard by the cathedral of good St. Magnus, and he rules not with a shepherd's crook but with an iron rod." Hafthorsson shook his head. "He will cross you at every opportunity and do all that he can to thwart your purpose. Make no doubt of it, my dear Lord, you have in William a foe to reckon with."

Sinclair smiled. "Not yet. Haakon—"

"Will make you jarl. He has to. He needs your strength, my friend. This land has suffered much in latter years. We have not yet recovered from the scourge of the Black Death. Why, a third part of the population was carried off, and the whole country lay in desolation. Crops rotted in the fields; the cattle starved; our once great merchant fleet is but a memory, and our treasury is still not recovered from the terrible drain of those dreadful times.

"Our late king, God rest him, did what he could, and more than any one man could be expected to do. But, I tell you, we were beggared by that cursed plague, and all of Haakon's power and skill are bent on reviving his ailing kingdom. The revenues from the isles are very much on his mind, and he will choose the man—Scot or no Scot—who is best able to bring the gold and silver in.

"He is a great man, our Haakon. I would to God he had come to the throne in a happier time, that he and our fair Queen Margaret might live out their days in peace and leave to our little Prince Olaf a secure and thriving land.

"But Haakon is a man. He deals in what is, not in what has been, and he will spend himself without stinting to bring about what ought to be. Wait until you meet him, my dear baron. You will see."

Sinclair waited. And in the hospitable interim, Ingram Gunn came forward with a piece of news. He and Sinclair were taking their ease in the castle gardens on one of those sunlit summer nights characteristic of that latitude, when Gunn announced, "We have sustained our first casualty."

"What? Is someone hurt? Clarke has not run afoul of some dairymaid's husband, has he? I'll send him packing in a minute if—"

"No, no. Clarke, so far as I know, continues to conduct himself with unwonted discretion. But one of our party hath sustained a wound that bids fair to do for him."

Sinclair looked grave. "Who's hurt?"

"Why, none other than your own brother."

"Johnny?"

"Even so." Gunn shook his head sadly. "I doubt he will recover, Harry His case is serious."

"But I saw Johnny not a quarter of an hour ago, and he—Hold! I know that look, coz. You are making game of me." Sinclair, half vexed, was obliged to laugh in spite of himself. "What is the nature of his wound?"

Ingram laughed. "'Tis mortal, I tell you. Your bonny brother's took a blow squarely on the heart."

"Ah-hah! The sly dog! Who is she, Ingram? What's the lady's name?"

"Why, 'tis none other than the fair Ingeborg, daughter to Denmark's King Waldemar."

"His natural daughter, as it happens," remarked Sinclair.

"Why, yes, sir, if by that you mean she was begot in the natural manner. And if there be any other way, I've yet to hear of it."

"Peace to your jesting, kinsman, pray. Humph. So Johnny's smitten."

"Fatally."

"How came you to know of this, and I did not?"

"Come, come, Harry. You are the very first man our Johnny would consult in matters of the martial kind. But when it comes to *amor,* he turned quite predictably to me. It is the mark of a wise man that, when he is himself in doubt, he seeks counsel with the best available authority. And I—"

"You are a most conceited ass!" Then Sinclair, a broad grin lighting his usually stern face, hunched forward confidentially. "What did he want of you?"

Ingram reached down, plucked a rose, and made a great business of inhaling its fragrance. "Well, sir, what he wanted was, in fact a rhyme for *bosom*."

"Ha-ha-ha!" Sinclair threw back his head and roared. "For—for *bosom*! Ha-ha! Oh, God and St. Katherine defend me! For *bosom*, you say?"

"Aye. Johnny knows, if you do not, the proper course for lovers. And that must include the inditing of verses to the fair object of a man's heart's promptings. He had got so far along as the lady's swanlike throat, but there he found himself at an impasse, and so turned to me. And very wisely too."

"And did you—could you help him?"

Ingram looked miffed. "My dear cousin, when in the long history of our two families have the Sinclairs ever looked to the Gunns for aid in vain? Help? Of course I helped. Johnny brought his little difficulty to the proper man, I assure you."

"Well?"

"Well?"

"Well, are you going to keep me on tenterhooks, man? What was the result?"

Ingram knit his brow and pressed his fingers to his forehead, the very picture of recollection. "Let me think," he said. "Hmm-mm. Ah, yes. 'Twas something in this vein, as I recall it:

> Each separate breast doth well combine
> To make a perfect bosom,
> And for to rest my weary head
> I could not help but choose 'em.

"Jesu, Mary!" Sinclair slid from the stone bench and collapsed helpless on the soft lush grass.

As he lay there all a-heap, shaking with laughter, the tears streaming down his face, a soft footfall was heard on the gravel walk and a silken voice inquired: "What ails my worthy kinsman, Ingram Gunn? Has he the falling sickness? Or has he imbibed too freely of the native beer?"

"No to both, Malise Sparre," retorted Gunn, eyeing the black-clad figure with undisguised distaste. "My cousin is very hearty, thank you, and when he has caught his breath he will so assure you and will convey his own thanks for your kindly interest."

Sinclair, propping himself up on his elbows and squinting against the light, favored Sparre with an ironic smile. "Well, Sparre, we meet again. You happen on us in our boyish folly, and find me prostrate before the onslaught of Ingram's wit. But," he got lightly to his feet, "as you see, I am quite, quite sound."

"I am glad, kinsman, for I would not have you absent from those ceremonies that must attend my investiture. In these affairs, family is everything."

"Well, well," remarked Sinclair, turning to Ingram Gunn, "'tis plain that though I have not the falling sickness, poor Malise suffers from the rising sickness still."

"Indeed, coz, he doth seem forever bent on getting above himself."

"A most laudable end," replied Sinclair, brushing the grass from his sleeves. "But, alas, although he stand on tiptoe and reach even to the stars, he cannot rise above his nature. Strive as he will, there is that within him which weights him down and will forever keep him in the dust."

Sparre's pale face flamed, and his long white fingers played about the ivory-hafted dagger at his belt. "Mock on, Sinclair. Much good may it do you. For, know this, my noble cousin, while you have been idling away these years at your pease-and-porridge keep, this rising star hath let his light be seen in high places, and I have won for myself such friends as will ensure for me favor with Haakon and a fast hold on Orkney's crown."

"Well crowed, old cock!" cried Ingram, capering about and flapping his arms. "Cock-a-doodle-do-oo! The king o' the dunghill speaks!"

"Fool! I am summoned to meet with Haakon on the morrow. We will talk of dunghills hereafter, you and I. In truth, I do not love you, Ingram Gunn. But if your manners improve in time, I may allow you sovereignty over a dunghill of your own choosing in some remote and uninhabited corner of the isles."

Ingram executed a many-flourished bow. "Your generosity, my lord, o'erwhelms me. I am—penetrated."

"Cross swords with me in place of words and you will find yourself so in short order."

"I tremble," murmured Gunn, clutching at his breast. "I faint with fear. Harry, hide me from this warlike lord lest—"

"Oh, hide your face," growled Sparre, "for I am sick of looking on it." And he spun on his heel and stalked off.

"Well, now," said Sinclair, "that was a pleasant interlude. I wonder what manner of folk he hath enlisted in his cause."

"They must be of poor stuff to ally themselves wi' that."

"Even so, Ingram, he would not brag and blow so did he not have some warrant for his confidence. I confess I do not like it that he goes before me to Haakon."

"Pah! 'Tis nothing, Harry. Why, you will shine all the brighter in Haakon's eyes by contrast with that crow."

Sinclair draped a fraternal arm around Ingram's broad shoulders. "Well, my best of friends, it may be that Sparre hath Haakon's ear, but I will not complain so long as I have hearts and hands like thine to rely on."

Ingram was for once quite dumb. This most uncharacteristic speech caught him all unwary. "Why—why, Harry, I did not—do not—"

"Heigh-ho!" cried Sinclair, thumping Ingram 'twixt the shoulders. "Let us go and stir up Johnny. You fetch your lute and I'll essay to sing his own verse to him. 'Each separate breast. . .' Ha-ha! 'Twill start him raving!"

Ingram giggled like a mischievous schoolboy. Then he sobered and said, "Go not too roughly, Harry, pray. He truly loves her."

Sinclair nodded. "I have seen her, Ingram. And I am glad for Johnny. Still, ye'd no deny me a little merriment at his expense. The fair Ingeborg will make it up to him anon, or I do much mistake her."

"Ye'd not oppose this courtship, then?"

"Not I. No, sir, I think it meet that one Sinclair at least shall have a prize. Come! Let's find the fellow out and ease his stricken heart with song."

16

Sinclair had passed a restless night; now, at first birdsong, he was up and dressed and out, pacing in the courtyard, a handsome figure in his sable cote hardie, with silver belt and wine-colored hose gartered at the knee. He had a baldric slung over his right shoulder, and his silver-hafted daggers—anlace and misericorde—winked and gleamed in the clear sunlight. His gloves, embroidered with the badge of his knighthood, he carried in his hand, slapping with them at his thigh as he strode along. Around his strong and sunburnt neck was hung a silver chain with St. Katherine's image pendant. His soft leather pouch, like his soft leather shoes, was stamped with gold and sewn with tiny pearls.

He looked that morning altogether the curled and elegant courtier. But not even his fine array could disguise the hard muscularity, the breadth of shoulder, and the bulk of limb that marked him for what he was, a man born to lead wherever duty, honor, and high adventure called.

A mingling of soft voices came to Sinclair's ear, and he looked down the walk to where a party of ladies, together with their children, floated toward him from the chapel where they had been at mass. As they drew near, he stood aside and bowed low. The party halted, and Sinclair heard himself hailed sweetly in the Latin tongue.

He raised his eyes to see a woman, as tall almost as himself and fairer than the morning, clad in a simple flowing gown of pale green cinched with a girdle of gold. She beckoned to him, smiling, and as he crossed to her, Sinclair noted the gold circlet crowning the snowy wimple that framed the lovely face.

"God save you, Queen Margaret of Norway," said Sinclair, also in Latin, as he went down on one knee before her.

"Come, sir, rise and let us have a word with you. Are you not the Scot, Sinclair?"

"I am, Your Highness. Henry Sinclair, baron of Rosslyn."

"You are welcome, here, sir. We trust you are well looked after."

"Admirably, Your Highness. We want for nothing."

The young queen's silvery laughter quite discomposed the stiff formality Sinclair essayed. "Not so, sir, Not so. You want what de Ard and Sparre so ardently desire. And what would you do to have it, I wonder?"

"Why, Your Highness, I would do as your lord the king requires, no less, no more."

"Well said. Very well said." Queen Margaret turned and shared her approval with the attendant ladies, some of whom gave way to birdlike titters that made the back of Sinclair's neck go hot and crimson. "You have an audience with my lord this morning, have you not?"

"Within the hour, Your Highness."

"Tell us, Baron. What is your condition in Scotland?"

"Why, it is a very happy one," replied Sinclair, smiling. "For I have an old house and an old name and two sturdy sons who, God willing, will maintain both house and name in honor after me."

"Ah, then you are twice blest. Two sons?"

"Aye, Your Highness, and a daughter; and another child is expected soon."

Queen Margaret beamed. "Why, these Scots are noble breeders! Splendid, splendid! You will people King Robert's realm with Sinclairs."

Sinclair grinned. "I will do my part, Your Highness."

"We have but one child ourselves. Olaf, come here." A frail, pale-haired boy of some seven or eight years stepped forward and stared at Sinclair with solemn eyes. "What think you of our prince, Baron Sinclair? Is he not a pretty boy?"

Sinclair nodded. "He hath borrowed his beauty from his mother."

"And left me poorer?" There was mischief in Margaret's tone.

"Nay, Your Highness. For you have been endowed so richly that no amount of lending could diminish your rich store."

"You are, sir, a wicked flatterer, I fear."

"Your Highness has but to consult her glass to confirm me an honest man."

"An honest man! Now there is a wonder rarely seen in these parts. My lord the king will scarce know what to make of you." Queen Margaret eyed Sinclair curiously. "Tell me, is your lady wife quite beautiful?"

"Quite beautiful, Your Highness."

"And is she also honest?"

"Indeed, she hath never given me cause to think her otherwise."

"Wonder of wonders! 'Twould be worth a journey to your country to meet with so much honesty."

"All Scotland would be honored were Your Highness to grace us with her presence there."

Margaret looked down at her son. "Would you like that, Olaf? To visit Scotland one day?"

"Yes, Lady Mother, for I would like to play with this man's boys."

Sinclair laughed delightedly. He bent down and addressed himself to the delicate child. "Do come, my prince," he said. "Henry and Willie will let you ride their ponies, and their mother will fatten you up with great plates of steaming porridge."

"What is porridge, sir?"

"Why, oats, my son," answered Margaret in Sinclair's stead. "Everyone knows that Scots dine on nothing but oats—oats in the morning, oats at noonday, and at supper oats again."

"Aye," said Sinclair, grinning. "And on feast days and in Lent as well."

The small prince wrinkled his royal nose. "I think I should not like it much."

"'Twould make you stout and strong, my prince," said Sinclair. "'Tis oats that make of Scots such hardy fighters."

Prince Olaf seemed to consider this for a moment. Then he said, "Shan't eat oats myself. But when I am king, I'll send to Scotland for men to fight for me."

"I hope, my prince, that you will send for me."

The boy nodded. "I think I would be safe with you," he said.

Queen Margaret took the boy by the hand. "Come," she said. "We must go in and break fast."

"But not on oats, hey?" Sinclair winked at the boy.

The young queen smiled at Sinclair. "We are glad to have met you, sir," she said. "We hope to talk with you again before you take your leave."

Sinclair bowed. "You have only to command me, Your Highness," he said.

Margaret started away, then turned and, from a little distance, called, "Baron Sinclair!"

"Your Highness?" Sinclair hurried to her.

"Haakon is much concerned with the decline of Norway's shipping. You would do well to think on ships, Sinclair." And with that, Queen Margaret slipped away.

"Oh, Janet," murmured Sinclair to himself, "'tis well you have not seen this royal lady, or I should never have been able to persuade you to stay at home at Rosslyn.

"But now to the king. And may God defend my cause."

Haakon, although he was not yet forty years old, showed in his pale and deeply furrowed face the weight of the cares of his kingship. He looked tired, Sinclair thought; tired and heavy-burdened. But his manner was open and kindly, and he appeared to study the Scottish claimant with keen interest.

"Welcome, Lord Sinclair," said Haakon, his voice firm, low-pitched, and clear. "We regret that we could not meet with you earlier, but a king, you see, is master of everything but his own time.

"We will dispense with ceremony here, for we have much to discuss. Do you avail yourself of this chair before us. My counselors and I have some questions to put to you, and we would not have you wearied with long standing."

"Thank you, my lord." Sinclair seated himself before the dais and coolly took in one by one the faces of the dozen grave nobles arrayed on either side of Haakon's throne. He felt heartened to see Hafthorsson there; the rest were strangers to him.

"Baron Sinclair," Haakon began, "we do not hesitate to say that your fame has run before you into Norway. We have heard many things to your credit, and nothing to your detriment—if we except your being a Scot bound by ties of blood to Scotland's throne."

"My lord—"

"In a moment, Baron." Haakon held up a thin white hand. "We will deal with that in due course. But we are curious to learn what you may have heard of us."

"Why, little, my lord, but that little is all in Your Majesty's favor. I know that Your Majesty hath the love of his people, the esteem of other nations, the respect even of his enemies."

"That is very little, and very good." A faint smile passed over Haakon's thin lips. "No more?"

"Your Majesty hath been sore beset by difficulties at home and abroad. The Swedish and the German campaigns, the Black Death, the decline of trade—all these have troubled Your Majesty's reign. The Baltic pirates harass Your Majesty's coasts, the Hansa merchants monopolize the sealanes, and the continuing strain on Your Majesty's treasury makes Your Majesty's kingly burdens more heavy than those most monarchs bear. But, so I have heard, Your Majesty does bear them, and does, despite their crushing weight, so conduct this state as to have won completely the minds and hearts of his people."

"God and His holy mother," murmured Haakon, sitting bolt upright. "What more do you know?"

"Why, that Your Majesty's little son hath thwarted the Mecklenburg claim to Denmark's throne, and that Your Majesty's wise policy in dealing with the Swedish nobles may yet result in that Scandanavian dynasty which was Your Majesty's father's fondest dream."

"Do your hear this Scot?" demanded Haakon of his counselors. "Ogmund Finnsson, what do you make of this?"

A grizzled noble, long-jawed and lean, hunched forward in his seat. "It appears, my lord, that this man is not the stranger we had thought him. May I have Your Majesty's leave to put a question to him?"

Haakon waved his assent.

Finnsson, his voice that of a field commander, turned to Sinclair and said, "How is it, sir, that you, a Scot, have taken pains to learn so much of state affairs in Norway?"

"That is easily answered, sir," replied Sinclair. "A shrewd man will make it his business to study those matters that most nearly affect his own hopes of preferment in this world."

"And what of the next?" demanded a barrel-shaped bishop, seated next to Finnsson.

"As to that, my lord bishop, the shrewd man puts no trust in himself, but rather clings to the rule of holy church that she may guide him safely through the hazards of this world to that which is to come."

But the bishop would not let go. "And whose claim do you support, sir? Urban's or Clement's?"

"My lord bishop, you must excuse me. I am but a layman and know little of these matters. I can only trust that our Lord will, in His own good time, set matters right and mend the rent in the seamless garment of His church." From the corner of his eye, Sinclair could see Haakon's lips twitch in a barely repressed smile.

"There's another matter we would lay before you," Haakon said. "Our ambitions for Orkney have been most sorely thwarted by a countryman of yours, William, bishop of those isles."

An angry buzzing rose among Haakon's advisers at the mention of William's name, but the king waved them to silence.

"This William is a sore thorn in our side, a great, gross, grasping, greedy churchman who hath usurped lands and revenues belonging to ourselves. He shifts allegiance with every changing wind, mulcts our people, lays harsh laws and harsher penalties upon them, and keeps at his great hall a body of men-at-arms whose sole duty is to enforce his will and to protect his person against an angry and disaffected people.

"We cannot think our rule in Orkney firmly secured so long as this clerical cormorant feeds his private coffers at our expense and at such cost to our island folk."

"My lord," Sinclair replied, "it would be our first business in those isles to restrain this bishop and to restore all things illicitly acquired."

Haakon pursed his lips shrewdly. "But he is a Scot."

Sinclair smiled, but his smile was thin and touched with grimness. "Alas, my lord, Scot fighting Scot is no new thing in the annals of my country. Besides, the earl's allegiance is to Your Majesty. The fortunes of Orkney and of Norway are so conjoined as to make disloyalty to the one rank treason to the other. Were I to serve this court in Orkney, I would deal with this William."

"But you would not attack his person?" interposed Haakon's own bishop, in some alarm.

"Why, no, my lord bishop, only his body—of armed men."

A murmur of approval ran through the chamber, and before the bishop could launch out on another tack, Sigurd Hafthorsson broke in. "You have, I am told, known what it is to lead men into battle. Can we suppose, then, that you would not shun a call to arms from our noble liege?"

"You may rely on me."

"Now come we to it," declared Haakon, fixing his gaze on Sinclair's face. "You say you would fight in our cause, and we believe you. But what if Scotland's Robert makes a like claim? Where will you stand then, Baron Sinclair?"

"Your Majesty holds the answer in his hands. And if those hands bestow upon this head the coronet of Orkney, then these hands shall wield the sword in Norway's cause whenever Norway calls."

A murmur ran around the tapestried hall, but Haakon stilled the buzz with an imperious raising of his palm. "That is well said, Baron Sinclair. But we know it is hard enough in this world to cleave to even one loyalty. The gospel itself tells us that no man can serve two masters."

Sinclair smiled. "I'd no gainsay the gospel, my lord. I can only say that, should Norway recognize my claim, I'll do as much for Norway. That, my lord, is the word of a Christian knight. I can offer no other surety."

"In this court, we deem that surety sufficient. But, tell us, you are in your own mind in fealty to Robert still, are you not?"

"I am, my lord, and will be. But if I am ever found wanting, he that gives can also take away.

"My lord, Robert, is not a man troubled by ambition. His only enemy, England, is in nowise prepared to disturb his reign. He seeks no conquests, covets no territories; he wants only to live out his remaining years at home and in peace."

"He is an uncommonly wise king," murmured Haakon, dryly. Then he added, "So you think he will make no demands of you?"

"I can foresee no occasion for it, my lord."

"Baron Sinclair, tell us, if you were to find yourself made jarl of Orkney, what would you do?"

"Why, my lord, having kissed Your Majesty's hands, and having offered a mass in thanksgiving, I would return at once to Scotland and set about building a fleet of ships."

"Ships?" Haakon's brows lifted, and a spark of interest lighted his tired eyes. "And why would you do that, pray?"

Sinclair's speech and gestures grew more animated. "Consider, my lord: a man suddenly finds himself possessed of an earldom made up of more than an hundred islands scattered over a vast expanse of sea.

How else can he establish his rule there, bring the populace into sub-mission, and collect for his liege those monies due him except he build, as it were, a navy, whereby he can with his men-at-arms make haste from isle to isle, redressing wrongs, quelling disorder, and collecting revenues owing to the crown? I think, my lord, it is the only way."

Haakon nodded, plainly impressed. "It would be the answer, Baron; it could well be. God He knows we have long wanted this business settled, and God He knows, too, how sorely we need the revenue.

"So you would build a fleet?" Haakon rubbed his jaw, musing. "And you could do that?"

"I could, my lord."

"Well!" Haakon got to his feet, and Sinclair and the counselors rose also. "Baron Sinclair, we thank you for coming here and for sharing with us your thoughts on this matter. We will not keep you longer, but I would know one thing more."

"Your Majesty has but to ask."

"What would you do if the earldom fell to another?"

Sinclair did not flinch. "My lord, I would return to Rosslyn and study to be properly thankful for all that I have there."

Haakon, his face inscrutable, nodded. "Leave us now, Baron. We and our counselors have much to think on. Our decision will not be long delayed, we do assure you."

Sinclair bowed himself out of the chamber and walked out into the salt-scented summer air. "My God," he said aloud. "I am soaked quite through with sweat."

17

Haakon's word was good.

On the morning of the second day following Sinclair's appearance before the king and his counselors, the three claimants were summoned to stand before Haakon and hear his judgment on the lordship of the isles.

Malise Sparre, in the funereal black he affected, stood pale and composed on Sinclair's right, with only the cold glitter of his feline eyes revealing anything of his hopeful apprehension. At Sinclair's left, Sir Alexander de Ard, a sly smile working the corners of his weak mouth, rocked softly on the balls of his feet, his thumbs hooked in his gold-and-enameled belt, his pudgy fingers twitching to some music he alone could hear.

Sinclair himself, clad in plain brown fustian, stood with his sturdy hands clasped behind his back, his legs well braced for the impact of what must come. If hope or dread disturbed his heart, his face at least was serene. He had slept the past two nights, really slept, having acknowledged to himself that he had done all that could be done, that his hopes were meager, that he was likely to have no more out of this than his honor and pride intact. But that, he reckoned, was much. And he would rather carry that much back with him to Rosslyn than go to Orkney with anything less.

The counselors filed in. Then Haakon, with the beautiful Margaret beside him, her hand resting on his arm, entered. He acknowledged the bows of those assembled and took his seat upon the throne.

"My friends," the king began, "this day has been long in coming, and our heart is easier now that it is here. This matter has been for too long unresolved, and it had been our ambition and our intent to have it settled long ere this.

"But affairs of this magnitude do not lend themselves to hasty resolution. There were considerations on several sides. These had to be weighed and sifted, not only in light of our own desires but also in light of what is just." Haakon's eyes rested briefly on the faces of the pretenders.

"We have, as you know, three claimants to the title of jarl of Orkney, each with some considerable merit and each with some considerable substance for his claim. We are well aware that, whatever we decree, there must needs be two men disappointed of the prize. We wish it were otherwise; and yet we count ourselves fortunate in having such proven, able men to choose from.

"For, mistake us not, there is more to this title than honors and rank. 'Tis true, the jarl of Orkney will stand first among the nobles of this realm, second only to the lords spiritual and to ourself. But this lord will have much to contend with in securing his position." Haakon smiled a wintry smile. "It is one thing, my friends, to receive honors. It is another thing to keep them. More especially is this true for Orkney.

"For, though it grieves us to say it, our subjects in the isles are a stiff-necked and rebellious breed. Separated from us by full sixty miles and more of open sea, their loyalties the plaything of various insubordinate lords, the people of Orkney and Shetland show a most unfilial disregard for their duty of love and service to their king.

"He who wears the mantle, coronet, and authority of jarl must, by whatever means, bring these people into submission and secure for us not only their loyal obedience and faithful service, but also those monies so long owing to our depleted coffers.

"These considerations were foremost in our thoughts as we weighed the several claims.

"Further, prudence led us to draw up some particular conditions concerning the conduct of the government of these isles. It seemed to us wise to forestall misunderstanding and its attendant discord by causing to be writ down plainly the duties, functions, and limitations which we judge proper to the office of jarl of Orkney.

"We ask now that our faithful kinsman, Sigurd Hafthorsson, stand forth and read out the particulars, that all may hear and understand." Haakon nodded to the doughty Hafthorsson, who then stepped forward and, in a ringing voice, declared:

"These are the conditions which our lord and king, Haakon, whom God bless and prosper, hath, with his council, set down for the governance of the isles. He who is chosen will be chosen on condition that he freely and without reservation subscribe to the articles set forth as follows:

"In the first place, therefore, we firmly oblige ourselves to serve our said lord the king outside the lands and islands of Orkney with one hundred good men or more, fully equipped in arms, for the convenience and use of our said lord the king, whensoever we shall have been sufficiently required thereto by his messengers or his letters, and fore-warned hereto within Orkney for three months, but so that when we shall come with them to the presence of our said lord the king, from that time he shall provide us and ours with victuals.

"Further, if any persons design to attack or invade with hostile intent the said lands and islands of Orkney, or even the land of Shetland, in any way, we promise and oblige us forthwith to defend the said lands with the men whom we shall be able to gather for this purpose, in good condition, not only from the said lands and islands but also with the whole strength of our kin, friends, and servants.

"Likewise, if it shall happen that our lord the king is obliged by any right or other reason or necessity to invade any lands or kingdoms, then shall we be forthcoming to him in help and service with our whole power.

"Further, we promise in good faith that we will not build or construct castles or other fortifications within the lands or islands aforesaid, unless we shall have obtained the favor, good pleasure, and consent of our said lord the king.

"And that . . ." But here, Hafthorsson's voice cracked; and Sinclair, in spite of himself, could not forbear to grin. Haakon himself signaled for wine to be brought to the laboring Shetlander. Hafthorsson gratefully drained the cup, bowed to Haakon, and said, "Thanks, my gracious lord. 'Tis wonderfully dry work."

"You shall be free to wet down thy throat full liberally hereafter, my friend. Pray, read on."

With a great clearing of his pipes, Sigurd continued: "And that we shall be bound to cherish and to hold the foresaid lands and islands of Orkney and all the inhabitants thereof, both cleric and laic, poor and rich, according to their rights.

"Moreover, we faithfully promise that we will not at any time alienate or sell the aforesaid earldom and that lordship or lands or islands belonging to the said earldom or our right which, by grace of God and our lord the king, we have now obtained in the said earldom, lands, and islands, away from our said lord the king or his heirs and successors or their kingdom, nor shall we make over the same to any one in surety or pledge, or otherwise deal with them contrary to the will and good pleasure of the king and his successors."

Christ and His Holy Mother, mused Sinclair to himself, is there no end to this? Hafthorsson will not have breath left to blow out a candle.

". . .if it shall happen that our said lord the king or his heirs and successors wish to come to the said lands and islands for their defense, or other reasonable cause, or to direct thither his councillors and men, we shall then be bound to assist with all our power our said lord the king and his heirs and councillors and men, and to provide competently on their expenses our said lord the king and his heirs, men and councillors, with those things of which they shall be in need and as necessity shall then require so to ordain from the said lands and islands."

Hafthorsson shot an anguished glance at Haakon, but got only an encouraging nod in acknowledgment. With a huge sigh, he sawed on:

"Further, we promise that we shall not raise or begin any war, litigation, or dissension with any persons, either strangers or inhabitants, by occasion of which war, litigation, or dissension, our lord the king and his heirs and successors or his kingdom of Norway or the foresaid lands and islands may receive any damage.

"Likewise if it shall happen, which God forfend, that we shall do any notable wrong and injustice to any person within the aforesaid lands or islands or cause any notable injury to any one, as loss of life or mutilation of members or depredation of goods, in that case we shall answer in the presence of our said lord the king and his councillors, and satisfy according to the laws of the realm for our faults.

"Moreover, whensoever our said lord the king shall call us to his presence for any reason, where or when he shall wish to hold his general assembly, then we shall be bound to proceed thither to him for rendering to him counsel and assistance.

"Moreover . . ."

Somewhere between "moreovers," Sinclair's eyes wandered, stopped, and inadvertently locked with those of Queen Margaret. To his utter astonishment, he saw her make a most unqueenly grimace, as if to say, Is this not ghastly?

But, almost before he could be certain of what he saw, the young queen had quite composed herself and resumed the cool blank look of royal longsuffering, leaving Sinclair to fight down as best he could the laughter stirring in his belly.

Almighty God, he thought, I am losing an earldom, and I will split if I cannot laugh. He passed his right hand over his mouth and bit hard into the fleshy pad at the base of his index finger. That tided him past danger, but he would not look again toward Margaret. Instead, he chose a unicorn prancing in the tapestry above King Haakon's head, fixed his gaze on that, and let the words roll on.

". . .we promise that we shall not infringe the truces and security of our said lord the king, nor in any manner violate the peace which has been made or confirmed with strangers or natives or with any whomsoever, but shall defend all such with our whole power and hold all those for our confederates whom our said lord the king of Norway desires to esteem his friends and supporters.

"Further, we promise that we shall make no league with the bishop of Orkney, nor enter into nor establish any friendship with him unless with the good pleasure and consent of our said lord the king, but we shall assist him against the said bishop until he shall do what of right or deservedly he ought to do in those things which our said lord the king desires or may demand of the said bishop.

"Further, when God shall be pleased to call us from this life, then this earldom and lordship, with the lands and islands with all right, ought freely to return to our oft-mentioned lord and king. . ."

That "oft-mentioned" drew a silent heartfelt "aye" from the depths of Sinclair's soul.

". . .and his heirs and successors, and should we have left male children, one or more, procreated of our own body, then that one of them who shall have claimed the foresaid earldom and lordship ought to seek herein the grace, good pleasure, and consent of our said lord the king and his heirs and successors."

Sinclair thought of Henry and Willie. Well, they have Rosslyn and a good name for their heritage, and require no man's consent or grace for those, at any rate.

"Likewise we faithfully promise that we shall be bound to pay to our said lord the king or his official at Tunsberg at the next feast of St. Martin, bishop and confessor, one thousand gold pieces which are called nobles in English money, in which we acknowledge ourselves to be bound as a just debt.

"And that," croaked Hafthorsson, "save for divers matters of preamble and postscript, concludes the reading of the conditions of the investiture of the jarl of Orkney."

The room went deathly still. All eyes now centered on the king. He, for his part, scanned the faces of the three nobles standing before his throne. Then he got slowly to his feet and in a low voice began:

"Sir Alexander de Ard, sometime governor of Orkney; Malise Sparre, lord of Skuldane; Henry Sinclair, baron of Rosslyn, we have studied your petitions and weighed your several claims.

"This day you have heard our desires for Orkney and Shetland, and our conditions for bestowing title to lordship over them." The king's voice gathered strength now, and he called out clear and loud, "Do you, Henry Sinclair, baron of Rosslyn, promise in faith and honor to fulfill all the agreements, conditions, promises, and articles which are contained in the writings read here but now?"

Lightning coursed along Sinclair's spine and crackled in his brain. All in an instant he could see Margaret smiling, could hear the air go out of Sparre's lungs, could feel his legs move in a step not solely of his own volition. His blurred gaze focused on the king's face, and he heard himself say, "My lord, I do promise it."

"Come forward, then," said Haakon, kindly, "and render fealty."

Henry Sinclair approached the throne, knelt, and kissed the king's hands, and received the king's kiss on his lips.

Cheers rang through the hall; but in the din, Henry's and Haakon's eyes met and held. In the older man's look were hope and a question; in Sinclair's, a pledge and his heartfelt thanks.

Ingram Gunn was first to come forward to greet Sinclair as jarl—although, as he said, it near to broke his jaw to say it—and he made as if to kneel. Henry forestalled him and drew him to his heart. "From you, Ingram, I ask only that you will bide with me in weal and woe, and be as it were my other self in all things."

Ingram's eyes misted over. "Harry, ye know it's what I'd ask."

The cousins clasped hands. "I thank God for you always, Ingram. Be patient with me if I sometimes neglect to tell you so."

Ingram laughed. "Be patient with me if I remind you now and then. But now we have work to do, coz, man's work. God, is it not glorious?"

"Aye, glorious, but so beset with conditions that I scarce know how I shall move my right hand without breaking half a dozen."

"Aye. I thought poor Lord Sigurd would never come to the end of 'em. But no fear, Harry. Once you are away about your business, the conditions will take care o' themselves."

More conditions were to come, however, before the actual investiture of Sinclair as lord of the isles and premier noble of Norway. Haakon wisely provided that hostages be comfortably kept at Tunsberg against the delivery of the thousand nobles on St. Martin's Day. Among those to remain were Sparre, de Ard, and, to his undisguised delight, the love-struck Johnny Sinclair.

"We think it well to keep the unlucky claimants with us for a time," Haakon had said to Sinclair. "For though we doubt not you will achieve all that you have vowed and more, we would not have you encumbered by any untoward actions from those who might hope to profit should you fail."

"That was well thought of, my lord," Sinclair had replied. "These waivers were not so gladly given into our hands as to make us certain of them that gave them up."

"As to your brother—"

"My lord, it suits him and me. I doubt he would come away willingly at any odds, and I am content to have a Sinclair here to keep Your Majesty mindful of me."

And so, on 2 August in the year of Our Lord 1379, King Haakon and Queen Margaret; their attendant lords and ladies; Alexander de Ard, all smiling, weak, good-natured; and Malise Sparre, sullen and withdrawn; together with all who had come to Marstrand to hear the king's judgment, gathered in the church to witness the investiture.

Henry Sinclair, in crimson velvet, stood and gazed down the long center aisle to where the lords spiritual waited to receive him. There was waiting for him, too, gleaming and winking in the candlelight on the altar where it lay, a coronet of gold.

PART III

18

Sigurd Hafthorsson could hardly be blamed for feeling just a little puffed up. For, from offers of divers kinds, the new jarl of Orkney had accepted the hospitality of Hafthorsson's hall in Shetland. Still, a man does not pride himself on the condition of his friends—not a real man with real friends; and Lord Sigurd was real enough and man enough and friend enough to value Sinclair for his qualities as a man. All the same . . .

"God bless us, friend Hafthorsson, these islands must be the very parliament of birds. I swear I have never seen so many kinds in all my life before." Sinclair, leaning on the rail of Lord Sigurd's bark as it plowed through a sparkling sea, was plainly enchanted. "Look there! Puffins, are they not?"

Hafthorsson shaded his eyes and stared at the rocky inlet, spied the yellow-billed black-and-white sentries, and replied. "Aye, my lord. I love the blessed creatures. Like neighbors, they are. But you should be here in nesting time. These flocks you see today are as nothing compared to what we have then. Why, the cliffs ring night and day with bird cries, and our skies are filled with all the feathered kind, from the smallest tit to the great sea eagles. The snowy owl comes down from the icy fastness, and there are geese and ducks and gulls of every description, gannets, gallinules, and birds that no man yet has put a name on.

"Our lads are busy then, I can tell you. They go out in droves to scale the cliffs and steal the eggs we all love so."

Sinclair eyed the soaring volcanic palisades dead ahead. "That is no boy play, surely. I think I am no coward, my friend, but 'twould take more than an appetite for eggs to make me attempt those heights."

Hafthorsson laughed. "You would not think it to look at me," he said, slapping his paunch, "but I was myself a clever climber in my youth, and risked my neck—aye, and my eyes, too, for the parent birds did not welcome our depredations—to bring home a trove of succulent eggs to grace our table. After a Lent of salt fish and coarse messes, eggs are very grateful to the palate, I assure you."

"Do your own boys also scale the cliffs?"

"They do."

Sinclair shook his head. "If my lads were to try it, I think my heart would cease to beat till they were safely down again. But then—ah, a good morrow, coz. Is this not a fair morning?"

Ingram Gunn appeared on deck, with little John Clarke at his heel. "Why, Harry, 'tis like the day God rested from his labors. All things seem fresh and new." Gunn stretched his strong arms high above his head. "God, it is good to be alive and at sea on such a day."

Hafthorsson smiled. "The sea is behaving nicely now, but wait, my friend, only wait till the first winds of autumn blow. Then will you see such fearsome surging storms as would strike terror in the heart of even the boldest mariner."

"I'll gladly wait," replied Gunn. "And, indeed, but for days like this, I am content to leave all the world's oceans for other men to play on. Gi' me a horse to ride, or set me down on my own two legs on solid ground, and I'm your man for any enterprise. But God preserve me from a storm at sea. I'd rather have St. Paul's stripes than endure his voyages."

Sinclair grinned. "You'll have your share of voyaging all the same, coz. Unless you mean to change your mind and leave me to rule the isles without your aid."

"Why, Harry, never think it. And if I prove no use as a shipman, you have but to dress me in full armor and make of me your anchor."

Sinclair laughed heartily and clapped his kinsman on the shoulder. "There spake my loyal Gunn."

"A good enough Gunn, I warrant ye," replied Ingram, wryly, "but like to misfire when wet."

Shortly before noon, Hafthorsson's bark made port. His household, having seen his sails from afar, were on the beach with mounts enough for the entire party, and to spare. After a deal of greeting and kissing of Sinclair's hands, the travelers swung into their saddles and followed Lord Sigurd to his island hall.

A short ride over the grassy meadows brought them quickly to the plain but massive stone manor house. Sigurd's wife, Lady Herdis Thorvaldsdatter, and their sons, Sigurdsson and John, hurried from the house to greet their returning lord.

Hafthorsson, with an agility that belied his bulk, swung down from his horse and, sweeping the plump Lady Herdis into his arms, bussed her heartily. "Hallo, love," he cried, pinching her ruddy cheeks. "Hey, Sigurd; hey, Johnny! We've brought you company."

Lady Herdis pushed back a straying strand of iron-gray hair and looked curiously at Sinclair, Gunn, and Clarke as they came smiling toward her. She had been a beauty, Sinclair judged, and was even now an uncommonly handsome woman, with more than ordinary intellect mirrored in her clear eyes and her high, unfurrowed brow.

"My dear," announced Hafthorsson, slipping one arm around his wife's waist, "this gentleman with the mischief in his eyes is Sir Ingram Gunn of Caithness. The Gunns are very great people there, and most highly esteemed in the court of King Robert."

Lady Herdis curtsied to Ingram's low bow. "You are welcome here, Sir Ingram," she said. "Our house is yours."

"This great hulking fellow here," Hafthorsson went on, "is John Clarke, a squire and a worthy man."

"You are welcome, sir," Lady Herdis said.

"And this gentleman with the red-gold hair and the look of eagles in his eyes is, my love, Jarl Henry Sinclair, lord of Orkney, baron of Rosslyn, and my very good friend."

"J—Jarl—" Lady Herdis clapped her hand to her mouth. "Oh, my lord, why did you not prepare me? We are all in disorder here. There is no fresh meat, no—"

"Lady Herdis," said Sinclair, extending his hand, "you must regard me as a friend to this house, happy to share your portion and honored to be counted among your husband's friends."

Lady Herdis made as if to kiss Sinclair's proffered hand. But he said, "No, madam, let us not have ceremony between us. Your lord has proved himself our loyal ally. We would have your friendship before your fealty."

"My lord," replied Lady Herdis, her cheeks grown redder still, "God give you long life and a happy reign. Do consider this poor house your own, and my sons and me as second only to my husband in friendship and fealty, too."

"Madam, I will, on condition that you make yourself no trouble on our account. Treat us, pray, as you would any comfortable friend. We shall have frequent occasion to require service of your husband, and one day, perhaps, from these strong sons of yours. We would have that not as a duty, but as a kindness from one friend to another."

Lady Herdis could only murmur, "My lord, you are the very soul of courtesy."

"Now, then," said Sinclair, "are we not to have the acquaintance of these two stalwart fellows? Their father has talked of them so often and so highly that we cannot be content till we have shaken hands with them."

"Ha-ha!" Lord Sigurd cried. "These are the knaves, in truth, my lord. Yonder great fellow of sixteen is Sigurd; the lad with the smutty face and the sheep's eyes is our Johnny, only thirteen but already a great favorite with the lasses hereabout."

"And a notable robber of birds' nests, too, or we much mistake him." Sinclair clasped hands with both lads and said, "Will you be willing to enter the jarl's service when you are of an age to bear arms?"

Sigurd, pale-haired like his brother, but taller and brawnier as became the elder, knelt and kissed Sinclair's hand. Then, looking up into the kind eyes, he said, "My lord, I would like nothing better."

Sinclair smiled. "There will be a place for you whenever you care to claim it," he said.

John Sigurdsson made also his profession of fealty, and Sinclair could not but grin at the earnestness shining in the unwashed freckled face. "We have a brother called John," he said. "And, like you, he is a younger son. But do you serve me as well as he has, and you shall not want for preferment."

"I will do my best, Jarl Sinclair," piped the boy.

Sinclair laughed and raised him up. "What man would ask for more?"

Despite the admonition of her noble guest, Lady Herdis outdid herself in hospitality, and Sinclair, Gunn, and Clarke were right royally entertained throughout their stay in Shetland. Sinclair's affection for this family grew, as did his liking for the place, and he would have been pleased to tarry longer at Hafthorsson's hall, but there were great matters to be undertaken, and he was—prompted perhaps by the warmth and geniality of this house—taken with a great longing for Rosslyn and the love that waited for him there.

Thus, at supper, toward the end of the week, he said to the hostess, "Lady Herdis, we would ask a boon of you."

"Anything, my lord."

"We have a need of your husband's services, and though he has been long away, we would ask him to absent himself again awhile from this happy house and go with us to Orkney to carry forward some business for us there."

"Why, my lord, 'twill be a blessing not to have him underfoot." Lady Herdis smiled. "He cannot be here for longer than a day without attempting to usurp my function. He is forever poking about in kitchen and pantry, upsetting the servants and meddling in the household arts, whereof he knows no more than Johnny there."

"Slander, slander!" cried Lord Sigurd. "Woman, I do protest. Why, Jarl Henry has but to look at me to see I know more of cookery and good feeding than any dozen womenfolk."

Johnny giggled and began to choke on the mouthful of mutton he had taken in.

His father, undisturbed, fetched his son a mighty thwack between the shoulders. "Go easy, young glutton," he warned. "Or if you must strangle yourself, go out into the yard so we will not have so far to lug you for your burying."

But Sinclair sensed that the boy was in a serious way. He leaped from his chair and, running to the boy, thrust a finger into the lad's mouth, with predictable and disastrous results.

"Jesu, Mary!" cried Hafthorsson, springing up from his chair. "Now you've gone and puked all over Jarl Henry's boots!"

The boy began to cry for shame and fear, but Sinclair put his arm around him and said, *"Pax,* Lord Sigurd. The lad could not help it. And what's a mite o' puking among friends, hey? By God, we cannot afford to lose this fellow for any number of boots."

The boy looked up at Sinclair with grateful, tear-filled eyes, and his whole heart from that moment belonged to Orkney's lord.

"Now go and wash your face, boy," said Sinclair gently. He roughed Johnny's hair with his hand. "Think no more about it. There's boys at my house, too, and they have made grander messes than this a score o' times, I promise ye."

Ingram grinned and said, "By the mass, Harry, will ye ever forget the time o' Willie's christening?"

"No more than I will forget my own name," replied Sinclair, laughing. "Stay, John, ye must hear this.

"We brought the little fellow to Friar Donal, a fat old priest whose dignity's as great's his belly. And came the time for the pouring on o' water, the fat old fellow takes the babe in arms and pours away. 'Tit for tat!' thinks our wee Willie, and lets fly a gill of piss all down the holy friar's gown."

"Ha-ha!" cried Lord Sigurd, smacking the table with his palm. "Willie's the match for you, Johnny. You've done only a discourtesy; he did sacrilege!"

The crisis past, and the small Hafthorssons dismissed, Sinclair now outlined his plan to Herdis. "Your husband will remain in Orkney to oversee our interests there till we return. Sir Ingram here will be going on to Caithness to recruit every shipwright for miles around to begin the building of our fleet. For our part, we will home to Rosslyn to see our kin, and to raise the payment due Haakon at Martinmas. In all, we shall be gone but a few weeks, and you shall have your husband underfoot again before the first snowfall."

"Take him and welcome, my lord," said Herdis, reaching across the table to pat her husband's hand, "so long as you send him back to me sometime. For all his meddling, he's a man I've grown uncommon fond of these nearly twenty years."

"He will be back ere you've had time to miss him," Sinclair pledged.

"Aye," growled Sigurd, "barring interference from the worthy Bishop William."

"Ah," said Sinclair, "now there's a subject I've meant to sound you on, friend Sigurd."

"I'd not presume to counsel you in the matter, my lord," said he, "but I pray you go most carefully into this. Yon William's not a man to trust, even out under God's own sky. The bishop is a by-Our-Lady weathercock, that shifts with every politic wind that blows. In my time I've known him to be so thick with the Norse gentles that none would know him for a Scot. But let the wind but veer to another quarter, and straightway the man's more Scots than yon King Robert or even your very self.

"But mind you," Lord Sigurd continued, with a knowing wag of his head, "let Scot come and Norse go, yon William's loyalty first and last is to his belly and his purse."

Lady Herdis, long silent in her place at table, spoke up, her voice urgent and strained. "I think, husband, you should take Jarl Henry to see Thorvald."

"Peace, woman," growled Lord Sigurd.

Lady Herdis speared a bit of herring on the point of her knife. "I do think it, husband," she asserted calmly, but it was plain to any that her calm was dearly bought.

"What's Thorvald?" asked Sinclair.

"A kinsman to this lady," muttered Sigurd, glaring at his wife. "There's nowt to see in him, Jarl Henry. Let it go."

Sinclair's quick glance took in the pain and pleading in Lady Herdis's wide eyes. He let his knife fall in his trencher. "I think we should see the man, friend Sigurd."

Hafthorsson sighed heavily, blotted his mouth on the back of a hairy hand, and said, "Well, then, come away upstairs, my lord. And, yes, Sir Ingram, you come, too."

The bulky islander led the way up a winding stair of narrow steps and, in the dim half-light, halted before a massive oaken door. "I'd suggest you hold your noses," he said dourly, "lest ye want to lose your dinners."

Hafthorsson shot back the iron bolt and swung the door wide. As he did so, a wave of fetid air assaulted their nostrils, and Gunn and Sinclair both let slip involuntary cries of disgust. Light from a narrow, barred window fell onto a heaped-up mound of straw in the corner of a small room, little more than a cell, virtually barren of furniture. Lying on the straw was a thing in the shape of a man.

The creature raised a pale, contorted face, wreathed in madly tangled, knotted hair, and at the sight of the three visitors, he began to growl and gnash his teeth until foam bubbled in the corners of bloodless lips.

"Jesu, Mary!" breathed Ingram Gunn, crossing himself in hasty reverence. "Is this your lady's kinsman?"

"Aye, or what is left of him."

Sinclair's shielding hand dropped to his side, and he gazed in mingled pity and horror at the afflicted man. Involuntarily, he took a step toward the sufferer, but Hafthorsson checked him with a firm hand. "No, my lord. There's danger."

"We have seen enough," Sinclair said.

As Hafthorsson led them out and turned to bolt the door, a wild cry rose from within, and the lunatic Thorvald flung himself at the oaken portal. Lord Sigurd was no slight man, and yet such was the violent force of Thorvald's assault, that the door did give way a little, and a thin, sinewy naked arm thrust through the opening.

"For Christ's sake, help!" Lord Sigurd cried. Gunn and Sinclair sprang forward, and strained their combined strength to thrust that wildly flailing arm back in. They dropped back as Hafthorsson shot home the bolt, and then right willingly followed him to the great hall below, where Lady Herdis waited.

"Well, they have seen the man," Lord Sigurd growled. "May it give you satisfaction."

"I thought 'twould steel Jarl Henry against his meeting with William," replied the lady, a look of defiance in her fine eyes, and no hint of regret in her voice.

"How so, lady?" inquired Sinclair. "What has that poor man to do with William?"

"That he is a poor man, and daft, is all of William's doing, my lord," replied Lady Herdis. "By birth and blood and station, Thorvald was in every way the equal to the best man in these isles, and he owned a fair estate in Skara Brae. Bishop William coveted those lands, and now he has them."

"But how, lady?"

"Why, my lord, yon Thorvald had a wife. Jocelyn she was called, a bonny thing and fair." Lady Herdis's voice broke, and tears brimmed on her pale lashes. "God and St. Mary, but I did love to hear her laugh and sing about this place when she and Thorvald sojourned here."

Lord Sigurd, mollified, came to stand by his wife's chair and placed a comforting hand on her shoulder. Her own hand stole up and clasped his thick fingers. "You see, my lord," the lady continued, "Thorvald and Lady Jocelyn were fourth cousins, and it was on this account that Bishop William, lusting after Thorvald's lands, declared their marriage no marriage at all, but—Christ help us—incest. And to punish Thorvald for this so-called sin, the bishop further declared his estates forfeit, and made my kinsman's fair estate his own."

"Incest?" muttered Ingram. "God's bones, these poor cousins were well cozened, truly."

"The way it is with us, Sir Ingram," Hafthorsson explained, "we are a place so sparsely peopled that when our young folks look to wed they must often look among the ranks of kindred. If it be sin, then God ha' mercy on these islands, for I doubt not that more than half the folk, both small and great, do marry cousins of some degree."

"Does Bishop William enforce this rule consistently?" Sinclair asked.

"Why, yes, my lord—whenever there are lands and wealth to be had, he does," replied Lord Sigurd. "I've never known him to trouble common folk about it."

"A most selective scruple," murmured Jarl Henry. Then he said, "And it was this that made your kinsman mad?"

"It was," said Lady Herdis. "For the fair Jocelyn on hearing that she was judged guilty of so great a sin, straightway left our cousin Thorvald's bed and sought refuge in a cloister. There she secluded herself from Thorvald and the world; and, after some several years of penitent prayer and labor, she died.

"Thorvald is as you have seen him."

"It is a sight I will not soon forget," Jarl Henry's tone was edged with flint, "and one I'll keep before my eyes when I meet this Bishop William."

The crossing to Kirkwall was accomplished next day. Sinclair immediately sent an emissary to Bishop William, but for his pains received only the word that the bishop was "indisposed."

"'Indisposed,'" growled Sinclair, when Clarke brought back the news. "I can well believe it. He is indisposed to see us sovereign here. Well, so be it. He'll rue this incivility ere he's grown much older.

"Sigurd, my friend, here's work for you. Do you serve notice to all able-bodied hereabout that Jarl Henry Sinclair offers them employment at twice the common wage."

"And what employment's that, my lord?"

"Why, sir, d'ye see that rising ground yonder? There. Looking down on the harbor."

"Aye."

"Well, my friend, 'tis there we mean to raise a mighty castle, well fortified and ample enough to garrison two hundred men-at-arms."

"Two hundred, Harry!" Ingram Gunn let go a low whistle. "I call that building on the grand scale."

"We are lord of these isles, cousin. We mean to house our family in proper condition, and we mean also to be so staffed and so equipped as readily to further our business here."

"But my lord," said Hafthorsson, "I—I have no wish to raise difficulties, but the articles of your investiture specifically prohibit the building of castle or fortress without Haakon's consent."

Sinclair turned a frosty eye on the stout Shetlander. "Lord Sigurd, do you but look over your shoulder at Bishop William's heap o' freestone there. Think you we will be content to walk about in the shadow o' that and yet call ourself master here? No, sir. Haakon calls me jarl; he bars any alliance 'twixt jarl and bishop, even were such an alliance possible; and he bids me rule in Orkney. We mean to do that, to have this realm and hold it secure for ourself and Norway forever. And we will build here, and that grandly.

"Doubt not our intent toward Norway, friend Hafthorsson. But neither doubt our purpose to be in full possession here."

"My lord, I never doubted either. But Haakon—"

"Is in Norway. And has his hands full. He wants these isles mastered, ruled, and properly subject to his authority. So they shall be. But leave the means to us, and Haakon shall have naught to complain of."

Sinclair looked about him, smiled, and nodded his satisfaction. "God, what jewels these islands are, my friends! How they gleam in this sunlit sea! These should be a happy people, prosperous and content with the bounty these waters and this land afford. We mean to have them so, and so to maintain them with all our strength and mind and heart.

"To that end, we will establish ourselves here, subdue the unruly, encourage the true and the honest, and so begin a time of peace and good order that shall endure so long as there is a Sinclair left in Orkney."

"God strengthen you in your purpose, my lord," murmured Hafthorsson.

"He has never failed us, my friend. We know that you will not either."

Sigurd smiled. "The walls will be a-building by the time you are again in Kirkwall. We shall raise such a castle here as will blot the sun from William's windows and keep him forever in your shade."

19

Ingram and Sinclair parted at Caithness.

"You are to consider the Sinclair holdings here your timber yard. Bid the men cut as they need, coz, only bid them work quickly. The sooner we are afloat, the sooner we shall begin to make our presence felt among the people of the isles."

"I wish only that I were a better sailor," Ingram said. "I fear I may be of little worth aboard ship."

Sinclair smiled. "We both have much to learn, coz. I am myself a most indifferent mariner. But what other men have done, we can do. Let the ships but carry us safe to land, then shall we give an account of ourselves that neither of us need blush for. But, lord, what I would not give for an hour's talk with Carlo Zeno."

"Who is he?"

"Did you never hear of the Lion of Venice?" Sinclair's eyes brightened. "Why, Ingram, he is the greatest admiral in Christendom. Only last year, there was a blackfriar come to our house who talked of little else but this Zeno, a quondam clerk turned soldier who defeated Padua and the Genoese."

"And a mariner too?"

"Aye, and what is more this Zeno hath devised a most ingenious means for using bombards to good effect."

"What? From a ship?"

"Aye, that's the wonder of it. He's found a way to mount the cannon

134

so as to compensate for the roll of the ship and, according to the Dominican, unleash a most uncommonly accurate broadside. 'Twas this that brought the Genoese to heel and won for this Zeno the acclaim and love of all Venice."

Ingram whistled low. "By the mass, Harry! And if you had a fleet so armed, the isles would be in your pocket by next Tuesday, and no rebel bishop or disappointed claimant would dare raise his hand against ye."

Sinclair nodded. "'Twould be worth a journey to Venice to pry this Zeno's secret from him. But we will do our best with what we have, my friend. Do you but get my fleet launched, and we will contrive to learn the mariner's art as we go along.

"And now, coz, adieu. The sun's already near his zenith, and there lies a long and weary way before me." Sinclair vaulted lightly into the saddle and gathered his reins. "I will be here again early in October. We have a rendezvous to keep at Tunisberg, you and I. For Haakon will have his thousand nobles, and we must not keep a king waiting."

"My love to Janet and the children, Harry. Godspeed!"

With a wave of his gloved right hand, Sinclair turned his horse's head and, with Clarke alone to attend him, set out for home.

It was old Duncan, warming his ancient bones in the late summer sun, who was first to spy the returning master of Rosslyn. That faithful soul bestirred himself and, like a startled duck, waddled rapidly into the main hall. "He's come," the old fellow shrilled, "Sir Henry's come! I seed 'im on the bridge."

Then was there great rejoicing in the halls. Sinclair had barely dismounted when he was surrounded by the welcoming throng. Henry and Willie seized his legs, and Betsy all but scaled her father, swarming up into his arms like a pretty monkey. Grizzled Oliver Knox, his face abeam with pride in this man whose molding was so much his own handiwork, shouldered his way through the ranks of the servants to be first to kiss the new earl's hand. And Davey Sinclair, awe in his face, could only stare in slack-jawed wonder at his triumphant older brother.

"Come, Davey," cried Sinclair, "gi' us your hand, boy, and tell us you are glad to see us home."

"Oh, I am, Harry. I am. And—are are you truly prince of Orkney now?"

"Prince, earl, or 'jarl' as they call it in Norway," replied Sinclair, crushing his brother's fingers. "Here, take Betsy, will you? She's near strangled her poor old father."

"We have a new baby, Father," piped Willie, looking up in worship at this handsome laughing hero-father.

"A new baby!" Sinclair caught Willie up and tossed him about in the rough loveplay that was the child's delight. "Now that is a prize!"

"'Tis only a girl, Father," Henry said.

"Oh-ho! Only a girl, hey? Well, my son, you have much to learn, I can see that." Sinclair touseled his firstborn's hair. "Where is this girl baby? And where, for heaven's sake, is your blessed mother?"

"She—"

"Harry!"

"Why, Mother, God save you. It is very good to see you again." Sinclair disentangled himself from his boys and strode to the doorway where Lady Isabel, cool and white as a marble statue, stood with her head held high, her pride shining in her eyes.

As her son embraced her, she said, "Oh, Harry, Harry, at last! At last! When your letters came telling us of Haakon's favor, my heart swelled to bursting with joy. The isles are yours, Harry. You have kept your vow."

Sinclair kissed his mother's cheek. "God willed it, Mother. All vows, all stratagems, all human endeavor come to nothing without God He sees fit to prosper the work. But, come, where's my Janet?"

"In her chamber, sleeping."

"She is not unwell?"

Lady Isabel smiled. "No, my son. But this last child you gave her is a most lusty crier and doth rob her pretty mother of some several hours' sleep six nights in seven."

"The little wretch," said Sinclair, laughing. "We'll pack her off to a wet nurse this very day."

"Ah, wait till you've seen her, Harry. The child's as fair a flower as ever bloomed at Rosslyn."

"Methinks I'll steal upstairs now, Mother, and have a look at this flower for myself. D'you instruct Friar Donal we'll have a mass in thanksgiving the morrow, and bid the cook outdo himself this night, for we shall feast and drink deep in celebration of this happy, happy day." Sinclair made to go past his mother.

"Harry, is Johnny well?"

Sinclair laughed. "Mother, Mother, fear you nothing on Johnny's account." He chucked the proud chin with his finger. "Our Johnny's well and well cared for, and will be here before Christmas with yet another flower to grace our gardens here."

With that, Sinclair passed through the archway and ran lightly down the corridor and up the stairs to Janet's chamber. Softly, softly, he tried the door, eased it open and slipped in.

There Janet lay, her sweet face soft and unlined as a child's, her hair spread out like tumbled silk on the pillows. She stirred not. There was only the gentle rising and falling of her breast, the soft whisper of her light breathing.

Then Sinclair heard a tiny noise, a sound no louder than the chirring of a pantry mouse, and he tiptoed over to the rosewood cradle. There, wide-eyed and solemnly sucking on her fingers, his infant daughter lay

"Well," Sinclair whispered, going down on one knee beside the babe. "Well! Thy grandmother spoke truly. Thou art indeed a lovely blossom. Here, let's have a look at you, you pretty rascal."

He lifted the child from the cradle and, holding her to his breast, walked over to the window where the sunlight mingled with the downy curls that crowned the tiny head. Sinclair's smile widened, and he bent and kissed the soft plump cheek. "You've a coronet fairer than my own, sweetheart," he said. "Afore God, you are a bonny, bonny thing."

A slight sound caused Sinclair to turn around. Janet was waking. He crossed to her bedside; as Janet's eyes opened, the first thing she saw was her husband smiling down on her, their child in his arms.

"Harry? Is it—is it you?"

"No other."

"Oh, dearest!" Janet's arms opened wide. "Dearest, dearest love. How I have missed you this long, long, weary while!"

Sinclair adroitly shifted the baby to his right arm, and with his left he crushed Janet to him and all but devoured her face and throat with kisses.

"Ah, Janet, sweetheart, 'twas a weary time for me also. Many's the night I could not rest for thinking on you and longing for to be in your white arms again."

"Did you truly miss me, husband?"

"Let me but stow this pretty baggage in her cradle, madam," Sinclair growled, "and I will prove the truth of it."

Janet nodded, her smile radiant, her eyes aglow. As Sinclair returned the babe to the cradle, Janet slipped out of her shift and lay there in her naked loveliness to receive her husband.

Sinclair made quick work of his divesting. All travel-stained and dusty as he was, he took her—almost roughly, for long abstinence had given him appetite. And when he was spent, he lay a little while beside his love and let his eyes and hands renew their old delight. Then, more gently, he took her in his arms again and soared with her to the very heights of joy.

Janet clung to him for a long while afterward, as if she would never let him go.

"Husband," she said, an hour after, as she sat brushing her shining hair, "is it sin, d'you think, for me to have so much pleasure from your body?"

"Sin?" Sinclair paused in the act of pulling on a clean shirt. "What silly talk is that?"

Janet turned to him a grave face. "It hath sometimes seemed to me that so much delight cannot be altogether fit for Christian folk."

"Jesu, Mary!" exploded Sinclair, laughing. "Why else did God He make two kinds of folk an He did not mean for them to couple and get children? Ye cannot think He meant for us all to be capon priests and neuter nuns, surely."

"No-o," said Janet, slowly. "But there was a mendicant friar stayed with us here some nine or ten days whilst you were gone, and he did preach most eloquently against the too great fondness of flesh for flesh, and did admonish all against the too frequent sating of the lower passions."

"Lower passions! God's wounds, woman! An I had been here, I'd ha' sent the fellow packing, him and his foolish notions. Look you, Janet. Do we not keep here an upright Catholic household?"

"Aye, but—"

"We keep the fasts, give alms, support the clergy, and mind always our duty to God and holy church."

"'Tis true, husband. And indeed you are by many called Henry the Holy for your great generosity to all the convents and religious houses hereabout. But this, this thing I feel when you are sporting with me in our bed, it—it gives me so much pleasure, Harry, that my conscience is not easy."

"Pox on your priest-ridden conscience, woman!" Sinclair pulled on his shirt, and striding over to the cradle, he picked up the infant and showed her to her mother. "D'ye see this bonny lass? And d'ye think this the fruit of sin, hey? And Henry? And Willie and Betsy?

"Think on them next time you hear a wine-soaked stupid cleric talk against our lawful pleasure, Janet, and trouble yourself no further on that account." He brought the baby to her and, in a softer tone, said, "My dear, dear love, look at this child and tell that what we did to get her was a sin."

Janet smiled and reached for the baby. "Husband, I cannot think it. It must have been my wanting you so hugely that made my silly mind susceptible to the foolish fellow's prating."

Sinclair sat beside her and slipped his arm around her slender waist. "These be strange times, Janet. The church is in schism, and all manner of crack-brained mendicants go up and down the land preaching strange doctrine. There is talk of a renegade priest in England, one Wycliffe, that goes about stirring up the common folk with wild ungodly ravings. He was for a time under John o' Gaunt's protection, but now he preaches and writes such evil stuff—even denying Christ's presence in the Eucharist—that Lancaster's abandoned him and he will end upon the gibbet, surely.

"Let us you and I hold fast to sound doctrine, and let no heresy take hold here. God He will not let this present state of things endure for long. 'Tis you and I and all true Christian folk must stand unwavering against this raging tide of disorder and dissension. For if great folk go under, what then will small folk do?"

" 'Tis well said, husband. And for this comfort, thanks. You ought not to stay so long away from me hereafter. Your strength is my strength, and without you I am but a poor weak thing that can scarce stand unaided."

Sinclair kissed her and said, "No more of this dry monkish talk. Come, what name shall we give this pretty lady at her christening?"

"I thought to call her Beatrix."

"Why, 'tis a fair name for so fair a child. I like it, Janet. I like it much. She is Beatrix, then, and shall be a fair ornament to our court at Orkney when you are ensconced there."

"Are we to live in Orkney, then?"

"In time, love. There's a deal to do ere then. But I have set the work in motion, and in a few years—"

"Oh, years."

"Aye, dear heart. I am afraid so."

"'Tis as well, Harry. I am in no hurry to leave Rosslyn."

"No more am I. But wait till you see the place, Janet. Kirkwall's a perfect jewel, green as an emerald, and kept immaculate by the house-wifery of the Orcadian winds. 'Tis a fair land, sweetheart. I think we will be happy there."

"Where you are, husband, there is my happiness."

Sinclair spent some sunny days in idleness at Rosslyn, walking about the place and renewing old acquaintance among folk of high estate and low. Then, toward the end of September, he began to talk of riding out again. "For," as he said to Janet, as they walked one golden afternoon along a narrow path winding down to the glen, "I am bound to deliver Haakon's levy on Martinmas, and I would not have him find me derelict by so much as a single day. He put his trust in me; I cannot this early give him cause to doubt the wisdom of his choice."

"Harry, would you take me with you?"

"Why, Janet, you're as bad as Davey." Sinclair chuckled and took his wife's hand in his. "No, sweetheart; although I would dearly love to have you by me, I will be in such a maze of business and will have so many matters to attend to that 'twould be no pleasure for you.

"In time, my love, in time, I mean to dazzle the envious islanders, and even the folk of Haakon's court, by marching about with the lovely Janet Halyburton on my arm. Alas, 'tis a pleasure that must be post-poned; but never mind, 'twill be the sweeter for that."

"Harry, what is she like?"

"Who?"

"Margaret, the queen. You told me it was she that put you in mind of talking ships to Haakon. But you have told me nothing of what she is like."

"Why," said Sinclair, bending back a resilient branch to let them pass abreast, "she is young, and a mother, and much loved by the people there. I think she is wise and good and kind. She has that repute in Norway."

"But is she pretty?" persisted Janet, skipping lightly over a fallen limb.

"I would not call her so."

"What then? What would you call her, Harry?"

"Beautiful."

"Oh." It was a very small, a very subdued "Oh."

Sinclair let the silence hang as he led Janet down to where the river wound its way to the fall. Then he said, "But not so beautiful as you." And he accepted without flinching the kiss that rewarded his gallant lie.

"Why, look, Janet," he said, as they rounded the bend of the river and came upon a clearing, "'tis old Meg's hut, fallen all to ruin."

"Oh, Harry, I had forgot all about her; she died while we were yet quite young, poor thing. D'ye mind the time when you and Ingram and Malise Sparre and I rode here to have our futures told?"

"I do indeed," said Sinclair, his voice wondering and low. "And I marvel now that I had forgot it for so long."

"Was Meg truly a witch, Harry?"

Sinclair shook his head. "Had you asked me that a year ago, Janet, I think I would have laughed and told you no. Now? Well, I can only wonder how much more of what she told us will come to pass."

20

Came the day of Sinclair's departure, a bright blue October morning with the smell of frost-nipped grapes and woodsmoke in the air. He left his bed full early, while Janet was yet sleeping, roused Clarke, and saw to the final preparations.

As he left the stable, having seen to it that his newly shod gelding and been well fed and thoroughly groomed for the run to the coast, his brother David caught up with him and took up an old theme: "Take me with you, Harry," he said. "Please. There's nothing doing hereabout, and I have a great mind to see new places and learn something of the world beyond those hills."

"Davey, Davey," said Sinclair, draping an arm over the youth's broad shoulders, "do but bide here a little while longer, till Johnny's come. Then, I promise you, I'll send for ye, and will give you work worthy of those stout arms."

"But damn it, Harry, I—"

"Enough now. You're needed here, Davey. Janet and our mother must have a man about the place for them to lean on. Do your duty here, and I promise you shall have a place beside me when we sail out to establish our sovereignty through all the isles."

"Oh, very well, then. If I must stay—"

"Ye must. And Davey," Sinclair's tone was stern, "mark you, I will not often engage in this kind of womanish debate wi' ye. We have great work before us. There will be hardships and, no doubt, some danger.

I must have men about me who not only are hardy and skilled at arms, but who will do my bidding without murmuring, without questioning either my commands or the authority behind them. D'ye understand?"

"Aye."

"Then pay heed, little brother. For, brother or no brother, I will not, cannot endure petulance, questioning, or anything that smacks of insubordination. There is an earldom to be won and made secure, Davey. This is no boy's play. There is room only for men in this enterprise—good men, loyal men, men who will cleave to duty and make their will one with my own.

"Serve me well, and you will yourself be well served. But if you presume upon our kinship to bait and check me at every turn, why, sir, I will bid you farewell and Godspeed and see you off on the shortest route home to Scotland. Understood?"

"Aye."

"Good, then. Here's my hand on it. Ye'll have your day. Now go and find our mother. I'll wait on her i' the great hall, for 'tis time I made my farewells."

Sinclair watched his brother depart. A frown knit his brows and he muttered to himself, "Davey, thou had better soon show thyself a man, or I fear we shall not long keep company."

He turned then, and made his way to the great hall. There his mother found him as he stood before the hearth, gazing up in undiminished reverence at the warrior Sigurd's sword.

"Good morrow, Mother," he said, turning at the sound of her soft step. "Slept you well?"

"Briefly, but well, my son. I linger not so long abed as formerly." Lady Isabel received his kiss with a smile. "Davey bade me come to you here."

"Aye. I would say farewell now, Mother, and ask your blessing ere I go." Sinclair knelt, and Lady Isabel brought her hands to rest lightly on his head.

"God and St. Katherine go with you, my son. May this and all your errands prosper."

"Thank you, Mother. God bless you." Sinclair rose. "'Tis a fair morning to be riding out in."

"Are you glad to be going?" A faint smile played about Lady Isabel's pale lips.

"Alas, madam, I fear I have come to that point where it is with me all business. And though I still delight to ride to the sea on such a day, I have lost something of that boyish spirit that loves a journey for the journey's sake, with no more thought than to enjoy the going. In truth, my mind's so full of Orkney that I can scarce summon up a pang o' regret at leaving my beloved Rosslyn."

"That's good, my son." said Lady Isabel, her eyes flashing. "'Tis as it should be with you. Oh, Harry, have I ever really told you how very proud, how very, very proud I am that you have won the earldom?"

"Not above a score o' times, Mother," replied Sinclair, smiling. "And I swear I am as happy for you as I am for myself. This prize was long in coming, and you have had a weary time o' waiting."

"But it has come, Harry. And all the waiting is forgot in my joy at this most happy resolution."

"Well, Mother, there's much to be done. I shall need something of your own tenacity to see it through. See that you keep well and guard your health against the day when I shall send for you to come to Kirkwall, where you may with your own eyes survey all that I have won as my legacy from your father."

"God speed that day, Harry."

"Amen. And now, Mother," he said, kissing her on both cheeks, "fare you well. With luck, I shall be here again in time to keep Christmas with you and give you full report of all that happens in the interval."

"God be with you, Harry. I shall have masses said for you daily."

"Do that, and do you pray for me also, for I shall have need of prayer." Sinclair turned and eyed the Viking sword. "I shall not rest content until that ancient blade hangs in my hall at Kirkwall."

"I think, my son, that you will never rest content—at Kirkwall or any other where. And for that as much as anything, I do love you."

"Why, Mother, I love you, too. But now it is really adieu. I must upstairs to Janet, then haste away to make the most of the sunlight hours. Again, fare you well; God keep you." And Sinclair, with a parting kiss, hurried away to Janet.

She was suckling their babe when he entered her chamber, and a fair picture they made, mother and child, seated in the spill of morning light that poured through the window. Sinclair's heart was in his eyes and in his smile. "Good morrow, my dearest love," he said. "It seems I am come at an awkward time for saying farewell."

"There is never a good time for farewells between us, my lord," replied Janet, rising from her chair. "But do you kiss me and take your leave. I will study to keep my thoughts on Christmas, and will make of patience my constant companion until you ride this way again."

"You know that I shall miss you all the while I am away," murmured Sinclair, bending to brush her lips with his.

Janet tried to smile. "I fear we shall have a deal of missing in the years to come."

Sinclair nodded. "No blessing comes unmixed," he said. "And though a part o' me rejoices in the work to be done, there is another part that longs to bide here with you and watch our children grow."

He placed his finger in the infant's tiny hand and smiled as the wee fingers curled around his own. "She's a strong grip, this one."

"Aye. All our children are hearty. 'Tis their gift from their father, I think."

Sinclair chuckled. "Well, thank God they look more like their lovely mother."

"Not Willie," Janet said, smiling. "When I look on him I see your miniature. I must arrange to keep him by me while you're gone, so as not to forget the look of you."

"Ah, Janet, Janet, I am sorry to be going. I wish—"

"Hush! You have great matters to attend to, my lord of Orkney. Give your mind to that, and fear me not. Only love me always and do what you must. I'll not complain."

"God bless you, Janet."

"And you, my dearest, dearest love. Now, go. I am resolved not to weep. But if you tarry longer, I cannot promise to keep dry-eyed."

"The children—"

"Are already in the courtyard, waiting to watch you ride off. Oh, love, kiss me and go. Take my heart with you, and bring it home again to me at Christmas to sing a joyful carol in my breast."

Sinclair, his eyes misting over, his own heart in his throat, choked out a last farewell and fled, like Noah, before the flood.

In the courtyard, he found Clarke mounted and ready, his own horse saddled and bridled, pawing the earth as if impatient to be off. He scooped up his children one by one and kissed them each farewell. Then he mounted and rode off, with their piping "God be wi' you" ringing in his ears.

Had he looked back—a thing he would not do—he might have caught a glimpse of Janet, with Beatrix at her breast, standing in the high window. And he might have seen another figure, that of his brother Davey, skulking by the stable door.

The weather held for their easy day's ride, and Sinclair's spirits rose with every mile accomplished. Earth seemed fair that autumn morning; the harvest was in; it had been a bountiful year, and the native hospitality of the Scots was only enhanced by the plenty now laid up in cellar and barn against the coming cold.

"Hey, John Clarke, would ye no love to be takin' this journey overland, through the high places nor'west o' Culloden moor?"

Clarke, who was not the horseman Sinclair was, shook his head. "Nay, my lord. My tail would be sore worn wi' such a pounding. 'Twould be many a weary day we'd have of it, let alone the cold at night. I had rather trust these bones to Hafthorsson's bark."

"Ha-ha! Well, God bless me, but I do love the feel of a stout horse between my legs."

"A stout whore's more to my liking," gritted Clarke, rising in his stirrups to give his chafed tailbone an instant's respite. "But every rider to his own mount, I say; and each man to his fancy."

Ere nightfall, the travelers found themselves in Edinburgh. Hafthorsson's men joined them in a hearty supper at the inn, and they went early to their rest against an early departure in the morning.

Dawn brought with it gray skies and a spit of rain, but also a brisk southerly wind most favorable to their journey. Sinclair, Clarke, and the crew were early on board, and well before the sky had lightened, their bark was scudding along over a light chop, bound away for Caithness. They hugged the coast past Dundee, past Aberdeen, their broad sails carrying them far and fast before the unfailing wind. Through the night, with a lone steersman, relieved turn by turn through the lonely watches, the little vessel made its way, and with the dawn of a brighter, colder day, the travelers watched the land fall away astern as they ventured forth into the open water of the North Sea.

During the last hours of the night, the wind had veered around to the west, the seas ran high, and the mariners' skill was thoroughly tried in that eighty-mile crossing to the fair village of Wick. But evening found Sinclair and his party safe ashore and enjoying the hospitality of the chief family of the place.

Leaving Hafthorsson's men behind, Sinclair and Clarke set out the following morning on hired mounts and made an easy journey to the Sinclair lands in Thurso. There they found Ingram Gunn in his glory as the self-styled clerk-of-the-works, presiding over an improvised boatyard there on the North Sea shingle.

"By St. Katherine," murmured Sinclair, as he stood with arms akimbo surveying the piled-up logs, the scurrying shipwrights, the coils of cordage, the rising skeletons of a pair of likely looking barks. "Ye've no been idle, kinsman. I gi' ye that."

Ingram beamed. "I have never enjoyed myself so much in all my life before. Had I another chance at another life, I think I would begin as a 'prentice to some honest joiner, and so make my way up through journeyman to masterbuilder. There are good fellows here, coz. 'Tis a joy to work with 'em. They may know nothing of mounting bombards, but they know ships. I'd trust my landsman's life to any craft they put afloat."

Sinclair nodded his approval. "When d'ye think the first of the fleet will be in the water?"

"Before the snow flies, with any kind of luck."

"No sooner? I had hoped—"

"Harry, Harry, this is no crew o' motley barn builders we have employed here. These are master craftsmen. They are about building ships, not coffins. Ye want strong ships, stout ships, ships as will weather the worst o' gales. Ye do not hurry a thing like that."

Sinclair slapped at his thigh with his gloves. "Aye, aye. But there's so much to do; so much work—"

"Come, come, coz, What o' thy family motto? 'Commit thy work to God,' hey? Well, commend it to Him, pray, and leave off fretting yourself into wrinkles and gray hairs."

"I do commit the work to God, coz; but 'tis I who must see it done."

"God and St. Mary!" groaned Ingram. "I had thought ye'd be so pleased, and here ye are grumping away as if we hadn't a stick o' timber cut, nor a single vessel framed."

Sinclair smiled and grasped his cousin's arm. "Forgive me, my friend. You have done much, and that much is well done. I am grateful. Here. Here's a purse for the men. Bid them drink deep tonight, for they have earned our thanks."

"Would ye have me go wi' them, my lord," John Clarke put in. "to see they do not drink themselves helpless?"

"Why, 'tis tenderly thought of, John Clarke," replied Sinclair, pursing his lips to hide a smile. "But we must ourselves be up early on the morrow to return to Wick, whence we sail to Kirkwall the day after."

"You will spend the night with me, then?" asked Gunn.

"Aye. And, if you can leave off playing shipwright for a time, I'd have ye go wi' me to Kirkwall and on to Tunsberg to meet wi' Haakon's men. Can this business here go forward without ye?"

"In truth, the men will be hard put to get along without the daily inspiration of my presence here, but if my lord wishes—"

"Your lord wishes that our Lord had blest you with brain as quick's your tongue," retorted Sinclair, laughing. "Come. Let us go and test the merits of your kitchen and your cellar, coz. And I'll regale ye with an account of the most beautiful babe yet born at Rosslyn."

"What? Another Sinclair?"

"Aye. Can there ever be too many?"

"No, no. God He knows I would gladly see the whole o' Scotland peopled wi' Sinclairs, so long as ye leave a wee bit o' room for us Gunns."

"Why, sir, and if we Sinclairs crowd you out, I promise you your pick o' the isles to build yourself a home in."

It was good and cheering and healthful, Sinclair found, to be again with Ingram. It was no slight temptation to let the work go, to ride after the red deer, to hunt and hawk, to keep late nights with music, wine, and laughter. But Sinclair's life had purpose now, and he would let no man's whim, not even his own, turn him from his path.

At Kirkwall, it was plain that Hafthorsson had not been idle either. Granted, there had been scant clearing to be done, for trees were sparse on that windswept isle, and granted, the abundant freestone gave the builder ready access to his materials. But Sinclair was amazed and delighted to find how high the walls were rising, and on how grand a scale Hafthorsson's men were building.

Hafthorsson himself insisted on conducting a tour of the site. His proprietary air caused Sinclair more than once to grin, as the stout Shetlander explained with many a gesture and many a choice word the advantages of the site, the thickness of the walls, the height, the bulk, and the overwhelming superiority of this to Bishop William's pile.

"Come up on the scaffolding with me, my lord," Hafthorsson bade. "I'll show ye where I've a mind to garrison your men."

Sinclair, Ingram, and Clarke all followed Hafthorsson up the several ladders to the top of the wall.

"We will command a fine view of the bay here," Sinclair said, nodding his approval. "When our walls are raised to their full height, no ship will come or go without our notice."

"Aye, my lord," said Hafthorsson, proudly. "And 'twill be a rare bishop can breach these walls when we've done our work. Yon castle will be quite overtopped by this. Why, look you—"

Here Hafthorsson turned. But what it was he meant to point out, whatever he had meant to say, Sinclair would never know. A slovenly workman had left behind his mallet, a small hammer of no very great weight. But it sufficed for Sigurd Hafthorsson. His foot came down on the head of it, his ankle wrenched suddenly under his own considerable bulk, and before anyone could raise a hand to help him, Hafthorsson went hurtling over the side. Those on the wall heard plainly the snap of the man's neck when he struck the ground below.

"Jesu, mercy!" breathed Ingram Gunn.

John Clarke covered his eyes with his hands, but he would see that fall again and again in his dreams.

Sinclair, his face dead white, crossed himself, picked up the mallet, and hurried back to the ladders and down to where Hafthorsson lay. A glance told all. The goodhearted Shetlander was dead. Workmen gathered like cows around a salt lick to stare down at this fearful thing that was but a moment before an upright, jovial, free-swearing man.

"Whose is this mallet?" Sinclair's voice cracked like a lash. His cold eyes surveyed the faces before him. "Whose is this, hey?"

The silence hung with a crushing weight above them all.

Sinclair folded his arms and, in a voice filled with scorn, cried out, "Are you the men of Orkney? Is it you we are called to lead and protect? Ye cowards! I think ye are not worth—"

"Sir! My lord!"

"Who speaks? Stand forth and let us see you, man."

A fellow of an age with the dead man, but thinner and stooped with toil, advanced from the rank of workman. "The mallet's mine, my lord," the man said, raising his eyes with an effort to meet those of his judge and his accuser.

"What is your name?"

"Hugh Croft, my lord." There was such hopelessness in the man's face and in his eyes that Sinclair hardly knew how to direct his own wrath. Had the man been defiant or defensive or merely sullen, he could have dealt with him swiftly and without a second thought. But this was despair as Sinclair had never seen it before. And it troubled him. It troubled his very soul.

He tapped his palm lightly with the mallet, uncertain as to his course. "A man is dead, Hugh Croft. A good man, with a wife and sons who need him, and friends who will long mourn him."

The fellow said nothing, only lowered his gaze and seemed to offer his bowed neck to whatever stroke it pleased human justice to deliver.

"Ye left this mallet on the wall, a thing no good workman would do. And because of your careless act, Sigurd Hafthorsson lies there wi' his neck broke." Sinclair's voice rose, crackling with rekindled anger. "Do you deny it?"

"The mallet's mine, the fault is mine, Jarl Sinclair."

"Not so!"

Sinclair's head went up like that of a startled horse. "Who is that?"

"'Tis I, your lordship," rumbled a deep voice. A great bear of a man in tawny beard and homespun smock came foreward and stood beside High Croft. "Tom Prentiss is my name, a neighbor to this man and, like him, an honest workman."

"What have you to say of this?"

"Why, my lord, that there mallet is High Croft's, as he himself telled ye. But it was no his fault that it came to be left there so as to trip up yon poor lord and bring him low."

"Was it you, then?"

"An it was, my lord," replied Prentiss, with a look and a tone that won Sinclair completely, "an it was, I would ha' telled ye."

Sinclair's face softened. "I believe you, Tom Prentiss," he said.

For a moment, the men's eyes met and held. Prentiss seemed to be reading the face of this lord that Norway had set over him. Then, apparently encouraged by what he saw there, Prentiss went on. "'Twas not Hugh, but his lad that done it, my lord. He could not speak against his own flesh, and I could not stand to see Hugh punished for what was no fault o' his."

Sinclair nodded, inwardly thanking God that he had not struck Croft down on the spot. "Where's the boy?" he asked, quietly.

And the men brought before him the mute, vacant-eyed fourteen-year-old innocent that was the only child of Hugh Croft.

"He's not right i' the head, d'ye see, my lord," said Prentiss, looking sadly at the uncomprehending child. "We lets him come about us as we works. There's no harm in him, sir, and if you was to beat him from now till sunrise, he'd no more understand what's happened here than yon block o' freestone would."

Sinclair covered his face with his hands for a brief moment. Then he looked to Croft and Prentiss. "There'll be no beatings," he said, softly. "You, Hugh Croft, keep closer watch over your lad hereafter. We would not have him come to any harm.

"You, Tom Prentiss, will oversee the work here. He who defies your authority, defies our authority, and will suffer the consequences.

"For ourselves, we and our friends will bear the body of this our friend to his home in Shetland. We commend his soul to God, and we ask you all as Christian men to pray for his repose."

Those nearest him could see tears brimming in Jarl Henry's eyes, but the deep voice held strong and unwavering: "Do you, Sir Ingram, appoint some two or three to prepare Lord Sigurd's body for his burial. We will ourselves take ship within the week and carry all that was mortal of him to his native place to see him honorably entombed, and to give such comfort as we can to Lady Herdis and her sons."

That evening, over the wine, Sinclair unburdened his mind to Ingram Gunn.

"God help me, coz, I do not relish this errand. In this sturdy Shetlander's dying I have lost a valued help and, for all that our acquaintance was so brief, a trusty friend. But the loss to Lady Herdis," Sinclair shook his head and frowned down at the dregs in his cup, "there is a loss that beggars mine."

"And yet, coz, she knew ere they were wed that one of them must needs outlive the other."

"Aye. Whenever two will love, one must remain to mourn. But I like it not to stand before that lady and announce to her her widowhood, her worthy lord gone thus suddenly and unshriven to his accounting—and this on our account, upon our business."

"In this I think you are too tender, Harry; pardon me. Lord Sigurd's not the first to die in your service, nor is Lady Herdis first to change to widow's weeds for a lord that's perished in your cause."

"Deeds of war are one thing," returned Sinclair, "but to oversee the building of a by-Our-Lady house—even so grand a hold as this will be—is not a cause a man would die for; nor should he."

Ingram Gunn eyed his lord and kinsman shrewdly. "Harry, I loved Lord Sigurd too. But you and I have seen men sell their lives for less by far than this. It is no small thing to have a share in the building of a noble house. Certain it is that the building of it is at least as honorable as the work of upholding it. My own work's not a whit more worthy than Sigurd's was, and should I die defending your walls, I shall have no greater claim than Sigurd to honors and to tears.

"It's good work, Harry. It's work that needs doing, in Norway's service and to the honor of your name. These isles will be beneficiaries of all that Sigurd has begun. Aye, and his lady and his sons will profit from it. For my own part, I would prefer to die in the course of such a labor than on some fool's errand for some paltry lord who'd spend men's lives like a purse o' groats to gain some tainted glory in a mean and venal cause."

Sinclair smiled at the warmth of Gunn's reply. "Give us your hand, good cousin. If you have not convinced me of your argument, you have at any rate confirmed me in my old belief that never a lord in Christendom was blest with such a friend as I have found in you."

Ingram made as if to speak, but Sinclair forestalled him. "Let it rest there, friend Ingram," he said, rising in his place. "And let us take our rest. We have a sad errand before us ere the week is out. That done, I mean to give all my thought to this work that Sigurd has begun so well. And then, sir, I mean to have it out with Bishop William."

Ingram grinned. "'Twill be worth the work and the waiting both, to see the dawning of that day, Harry."

As it happened, Ingram Gunn had not so long to wait.

21

William of Orkney was in no pleasant humor. Servants, clerks, and men-at-arms walked softly and kept well away from the episcopal apartments within those towering palace walls. Tremors of his princely wrath were felt from scullery to battlement, and even the hardiest of his household thought it prudent to stay wide of William's path.

The priest Giles Weyland was not so lucky. It was his dubious honor to serve this bishop as confessor and scribe, and more than once it was only prayer—that and a native gift for politic silence—that sustained the unfortunate Giles under the load of these two considerable crosses. Again this morning he wished, with all that fervor that had so marked the fasts and vigils of his novice years, that the abbot had never chosen to honor him by the free gift of his services to the irascible William.

"My son," the abbot had told him, "this can be a great thing for you and for our abbey."

Well, it had been a great thing for Giles—a great and crushing burden and a sore trial of his vows. As for the abbey, beyond a tun of no very excellent vintage, there had come, so far as Giles was aware, no benefit beyond the slight reduction in expense that resulted from his own absence.

He stood now, knees a-tremble, the sweat prickling under his hair-shirt, while the portly prelate paced and raged.

"Now damnation take this Norse-Scot tool of Haakon's!" cried the bishop, smiting a little used bog-oak *prie-dieu* with the flat of a hammy

151

hand. "He dares, dares, mind you, to think of raising a by-Our-Lady fortress in the very shadow of our cathedral; nay, not more than a bowshot of our very walls."

"Perhaps, my lord—" ventured the priest.

"Silence!" roared Bishop William. "God's bones! How's a man to think as you stand there nattering like any fishwife?

"We'll send letters to Haakon. We—no, no! Blast and damn Haakon! He made this creature. He will not this early be moved against him." The bishop gnawed at his pendulous lower lip. "What's to do? What's to do?"

"If my lord were to see this jarl—"

"Will you be silent!" William's roar was heard clear away to the very chapel where his own Lord reposed. "By the mass, if you speak again unbidden, we will send you packing back to that hive of idleness whence ye came, and that instanter."

Giles Weyland in that moment faced a temptation as strong as any he'd encountered since his ordination. But he held his peace.

Bishop William rocked back and forth on the balls of his slippered feet and patted his great paunch with his hands. He chewed his lip and rolled his eyes; he was thinking.

"I have it!" he cried at last, smacking his fat palms together with a crack that made poor Giles Weyland jump. "We will send for this jarl; we will confront him; we will serve notice that his actions are in defiance of church and crown, and if he persists, we will crush him utterly.

"What think you of this notion, Giles Weyland?"

"It has merit," murmured the anxious priest.

Bishop William chortled. "Only see what a little thought can do. If you mean to rise, my friend, try thinking. We commend it to you."

"I will try, my lord," said the priest.

"Now, then, do you dispatch yourself to this upstart princeling this very hour, and bid him come to us at this same hour tomorrow. Oh, we will put a flea in his ear, I warrant ye!"

"My lord," began Giles Weyland, in deep distress. "I do not think that I—"

"Christ's wounds, man! Will you drive us mad? What have you to do with thinking?" The bishop's jowls pinked with choler. "Get you to Sinclair, and let me not see your silly face again till you have done our errand!"

Giles Weyland departed quickly.

Not more than one hundred yards to the north of St. Magnus' Cathedral, on a spit of land that formed the shore of Kirkwall's harbor, Henry Sinclair walked that morning with his kinsman Gunn. Tom Prentiss, in his new role as clerk-of-the-works, was full of a most infectious exuberance for carrying out Hafthorsson's plans.

"Ye see yonder rise, my lord?" said he to Sinclair, pointing to a slight elevation that ran from a point on the shore out into the bay.

Sinclair nodded.

"In old times, there stood on that very spot a stronghold of Norse lords. The foundations are yet in place, going down below the water and rising to a point level with the highest tides. Lord Sigurd's purpose was to raise your fortress there, built solidly of great blocks of hewn stone with walls so thick that no gale nor no bombard can make a dent in 'em."

"It is a grand spot for a sea-lord," murmured Gunn, nodding his approval.

"Ye've a long head, Sir Ingram," said Prentiss. He unsheathed his dirk and squatted heavily, with a great expulsion of windy breath. "Look here, my lord. I've a plan will strike your fancy."

In the sandy ground at his feet, Prentiss sketched an arch within the rough outline of a wall. "What Lord Sigurd wanted was a water passage here, so that your goodly ships can sail as it were into the very castle, and load or offload wi'in the very shelter of those same tremendous walls."

"God bless us," murmured Sinclair, himself squatting down for a closer look. "That was right cleverly conceived of."

"Aye," remarked Gunn, "but could not an invader take advantage of this bit o' cleverness, and fill your castle with men-at-arms some moonless night whilst we are all of us asleep? For my part, I should not care to waken to the pricking of a steel point at my throat—or, what's worse, not to waken at all."

Tom Prentiss's smile faded. "Lord Sigurd was no fool, Sir Ingram," he said. "We've men here who can craft a gate. And surely, Jarl Sinclair would not mean, however thick the walls, to leave those walls unguarded?"

"Yield, coz," said Sinclair, smiling. "Lord Sigurd anticipated any doubts, and that right handily.

"It seems to us a splendid work. And I can envision a vast cellar filled with stores, so that the outfitting of a ship, or the housing of cargo, can be most efficiently disposed off. I like the plan, and you have our leave to prosecute the work full swiftly, for I mean—" Sinclair broke off. He rose to his full height, and squinting in the autumn glare, he shielded his eyes with a cupped palm and stared southward.

"A rider comes," he said, "a clerk, by the look of him."

Prentiss and Sir Ingram rose and stood by their lord, watching the approach of black-and-white-robed slender figure, mounted on a shaggy palfrey.

"It is the priest, Giles Weyland, or I do mistake myself," muttered Tom Prentiss.

"What's his condition here?" asked Sinclair.

"He's of William's household."

"Not a condition to be envied," said Sir Ingram, smiling.

"No, sir," replied Prentiss. "Yon Giles is, I think, an honest clerk. Folk hereabout speak kindly of him, for all they do despise and fear his master. But that he is by birth a Southron and by misfortune linked to Bishop William, I know nothing to his discredit."

"He hath spied us," Sinclair remarked, "and he comes this way. I little doubt we are the object of his errand."

Giles Weyland soon erased whatever vestige of a doubt there might have been in Sinclair's mind. He reined in before the jarl and his men, and bid them a subdued good morrow.

"Good morrow to you, sir priest," replied Sinclair. "Pray, dismount and make yourself known to us."

While Ingram Gunn held his mount's bridle, Giles Weyland got himself down with no remarkable grace, and shook out the rucked-up skirts of his friar's habit. He came forward then and knelt to kiss Sinclair's extended hand.

"You know us, then?" Sinclair murmured.

"No, my lord," replied the priest. "But there is that in you bespeaks the rank you bear. I should have marked you for what you are as readily among three thousand as among this threesome."

"Well, Sir Ingram," said Sinclair, smiling, "I think we have been complimented, and that exquisitely."

"You have been complimented, coz," returned Gunn. "As for myself, I am less certain."

Sinclair laughed. "Come, good father, rise and give us your name and your purpose."

"I am Giles Weyland, my lord, come from Bishop William's house on purpose to deliver a message."

"From him?"

"Yes, my lord,"

"To us?"

"Yes, my lord."

"Well, then?"

Giles Weyland looked unhappy. He slipped his pale hands into his sleeves, bowed his tonsured head, and said, "My lord William bids me ask that the jarl of Orkney attend him in his hall at about this hour tomorrow."

"To what purpose?" Sinclair asked, his voice neutral and mild.

"I cannot say, my lord."

Sinclair's smile was doubtful. "Or will not? Well, Giles Weyland, we are sorry to have been the occasion of this fruitless journey, but you must inform your master that we are—indisposed."

Sinclair nodded by way of dismissal, and turned as if to go.

"My lord?" Distress was plain in Giles Weyland's voice.

"Father?"

"Do you mean never to see him?"

Sinclair shrugged. "Who was it spoke of 'never'? Indeed, 'never' is a thing I cannot grasp. It may be that we shall hear a mass at yonder cathedral, and see the bishop there. It may be that as we move about this place we shall even pass him on the way. No, sir, I do not speak of 'never.' I speak of tomorrow, when we shall be, as we told you, indisposed.

"'Indisposed,'" he repeated, savoring the word on his tongue. "That is a word familiar to your lord, I think. Do you relay it to him and see if he but recognize the expression."

Giles Weyland seized Sinclair's hand. "My lord," he said, "think me not presumptuous in this. I know myself to be but a simple friar, and one not accustomed to policy and great matters. But there is this to consider.

"My lord bishop and yourself, my lord, have the peace of these isles in your keeping. If there can be harmony between you, then we can look for a kind of perpetual summer, as it were, a long and happy season such as these lands have never known, when crofter and prince alike may enjoy their several states in peace. Such an epoch would, my lord, redound to your great honor, and would serve as an exemplar to kings and lords through all the world."

Sinclair scanned the anxious face of this earnest clerk. "Sir priest," he said at last, "we take you for an honest man."

Giles Weyland made as if to speak, but Sinclair forestalled him. "We, for our part, would deal honestly with you. It is very much to our purpose to have peace here. But our love for peace is neither so great nor so all-embracing that we would purchase it at the price of honor.

"From all reports that have come to us from men whom we deem trusty, we have drawn no very encouraging account of your bishop. Indeed, we have heard not one thing that would commend him to us. Can you, sir, as an honest clerk, offer us any proofs to the contrary?"

Giles Weyland's dark eyes seemed to look for answers in the dust. At length he raised his gaze to meet Sinclair's and said, "My lord, I cannot. There is only this. William is bishop here. The souls of all here are in his keeping, and my duty is to serve him."

Sinclair managed a wintry smile. "We do not envy you your duty. It takes no great imagination to picture what awaits you at William's palace when you return to him with our answer."

The doleful expression in Weyland's eyes confirmed Jarl Henry's speculation. "My lord is a shrewd appraiser of men's nature," he said.

Sinclair sniffed. "That's as may be. We'll go so far as to say that, were you bishop here, we would not hesitate to treat with you."

"You do me too much honor, my lord."

Sinclair's smile widened and warmed. "If you knew us, you would not say so. But here it is. We like you, Giles Weyland. We do not love your bishop.

"To spare you pain, and to afford him opportunity to prove false or true the accounts we have had of him till now, we will meet with this William."

"Thanks, my lord," murmured the priest.

"But not tomorrow, and not in his hall."

"No, my lord?" The priest's brief smile faded.

"No, sir. You may tell your lord that we can be found here, under this open sky, at about this same hour in two days' time. Tell him that we welcome this meeting, but that we are obliged to plead a great press of affairs that must deny us the pleasure of his hospitality. And now, Giles Weyland, we must bid you good morrow, for in truth we have much business to attend to."

Giles Weyland was no fool. He knew that he had gained all that could be gained from this stern Norse-Scots noble. With a bow and a hoarse "God be with you," he clambered aboard his palfrey and jogged back to William's palace, composing a softened version of Sinclair's reply as he rode.

Sinclair and Sir Ingram sat very late that night. Next day, riders—including the late Lord Sigurd's sons and some three or four of his picked men—made a great many comings and goings in the region around Kirkwall. By the time night had unfurled the sable banner of her brief encampment, Jarl Henry's plans for the morrow were well and truly laid. It remained only to see if Bishop William would rise to the bait.

He did. Perhaps his curiosity overpowered his wrath at Sinclair's refusal to come to him. Or perhaps Giles Weyland's sly persuasion tipped the scales. "For," he said, when the bishop did at last give him leave to speak, "my lord would make a very fair showing before this jarl of Orkney were you to ride out at the head of your men-at-arms. That, I think, will speak to him more plainly than ever words could do."

William, whose fondness for display was only a little less than his love of possessions, allowed himself to be persuaded. And so it was that on that fair autumn morning, William of Orkney, bishop, mounted on a richly caparisoned white mule, sallied forth from his palace at the head of a company of fifty riders in full armor. The bishop himself was clad in churchly purple, with a most unclerical steel cap covering his hairless pate. A gorgeously outfitted little page jogged at his lordship's elbow, bearing William's banner—a task made awkward by a frisking wayward breeze.

William of Orkney reined in as his party came to the broad low area of Sinclair's building site and, squinting against the sun, rose in his stirrups to survey the scene. "Now, plague take him, where is this fellow? Giles Weyland!"

Trotting from the ranks of armored men came the bishop's secretary. "My lord?" he said.

"Where is this Sinclair?" And before the priest could make the obvious reply, his bishop belabored with a half-dozen questions more. Was he sure of the time? Could they have come too early? Too late? Was this the appointed place? Had Weyland not, as usual, botched the business altogether?

Mercifully for the beleaguered friar, the bishop's page piped up: "Look, my lord. Someone comes."

The bishop left off tormenting Weyland and turned his pouched and glittering gaze to where a lone man, cloaked and hooded, came striding down the slope from the rise that overlooked the plain.

"'Tis some emissary of his, no doubt," muttered the bishop, "come full of lies to explain away this delay and so work off some tricksy plot to humiliate us further."

The man in the shabby cloak drew near and, with a preliminary bow, approached the bishop's mount. "Good morrow, my lord bishop," he said, his voice strong and forceful, and very like that of an equal for all that he dutifully kissed plump William's hand. "Come, dismount and take your ease. No doubt we can conclude our business quickly, and you and your little troop can then make trial of a jarl's hospitality."

"What's this? What's this?" The bishop puffed and blew like a beached whale. "We will not treat with you, sirrah. Summon your lord instanter. Does he mean to insult us by this sorry tactic?"

"My lord," began Giles Weyland, urging his mount level with the bishop's own. "This man—"

"Peace!" cried the bishop. "Hold your tongue, sir! I do not hold you blameless in this."

The man in the cloak chuckled, fueling William's ire and making the poor friar tremble—and not on his own account solely. "My lord bishop," said he, "the fault is mine. I am Sinclair."

"You?" the syllable exploded in wonder and disbelief.

"Aye, my lord, Henry Sinclair, baron of Rosslyn and jarl of Orkney."

A sneer distorted the bishop's mouth as he again surveyed the un-prepossessing figure before him. "Indeed, you wear your honors lightly," William drawled.

"Aye, my lord, for I have long since learned the folly of holding too hard to that which thieves can steal or moth or rust corrupt."

William loosed a snort of mirthless laughter. "If you mean to preach, sir, I wonder that you do not take orders. For ourselves, we have a chaplain and do not need another."

Sinclair laughed. "Your pardon, my lord. Come, dismount and walk a little way with me. We will dispatch our business, and then—"

"No, sir," replied the bishop, gathering in his reins. "It takes but an instant to say what we will say, and we have other and more pressing business elsewhere this morning."

Sinclair bowed. "Say on, my lord."

"Hear this, then. As bishop of this place, and as a loyal servant of Norway's lord, we command you to give over this plan of yours to build a stronghold here. It is a project much to our disliking and wholly at odds with the very patents by which you hold your title. Defy us in this and it shall be at your peril.

"And now, Jarl Henry, we must bid you a good morrow."

As the bishop made to turn his mount's head, Sinclair seized the animal's bridle. "A moment, my lord bishop, pray."

"What's this?" Bishop William fairly spluttered. "How dare—?"

"My lord, you appear to misapprehend the purpose of our meeting." Sinclair's tone continued mild. "I came this early from my bed not to listen, but to speak. Sit easy in your saddle, pray, and hear me."

"That will I not!" huffed the bishop, a rosy flush pinking his gills.

"My lord, you will," asserted Sinclair, and putting his fingers between his teeth, he raised a shrill whistle.

"Now, by Christ's winding sheet," began the bishop, but before he could complete his oath, he saw that which gave him pause. For over the rise, their armor glinting in the hazy sun, came some sixscore men on horse and foot, moving at a pace as purposeful as it was slow. One horseman gave spur to his steed, and came at a canter up to where Sinclair was standing. There the knight dismounted and said, "Will ye have my horse, Jarl Henry?"

"Thanks, Sir Ingram," said Sinclair. He let his hooded cloak fall to the ground, and swung lightly up into the saddle. Bishop William now found himself gazing up at a brawny, broad-shouldered noble clad in blue and scarlet, and looking every bit of what he was.

"Oh, and here's this, my lord," said Ingram. Sinclair took from his kinsman's hands a circlet of white gold and settled it securely on gray-flecked reddish thatch.

Sinclair, appearing not to notice that his men-at-arms had by now encircled the bishop and his minions, fixed William with his slaty eyes. "Now, sir," he said, "you will hear us."

The bishop seemed to shrink within his costly robes as Sinclair said:

"First, we are by Haakon's will, prince of these isles. To those who give us fair allegiance, we will give our faithful friendship in weal or woe.

"Second, we will cause to rise here a stronghold sufficient to our private need, and so strongly built as to ensure the safety of our lands and people.

"Third, we will keep faith with Norway and with holy church in all things. And," he added with an edge to his words no man could mistake, "we will see justice done.

"We have," he added more mildly, "some few good men to do our bidding, as you see. And there are many times as many more in Scotland and in Norway who will, at our summons, ride out to defend our cause."

The ruby in stout William's ring winked at the trembling of his plump hands, and his padded cheeks seemed drained of blood as his foxy brain took in the numbers Sinclair had laid out for him.

"Finally, my lord bishop," said Sinclair, his eyes boring into the bishop's own, "we mean to redress the wrongs that you yourself have done this people, to restore such lands as you have usurped, and to keep so close a watch on you as will ensure no further straying beyond the bounds of what a bishop's business is."

It was then a shout was raised, "God save Jarl Henry!"

And when the echo died away, Sinclair made taut his reins and said, "Look you, lord bishop, make no mistake. We would be in all things and to all men friendly, but if you stray so much as a hair's-breadth from the course we have laid out for you, you will find yourself adrift in such a welter of troubles as have not befallen any man since saintly Job's day."

"Sacrilege!" roared the bishop, his jowls aquiver. "Jarl or no jarl, I'll see you excommunicate!"

A collective gasp went up from the bishop's retinue, and the priest Giles Weyland crossed himself in horror at his master's wrathful word.

"Remember England's Henry, my lord Sinclair," the bishop continued, his voice barely under control even yet, "how he was made to submit to flogging at Becket's tomb. Do not imagine your own back so well armored as to escape the bit of the penitent's lash. When Rome shall hear of this, this realm of yours may well find itself under an interdict. Not a mass shall be heard, no wedding or funeral solemnized, no sacrament administered until you bend your neck to the authority of holy church."

"Pax, pax!" cried Sinclair, his forehead creased in a frown. "What is this talk of Rome and interdict? You rage at phantoms, my lord. Nothing we have said can warrant—"

"You have threatened our person," growled William. "And that is sacrilege."

Sinclair's expression was bleak. "No, sir," he said. "Your person's safe as if 'twere guarded by a troop of holy angels."

"Hah! We are glad to see some sign of proper reverence—" began the bishop.

Sinclair, with an impatient gesture, broke in. "Your person is safe," he repeated. "Indeed, it never was in any danger from us. But not so your place, my lord."

"What?" The bishop's pursy mouth worked furiously, but Jarl Henry forged ahead.

"A word from us to Bergen, and thence to Rome, will dislodge you and this petty troop as readily as any turnspit may dislodge a flea. We have a kinsman, Robert, now dean of Moray, who would in our estimate make a better shepherd here. Do you but continue in this present course, and you will live to see another in your place."

Outrage clouded the vast expanse of William's shaven face. His great chest heaved with volcanic wrath. "Rome shall hear of this!" he cried, his voice cracking and shrilling with emotion. "We will dispatch letters to holy Urban this very day."

William made as if to turn his mount's head, but Sinclair deftly snared the bridle. "My lord bishop," he said, "reflect. I rule here as Haakon's deputy. And Haakon's worth to Urban is beyond price—at least so long as Clement claims the chair of Peter from his hold at Avignon. Before I spilt much ink in this, I'd ponder well the likelihood of Urban's risking Haakon's loyalty. Rome needs the king's allegiance more than she needs your happiness."

Sinclair let go the bridle and, wagging his head, added, "I would think on it, my lord. I would make of it a matter for grave study."

The bishop puffed and snorted like a blown horse. "You will find that with me, Jarl Henry, to think is to act. The sun will not have set ere I have set my seal on letters to Urban in this cause. An I were you, my lord, I would make this text my study: 'What doth it profit a man if he gain the whole world but suffer the loss of his own soul?'

"Look well to your soul, Jarl Henry, I charge ye. Look well to your soul!"

For a perilous moment, Jarl Henry grappled with a surging impulse to commit that very sacrilege William had charged him with intending. He longed with a terrible longing to vent his anger with a resounding smack of his gloved hand across the veal-like slab of William's pale and bloated face. The very tension of sinew, however, caused his horse to skitter, and in controlling his steed, Sinclair gained control of his own coltish emotion.

Gathering in the slack in his reins, Sinclair, his voice taut and strained as the reins themselves, brought an end to the parley: "I will look to my soul, my lord," he said. "See you look well to yourself. For if a knight may take a bishop, think what a jarl might do."

With that, he turned his horse's head and led his troop away.

That night, over the wine, Ingram Gunn sounded out his kinsman: "What will ye do, coz, an this William succeed in placing us under the ban?"

"Pray he does not succeed, coz." Sinclair traced a pattern on the oak with a finger dipped in the wet rings left by his goblet. "There are three things I value more than my life—Janet, my honor, and my immortal soul. If Urban were to heed this grasping prelate's plea and deny me the sacrament, then all my power and all my plans would as dust and ashes."

Sinclair shook his head. "To you I own it, Ingram, in trust and in secret. I'd break faith with Norway and Scotland both before I would defy the sovereignty of holy church."

"But is Urban pope, or Clement?"

Sinclair's laugh was rueful. "God He knows. But only let the word go forth that Orkney's jarl's an excommunicate, and all my usefulness is at an end."

"But you think Urban will not listen to William in this?"

"So I think, coz, and so I hope, for—but here's John Clarke!"

"Aye," said Ingram, laughing, "come from his bed—or someone's bed—by the look of him."

And indeed little Clarke presented a frowzy specimen of himself—hair tousled, hose wrinkled, and doublet awry. He dug at his eyes with his fists, gaped, and said, "Your pardons, masters, pray, for this intrusion on your revels."

"It seems that we intrude upon your own," returned Jarl Henry, smiling. "For that we ask your pardon, John Clarke."

"Granted," mumbled Clarke, with a careless wave of his hand. "My lord is the very soul of courtesy."

"Humph! And you, sirrah, are the very prince of impertinence," Sinclair replied. "But come, what is it drags you from your night's devotions? We readily conceive it must be a weighty matter that summons you so late—or so early—from your labors."

"God bless us, my lord, talk not of conceivings and labors. 'Tis early days to speak o' that, and it fair gi'es me the grue to hear it." John Clarke shuddered and hugged himself against the chill in his bones.

"Take a little wine to warm ye, John, and deliver yourself o' this news that brings you hither."

Clarked drained off the proffered cup, smacked his lips, and wiped his mouth on his sleeve. "I'd take it kindly if ye'd no speak o' deliverin's neither, my lord," he said. "These are delicate matters, not fit for gentle conversation."

"My boot will have no gentle conversation wi' your arse an ye do not give over playin' and state your business," growled Sir Ingram, half laughing in spite of himself.

" 'Tis no great thing, Sir Ingram," replied Clarke, pretending to take offense. "'Tis only some priest come from William's palace to have a word wi' Jarl Henry."

Sinclair's eyes widened. "So? This is some trick our canny bishop's hatched, I make no doubt. But do you show him in, John Clarke, and retire to your rest."

"Or to your wrestling," amended Sir Ingram, pulling a sour face.

Little Clarke bobbed a bow, pattered off, and returned promptly with Giles Weyland in tow.

"Here he is, my lord," chirped the squire. "And now my work is done I'll bid all here good night."

"We trust you'll have a good night of it yourself, John Clarke," replied Sinclair. "To bed, to bed."

And as the small squire padded off, Sinclair turned his attention to the cloaked and hooded Giles Weyland. "Now, sir priest, what is it brings you to our hall this late, late hour? Take a little wine, I pray you, and state your errand."

"No wine, my lord, I thank you," replied the priest. "I dare not stay a moment longer than it takes to tell my news."

"Say on, then." Sinclair folded his hands on his belly and leaned back in his chair, coolly scanning the pale strained face before him.

"I am sent to Rome, my lord. Bishop William commands me to take ship this very night for England, from there to make my way to Urban's court." Giles Weyland drew from his sleeve a sealed roll of parchment. Tapping the cylinder lightly on his palm, he said, "These writings plead with Urban for your excommunication and your ruin."

"So." Sinclair's tone was mild and even. "And you come to us, Giles Weyland. Why?"

The priest's spare frame seemed to lock itself into a posture of erect determination. "I do not mean that Urban shall ever see these letters."

Sinclair and Gunn exchanged a glance.

"You will not go to Rome?" asked Jarl Henry.

"To Rome I will go, indeed, God willing. These writings, however, I will not carry. I have come here to place them in your hands, my lord, and to bid you farewell."

Sinclair leaned forward, chin on fist, curiosity brightening his shrewd blue eyes. "And how does this purpose square with your vows, sir priest? Forgive me, but you seem to us no rebel, nor in any way a man lightly to cross the will of his superior."

A thin smile briefly lightened Weyland's somber face. "'Tis no light thing, my lord, to have for so long forgot Who is my superior and where my true allegiance lies. I came to William's service in obedience to my father in religion. And in obedience, I have done Bishop William's

bidding in all things, even when the bidding of my conscience directed
otherwise.

"Will you take these letters, my lord?"

Sinclair ignored the question. "But if you do this thing, is there not
some risk?"

"Nothing to the risk an I do not, my lord." Weyland smiled a second
time, and his smile was wintry. "I am a selfish man, believe it. And so
careful of myself am I that I will not risk my hope of heaven for another
man's convenience—not even Bishop William's."

"And you believe you hazard your salvation in William's service?"

"I know only that it is so for me. What another man might do, how
well he might walk the narrow way between serving Christ and pleasing
William, I cannot say. It is Giles Weyland I judge, my lord, not William.
And I know this Weyland lacks the mountebank art to juggle Christ's
and William's business while dancing on rope across the pit of hell.

"I mean to go to Rome, my lord, and by God's grace to heaven at the
last."

Sinclair nodded, approval plainly written on his face. "And have you
assurance of refuge in Rome? William, once he hath smoked your purpose, is not likely to overlook it."

"Our order has a house there, my lord. I will be quite safe, and very
happy to be again what I was before I came to Orkney." Weyland's
evident joy at the prospect made his face youthful, radiant, and kindled
a responsive warmth in Sinclair's breast.

Jarl Henry rose and came around the table to take Giles Weyland's
hand. "Is there any way that we can serve you?" he said.

Weyland shook his head. "Only take these writings, and keep me in
your prayers."

Sinclair took the parchment. "Will you give us your blessing, father,
before you go?" he said, and he knelt before Giles Weyland.

"And I," cried Sir Ingram, coming forward to kneel beside his kinsman.
"If ever a man needed blessing, I am he."

The priest smiled and raised his hand above the heads of the nobles
at his feet. *"Benedicat vos omnipotens Deus, Pater, et Filius, et Spiritus
Sanctus, Amen."*

"Amen," echoed Sinclair and Sir Ingram.

They rose, and embracing the priest, Sinclair said, "Godspeed, Father
Giles. This service to us—"

"Not to you, my lord, but to our Lord," said Giles Weyland. "God
keep you both. Adieu."

With a slight bow, Giles Weyland turned and walked swiftly out of
the great hall and into the kind, concealing night.

"There goes an upright man," murmured Jarl Henry, his gaze still focused on the portal through which the priest had disappeared.

"Aye," said Sir Ingram, "he would have made a grand knight."

Sinclair smiled. "He serves a grand King, surely. And in serving Him hath served us very well."

"Let's see what William's written, since Urban never will."

Sinclair stared down at the cylinder in his hand, then slowly shook his head. "No, coz," he said, "'tis a thing I'd like to think beneath our dignity, however much our curiosity gnaws."

With that, he tossed the parchment in a low arc that landed it squarely amid the dying embers on the hearth. As tiny tongues of flame rose up to lick the waxen seals, Sir Ingram shook his head in wonder.

"Before God, Harry, I could not do so. Ye're a better man than I, that's certain."

Affection for his cousin shone in Sinclair's eyes. "That, friend Ingram, is just what I should have said to the priest Giles Weyland. Before God," he said.

22

With his bishop effectively in check, Sinclair now made haste to keep his appointment in Norway, to deliver up to Haakon the monies due him under the terms of Sinclair's investiture as Orkney's lord. For all his haste, however, Jarl Henry did not neglect his opportunity to visit Lord Sigurd's widow on his course through the Shetlands.

Herdis Thorvaldsdatter, he found, bore her grief with simple grace. "I had thought to grow old with him here," she told Sinclair. "I would have been content with that. We had friendship between us, Sigurd and I, over and above the love that gave us two strong sons. We talked well together. I think we could not have been happier in the court at Bergen than we were here. Our life was simple; we took joy in the turning seasons, the comings and goings of the birds, the changing moods of sea and sky. I wanted nothing more; neither, I think, did he. Except," she smiled and shook her head, "he wanted to feel useful, wanted still to play a young man's part. That is why he—he was so pleased when you asked service of him."

"We received from him in full measure," Sinclair said. "He was a very able man, and a good one. We shall not forget him ever."

"Forget not his sons, Jarl Sinclair, pray."

Sinclair took the woman's hand in his. "Lady Herdis, we give you our solemn pledge to be your protector and to foster your sons in their growing toward manhood, to find places for them in our household when they are to manhood grown."

"My lord, I can ask no more than that."

Sinclair shook his head. "You may ask of us anything, Herdis Thorvaldsdatter; you will not find us unmindful of our obligation to this house. My men and I are bound away to Tunsberg with the morning tide. We have business there that will not admit of delay. But be assured, lady, we shall be often in Shetland, and as often under this roof. Our love and duty to this house will take precedence over all, save that we owe to Haakon himself."

Lady Herdis sought to kiss Sinclair's hand, but he instead embraced her and kissed her on both cheeks. "Fare you well, Herdis Thorvaldsdatter," he said. "We shall look in on you as soon as we return from Norway."

It was a rough crossing, but Sinclair and his party were in the appointed place on the appointed day. On hand to greet them was Ogmund Finnsson, Haakon's chief counselor, with some several courtiers, Johnny Sinclair, and Alexander de Ard.

"Well, Jarl Sinclair," said Finnsson, offering his hand, "you are prompt upon the day."

"Aye. We mean to be diligent in all the king's business. Ah! We spy our rascally brother! Greetings, Johnny. Come, gi' us a hug. How fares our bold suitor in his campaign?"

John Sinclair embraced his brother. "Before God, Harry, it is good to see you. How's Mother? And all at Rosslyn?"

"Well, Johnny, very well. Ye've a new niece to your string."

"A sister for Betsy! I'm glad of that."

"And what about a sister for us, little brother? Are you and the fair Dane yet handfasted?"

Johnny nodded, grinning from ear to ear. "We have her mother's blessing, Harry. Have we yours?"

"With all my heart, Johnny. Did ye doubt it? I told the folk at Rosslyn ye'd turned fortune hunter and gone and pledged yourself to a twice-widowed brewmaster's daughter, twelve years older and thirty pound heavier than yourself."

"Ah, God, ye didn't?"

"And warts. I added warts too." Sinclair burst into laughter. "No, no, John. I was playing with ye. I told 'em ye were bringing home a beauty, and so ye are. So ye are."

"It will be good to see home again."

"Aye. We'll not be long here, I promise you. But where's our sweet kinsman Sparre, hey?"

Alexander de Ard spoke up. "He thought you might not be coming, noble cousin, and so he has gone off hunting."

"A pleasant day he'll have of it," muttered Sinclair, eyeing the brooding sky. "Well, to business. What say you, Ogmund Finnsson? Shall we have our men carry the gold within? I suppose the king—"

"Haakon remains at Bergen, Jarl Sinclair," said the old counselor. "He hath been very low of late, and the physicians are daily in attendance on him."

"Why, we are truly grieved to hear it, sir. Truly. What is the nature of the king's complaint?"

Finnsson shook his head. "The physicians argue among themselves on that point, my lord. And while they debate, poor Haakon grows daily weaker and so pitifully thin that we are all in fear for his life."

"So bad as that?"

"Aye. He hath had the extreme unction, but he gets no better. the archbishop himself hath shriven him and given him the sacrament. Masses are said daily for his recovery, and all our hope is in God's providence." Finnsson crossed himself, then said, "But, come, my lord, I do not mean to keep you and your men standing out here in this wind. Let us go in and complete our business. Then shall you try our hospitality here at Tunsberg."

"How fares the queen?" Sinclair asked, as he and Finnsson led the way into the castle.

"As becomes a queen, my lord. She keeps a cheerful countenance, and hides her care from all but a very few. Margaret has something of Haakon's fortitude. She is, my lord, a most remarkable woman."

"So I thought her," murmured Sinclair. "I pray you, tell her she and her lord are in our prayers, and say that Orkney stands ready to do her bidding in any and all things."

"I will tell her, my lord, so soon as I am again at Bergen."

Finnsson called for spiced wine. And when the travelers had quite rid their bones of the November chill, Sinclair made over the gold to Finnsson with due ceremony. The documents were witnessed and sealed, and Sinclair and friends were then conducted to their several chambers where they might refresh themselves and make ready for the dinner Finnsson promised them.

"So you're to be a happy bachelor no more, eh, Johnny?" teased Ingram Gunn, as he lounged in the window of Sinclair's chamber.

"Pay him no mind, John," advised Sinclair, who was industriously scraping away at his jaws with his razor. "He is green jealous, is all. You've plucked the fairest flower o' Denmark, and our poor Gunn hath not one blossom to call his own."

"Ah, there's your mistake, Harry," replied Gunn. "Flowers were not meant to be owned. Pluck 'em and they fade. Keep 'em, and they lose their sweetness. Study the butterfly, my friend, and the humble bee. Do they pluck? Do they keep? Not so. Yet they have such a store o' sweetness as no mere husband can ever hope to own."

Sinclair grunted. "Even a humble bee can get himself stung, my friend. And he that flits from flower to flower may find himself stinging in such a part and in such a fashion as quite to make his honey sour."

"Ha-ha!" Johnny Sinclair fell back on the bed and kicked his legs in the air. "A gold! A gold! My brother hath hit the bull's eye."

"'Twas not the eye I aimed at," drawled Sinclair, wiping the soap from his chin.

"In truth, sir, ye did aim low," growled Ingram.

"Why, sir, 'twas low talk and low companions put me off my aim."

"Why, as to that, my lord, you are lowest here. I have you topped by an inch or two, and our eager bridegroom here is as much above me."

"Height, sir," replied Sinclair, mildly, "is one thing among bean poles, quite another among men. If we were to accept your standard, then any six-foot rustic might be king. You have heard how Jack slew the giant—"

"An old tale, sir, and not to be credited."

Sinclair laughed. "There's more of truth in the old tales than in some I have heard lately. But, come, this idle talk hath whet my appetite. Let's try this northern fare, what it can do to still the grumblings of a Scottish gut."

At table, Sinclair informed Finnsson of Hafthorsson's death.

"What, Sigurd?" Finnsson's jaw went slack.

"Even so," Sinclair replied.

"How came he to die?"

"Why, sir, it was a foolish thing. He only tripped and fell, but that was enough. It did for him as well as sword or lance might for another. God ha' mercy on him."

"Amen," muttered Finnsson, splashing some wine into his cup. "God! What a pity. I liked him, my lord. I liked him very well."

Sinclair nodded his sympathy. He thought it prudent to avoid mention of walls and buildings in this circumstance, so he said only, "We ourselves had come to love him, sir."

Finnsson stared down into his cup and sniffed noisily. "Poor Lady Herdis. She will be quite alone now."

"Not quite alone," Sinclair said. "She has her two boys and, so long as we live, she has in us a friend and protector."

Finnsson eyed his guest keenly. "I think, my lord," he said at last, "I think Haakon's judgment is confirmed. Oh, I confess it, I was uncertain, had doubts, reservations. I freely own it. There's no shame in that. But neither is there shame in saying now that I am right glad that you are jarl of Orkney."

Sinclair smiled. "I like your candor, Ogmund Finnsson. And I am heartily glad of your confidence."

"You have that, my lord," the older man said. "And you have in me a friend at court in Norway."

Sinclair lingered but a few days at Tunsberg, chiefly to give Ingeborg time to gather her things for the long journey before her. But also he hoped to have some word of Haakon—and of Margaret.

None came.

The day of departure dawned clear and cold. And on that morning Malise Sparre put in an appearance.

He had come riding in late the night before and gone straight to his bed, bone-weary and chilled through. But there was a toughness in this pale Swede for all his dancing master's airs and graces. He was up with the sun—before the sun, in fact, for the sun was last to rise in that season in that clime—and caught up with Sinclair over the cold meat on which he broke his fast.

"So, kinsman, we meet again."

"So it seems," replied Sinclair, coolly. "How fared you hunting?"

"Indifferent well." Sparre shrugged his narrow shoulders. "I speared a boar before he speared my horse. That was something."

Sinclair nodded. "'Tis fair sport, boar hunting."

"I have known better. But it is so dull here that I am glad of any little diversion that takes me out of myself."

Temptation pricked at Sinclair's lips, but he withstood it.

"As you are here," Sparre went on, shooting a furtive glance at his sometime rival, "can I assume that you have met Haakon's demand and I am no more hostage?"

"That must come from Haakon, surely. But the terms are met. We sail today with my brother and his betrothed."

Sparre rubbed his white hands, making a dry, whispery sound. "Then I shall no doubt be leaving soon for Skuldane."

"Bon voyage."

"Merci." Sparre nibbled at a crust of rye bread. "How—ah, how do you find matters in the isles?"

"To my liking, kinsman, thank you. There's a deal of work to be done, but the work's very much to our taste."

Sparre nodded. "You were ever an enterprising man, cousin. Still, I daresay you've learned already that 'tis no small task you've undertaken. I mean, it's all very grand being called jarl of Orkney; but, dear, dear, all those little islands scattered over so wide an expanse of sea! Unless a man can contrive to be in an hundred places at one time, I confess I do not see how he can hope to maintain his authority."

"'Twill try our mettle, surely."

"I should think so. Why, 'tis like trying to carry a dozen eggs with no basket. Something must be let fall, and if you try to retrieve that one, you must surely lose another." Sparre shook his head. "I marvel that you would even try, kinsman. Truly, I do marvel."

"And I marvel, sir, that you troubled yourself to the extent of contesting our claim for so poor and worrisome a prize. Indeed, sir, we see now that it is you who are to be congratulated on having escaped our burden. We do rejoice for you, and that most heartily." Sinclair's voice dripped with irony. "We wish you Godspeed to Skuldane, and we shall study to overcome our envy of your great good fortune in having avoided this cross we bear."

And Sinclair, with a very slight bow, turned on his heel and left Malise Sparre to digest his spite along with his breakfast.

Their farewells said, Sinclair, Ingram, Clarke, and Johnny, with the blushing Ingeborg and her maid, boarded ship and set sail for Caithness.

"Ingram and I will bide there and go about our business," Sinclair told his brother. "The ship will carry you on to Edinburgh, where you can take horse for Rosslyn."

"But you will be coming soon after?"

"Aye. Tell Janet to expect us in time for Christmas. We mean to stay and see you decently wed, for I mean to be groomsman to you, if ye'll have me. And then, well, I shall need a day or so to count the children, and another week at least just to be with Janet and wander about the old place and restore myself for the work ahead."

"Won't it be fine for Mother to have us all home at Rosslyn again?"

"Aye, John, and maybe for the last time. Who knows?" Sinclair smiled and clasped his brother's hand. "Get ye gone home, lad, you and your girl. Oh, and tell Davey I've no forgot my promise. He'll come with me when I go north again."

"And I?"

Sinclair laughed. "Johnny, Johnny, ye'll be main busy for a time now. Make Rosslyn your home and take your ease. Ye've fairer employment before ye than any I could offer ye."

23

Spring's first green had touched the land by the time Sinclair returned to Kirkwall. For while he was yet at Rosslyn, word had come from Bergen that Haakon was dead.

Although he could not possibly travel thither in time for Haakon's burial, Sinclair felt it his duty as premier noble of Norway to make an appearance at the mourning court. So it was that, in the dead of winter, he made the arduous northward journey, taking with him John Clarke and young David Sinclair.

"And will I go with you to Bergen, Harry?" David had asked.

"Nay, lad. Another time, it may be. But I think there would be little pleasure for you in it now. God He knows there is none for me. You will bide the while with our cousin Gunn and have a chance to see my ships a-building. When I've done my business at court, I'll come to Caithness and we will go together over to Orkney."

"Well, I suppose I shall have some sport with Ingram," had been David's reply. "But I would like to see the court and be presented to the little boy king."

Sinclair refused to quibble. He had neither time nor appetite for it. He could think only of the widowed Margaret—of her and of the possible effect of Haakon's death on his own small seagirt realm.

Ogmund Finnsson was first to receive Sinclair on his arrival. The two men clasped hands with new warmth, and soon they were deep in talk over hot wine in Finnsson's chamber.

"She bears it very well, my lord," Finnsson reported. "But she is sorely grieved. And so are we all. For Haakon was a goodly king, and greatly loved by folk of all degrees."

"We hardly knew him," Sinclair murmured, "yet were we most taken with him. He was a man you could readily give allegiance to."

Finnsson nodded. "Oh, he had his troubles. And he made some—some errors of judgment, no doubt. But he was king in a difficult time. We are far from recovered from the Black Death here, my lord, even now. The great plague of '49 carried off a third of our people; and the lesser outbreaks in '59 and '71 depleted us further still.

"Our economy is far from robust. Without people to plow and reap, without people to carry on trade, without people earning and spending, no country can prosper.

"Why, Norway was within my lifetime the very queen of the sea. But now, such ships as we have are too small and too slow to compete effectively, and those upstart Hansa merchants now have a stranglehold on commerce in these parts.

"Christ! In the worst of it, when our treasury was depleted, Margaret was actually hungry. Hungry, mind you! And had Haakon not put by his pride and sought credit from the German merchants, who knows what she might have come to?"

Sinclair shook his head. "We have heard, of course, that times were bad here; but for Margaret to be in want—"

"Oh, I tell you, my lord, that woman knew hard days, the harder for her just because she was queen. And the people know it, and they love her the more for it. She stood by Haakon through all the troubles, when any lesser woman might have sought refuge in her father's court where at least she would not starve, nor have to go a-begging of a damned German."

"What happens now?" Sinclair asked, masking the emotions that warred within him.

"Why, my lord, I shall serve as regent here for the young Olaf. When he is of age, he will have the crown of Norway as well as the crown of Denmark. Then, who knows? We may yet live to see Haakon's dream become reality."

"The union?"

Finnsson nodded. "If we can unite Norway, Denmark, and Sweden under the one crown, then can we hope to regain our former strength, and then will we be once more a power to be reckoned with.

"'Twill take time. You do not rebuild a nation in one year or ten years. But Olaf is very young; time he will have in abundance. If he have health and wisdom, too—and a measure of luck; let's not leave that out—why, he may one day rank with the grandest rulers in Christendom. But I do wish the boy were hardier. I do wish that very much."

Sinclair, troubled by the older man's tone, said, "Is he sickly, then?"

Finnsson gnawed at his lip, then let go a great sigh. "In truth, my lord, he strikes me as a very frail little boy. You are a father. What do you think of him?"

Sinclair shrugged. "I am a father, not a physician, Ogmund Finnsson. But I do confess he seemed to me—delicate, by contrast with my own brood. But then, my lads are such rough-and-tumble fellows as keep the whole house in constant uproar with their doings."

"There!" cried Finnsson. "That it is that troubles me. If the young king would show some spirit, if he would act the boy—climb trees, steal tarts, abuse the servants, worry the dogs, that kind of thing—why, I would, even in my grief for Haakon, rejoice at Norway's prospects.

"But this small king only moons about, shuns rough play, and likes best to hug the fire and listen to tales about trolls and the nisse, the goblin that loves to play tricks on dairymaids. Now if *he* would play tricks on dairymaids—"

"Then you would no doubt complain he was unruly," said Sinclair, laughing. "Come, come, my friend. Put not so gloomy a cast on things. Each child is different. This little king may yet prove a very large hero. And with you as regent, it seems unlikely he can come to any harm."

"Thank you for that," replied Finnsson. "But I still wish that he were more like your boys. Before God, I do wish that."

Sinclair did not see Margaret until late in the following day. She received him in her chamber. Her page, her tiring maid, her chaplain, and an attendant dame or two were with her, but these she dismissed almost immediately on Sinclair's arrival.

He came forward, knelt, and kissed Margaret's fair hand.

"You are welcome here, Jarl Sinclair," Margaret said. "We had hoped you would come."

"And I would have come sooner, had it been possible, madam. But, alas, I was away home in Scotland when I learned how matters stood here."

"Early or late, we are glad to see you here."

"Madam, I am grieved for you and for Norway. We have ordered masses sung for your late lord at all the churches round about Rosslyn."

"That is a comfort to us," Margaret said, "and kindly thought of. A king needs prayers and masses at least as much as another. Perhaps more. But how did you leave your family?"

"Well, madam, I thank you."

"We are glad to hear it. You must bring them to Bergen one day. We should like to meet your lady wife and all those lusty children."

Sinclair smiled. "I fear my boys would quite overrun this palace, madam. I know they would quite beggar pantry and kitchen."

"Bring them soon, then, for it would do us good to have some liveliness and laughter here."

A silence grew up between them, and in the interval, Sinclair studied Margaret's face. She looked younger still in her mourning dress. But then, she had been but a child when wed to Haakon, and was now not more than five-and-twenty. How lovely she appeared to him, with the firelight lending its glow to the warm ivory of her skin, the fine gold of her hair. Tall she was, and proud, and altogether beautiful, this young queen. But Sinclair grew troubled in his heart, and rather than remain at the mercy of his thoughts, he forced himself to speak.

"Ogmund Finnsson tells me he was named regent for your son."

Margaret started, as if waking. "You—oh, yes. Yes. The council chose him, and Haakon almost with his dying breath confirmed him."

"A good choice, I think."

"We are pleased. We have known Finnsson since first we came here as a child. He is an upright, wise and altogether trustworthy man. Our son will have need of such." Margaret looked directly into Sinclair's eyes. "And you, Jarl Sinclair, will you see Haakon in our son, and serve the son even as you were pledged to serve the father?"

"I regret that Your Majesty felt a need to ask that," returned Sinclair, with something of his old stiffness.

"It is a mother asking, Jarl Sinclair, not a queen."

"And it is a man who answers, madam. Even were I not what your late lord hath made me, still would I behave me as would any Christian knight toward a fatherless boy.

"As lord of Orkney, I know my duty also. Your Majesty, Ogmund Finnsson, or the king has only to try my loyalty at any time, in any circumstance. I will not be found wanting."

Margaret sighed. "We did not mean to give offense, but surely you are quick to take it."

"Madam, I am sorry. I want only to be of service, to give such comfort as I can, and to assure you I am loyal."

Margaret smiled, and the light of mischief sparkled in her eyes. "So you are loyal, Jarl Sinclair?"

"Aye."

"Then tell us, pray, how is it that you have set about building a monstrous great hall in Orkney, in direct defiance of the conditions of your investiture."

Sinclair's jaw dropped.

Margaret clapped her hands. "Caught!" she cried, her delight evident in her eyes and in her voice. "There now, proud Scot. So you are quite human after all. And we are glad of it. Perfect men are very unpleasant company, at least it is so here on earth. How it is in heaven is something we are content to wait to see."

Sinclair laughed, albeit ruefully. "I never thought me perfect, madam. Far from that, I think."

"Far enough to our liking, at any rate," Margaret said. "But you are in the right, surely. Haakon was not well advised in setting such a condition. He knew how matters stand in Kirkwall. Have I not heard him rage against that tricksy bishop a score of times? And how did he think you were to wrest control from that meddler if not by a show of strength?"

"Madam," said Sinclair, with a slight bow, "I see now the source of Haakon's strength. He had in you no ordinary queen."

"Pray, sir, do not flatter."

"I do not mean to. Indeed, I have no gift for it, or I might have had my coronet from Magnus long ago."

Margaret nodded. "Then we shall take you at your word. 'Tis true, sir, I am not one of those ladies who are content to stay apart from high affairs, to pass my days with music, needlework, and idle talk.

"The king my husband deserved better; so does the king my son. A woman may be a woman and not a fool, Jarl Sinclair. God gave us brains as well as breasts. The pity is so few of us will use the brains God gave us.

"As for this woman, sir, I assure you she means to use her brain. Look, you, I was but a girl of ten when my father married me off to Haakon. That was his right and even his duty, as he saw it. A union of Norway and Denmark was the advantage he sought. Both peoples stood to benefit therefrom. And I have neither illusions nor regrets concerning that.

"Haakon was a good man, a kind husband and an able king. In time, I came to love him. I always respected him. And in nothing save his dying did he give me cause to complain." Margaret smiled, and a faraway look came into her eyes. "We came through hard days together, he and I. And if our marriage was a politic contrivance, what then? As compared with many marriages I have seen, ours was among the best."

"That is a tribute to both Your Majesties," Sinclair said.

"Perhaps. I do not know. I do know that I learned from Haakon. He honored me by talking to me, by seeking my opinion, by unfolding his own to me. That, my good jarl of Orkney, is the only kind of compliment I understand. It is the only kind I welcome.

"Do you but pay me a like compliment by speaking plainly to me of your plans for Orkney, and you shall stand first among our nobles not in rank only, but in our trust too."

Sinclair bowed. "Madam, I can aspire to no loftier thing. You shall know all that I intend, and if you will favor me with your judgments on these schemes, I shall be more than ever obliged to you."

In the days that followed, Margaret met often with Sinclair. There was a new openness between them, and a growing regard on both sides. The young queen heard and approved all that Sinclair proposed by way of securing the isles. His fleet interested her hugely.

"Ships are the great need here," she said. "Our coast is too vulnerable by far, and our trade is paltry. In former times, our realm was divided into naval districts, with each district obliged to provide a certain number of vessels. Then did Norway boast a navy and a merchant fleet such as any ruler might be proud of.

"With the Black Death, shipbuilding ceased, and our existing fleet fell into disrepair. Since then, other nations have greatly improved and enlarged their ships, while poor Norway sits upon the beach and watches her opportunity slip away."

"So Finnsson has told me."

"And that is why we hinted you should talk of ships to Haakon," said Margaret smiling. "When you have done what you must in the isles, we expect to call on the services of your fleet, Jarl Sinclair. Be prepared for that."

"Madam, I only regret I am not a better sailor. But, such as I am and such as I have are yours to use as you see fit."

Margaret unfolded in detail her own ambitions. Having secured for her son the crown of Denmark, and being assured of his succession here in Norway, her thoughts all turned now on stratagems for Sweden. "For if I cannot be myself a king, yet will I do king's work," she said.

"I do believe it," murmured Sinclair. He felt—something, he knew not what, for this royal widow. He sensed that her mind was extraordinary, that her will was adamant. Yet he could not separate the woman from the queen. He thought her beautiful, admirable, and—what?

The man's bluntness was not limited to his dealings with others. He could be, and was, quite as direct in dealing with himself. He admitted—to himself—that he could love Margaret. He admitted, with like readiness, that it would be folly. And folly was not his game.

Having faced his own feelings and having acknowledged that he was indeed vulnerable, Sinclair straightway mounted his defense. In his meetings with Margaret, he was studiously correct; away from her, he did not attempt to forgo the pleasure of thinking on her. Instead, he flung himself into his plans, wrote daily letters to Rosslyn, sought out Ogmund Finnsson for long and frequent talks, and spent hours poring over such books as he could find on shipping and navigation.

Yet it was with a profound sense of relief that he departed Bergen. He had, he knew, been in mortal danger. And he was grateful to get away but with a superficial wound.

Once back at Caithness, Sinclair seized the advantage of the lengthening days and commissioned Ingram to recruit more shipwrights. "Send to the south, if you must; or to Norway, or wherever such skills may be found. Offer them any reasonable wage above what they earn presently, and work 'em, kinsman. Work 'em in earnest. I mean to have my fleet afloat by the time my hall's roofed over."

"I can find more builders, certainly," replied Gunn. "But where you will get men to sail your ships is another matter."

"Oh, we'll find 'em, never doubt it. There's many a stout Norway man who'd give his all for the chance to feel a deck beneath his feet again. And there are Orkneymen and Shetlanders who will gladly enter my service. If God He send me but one true navigator, all will be well." Sinclair took up a stick and traced the outline of a shield in the sand. "Look you, Ingram. Here is a thought I have been playing with since first this work began. D'ye see? Here are the Sinclair arms. Now, if I but quarter the shield thus, and cause to be placed here a golden galley, we shall have in our arms a true picture of our state."

Gunn nodded. "I like it," he said. "'Tis very proper for a prince of an island realm."

"Good, then. I'll order this alteration made when next I find myself at Rosslyn."

Satisfied that all that could be done was being done to further the building of his fleet, Sinclair now embarked with David for Kirkwall. There he found not only the most encouraging progress in the construction of the great castle, but also late news of some import.

"The bishop's dead," Tom Prentiss told him, as Sinclair came up to shake the hand of his doughty clerk-of-the-works.

"What, William?" Sinclair was incredulous.

"Aye, my lord. But two days ago."

"But was he ill?"

"Nay, only ill disposed to yourself, my lord. I cannot get at the whole of it, but he hath been indifferent busy in Your Lordship's absence, stirring folks up and trying to foment discontent among 'em. He preached a powerful sermon against you and yon castle only last Sunday, thinkin' no doubt that with Haakon dead he'd have some advantage here."

"Well," said Sinclair, with some humor, "we have heard some preaching in our time that well nigh bored us to death. But surely the bishop was not done in by his own droning?"

"In a way, ye might say so, my lord. Folks hereabout are uncommon glad of the wages this work is bringin' in. My guess is, they feared the bishop's words meant an end to their prosperity, but who can say what folks think? I know only that there was a tumult outside the cathedral, and it happened that some fellow or other got his fingers on a handsome stone and—"

"Oh, no!"

"Aye. The bishop went down like a felled ox, my lord, and did not rise again. Nor will he, till the last day."

Sinclair's face went grim and hard. "We must find this fellow out and bring him to an accounting for his crime."

Old Prentiss hawked and spat in the dust. "My lord, 'twould be lookin' for dew in the ocean. There be no means for findin' him; none would come forward to name him, unless ye mean to stir up more difficulty by offering a bounty or holding inquiries. Ye might then come to the culprit. Ye might. But, sir, folks here is close-knit, d'ye see, an' they could no more forgive an informer than they could forgive yon William for threatenin' to take away their livelihood."

"But, Christ, Tom Prentiss, we cannot blink this—this murder."

The old man nodded. "I understand, my lord. Even though 'tis a thorn out of your side, so to speak, to have the bishop unthroned, as ye might say."

"Tom, we'd be lying if we said we wept for William, but if we countenance murder, then—"

"Then do not countenance it, my lord. Let folks know you are wroth. Write a paper saying the guilty man will be punished if he is found, say he is excommunicate, say anything, but don't offer money for his capture or too diligently press the matter." Old Prentiss shuffled his feet in the loose earth. "Forgive me, my lord, if I meddle. 'Tis not for me to counsel you, surely. I—"

"No, no, my friend. We are in need of counsel and glad to have it from one who knows something of the ways of these folk." Sinclair squeezed the man's arm. "In truth, Tom, we are in your debt. But it does not sit easy, this sudden and convenient dispatching of a foe. We must profit by it, but we must study so as not to appear to be glad."

"So I think, too, my lord."

"Well, God pardon us—yes, and William, too; we'll write a paper, Tom. But we will not too eagerly seek the identity of our benefactor."

David Sinclair was less restrained. "By God, Harry," he declared, on hearing the news, "that is fortunate! You would have had to confront him sometime, to test your might against his. I am glad for you, really glad."

"Are you, Davey?" Sinclair eyed his brother curiously. "The man was my enemy. But he was a man, and a prince of the church. Does it not trouble you that he could be murdered in the very shadow of the cathedral?"

Davey shrugged. "I see it as a providence; no less, no more."

"Davey, you heard the late news from England, of how this fellow Tyler and the renegade priest John Ball led the peasants in revolt against their king."

"Aye, I heard something of it. Young Richard had the wit to win the lousy beggars back to him, more's the pity. Christ, if they had succeeded in their rebellion . . ."

"If they had, how long do you think Scotland or France or Norway or any other kingdom would stand secure? I tell you, Davey, I do not like this murder, much as I may be for the moment helped by it. If there are men here who would kill a bishop, there are men here would kill an earl."

"But, Harry, you are not William. You are—"

"I am a person in authority. Mark you, Davey, when any proper authority is threatened, all authority is threatened. No, sir, I do not rejoice in William's death. It may prefigure my own."

"Surely—"

"Hush, Davey. No more about it. But let us go circumspectly here till we are fully settled and sure of our strength."

"When will that be, d'ye think?"

Sinclair shrugged. "Three years, five years; I cannot tell."

"Five years! But, Christ, Harry, I hope you do not mean for me to sit idle for five mortal years and—"

"Boy, shut your mouth!" Sinclair's eyes flashed cold fire. "Look you, Davey, I will not have insubordination—not from peasant or bishop or you. Least of all from you. Is that plain?"

"Aye."

"Then give over those dour looks and childish sulks. You will have work, and that in plenty. If you prove yourself able and trusty, you shall have every opportunity this realm can offer. If you prove otherwise, well, Scotland lies that way."

"I'm sorry, Harry," said Davey, with no very good grace. "It's—it's just I get impatient, is all."

Sinclair sighed, then smiled and said, "I know of patience, Davey. I learnt it well in waiting for this prize. Learn patience from me; I'll be thy stern schoolmaster. A few years, lad, a few years more is all. Then shall we have great work before us. Only bide your time, Davey. Bide your time."

24

In the years that followed Haakon's death, Sinclair busied himself with establishing his base in Kirkwall and with the construction of his fleet. He had envisioned a modest navy of a dozen vessels; Ingram made it a baker's dozen, with eleven barks and two oared galleys. When his entire fleet was in the water, Sinclair was capable of mounting a very respectable fighting force.

In the matter of Bishop William's successor, Sinclair moved swiftly but with indifferent success. Avignon was willing that Jarl Henry's kinsman Robert be named bishop of Orkney, and he was indeed so consecrated. But Rome was another matter, and it was to Rome that Margaret and Norway bore allegiance.

"It does not please Clement," Margaret had written to Sinclair, "that a Scot should also rule the church in Orkney. Our own mind is not set against your will in this, but so highly do we esteem our ties to Rome that we would have you yield to Clement on this point, and consider us your debtor when next you bring some cause before our throne."

For the space of a day, Sinclair was angry, calling down plagues and poxes in great number on all politic ecclesiastics. But he knew where his own allegiance and his own best interests lay.

His letter to Robert was an artful document, filled with assurances of all Orkney's disappointment and of Sinclair's own regret. Robert, a realist, was not distressed. In a cheerful reply to Jarl Henry's letter, he averred that he, for his part, was relieved at not having to abandon Moray for the isles. "And, kinsman," he added with evident good humor,

180

"it will ever after give us pleasure to style ourself as titular bishop of Orkney. If the world may have the luxury of a pair of popes, shall not small Orkney have at least two bishops to her name? Let Clement and Margaret have their way, dear cousin. I am content to bide in Scotland still."

Sinclair chuckled over Robert's lines. "Before God, I should have liked to have him here," he said to Ingram Gunn. "But let us see what Clement sends, and try if we can make do."

As Sinclair soon learned, the new spiritual overseer of his realm was, if not a Robert, at least no William.

"Our will is," said Sinclair, in his first interview with Bishop Henry, "our will is that you will exercise your authority fully in the governance of souls, and that you will leave to us the managing of all things else."

Bishop Henry's strong Nordic features relaxed into a smile. "Fear me not, Jarl Henry. My allegiance to yourself will be second only to my allegiance to our Lord."

Sinclair returned the smile. "A pity, my lord bishop, that not all princes of the church see their duty so clearly."

Bishop Henry's smile faded. "There is something in what you say, my lord. I wish it were not so. But, for my own part, I mean to be about Christ's business here. Right gladly do I yield all temporal cares to you."

The two Henrys parted content. Bishop Henry proved true to his word, and Jarl Henry, satisfied that the souls of his people were ably shepherded, now gave his attention to affairs of state.

His Orkney stronghold took shape even as his navy grew. Tom Prentiss drove his men hard. They built in Kirkwall a fortress with walls high enough to discourage assault and thick enough to withstand not only the projectiles of bow and bombard, but also the penetrating blasts of the Orcadian winds. For Sinclair meant to have his family there, and he would not have Janet or the children suffer from the cold in that open island place.

While all this work was going forward, affairs in Scotland altered little. The old king clung to life and throne with a tenacity unexpected in so weak and vacillating a man. At Rosslyn, the Sinclairs were all thriving. The years made little impact on either the face or the spirit of Lady Isabel. Janet was blooming, the children hearty. John Sinclair and his Danish bride seemed well content with one another and with the life at Rosslyn.

Only Knox—stout, loyal, old Oliver Knox—seemed to be yielding to the years. His last pupil had been young Harry Sinclair, eldest son to Orkney's lord. And now he had given over even that proud duty to his successor. Knox was simply old. He had lived a long time, for a soldier. He had fared well, as this world goes. He would have liked to continue young Harry's training at least. And Willie—there was a lad after Knox's own heart, spirited, hardy, as quick to laugh as to fight. He'd make a proper champion, Knox knew. But it was time, it was time.

And so Knox withdrew from the tilt yard and the armory to take such warmth and comfort as he could from chapel, hearth, and old acquaintance over the cheering cup.

In Norway, Olaf came of age and, at fifteen, was crowned king—just five years after his father's death. Ogmund Finnsson continued to serve as chief counselor, and Margaret's presence was very real in every decision from the throne.

As Sinclair came close of his fortieth year, he found he had little to complain of. The main body of his Orcadian castle was complete and habitable; his fleet was ready, his men were ready to venture out on the open sea; his family were all well and, apparently, content. Neither Norway nor Scotland seemed inclined to demand from him anything that would keep him from pursuit of his own ambitions. He was, he felt, as ready as ever he would be to take up the work.

So he removed his family to Kirkwall, leaving John to keep a trusty eye on matters south in Scotland.

"Well, Janet," he said, when first they stood together in the castle at Kirkwall, "what d'ye think o' your new home?"

"It—it's very big, isn't it, Harry?"

"And not so very handsome, hey?"

"We—ell, it is not Rosslyn."

"Nor Dirleton, neither." Sinclair chuckled. "You were spoiled, woman. 'Tis no fair that you were raised up in the loveliest castle in Scotland. What can a rough fellow like me provide to match it?"

"Don't talk so. You know you do it only to tease me."

"Aye, I never tire o' teasin' you, lass. When ye go all pink like that, I think we are both of us young again and running the woods and the glen at home.

"But you are in the right, Janet. 'Tis no pretty palace you see here. 'Tis a fortress as well as home, big enough to garrison an army and stout enough to withstand any foe."

"Are you expecting attack, then?"

Sinclair smiled. "Would I bring you and the children here if I were? No, no. But I mean to loom large in the isles, my dear love. 'Tis better to show a strong hand at the outset; it can mean less occasion to use it thereafter.

"But come, woman, where's old Sigurd's sword?"

"Young Harry's got it," Janet replied. "Indeed, he would not let Clarke or anyone else so much as touch it."

"Would ye fetch the boy, then? I'll not feel truly settled here till I've hung the sword in its place."

Janet found the boy and brought him to his father.

"Well, Harry," said Sinclair, smiling down at his son, "you have the sword, hey?"

"Aye, Father, I brought it safe. I even kept it in bed with me o' night aboard the ship for fear of robbers."

"Good lad!" Sinclair clapped the boy on the shoulder. "'Tis good to know I've a son I can lean on in matters o' trust. Give it here, young Harry. Ah, ye had a heavy burden in this, and no mistake."

Sinclair turned and, reaching up, fixed the sword in place above the mantel. "Now, boy," he said, "our great ancestor can rest in peace. We have come home to what is ours."

"But is not Rosslyn ours too, Father?"

"Aye, it is, certainly. 'Twas my father's and his father's before him. And we have lands in Caithness and in Aberdeenshire too. But this is mine—ours—through your grandmother's line, boy. And we shall have this too, and hold it in fealty to Norway even as we hold our other lands in fealty to Robert away home in Scotland."

"And shall I rule here one day?"

"Aye, one day. 'Twill be my task to win the loyalty of the isles. God grant you will rule them in peace."

"Must you make war, then, Father?" The boy's face was grave, his eyes troubled.

Sinclair roughed the boy's hair. "I hope not. Indeed, I do not think so. Ye see, Harry, by being always ready for war, I plan to discourage those who might think to make war on me. We will talk o' this again when you are older, but remember if ye can that even the gospel tells us that a man fully armed who guards his courtyard is not a man who finds himself surprised by enemies. Readiness is everything—that and letting folk know you are ready to oblige 'em anytime they have a notion to take arms against you."

The boy nodded. "I'll remember that, Father."

"Good boy. Now run along and find your blessed sisters and Willie. Night's coming on, and I would take it sorely if any of you was to walk off into the sea."

"It's as if we were on a ship here, isn't it, Father?"

"Aye, a strong ship too, I trust; one that will carry us far."

It was during the first months of her stay at Kirkwall that Janet discovered herself to be again with child. Sinclair was delighted.

"Now, by God, we'll have an Orkneyman to mingle with our brood o' Scots."

"You are pleased, then, husband?"

"Aye, and why not?" Sinclair kissed his wife heartily. "I have the pleasure o' gettin' the creatures; 'tis you must bear 'em. God! D'ye mind the time ye had bringing yon Harry into the world? I thought I would run mad with fear and grief."

Janet shook her head. "I—I know it was not an easy birthing, but I cannot recall the pain of it. Were you truly afeared, Harry?"

"Aye, God bless me. I would not go through that night again, not if there were twins in it."

Janet laughed that girlish laughter that was her husband's joy to hear. "You are yourself a great baby, Earl Sinclair."

"Jarl, woman; say jarl, or they'll take you for a foreigner. And what d'ye mean calling me a baby?"

"You are. Look at you, a great bold warrior knight that's slain the Southron by the cartload and talked with kings and queens, and yet you say you'd not go through another birthing like the one that gave us Harry." Janet shook her head. "Do you not love Harry, Harry?"

The doubled "Harry" struck Janet as so comical, that Sinclair was obliged to hold his answer till she was quite over her silly fit. Then he said, "Love Harry? O' course I love him. He's my son, isn't he? And a smart boy and a good one too. What's that got to do—"

"And what of Willie?" Janet demanded. "D'you care for him at all?"

"Dammit, woman. Don't talk nonsense. O' course I like Willie. He's a damned rascal and a great worry to you—always breaking his crown or skinning his knees. But he's a bonny, bonny lad, and I dote on him. And ye know it."

"And Betsy and Beatrix?"

"God in heaven, woman! Ye've seen how they bully me and get round me and make me do everything but stand on my head. How can ye ask if I like 'em?"

"Then is it worth my going through another birthing to get another child?"

"Whew!" Sinclair let out his breath in a great windy sigh. "I tell ye, Janet, I'd rather stand before the Parliament in England or that body they call the Lawting there in Norway than ever bandy words wi' you again. All I said was, I grieved for ye when ye had your trouble wi' yon Harry."

"Oh."

"'Oh'?" Sinclair yelped. "Is that all you have to say? Just 'Oh'? Ye tie me up in knots, Janet, I swear to Peter. It all comes because ye don't listen to me. That's what it is. Ye don't listen."

"Humph. An I hadn't listened to you the last time you came stealing into my chamber, we'd not be having this pleasant conversation now."

Sinclair shook his head in despair. "Janet, dear, have your baby. Have two babies. Have all the babies ye want. Only don't let's talk of it anymore. It makes my head hurt, truly."

But the happiness at Kirkwall was quickly overshadowed. For, some days after Janet told her news, Sinclair received news from another mother—Margaret of Norway. Her only son, the king, lay gravely ill at Bergen.

"I must go there, Janet," Sinclair said. "If the boy does not recover, Margaret will have more than sorrow to contend with. It is important that folk great and small see the lord of Orkney at her side, should Olaf die."

"Which God forbid," murmured Janet.

"Amen. Poor little king."

Sinclair, in anticipation of the worst, decided he would make a show not only of loyalty but of strength. He summoned Ingram from Caithness with the entire fleet. "Let's make this a trial of our seamanship, coz," he said. "Let's sail into Norway's waters like eagles o' the sea. 'Twill be our proclamation to the world that Orkney's strong at last, and strong in his support of Norway's Margaret."

Thus did Sinclair's fleet make its first venture into his watery realm. In the lead bark, Sinclair, his brother David, and Ingram Gunn sailed, with a sometime fisherman from Shetland at the helm. The cracking canvas, the blown spray, the lively pitch and roll of the ship as she plowed the sparkling sea gladdened Sinclair's heart, and despite the gravity of his errand, he could not help but exult in the sheer joy of the thing.

"Christ, Ingram, is this not fine? Is this not truly fine?" Sinclair's eyes danced and glinted like the waves that broke under their vessel's prow. "Look at 'em, coz. Look at the sails! By God, we'll rule in Orkney now. Wait till they see us coming at Bergen, hey?"

"They'll think us pirates, more than likely," muttered Gunn, whose stomach was in a state of mutiny. "We'll be lucky if they don't fire on us before we've had a chance to make ourselves known."

But it was bells, not bombards, that greeted the fleet at Bergen. Only bells. No need to ask the reason for their slow tolling. One had only to see the faces in the streets to know. The king was dead.

"Jesu," murmured Sinclair, crossing himself. "Poor Margaret. And poor Norway. Twice in five years bereft."

Ambassadors, churchmen, kinfolk came and went. But steadfast beside the grieving mother through the long days of mourning stood the stalwart figure of Orkney's lord. There could be no doubt in any mind as to where his allegiance lay. And the force of that allegiance was plainly to be seen riding at anchor in the bay.

Margaret herself seemed to draw strength from the muscular Scot at her side. Now and again she murmured to him, was seen to lay her hand upon his arm as if she would borrow of his sinew and steel. His presence was a declaration none could misread. The chief noble of Norway was loyal, and in him Margaret had a champion and a friend—a friend such as no man and no faction would care to have as foe.

When the rites of death were over, and all ceremony had been dutifully fulfilled, the all but exhausted Margaret withdrew to her chamber and bid Sinclair attend her there.

"Madam," he said, his voice low and near to breaking, "you sent for me."

Margaret, her face pale as her child's had been in death, raised her darkly shadowed eyes to his and said, "My very good friend, we did. We are tired even to the point of dropping, but—please, be seated, for you are surely weary too—we wanted very much to have some private words with you at this first opportunity."

Sinclair took a seat, his eyes fixed on that noble sorrowing face. "I wish, madam, that there were something, anything at all, that I could say or do to ease your pain."

A tear, the only tear Sinclair would ever see from Margaret's eyes, slipped down the wan cheek. "God bless you, Jarl Sinclair. You have already done a great thing by coming as you did, with your fleet at your back, to stand by us in this—this crucifixion.

"As for our pain, my friend, God sent it. We can only give it back to Him from the altar of our heart."

Sinclair could feel his own eyes stinging. He fought down an impulse to hold this wounded woman in his arms, to urge her weep, to let his breast be pillow to her grief. But, no, he could only speak and listen. This woman, for all that she was and all that she had been, was denied a woman's haven in distress. No arms could hold her, no hand could brush away that tear. She must stand alone and bear alone this heavy crushing cross.

"Jarl Sinclair, what's to become of us?" It was not a plaintive cry, only a question. Nothing more.

"Madam, I do not know. But if there is aught that I can do, any service however slight, however difficult, you have only to ask, and it will be done."

Margaret nodded. "We know," she whispered. "We know. And we are profoundly grateful."

There was silence for a time, restful healing quiet. Margaret seemed to gather something of her former strength in the interval. She sat forward in her chair and, in a firmer voice, said, "Well, here we are of husband and child deprived in such a little, little span of time. Widowed and childless; widowed and childless." She shook her head. "God must love us very much to have laid such burdens on so frail a thing. But forgive us, we do not mean to keep you so long from your own family and your own tasks.

"Look you, Jarl Sinclair, despite all—all that has happened, we do not intend to abandon our dream of union. We will enlist our friends to favor our nephew, Eric of Pomerania, as heir to this throne. In him, perhaps, this people can have at last a king who will bring these lands together in one strong nation that will dominate this quarter of the earth.

"Finnsson, we know, will stand with us in this. So will the others of the council. Will you, Jarl Sinclair, lend your voice to Eric's cause?"

"Madam," replied Sinclair, smiling, "if Eric is your choice, he is mine also."

Margaret slumped back in her chair. "Then it is done," she said, her voice gone weak once more. "We shall forward this matter with all our skill and all our strength. When the people know that the council and the archbishop all support Eric, why, the thing's as good as done."

"Madam," said Sinclair, rising, "I beg you, take some rest."

"We shall rest, my friend, and rest the better because we have you for our friend."

Sinclair bowed. "I will leave you now, madam. Tomorrow, my men and I return to Orkney. But know that you have only to send for me at any time, in any need, and I will be here so fast as the winds allow me."

Margaret managed a faint smile. "You, sir, are truly fit to be chief noble of this realm."

"And you, madam, are more than fit to rule here."

A strange light glowed in Margaret's eyes, and a flush mantled the pale cheeks. "Sinclair, my friend, as you are my friend, do not say so outside this chamber."

Troubled, Sinclair began to stammer a reply. Margaret cut him short. "No, no. We know your meaning, and that you do indeed mean it. But—God help us, have we not ourself thought—no, please. Say nothing further on that head. Do go now, with our love and our thanks. God grant we meet in happier times hereafter."

Sinclair bowed once more. "Fare you well, madam. God keep you in His care."

Sinclair sailed for Kirkwall that next morning. Once home, he brooded much on Margaret and her woe. Janet wisely questioned him but little. She could see that he was greatly troubled by all that had occurred at Bergen. Now and then she observed him, saw him look at Willie or Harry and shake his head as if he were questioning his own ability to endure that which Margaret must. And she herself, as the babe in her womb stirred with waking life, felt a tender pity for the grieving queen.

No doubt Janet's sympathy would have been much abated had she known which way her husband's thoughts were tending. Sinclair, at the mercy of those thoughts, passed a wretched, restless night, hounded by memory and desire.

He could imagine a pale hand resting on his arm, a pale face raised to his in an unspoken plea for his protecting and unswerving love, pale hair cascading over his eager breast as he sought to lend warmth and comfort to that fair northern queen—a lady whom affliction had rendered fairer still.

Sinclair lay in a pool of moonlight, listening to Janet's rhythmic breathing. God, if he could but sleep!

He propped his head in his hand and looked down on the innocent face of his Janet. It would, he was aware, be no new thing in the chronicles of courts and kings were he to leave her for Margaret's bed. Rome itself had blinked more than once at such behavior in high places.

Would Margaret have him? He did not doubt it. Things unspoken lay between them, unsaid, and yet so plain a blind man might read them. Her marriage to Haakon was, by her own account, a political union. It had, it is true, flowered into friendship. But friendship, Sinclair knew, could hardly hope to slake the fire that smoldered deep within that sculpted ivory breast.

"Christ help!" muttered Sinclair.

Janet stirred and murmured in her sleep. Unconsciously, her delicate fingers grasped her husband's hand.

Sinclair smiled through his pain. "Ah, Janet," he whispered, "ye little dream what power lies in the grip o' that little hand."

Jarl Henry was still smiling when, just before first light, he drifted into sleep.

25

As we see it, Ingram," said Sinclair, stretching his legs out before him as he settled comfortably in his accustomed chair in the vast hall of his island stronghold, "the Faroes come first.

"Orkney seems stable enough, especially now with William removed from the center of that episcopal hive over the way there. And Shetland, for our poor friend Sigurd's sake, seems disposed to accept our authority. At least, there's no outward sign of opposition. But the Faroes we have not yet so much as visited. And from such accounts as we have received, folk there are of a less tractable disposition than these here.

"I have about concluded, then, to muster a goodly number of men-at-arms and make an expedition to those outlying isles. Some show of strength on our part may serve to exert a pacific influence and win for us that acceptance essential to our governance."

"That's sound enough," drawled Gunn, crossing his ankles and leaning back in his seat. "But, from what we've been told, I think you must spare nothing in making a display of might. Those Faroe men are a hardy desperate breed, accustomed to hard living and hard dealing. 'Tis said they are not above luring ships onto the rocks that they might have the plundering of them."

Sinclair's smile was grim. "Aye, we have heard that. We need not look for much courtesy in those parts, my friend. The people can hardly be expected to rejoice at our coming, the more especially since we mean to establish the rule of law and put an end to this highly original method of getting a livelihood."

"And levy taxes."

"That too." Sinclair rubbed his jaw thoughtfully. "We shall have to go warily among 'em, Ingram. I do not mean to have some hairy fellow put a period to my career with the point of his fish knife. We will go in force, and we will strive to win their best men over to us in hopes that their followers will follow still."

"What will ye do for soldiers, Harry?"

"Why, I mean to—yes, Janet? What's the matter?" Sinclair looked up as Janet, her sweet face puckered in an anxious frown, entered the hall. "Husband, pardon me. I did not mean to intrude. Good morrow, Ingram."

"Good morrow, lady," said Gunn, rising and bowing. "Pray, take this chair. I'll slip away and leave your husband to you."

"No, sir, do not go. 'Tis no private matter. Only, Harry, letters have come from Rosslyn. Your dear old Knox is very low. Your brother says he cannot live long. I thought you would want to know."

"Old Oliver Knox." Sinclair sighed and slumped deeper in his chair, shielding his eyes with his hand. "Before God, Janet, I am sorry to hear it. I love that old soldier dearly."

Janet crossed to him and took his hand in both of hers. "I know, Harry. And he loves you. I am sorry to bring this news, but I thought—"

"Yes, yes." Sinclair rose and kissed her lightly on the brow. "Dearest, will you find Davey and send him to me?"

Janet left to do her husband's bidding. Gunn studied his noble kinsman's face for a long moment, then he said, "This pains you, Harry, I know. I am sorry."

Sinclair nodded. "Thanks, coz," he said. "I wish—I wish I had shown myself more grateful to the man. I owe him much. Now, most likely, he will die and I shall never get said what I ought to have said so very long ago."

"Surely he knew, Harry. He was a soldier; he had no need for words."

"Even so, Ingram, a man likes to keep his accounts in order. There's Haakon gone before I could even begin to prove my gratitude to him. Knox is going. Who's next, I wonder."

"Ah, Harry, don't—"

"No, Ingram, it troubles me. It does, truly. So much I take as my due—from poor Hafthorsson, from Janet, and from you, my loyal friend and kinsman. And when do I say thanks? Tell me, Ingram, when did I last thank you for anything?"

"Harry, I—" Ingram shook his head, raised his hands and let them drop to his sides. "Man, I don't want your thanks. I have your friendship. What more—?"

"Harry?" David Sinclair hurried breathless into the hall. "Janet says ye sent for me."

"Aye, lad. There's something ye can do for me."

"What is it?"

"I want you to order the servants make ready for a journey."

"Where are we going, Harry? Norway?"

"No, Davey. We're going home to Rosslyn. Oliver Knox is dying."

"Rosslyn? But—" Disappointment was plain in the younger man's face. "Surely, Harry, we're no going clear to Rosslyn because of old Knox. Ye cannot mean to lose the fine weather to go and bury a servant?"

"Ingram!" Sinclair's voice was sharp as a winter wind.

"Harry?"

"What did I tell this boy?"

"To order the servants make ready for a journey."

Sinclair nodded. "'Tis what I thought I'd said." He turned a cold eye on his brother. "How is it, Davey, that our cousin Gunn heard me and you did not?"

"I—I heard ye, Harry."

"Ah! Did ye, then? Well, sir, then heed me."

"Yes, sir. And will all be going?"

"Aye. Janet and the children too. God grant we get there in time. I'd have my sons look once more on that face so they might, in future time, remember it as the very archetype of the face of an honest man."

"I'll go at once, Harry."

"Davey!"

The younger Sinclair turned. "Harry?"

"Davey, as it happens, I meant to go to Rosslyn before I had word of Knox's dying. I mean to raise my army there."

"Oh!" Davey's face brightened. "Well, now, that's a different matter. I thought you meant to go only for old Knox's sake. I—"

"Davey," Sinclair broke in, his voice ominously low, "ye still mistake me. Oliver Knox is my oldest friend. So long as there was a chance of seeing him one last time alive, I should have undertaken this journey no matter what my own plans might have been."

Sinclair held his brother's eyes with his, till Davey was forced to look away. Then he said, "Go. Bid the servants pack."

Ingram Gunn, in the awkward silence that followed Davey's departure, seemed suddenly to have taken a profound interest in the ceiling.

"Well?" Sinclair demanded, finally.

"Hum?" Ingram directed his gaze away from the ceiling and toward his cousin. "Ye spoke, Harry?"

"Come, Ingram, I know you. You heard him. I've a mind to take him back to Scotland and leave him there. Damn me, Ingram, I cannot abide that—insubordinate quibbling questioning. What ails Davey? Can you tell me? Hey?"

Gunn shook his head. "'Tis no my place—"

"Damn place! You are my friend, my friend of friends. If ye can gi' me any hint as to how I can best deal wi' that sulky little brother o' mine, I'd take it as kindness. I truly would."

Ingram rubbed his nose with the flat of his hand. "In truth, coz, I do not know. I confess, I have sometime thought you overharsh with him. And yet, well, I have had time to observe your brother here and at Caithness. I—I do not like to say so, Harry, but, well, did ye ever think that Davey is too much in your shadow?"

"In my shadow? What d'ye mean?"

Gunn sighed. "I shall put it badly, I know it. But, look you, Harry, you are all that Davey dreams o' being. He would give all that he has if he could command even half the respect that's yours. And so he tries too hard to show himself the man of action, rash, bold, ready for any enterprise. But he's had no opportunity to prove himself—to himself, I mean. And so he blunders about and chafes and frets and makes of himself a great nuisance. He wants only to be doing something so he can show himself a man."

"But you know and I know that proving begins in little things, Ingram. Like obedience, say, and loyalty, and giving what ye have to give to the task at hand, however small it may measure against the task ye dream of."

Gunn nodded. "Aye. You and I know that, Harry. But we are more than a little older than yon Davey. If we would let ourselves reflect for a little, we might remember a time or two when we made little enough of the task at hand."

Sinclair sighed. "Ye may be right in that, Ingram. But, dammit, I want that boy to show me something, and that quickly, or I'll no trust him to any greater business than he's employed in now."

Gunn shrugged. "Maybe ye should have him go into Robert's service at Edinburgh, Harry. Let him be on his own, to stand or fall. In time, if he prove himself trustworthy, ye could send for him again and make a place for him here. 'Twould ease the rub between you, and 'twould give him a chance to stand out o' your shade and discover for himself what he can do."

"Ah, God, I don't know, Ingram. I swear I don't. My mother, ye know, looks to me to give Davey his chance in the world. I do not like to have her think I've failed him. Indeed, I do not like to think I've failed him."

"I can understand that, coz," Ingram said. "But if ye explain matters to Lady Isabel, surely she'd see ye meant for the best."

Sinclair nodded. "I will think on it, Ingram. And for this counsel, thanks."

"Ah-hah!" cried Gunn. "There now. Ye've gone and done it."

"Done what, you merry lunatic?"

"Ye've gone and thanked me. Now will ye no give your precious tender conscience a wee rest?"

"Damn you, Ingram Gunn, but you're a dear man." Sinclair's smile was warm and wide. "And did I never tell ye that I love ye?"

Summer walked the Pentland hills and all was green and gold at Rosslyn when Henry, baron of that place and lord of Orkney, together with his wife and children, his brother David, and his cousin Ingram Gunn, arrived there. Sir John Sinclair and his wife, Inge, herself also with child, were on hand with Lady Isabel to greet the travelers.

"How fares poor Knox?" asked Henry Sinclair, when all greetings had gone round.

John Sinclair replied, "He is past speaking, Harry. But come, I'll take ye to him. It may be he will rally somewhat on seeing you."

John led his brother into the castle. "I had him bedded here. I thought ye'd want that for him."

Sinclair squeezed his brother's shoulder. "Thank ye, John. 'Tis what I'd want, certainly. Would to God I could do more."

The younger Sinclair showed his brother into the sickroom. The labored breathing from the bed told all. Beside the bed, a figure all in gray bent over the dying veteran.

"What? Brother Ambrose?" Sinclair's voice, though scarce above a whisper, conveyed his astonishment.

"My lord," said Brother Ambrose, "it is very good to see you."

Sinclair took the leech monk's hand. "Ye cannot guess how glad we are to see ye still among the living after so many, many years. If any doubt your mastery o' healing arts, you have but to show yourself in evidence."

The old herbalist smiled. "Alas, no, my lord. It is only that I am never sick, so I am never obliged to put my skill to that ultimate proof."

"And how fares our old friend?" asked Sinclair, glancing over to where Knox lay.

Brother Ambrose shook his head. "He has one foot on the stair already, my lord. Ere sundown he'll stand before the throne of God."

"And without trembling too, I'll warrant," murmured Sinclair. He went over to the bed and looked down on the shrunken visage of the old soldier. "Knox, Knox, my dear old friend, 'tis I. 'Tis Master Henry come to say farewell."

The dying man's eyelids fluttered, then opened. The glazing brown eyes seemed to clear, and the pale, bloodless lips moved as if they would speak. Sinclair bent low over the old man, and his ear caught a faint whisper: "——ster Henry. Best. Best."

Sinclair's fingers found Knox's hand and softly closed around it. "I love you, Knox," he whispered, directly in the man's ear. "Thank you. Thank you."

The old man started, sat bolt upright in his bed, a look of radiant joy lighting his face. "I see Jesus, Master Henry!" he cried. Then he fell back, dead.

When Knox had been sung to his rest, and all the decencies of death had been accomplished, Sinclair put away his private grief in the vault of his own heart and set briskly about recruiting men-at-arms.

"A pity ye cannot ask our noble cousin, baron of Longformacus, to be your captain, Harry," Johnny said, as the men sat late over the wine one evening, some days after Knox's burial.

"What, Jamie?"

"Aye. God bless me, but he's a rare bonny fighter, that man. 'Twas he that rode wi' Lyndsay and me at Otterburn. Oh, Jesu, Harry, ye'd ha' loved it. Ye surely would ha' loved it."

"Ah, that! We've had too little time for talk, John. I meant to hear more from you ere now. Ye told me that Douglas was killed—"

"Aye, God ha' mercy on him. There was a chief, Harry, a Douglas every bit as fine as the Douglas our grandsire rode with against the Saracen.

"Well, sir, we were main busy that day. The Southron met us with a mighty force. But we were better men. Along o' Douglas and Lyndsay and myself, there were Alex Ramsay and the earls of March and Moray, with many a hardy fighting Scot to help us carve the English mutton that God He set before us on that day."

"Did ye kill your share, Johnny?" asked David Sinclair, his eyes shining, his cheeks flushed with more than wine.

"Aye, Davey, I did what a Sinclair does in that situation. But Douglas, God ha' mercy, he was early struck down by as hard a blow as ever England dealt to Scotland yet. And seeing him unhorsed, I rode over to where he lay and asked him how he did.

"'Right well,' he said, 'but thanked be God there hath been but few of my ancestors that hath died in their beds.' How like you that, hey, Harry?"

Sinclair smiled. "'Tis like a Douglas," he said.

"Aye, and then he said to me, 'Cousin, I require you, think to avenge me, for I reckon myself but dead.' And then he prayed me take up his banner that lay there on the ground beside him, and he said, 'Show neither to friend nor foe what case ye see me in, for if my enemies knew it, they would rejoice and our friends be discomfited.'"

"And what did ye do, John?"

"Why, what the man bid me, Harry. I took up his banner, and Jamie and Lyndsay and I charged the Southron host, crying, 'A Douglas! A Douglas!' And so we scattered them like sheep and carried the day. Or Douglas did, although he was already dead before the battle was decided."

"Jesu, Mary!" breathed David Sinclair. "Now that is something like! Damn it, Johnny, I should ha' been here instead o' lollin' about yon Kirkwall a-starin' at the sea. I could ha' rode wi' ye, and maybe could ha' cried 'Douglas' too, and chased the Southrons back over the border.

"Why, Christ, instead of—Ingram! Your drink, man! Ye've gone an' spilt your drink all down my doublet!"

Ingram pushed back from the table. "Dear me, Davey. I must be gone lightheaded and heavy-handed all at once. Come away, lad, and let me see to your clothes, hey? We cannot have ye sitting here all slobbered over."

As Ingram led the spluttering, damp, protesting Davey away, he saw what Davey did not see—the wrath in Henry Sinclair's face.

In the days that followed, Sinclair completed the recruiting of his band. It was decided that Janet should remain at Rosslyn with the children, to have her baby there and to be company for Inge and Lady Isabel. "For," as Sinclair told his wife, "'tis sure we will be much away from Kirkwall now, and though this child was got at Orkney, 'twill please me to have yet another Sinclair see Rosslyn as his first sight o' this world."

On the evening before his departure, Sinclair made it a point to talk alone with Lady Isabel. He came to her chamber toward eight o'clock, and for an hour or more they talked quite comfortably together.

"I regret, Mother, that we have not had more time for talk. But what with poor Knox and the raising of my troops, I've scarce had a moment ere now."

"No need to apologize to me, my son." Lady Isabel's fine eyes showed unwonted warmth. "You have so much to occupy you now, and that is as it should be. I cannot tell you how much it gladdens me to see you this way—in command, planning, ordering, directing affairs of great moment. 'Tis worth the sacrifice of some hours of talk to see you as you are."

Sinclair smiled. "'Tis true I've no been idle. God He knows there are days when I could wish I were. But it is grand, Mother, truly, to see the work go forward. Before another year is past, I mean to carry you off to Kirkwall so you may see for yourself what I have been about all this long while."

"I should like that, Harry, to see your castle and your fleet."

"Ah, they're bonny boats, Mother. I was tempted to lead them here, in part for show and in part to transport the soldiers back to Orkney. But I wished to make all speed in hopes of seeing Knox alive. So I shall hire passage for the men, and you shall have to wait awhile longer to see the Sinclair navy."

"I have learned how to wait, my son."

Sinclair frowned. "I wish that Davey had learned so much. Mother, I wonder if ye know aught of my troubles with that brother o' mine."

"He has spoken of it."

"To you?"

Lady Isabel smiled. "To any who would listen. And that included his mother."

Sinclair stood and paced the room. "What make you of his grievances?"

"Why, very little. I have no illusions about my children, Harry. At least, I hope I have none. Davey is weak, impatient, and inclined to be—difficult. It was my hope that your influence would alter him somewhat, for I knew that he adored you. But that, plainly, was not to be."

Sinclair took a stand before the cold hearth. "It's this way, Mother: If I cared to give half my time to it, I could no doubt bring him farther along toward manhood. He does listen, at least at the time, when I am obliged to admonish him. But the lessons do not stay with him. I cannot fault his intention. Indeed, I think he wants nothing more than to be of useful service. But, God help me, I cannot be father to Davey and lord of Orkney, too. Something has to suffer."

"Then let it be Davey." Lady Isabel's voice was sharp, decisive.

"But he is my brother."

"And my son." Lady Isabel nodded. "I understand your dilemma, Harry, and I thank you for your concern. But there is a choice here between one recalcitrant boy and a whole kingdom.

"We have suffered much, you and I, each in several ways, to secure that realm. And though I love Davey with that doting love all mothers feel for the youngest child, I say the work comes first. You've your own children to think of, Harry. And theirs after them. If Davey is too much a hindrance, let him go. You'll hear no complaint from me, I promise you, though it was from the first my wish to have him with you."

Sinclair crossed to where his mother sat, bent, and kissed her cheek. "I'll try a little longer, Mother, give Davey one more chance. Then, if he fails, I shall make provision for him elsewhere, and get on with what I have to do."

"'Tis kind of you, Harry. But you need not trouble further on my account."

"I know. But I had resolved this much before we talked."

Lady Isabel smiled. "Harry, Harry, you never really change."

Sinclair returned her smile. "I hope I do change somewhat, Mother. And you should know that I am more comfortable in my resolution for knowing that you do approve it."

"Thank you, Harry. Thank you. 'Tis flattering to have one's opinion valued, the more especially if one is, like me, an old, old lady."

"Old!" Sinclair laughed. "Woman, you slander yourself. You'll never be truly old."

Lady Isabel shook her head. "You cannot gainsay the years, Harry. But never mind. I am content. My son is earl of Orkney."

Sinclair, with Ingram, Clarke, and Davey, set out next day for Kirkwall. His men-at-arms would follow after, so soon as they were able. Near two hundred strong they numbered, and these would be augmented by such of the late Orkney bishop's men as Sinclair chose to hire into his service. He had now, he reckoned aloud to Ingram, sufficient ships and men; and if he could not hold the isles with these, he said, then he deserved to lose them.

"We'll make a stir now, Harry," Davey crowed. "God, I'm glad to be going back to Orkney."

"So am I, Davey," Sinclair replied. "So am I."

26

Shortly after his return to Kirkwall, and even before his Scottish troops arrived, Sinclair was in receipt of astonishing news from Norway. In the soft evening hours of the "simmer dim," as Orkney folk dub the perpetual daylight of the island summer, Sinclair walked out in his courtyard with his faithful Ingram. Together they watched as an oared galley made its way into the harbor's mouth; they saw a boat put over the side and watched its progress as the stout rowers pulled for shore. One man leaped lightly from the craft as it beached, and came on the run up the slope to Sinclair's massive hall.

"The fellow's bound here, coz. Look, Clarke's intercepted him. Ah-hah! They come this way."

Sinclair's small squire took the tall sunburnt visitor in tow and piloted him directly to his master. "Lord Sinclair," Clarke reported, "this gentleman's come from Bergen bearing messages for you."

"You are welcome, sir," said Sinclair, offering his hand.

The Norwegian bowed low. "Jarl Sinclair, I have but little English. Pardon me. I am called Nils Eriksson, nephew to Ogmund Finnsson and knight in the service of Queen Margaret."

Sinclair smiled. "We ourselves are more at home in French than in English, sir. Though we would say your English is passing good."

The honest knight blushed like a schoolgirl. "In truth, my lord, I have been practicing that speech for three days. And now my English is used up."

Sinclair laughed. "God bless me, Ingram, the man's devoid of guile. Well, sir, we will talk Latin, then. How fares your worthy uncle? And how is Margaret, pray?"

"Both are well, my lord. My uncle sends you greeting and hopes you sometimes think of him."

"We do, and fondly. But do sit down, Nils Eriksson, and rest yourself. My squire will order some refreshment. Then he will go and bid your mariners pass the night with us."

"Alas, my lord, we may not. We are bound for your King Robert's court, and from there to Richard's in England. My errand will not admit delay, although I would gladly tarry here, for my uncle has spoken of you in such a vein as to make me wish to know you better."

"Your uncle is ever kind," replied Sinclair. "But this errand, it can only be a matter of consequence to require such dispatch. Is it the same business treated of in these writings?"

"It is, my lord."

"Indeed. Well, now, we are curious. Excuse me." Sinclair drew apart and broke the seal on the letter. His eyes ran quickly down the single sheet. "Jesu, Mary! Ingram! Hear this: Margaret rules! She rules, Ingram. Norway and Denmark together have chosen her to replace her son."

"God bless us, Harry. This is news."

"Aye, and good news too." Sinclair paused, lost in thought. A woman monarch! But what a woman! He turned to Clarke. "See to this gentleman's comfort, John Clarke, and then escort him to the beach. Nils Eriksson, we are glad to have seen you. Fair winds attend your journey. God grant we meet again.

"Ingram, I would be alone awhile. Pardon me. We will talk more of this presently." And with a nod to Eriksson, Sinclair walked away.

His easy, loose-kneed stride carried him quickly to a slight rise that overlooked the shimmering expanse of sunlit sea. Long, long he stood there, gazing out over the endlessly rolling waters, his thoughts churning as the sea itself churns where crosscurrents meet.

Then, quite suddenly, he felt a great stillness of spirit, and a deep sweet calm filled his breast. Matters were so ordered now that he need no longer be troubled by fear of loving Margaret. He could, would love her as her loyal subject, her liegeman of life and limb, her chief among the nobles of her realm. This was a relationship he could adapt to, one that would accommodate heart and conscience both. Just as there are loves, like his for Janet, that naturally and needfully flower into physical expression, there are loves that go beyond even that holy melding of spirit and flesh that makes true marriage.

Sinclair smiled, assenting in his heart to this resolve: that he would love and serve his queen with due reverence and subordination, that he would forever put by all carnal thought concerning her.

Margaret was no longer the pitiable childless widow, caught in the maelstrom of fate. She was more, much more; more even than the fair and desirable woman who wore the crown. She was the crown. And Sinclair would do what he could to strengthen and support that majesty.

Let Scotland endure the torpor fostered by its aging and ineffectual king. Norway and Denmark need not. Margaret had youth, intelligence, courage, ambition, zeal. And she had Sinclair.

Lighter in heart and spirit, Sinclair returned to the castle. That night, he slept quite through. No dreams disturbed his rest. One dream would never trouble him again.

With the arrival of the vanguard of his Scottish troops, Sinclair began preparations for his call on the Faroes. He and Ingram were often together, discussing strategy for what would surely be a difficult, delicate, possibly dangerous mission. Events, however, were to shape Sinclair's course along lines he could not foresee.

While the remaining Scots were still making their way northward, Herdis Thorvaldsdatter and her sons, Sigurd and John, arrived unannounced and unexpected at Kirkwall.

"Lady Herdis, we are very glad to see you here," said Sinclair, when his guests' comfort had been seen to. "And we are pleased to see your sons so hearty. Their father would be overjoyed to see how his line continues in these strong young men."

Sigurd and John beamed at this compliment to their stature. Although both in their early twenties now, neither was above a surge of vanity at this praise—if only for their brawn—from such a worthy as Jarl Sinclair.

"I have no doubt Sigurd would be proud of his sons, my lord," replied Herdis. "But he would be sore grieved at how matters stand in Shetland."

Sinclair bade the widow and her sons be seated. "Anything that grieves your house grieves us, Lady Herdis. Tell us, what's amiss?"

Tears welled in the fine eyes of Hafthorsson's widow. "Our land's usurped, my lord. Stolen. And had I not other holdings in my own right, my sons and I would be without a roof to shield us from the rain."

"Stolen? Your lands? But how can this be, madam?"

"My lord, I know not. I know only that a week ago we were snug and content in our house in Shetland. Now we are as you see us, turned out, robbed, and come to you as our friend and lord for succor and redress."

Sinclair replied, "You have not come in vain. Lady Herdis, we promise you. But tell us, who is it dispossessed you?"

"Why, sir, it was the lord of Skuldane."

"What? Our kinsman?"

Lady Herdis nodded. "Yes, my lord. 'Twas Malise Sparre."

Anger boiled up in Sinclair's breast. Little knots of muscle worked violently at the corners of his jaw, and for a moment he could not trust himself to speak. Then, with a control that cost him dearly, he said, "Sigurd, would you oblige us by seeking out our cousin Gunn and bidding him come to us here?"

Sigurd bowed and hurried from the chamber.

"Now, Lady Herdis," said Sinclair, with deadly calm, "on what pretext or by what reasoning does Sparre claim your land?"

Lady Herdis shook her head. "He had some trumpery bit of paper, my lord. But it was the thirty armed men at his back that moved us. I may be a lone woman, with but my servants and my sons, but I am not one to give way before a scrap of paper, I assure you."

Sinclair nodded. "We know that, Herdis Thorvaldsdatter. We are only glad that you did not try to resist. Jesu, Mary! If Sparre had harmed your person, he should have died horribly."

"Then I am sorry we did not resist, for 'twould have been worth many injuries to see that cat flayed."

"O Viking woman," said Sinclair, with a smile and a shake of his head. "Thirst not for gore. We'll tend to this thief, have no fear. But all shall be done lawfully."

"As he hath served me?" Lady Herdis was indignant.

"Madam," Sinclair replied, "we mean to bring the isles to peace and the rule of law. If we ourself work outside the law, even in this grave provocation, how can we command others to live by law? No, Lady Herdis, we mean—ah, Ingram!

"You remember Lady Herdis and young John Sigurdsson."

Ingram bowed to Lady Herdis. "Indeed I do remember this lady, and that most fondly. As to yon young giant, I do recall me that he once caused quite a stir by baptizing your boots wi' his dinner."

John's cheeks flamed and a sheepish grin spread over his face. "You have an excellent memory, sir," he said.

"'Twas I that buried the boots," replied Ingram. "'Twas an occasion so moving that I was myself moved in a memorable way. Hence, I can never think of you, sir, without I think of boots."

"Ingram," said Sinclair, breaking in on this pleasant exchange, "we've some business before us. Our loving kinsman Malise Sparre has dispossessed this lady, and even now swaggers about her courtyard and calls her house his own."

Ingram's eyes widened. "My lord, I scarce can credit my own ears. I know the fellow for an arrant rogue, but I never thought him a fool. How can he dream to achieve this thing? He must know that you will not suffer him thus to challenge your authority. The man's gone mad, coz, surely."

Sinclair shook his head. "Sparre may be mad, Ingram, but he is a canny creature all the same. It must be he thinks himself secure in some wise, else he'd not dare this thing.

"It may be that, with Olaf and Haakon dead, he assumed that Margaret is too weak or else too busy to involve the crown in this affair."

"But he knows you," Ingram said.

"Aye. And he knows that we will do all things seemly. He may think that, should we bring him to law, certain powerful Swedes will back his former claim and create such difficulties as will impede our business here. If he can stir up sufficient unrest and dissension—"

"But surely Margaret will support you."

Sinclair's eyes took on a bemused expression. "So we believe, Ingram. And yet, we cannot blink her Swedish ambitions. 'Tis that that Sparre may be thinking of. If it come to a choice between ourselves and the Swedish nobles, well, 'twould be no very slight temptation, would it? To sacrifice a Scot and gain sovereignty over Sweden?"

"D'ye think Margaret would do that, Harry?"

"No, coz, we do not. But Sparre may think so. And that would account for his unwonted daring." Sinclair nodded. "That must be it. It has to be."

"What will you do, my lord?" asked Lady Herdis.

"Do?" Sinclair smiled. "Why, my dear friend, we will go to Shetland. We were most hospitably received there once some years ago. We are of a mind to try that hospitality again.

"Ingram, order three ships readied for our expedition. Assign a score of able men-at-arms to each, and bid them make ready to sail at dawn."

"Aye, coz. 'Twill be done, and quickly." Ingram grinned. "I do believe there will be some sore disappointment that only sixty men may go."

Sinclair nodded. "We can expect that. But we do not mean to make a show of belligerence in this. Let us try what reason and law can do. Oh, and Ingram, my brother Davey—"

"Aye?"

"Include him among the chosen."

"Aye." Gunn nodded and hurried off.

"Jarl Sinclair?" Sigurd Sigurdsson spoke up. "What of my brother and me? Are we to go with you?"

Sinclair glanced at Lady Herdis, then back to Sigurd. "'Tis your house that's taken. It seems fit ye should have a hand in taking it back."

Sigurd and John exchanged jubilant looks. "My lord, thank you. We are in your debt," said Sigurd.

"No, sir," replied Sinclair. "It is we who are in debt—to your late father. Go to my cousin Ingram now; tell him you are to come with us. He will see you fitted out and properly armed for this enterprise."

At first light on the following day, Sinclair's barks put to sea. Ingram, David, and the Sigurdssons were in the lead vessel with Sinclair. The three younger men were ecstatic, full of warlike thoughts and martial spirit, as they watched the coast of Kirkwall fall away that fair September morning.

"Let me but cross swords with Malise Sparre," declared Davey, "and I will carve you up a Swede for your table."

"Better feed him to the gulls," said John Sigurdsson. "Or the fishes."

Henry Sinclair smiled. "Enough, young warriors," he said. "We mean no fighting if we can avoid it."

"Then wherefore these swords?" demanded his brother.

"Why, Davey, to help you pick your way up the beach. 'Tis marvelous hard going over the stones."

The Sinclair party raised the coast of Shetland in the twilight, but Henry Sinclair elected to lie at anchor through the night, delaying till dawn his encounter with Malise Sparre. That his sails were observed he little doubted, nor did he trouble himself with concealment. He was certain Sparre courted a confrontation. He was content to let him wait another night.

With the morning, Sinclair ordered boats let down, and he and his men pulled briskly for the beach. Sparre and his band were awake and alert. They were on the beach, armed and waiting, when the Orkney boats nosed in.

Sinclair, with Ingram beside him, led his party up the sloping sands to parley with the usurpers.

It was a golden morning. A bright blue sky arced over a bright blue sea. Shining flecks glinted like diamonds in the sun-warmed sand, and the breeze coming in from the sea was cool and sweet. But for the clink of mail and the lapping of the wavelets, all was still.

"Well, kinsman," said Malise Sparre, his harsh voice the harsher for the breaking of the hush, "to what do we owe this courtesy?"

"Why, kinsman, to your own discourtesy," retorted Sinclair.

A smirk creased the bloodless face of Malise Sparre. "You were ever fond of a jest, cousin. We are delighted that your present lofty station has altered nothing of your former lightness."

"You will find us heavy enough, Malise Sparre, we promise you. Now, sir, what means this theft?"

"Theft?" Sparre's tone was silken with undisguised irony.

"Aye, theft. For you have overreached yourself in taking the house and lands of Lord Sigurd Hafthorsson's widow, a loyal subject of this realm who hath appealed to us for justice."

"Justice. A most commendable thing." Sparre crossed his arms on his breast. "We ourselves seek justice, cousin. We have, as well you know, an old claim to these lands. That our claim was dishonored by the late King Haakon in nowise lessens the justice of it. We mean to have justice, sir. We do mean to have it."

"This land is my father's," cried Sigurd Sigurdsson.

Sinclair held up a gloved hand. "Silence!" Then, addressing himself to Sparre, he said. "We are glad you share our love of justice, sir. It will ensure the peaceful resolution of the issue. We will take the question to the Lawting, and will abide by the ruling of that body."

"D'you think me a fool?" retorted Sparre. "You are the law here in the isles. It would be madness for us to bring the question before you. You are yourself a party to the matter."

"Not so," replied Sinclair. "The matter lies between yourself and Lady Herdis Thorvaldsdatter. It is our duty, as lord of these isles, to give judgment in the matter. And we will do our duty."

Sparre shook his head. "We will take our case to Bergen, sir, not to you."

Sinclair frowned, his eyes narrowing to mere slits. "You question our authority here?"

"We do. We question your authority, your title, and your competence to give judgment in this matter. We will have Margaret's judgment, not yours."

Sinclair nodded. "Very well, sir. Your leave us no choice. We are sovereign here by authority of Haakon, late king of Norway. If we suffer you to challenge that authority, we will forfeit the respect of our people. Indeed, we will forfeit our own respect, and that will we never do.

"Is that your galley yonder?" Sinclair, with a jerk of chin, indicated the six-oared vessel standing some few rods offshore.

"It is," replied Sparre.

"Then, as lord of Orkney, we command that you, together with these men, board your galley at once." Sinclair put on his helmet. "Our ships will escort you to Orkney, and there will we convene the Lawting and give judgment of your cause."

Sparre's pale eyes flashed right and left. He was, he saw, in a serious way. Sinclair made it plain that this affair would not be laid before Margaret, and Sparre had no illusions as to what judgment Sinclair himself would give. But if he could elude these people and make his way to Bergen—quick almost as thought, Sparre's sword seemed to leap into his hand. What he may have intended, whether it was only to create a diversion and so flee to his ship, or whether he meant something more, it was never discovered.

The sight of the naked blade threw Sinclair on the offensive. His own sword was out in the instant, and Malise Sparre, whatever had been his purpose, now found himself in a fight.

He backed, backed, backed before the onslaught of Sinclair's flashing blade. His own men and Sinclair's, as if on signal, were lustily flailing at one another, waking the echoes in the rocks with their clashing steel.

Sparre, busy as he was, spied some of his band making a run for their galley. Desperately fearful that they should make their escape without him, he summoned up all his reserves of strength and countered Sinclair's attack. Now was Sinclair obliged to retreat before a frenzied rain of blows. Deliberately, steadily, Sinclair backed away, parrying the wild slashing strokes Sparre laid about him. Then, just as the Swede's frantic outburst peaked, Sinclair, with an adroit twist of his wrist, turned the point of Sparre's sword away and, with his own, thrust home.

Sparre's face contorted horribly; his mouth stretched in a soundless scream; blood gushed from his lips, and he fell dead upon the sand.

Sinclair crossed himself. "God and St. Katherine, thanks for this victory. Christ, have mercy on his soul."

He withdrew his stained sword and turned his attention to the skirmish on the beach. A dozen men lay dead or dying. Near a dozen more could be seen scrambling aboard Sparre's galley, with Sinclair's men hurling stones and curses after them. Then he saw his brother Davey sitting on a rock and clutching his left arm.

Sinclair ran to him. "Davey, are ye hurt?"

The younger Sinclair, his face pale, his eyes shining, replied, "Aye, Harry, I've taken a cut above the elbow. But I killed a man, Harry. I killed a man."

Sinclair himself tended to his brother's wound, and was relieved to find it of no consequence. He clapped Davey on the shoulder. "Good lad," he said. "Ye'll live to fight another day. Where's Ingram?"

Davey laughed. "Up to his middle in water. Look! The galley's under way! The remnant's escaping, Harry. Damn them! They'll get away!"

"Perhaps. But Malise Sparre will not."

"Ye did for 'im, then?"

"Aye."

"God, Harry, that's great news!"

Sinclair's mouth was grim. "'Tis not what I'd hoped, Davey."

"Ah, he needed killing."

"It may be so, but I take no joy in it." Sinclair turned, cupped his hands to his lips and called, "Ingram! Ho!"

Gunn responded by waving his sword in the air. He waded with difficulty to the beach, nearly losing his footing a dozen times as he picked his way over the slimy stones. At last, however, he made the sand and, rallying the men to him, led the way to where Sinclair stood.

"Well, coz," panted Ingram, as he came up, "that was a day's work, hey? What, Davey? Not hurt, are ye?"

"Only a nick," said David proudly. "He that did it will not take up his sword again."

"Ingram," broke in Sinclair, "how stand we?"

"None dead, thanks be to God. One or two have taken a slash here and there, but our foes ran better than they fought. We've not a man seriously disabled."

"Good. We did not mean that any should die this day; this fight was not of our making. If Sparre is dead—"

"He's dead?"

"Aye. He lies yonder." Sinclair pulled off his helmet and rubbed his crown. "I could not like him, Ingram. I never could. But I came not here to kill.

"Well," Sinclair heaved a great sigh, "let us give these decent burial.

Sigurd and John can go with the wounded on one ship back to Kirkwall. We'll take the two others and give chase to what's left of Sparre's men. We mean to take them to Kirkwall and hold them there for a time as an object of instruction to any who may incline to like folly."

Ingram squinted after the escaping galley. "We had better leave the burying to others, my lord. Those fugitives will be halfway to Skuldane ere we've opened graves enough for those they leave behind."

"No doubt you are in the right." Sinclair nodded. He told off the men for Kirkwall, bade them bury the dead, and be on their way with their report to Lady Herdis. "We will join ye there in Orkney so soon as we have finished our business with those adventurers."

David Sinclair approached his brother. "Ye do not mean for me to return to Kirkwall, do ye, Harry?"

"You are wounded, are ye not?"

"A scratch. 'Tis nothing. Let me go with you."

Sinclair eyed his brother curiously. 'Twas plain the man's blood was up. He'd found the day's doings much to his liking. Still, he had behaved well.

"Come along, then," Sinclair said. "We must seize this wind and tide or lose our chance entirely."

27

Sparre's men made the most of their advantage, and although Sinclair pressed his pursuit, his mariners could not overtake the fleeing galley. After two days and nights of this, the Swedes effected an escape under cover of a thick fog that had rolled in during the night and did not begin to lift until after noon of the following day. Whether they chose to seek refuge in some sheltering fjord along the Norwegian coast, or whether they altered course and made for Iceland, none could say. Their sail was lost to view, and in all that trackless watery expanse, there was nothing to indicate which course they had taken.

"We have lost 'em," Sinclair conceded. "Damn the luck. It would have been a most instructive thing had we brought them prisoners to Kirkwall."

Gunn put a cheerful face on the matter. "They'll no trouble you further, at any rate. That's sure. And the Sigurdssons have their home restored. We might have done worse, coz. Far worse."

"Aye. At lease we lost no men, for which God be thanked. But this chase is now a fool's errand. We've nothing to gain by running northward. Bid the mariners come about and bear southwesterly. We've come so far, let us make for Fer Isle and let ourselves be seen there ere we return to Orkney."

So it was ordered. And on a gusty day toward the end of September, the few inhabitants of Fer Isle, a bleak outcropping of some six square miles anchored in the turbulent North Sea, came running down to a short stretch of stony beach to see Sinclair's arrival.

"God bless us, Ingram, but they are a wild-looking folk," Sinclair remarked, as the boats pulled for shore. "Look at yon great red hairy fellow there with the knife at his hip. He'd as soon slit your throat as gi' ye good morrow, I warrant ye."

"I think they'll no be overjoyed at our coming," murmured Gunn.

"Let's draw swords, Harry," put in Davey Sinclair. "Let's show 'em we mean to be masters here."

"*Pax*, Davey. Give over this bloodthirst o' thine and let us go softly among 'em till we know more of the situation." Sinclair turned and called out to the oarsmen. "Does any man here know the language of this place?"

"I do, sir," spoke up a swarthy fellow astern.

" 'Tis Bjornsson," said Gunn, "a Shetlander and a good man."

"Well, then, Bjornsson," said Sinclair, "when we land, stay you by me so we can parley with these folk."

In a little time, the pulling boats ground to a stop in the shallows, and Sinclair and his men leaped out and splashed ashore. The islanders stood huddled close together, their faces surly, hostile, hard. None spoke. They only stared at the strangers, nothing of warmth or welcome in their eyes.

"Bjornsson," Sinclair commanded, "find out their leader."

Bjornsson, haltingly at first, called out in the dialect of the place, "Who is best man? Come forward. The jarl of Orkney bids it."

A muttering ran through the crowd. Then a tall, lantern-jawed man, black-haired, with a cast in his right eye, stepped forward a pace. "I am best man," he said to Bjornsson. "I am called Kol Ofeigsson. Who is this jarl of Orkney? And why does he not speak for himself?"

Bjornsson, with a glance at Sinclair, replied, "My lord knows not the language of this place, Kol Ofeigsson. But he comes, as you see, in peace and strength to establish his rule here under the crown of Norway."

Again, a buzzing went up among the people. Ofeigsson's eyes swept the ranks of the strangers. "Which of these calls himself jarl?" he demanded.

Bjornsson gestured toward Sinclair. Ofeigsson approached and, in a bastard Latin, said, "You are jarl of Orkney?"

Sinclair acknowledged himself to be so. "We have that title from Haakon, late king of Norway," he said. "We are called Henry Sinclair, a Scot by birth and baron of Rosslyn. Our mother was daughter to Malise, earl of Strathern, Caithness, and Orkney. Through her line we are become prince of these isles."

Ofeigsson was a time digesting this. He scrutinized the face of this jarl, surveyed the armed men at his back, took in the barks standing offshore, the boats beached on the shingle. Then he scratched the stubble on his chin and said, "We know nothing of jarls here."

Sinclair nodded. "We are not surprised to hear you say so, Kol Ofeigsson. Fer Isle has too long lain neglected while Norway was otherwise occupied. We've come to bring peace and the rule of law to these lands, that your people may prosper and live out their lives secure from all danger."

"We fare well enough," Ofeigsson replied. "There is fish in the sea. Ships are sometimes wrecked on our coast, and these provide us with things needful. What need have we of jarls, or Norway either?"

Sinclair's smile did not lack warmth, but there was an easy confidence in it that made Ofeigsson blink and frown. "We have heard how providence will send from time to time unfortunate vessels onto these rocks," he said. "But, my friend, surely there is a better way for able men to get their living. And, mark you, Norway has need of this island, whether this island needs Norway or no. We mean to rule here, Kol Ofeigsson. We mean these lands to prosper. And we mean Norway to have its due."

"You mean to tax us," Ofeigsson stated, rather than asked.

"Fairly," replied Sinclair. "And to govern fairly, and do all things for your good and our own."

Ofeigsson showed great snaggleteeth in a mirthless laugh. "We are but one of many isles, my lord."

"And we have many eyes," Sinclair replied, "and a long arm."

Ofeigsson frowned. "Are these your army?"

"Not the tenth part of it. But even this fragment will, at our bidding, give good account of itself, we do assure you."

Ofeigsson abruptly turned his back on Sinclair and shouted something to his people.

"What says the fellow, Bjornsson?"

"My lord, he says that you have come to take away their livelihood and to lay a heavy burden on them."

An angry muttering from among the Fer Islanders made plain that Ofeigsson's shot had gone home. A knife showed here and there, and the air grew thick with tension.

At Sinclair's elbow, his brother said, "Let's take 'em, Harry."

But Sinclair called to Ofeigsson, "Friend, will ye have bloodshed or will ye have peace?"

Ofeigsson scowled. "Jarl of Orkney, if you rule here, what will become of me?"

"Why," returned Sinclair, mildly, "we shall need your help, certainly. You are known here. The people look to you to lead them. We would have you make common cause with us, be as our right hand here, and help bring a better life to the people."

Ofeigsson nodded. He turned and again spoke to the ragtag assemply. Bjornsson reported: "He says, my lord, that you are a mighty prince, with many soldiers and many ships. He says you mean no harm here, that you have asked—Jesu!—that you have asked him to help you govern here."

"That is very near what we said," allowed Sinclair, smiling.

"He says, too, my lord, that you come in great numbers and with sharp swords, that your force is such as they cannot resist. He—he counsels patience, policy, and shrewdness. He says that this could be a good thing, that it would be well to bide their time and see how you conduct matters here."

"Sound advice," murmured Sinclair.

"He says also, my lord, that you will surely not stay here for very long; that when you are gone, they may go on as before."

Sinclair laughed. "By the mass! It is an able governor. We could not have hit upon a better. Tell him—wait! Who is this that comes up the beach. 'Tis a churchman, surely."

Hurrying along over the sands came a black-clad figure, slight and of no very great height, but from his gait a very brisk and hearty man. As he drew near, the islanders fell back and made some show of pacific reverence. Ignoring them, the small priest marched up to Sinclair, bowed, and said in Latin, "Henry, jarl of Orkney, welcome to Fer Isle."

"You know us, sir?"

"Verily. I have seen you ere now in Shetland, and I know too the bearings on your shield. I am Walter de Bochane, archdeacon in Lerwick, brother to William de Bochane, canon at Orkney."

"Reverend Father," said Sinclair, "we are glad to see you. We have but just arrived in this place, and have had some windy talk with these good folk in an effort to persuade them not only of our benign purpose but also of our sovereign right to be here."

The little priest laughed. "I can well imagine your difficulty, my lord. These are no meek people. Hell itself could not cow them, unless all hell's legions stood by with drawn swords. And even then, it would be in doubt whether they would submit or no."

"And how fare heaven's legions here?"

"Alas," replied de Bochane, "heaven can spare but an occasional stray legionnaire, and it is touch and go 'twixt us and Satan, with the advantage all on Satan's side."

Sinclair grinned. "We can well believe it."

Walter de Bochane shook his head. "'Tis a lonely savage place, my lord, lying as it does midway between Lerwick and Kirkwall. The life is hard here; it makes the people hard also. They are Shetlanders, but in name only. Their loyalty is to their bellies, not that I blame them; but I think you will not have an easy time of it."

"Well, sir, we do not look for ease. Or if we did, we'd not look for it here. But we mean to assert ourself, to establish our rule, and to have all things seemly."

"I am glad of it, my lord. These people understand strength. They see the strength of the sea, the wind, these very stones that withstand the assault of wind and sea. If they see strength in a man, they respect it. And even if they do not love the man, yet will they submit to him that is strong."

"Why, then, we shall pray God strengthen us, for we mean to go about all the isles, even to the Faroes, and let folk know they have a ruler now, one who seeks their good, but who will have first their fealty."

"My lord, if you mean to stay for a time, I offer you the hospitality of my poor house. As for your men, you may quarter them on the people, if it suits you; or else they may encamp on the high ground yonder. Indeed, I think they might encamp in greater comfort, for the houses here are very mean."

"Reverend Father, we thank you for this counsel and this courtesy. We will bid our men set up their encampment, and we ourselves will, with our dearest friend and our brother, accept the hospitality of your house."

"I am honored, my lord."

"Let me but conclude matters with this fellow Ofeigsson, and we will come away with you."

To Ofeigsson, and through him to his people, Sinclair repeated his intent to bring the isles into lawful submission. "This will we do, Kol Ofeigsson. We will do it peacefully if we can; but we will do it however we must. Give us your allegiance and your aid, and you shall prosper. Oppose us, and you do so at your peril."

"My lord," replied Ofeigsson, with a fawning smile and in a servile whine ill suited to his hardy frame, "if Haakon called you jarl, then you are indeed jarl and sovereign here. I am content to be your man, for I am certain you will prove a mighty and generous lord.

"Look now. I will kiss your hands, and these folk will know you to be our master." Ofeigsson stepped forward, went down on one knee and wet the backs of Sinclair's gauntlets with his lips.

"Well done, Kol Ofeigsson," murmured Sinclair. "You may tell these people that we will bide here some days. They are to afford our men such victuals as they can. We will talk with you more anon, concerning our purpose for you and for these folk." Sinclair turned to de Bochane. "Sir, if you will lead us to your house, we will be very glad of some refreshment and a little rest."

Walter de Bochane proved a genial host, and if his low stone, turf-roofed house was small, yet was his spirit large and generous. "Avail yourselves of what you will, my lords," he said. "God He knows there's little enough, but such as I have you are most welcome to."

Sinclair, Gunn, and Davey made the best of their meager fare, finding themselves well entertained by de Bochane's account of himself. He was, he explained, not a permanent dweller in Fer Isle, having a parish in Bressay. He and his fellow clergy came by turns to this lonely outpost to minister to the few souls native to the place.

"I confess, my lord," he said to Sinclair, "I never thought to see you here."

Sinclair smiled. "We hardly expected to come here, Reverend Father. But some business took us in this way, and it seemed opportune to come ashore and make our presence known."

"That you have done," remarked the priest. "Kol Ofeigsson is something of a tyrant, albeit a very petty one, for this is a very petty rock. That he kissed your hands today signifies everything for these folk. His submission is theirs."

"He strikes me as a scurvy dog," drawled Davey, stretching out his hands to the smoldering turf fire. "Ye should ha' slit his gullet for him, Harry, and had done wi' him."

"We are no murderers, Davey," said Sinclair, sharply. "This place is ours by right, but these folk live here— if one may call it living. Were we in their place, I think we'd no rejoice at the coming of a stranger lord."

"All the same, I do not trust the fellow."

"No more do I. But if we go about killing every man we do not trust, there'd be no end of slaughter. No, sir, Ofeigsson may be an arrant rogue, but alive he may prove useful."

"Even Judas had his uses," murmured de Bochane.

"Well," put in Gunn, laughing, "maybe this Ofeigsson will also hang himself, but where he'll find a tree in this place I'm sure I cannot say."

The little priest chuckled. "You would have to send to Norway for one, sir, or else to Scotland. The gales that blow about these isles will not suffer a single tree to stand."

That very night, a great southwesterly gale came roaring in. On through the night it raged, and well into the following day. Sinclair's men were obliged to strike their tents and take shelter with the populace in their poor smoke-filled hovels. Sinclair himself kept indoors, talking long with de Bochane to learn all that he could of the folk and their manner of living.

By late afternoon, the wind abated, and the heavy clouds dispersed sufficiently to allow some rays of sunlight to touch the barren land. Sinclair began to think of stirring himself and walking out when there came to his ears the sound of running footsteps and a sudden great banging on the door.

Walter de Bochane crossed himself in haste and cried, "Enter!"

Bjornsson, Sinclair's Shetlander, burst in. "My lord, my lord! A ship is breaking up on the rocks. Come quickly."

"Jesu, Maria!" cried the priest. "The folk will be after plunder."

Sinclair belted on his sword. "Davey! Ingram! To the beach! Muster the men as ye go!"

Pell-mell the Scots ran down the slope to the cove, crying out the alarm as they ran. Armed men, their helmets glinting dully in the pale watery light, burst from a dozen doors and fell in behind their chief. Over the sodden ground they flew, splattering, splashing at every step, till they came to the narrow shingle.

"Christ have mercy," muttered Sinclair. "Look!"

Some fifty yards offshore, a ship, her sails in tatters, pitched and wallowed in that wildly surging sea. On deck, tiny figures ran to and fro, as if unable to decide between clinging to a craft that must surely wreck or flinging themselves into the angry waves.

"That is no vessel I know," Ingram said, panting. "What d'ye make of her, Harry?"

"God bless me, Ingram, she could be anything; Spaniard or Portingale, for aught I know. But she'll be driftwood presently."

"Harry, look!" Ingram seized Sinclair's arm and pointed to where a party of islanders, Ofeigsson at their head, came running up the beach, yelling like demons and brandishing wicked-looking knives.

"Ingram, take Bjornsson and four of the strongest men. Man the boat and pull for yonder ship. Save whom you can. Davey! You and the others come wi' me. We'll intercept these gentle folk and teach them to behave more mannerly."

Ingram, Bjornsson, and four brawny oarsmen leaped to the boat and pushed off into the hurling surf. Sinclair, meanwhile, led a hard run down the wet unyielding sand and, sword in hand, came panting up face to face with the hungry-eyed islanders.

"Now then, Kol Ofeigsson, what means this riot!" Sinclair demanded.

Ofeigsson's foxy eyes shifted left and right. Then he said, "'Tis no riot, Jarl Sinclair. Yon ship is breaking up. We mean to salvage what we can of her cargo."

"And for that ye need these ugly knives?"

Ofeigsson looked down at the thin blade in his fist as if seeing it for the first time. Then he looked back to Sinclair with an uneasy smile. "We always carry knives, my lord, for our protection."

Sinclair snorted. "Protection? From what, pray? Sea serpents?"

Ofeigsson took refuge in weak laughter. He turned and translated for his un-Latined neighbors who had missed the jarl's jest. Some two or three among them covered their mouths with chapped red hands and echoed their leader's laughter.

"Let us be understood, Koll Ofeigsson," said Sinclair, sternly. "If any man among you raises a hand against those stricken mariners, he will not see tomorrow's sunrise. We are lord and master here, and we will have no discourtesy, no plundering, and above all no harm done to the unfortunate. Bid your men put up their knives. Now!"

Gracelessly, Ofeigsson turned and muttered to his followers. Some were inclined to grumble; but, whether it was the menacing look of Sinclair or the sight of Davey waving his sword before him as if seeking a breast to pierce, they one and all were cowed. Knives disappeared into sheaths, and the sullen crowd now turned their attention to the dying ship.

Ingram's crew had battled their way to within a dozen yards of the wreck. A figure was seen to leap from the ship and strike out for the boat. Another followed; and another. One by one, seven men were pulled into Ingram's boat, and now the oarsmen set their course for shore. Great waves rolled under them, heaving their craft high and casting it forward at a breathless, dizzying speed.

In a very little time, the oarsmen made the calmer shallows; and, as Sinclair and his men came down to the water's edge, a last swell drove the boat ashore with force sufficient to half bury its bow in the sand.

Ingram half stepped, half fell from his place in the bow and went down on all fours on the beach, his head down, his sides heaving. Sinclair ran to him and circled his shoulders with his arm. "Ingram, are ye all right, man?"

Ingram blew and puffed like a grampus. "Ch–Christ, Harry!" He shook his head and gulped for air. "My heart's about to burst."

"Ingram—"

"Nay. Look to the mariners. I—I'll be myself again presently."

"You, Ofeigsson! Bid some of your men bear Sir Ingram to the priest's house. And carefully, mind. He is dear to us."

Four Fer Islanders were told off to bear Ingram away. Then Sinclair, turning to help Bjornsson out of the boat, called to his brother: "Davey! Go with those men and see to Ingram's comfort."

Bjornsson, only a little less battered than Gunn had been, sat down on the wet sand and cradled his head on his knees. One by one, the oarsmen and the mariners, rescuers and rescued, were handed out of the boat. If Sinclair's men were beaten, the strangers were half dead. Two were barely conscious; the others in varying states of exhaustion.

Sinclair ordered them carried to higher ground, there to rest for a bit before being carried off to shelter. Bjornsson, somewhat recovered, presumed upon his own strength and made as if to bear a hand.

"For the love o' God, my friend," protested Sinclair, "go easy. Ye've earned your rest."

"Ah," growled Bjornsson, "we Shetlanders are hardy folk. I've got my wind back. I'm sound as ever."

Sinclair smiled. "Look at your hands, man. I never saw them shake so, save when first you met our lady wife at Kirkwall."

Bjornsson's honest face reddened. "I never was no hand with ladies, my lord."

"You're a great hand in a hazard, friend Bjornsson," said Sinclair, squeezing the Shetlander's arm. "We'll no forget your doings of this day. But tell me, what are these mariners? Learned you anything from them?"

Bjornsson shook his head. "We had no time for talk, my lord; saving a bit o' prayer and a bit o' swearing. But from the swarthy look of 'em, I'd guess them to be Gascons."

Sinclair and Bjornsson labored up the slope to where the shipwrecked mariners lay. It was true, as Bjornsson had observed, that the men were all of a dark complexion. Their garments, soaked and shapeless as they were, gave no hint as to their native place. Nor was there ornament or weapon about them to reveal anything significant.

As Sinclair stood looking down at the reclining figures, pitying their wretched state, he was startled to hear a weak chuckle. It seemed to come from a slender, handsome fellow whose dark curly head was cradled in the ministering arms of little John Clarke.

Sinclair hurried to the man. "Is he conscious, John Clarke?"

"So it seems, my lord. I moistened his lips with a little sack from my flagon, and he gabbled something I could not make out."

"Here, let me have him." Sinclair took his squire's place and, gazing down at the finely sculpted features, he was delighted to see the eyelids flutter, then fly open to reveal wide brown eyes, their rims and whites all reddened by the salt sea.

"Softly, friend, softly," murmured Sinclair. "All's well."

The man, his voice little more than a whisper, asked in Latin, "Who are you?"

And in Latin Sinclair replied, "Jarl Henry Sinclair, prince of these isles and liegeman to the crowns of Scotland and Norway. And you, sir?"

The mariner licked his salt-caked lips with his tongue. "I am, my prince, a Venetian, Nicolo Zeno by name."

"Zeno! Jesu, Mary! You are called Zeno?"

A faint smile played about the man's mouth. "I am truly Zeno, my prince. But—"

"Sir," broke in Sinclair, "we know you are weary and weak and all but worn out by this fearful brush with death. But one question more, and we shall carry you to shelter and rest. Are you, sir, kin to Carlo Zeno, the Lion of Venice?"

The Venetian's smile widened, and though his voice was yet weak, pride shone in his bright eyes. "Carlo Zeno is my brother, prince," he said.

28

It was late in the following day before Zeno woke. Although still quite weak from his harrowing adventure, the Venetian seemed eager to talk with his benefactor. After downing a bowl of broth and a cup or two of hot spiced wine, he felt himself sufficiently revived to sit up in de Bochane's best bed and further his acquaintance with this Lord Sinclair.

"We are very curious to know, sir," Sinclair said, taking a chair beside the bed, "how it is you came to be in these waters, so far from your native Venice."

Zeno flashed a brilliant smile. "Ah, my prince, that is because I am possessed of a curious ambition. It is my desire to see the world and learn the various languages and customs of mankind."

Sinclair could not miss the self-gratulation in Zeno's voice, and he smiled in his turn. "That is a curious ambition, sir, and a laudable one."

"My wife, alas, does not share your view of the matter, my prince. But," Zeno shrugged, "a man must do what he is called to do, or he is not a man. My illustrious older brother now, supposing he had been willing to stay at home and be ruled by his wife, where would Venice be today? Under the heel of the Genoese, surely."

"This brother of yours—"

"Oh, a great man, my prince, truly. Of course, I am myself of some consequence in my own country. I was an elector, ambassador to Ferrara, and one of the magistrates of Treviso."

"Indeed, sir," remarked Sinclair, shooting an amused glance at Ingram Gunn, who was with great difficulty following the tangled thread of the voluble Zeno's discourse, "you must be a man of mark in Venice."

"Truly," replied Zeno, folding his arms complacently on his chest, "and one of the richest. Not that that signifies, to be sure. The world can point to any number of wealthy fools. Nevertheless, the returns on my loans to our city during the war have made me quite, quite rich."

Ingram rolled his eyes to the ceiling, as if beseeching heaven to send him patience; but Sinclair pursued his quarry: "Are you yourself a seaman, sir?"

"Ah, a very fine navigator, yes. My brother Carlo, of course, he had made as it were a profession of seamanship. But I myself was captain of a galley and sailed against the Genoese. Moreover, the senate dispatched me at the head of a fleet of five galleys to transport the Holy Father and his court from Marseilles to Rome.

"The Pope gave me his personal benediction—when he recovered from his seasickness. I was very proud and honored, I assure you."

Sinclair nodded. "We can well believe it."

Zeno seemed to be reviving before the very eyes of his hosts. Clearly, he loved to talk. "We Zenos," he went on, "are all sailors. But what Venetian is not, eh? While the rest of the world occupies itself with war on land, we pursue commerce at sea. Of course, if war comes, we can readily convert our merchant vessels to war galleys, and we will give a good account of ourselves against any fleet in the world.

"We know ships, and we know the sea. You have heard, no doubt, of my countryman, Marco Polo?"

"We have," Sinclair said.

"Well, there you are. A Venetian! We are all of a kind. Cut us, and we bleed salt water." Zeno chuckled. "No doubt you thought me in grave peril yesterday. But it was not so."

"No?" Sinclair's brows arched in astonishment.

"No, no, my prince. You may stab a Venetian, or hang him, but you can never drown him. He is half fish."

"And your brother is a lion," murmured Ingram Gunn. "Interesting."

Zeno clapped his hands. "This knight makes a jest! I like that. Carlo says to me I talk too much, laugh too much. But I tell him I cannot help my good nature.

"There was a great Venetian once, the Doge Marini Faletro. Now he was not good-natured. No. And he became angry with a young noble, Michele Steno, who wrote some naughty verses on the Dogaressa. The doge brought Steno to law, but this Steno was known to be a good-natured man, and he was let off lightly. This angered the doge still more. And he contrived a plot to be avenged on all the patricians. You see what ill nature will do.

"He caused an alarm to be sounded, a false alarm of a Genoese attack.

The patricians came running to St. Mark's piazza, and there the doge's men surprised them and killed them.

"You are horrified, of course."

"Of course," murmured Sinclair, giving his head a shake to clear his benumbed brain.

"Well, then, as will happen, the truth came out. And this doge was tried and put to death. On his monument it is written: 'He lost his temper; then he lost his head.'

"You see! So when Carlo reproves me for my too much good nature, I tell him, 'Never mind, dear brother. At least I will keep my head.'"

"We sincerely hope so," said Sinclair, politely, although his own head was buzzing like a hive.

"But you asked about Carlo."

"Yes, you did," Ingram threw in, not without irony.

"We are very eager to hear about him," said Sinclair, rising. "But we must not tire you, my friend. Rest now. We will talk with you more anon."

"But I am not fatigued," protested Zeno. "No, indeed I am not."

"Rest," said Sinclair, with some firmness. "Sir Ingram and I will look in on you again in a little while. We must go now and see to your companions. Adieu. Ingram, come."

Zeno was still talking as Sinclair and Gunn passed through the door into the soft gray September afternoon.

"Whew!" Ingram exhaled noisily. "Christ, Harry, the fellow's a by-Our-Lady magpie!"

Sinclair chuckled and slipped an arm across his kinsman's shoulders. "He talked me deaf and dumb, I swear it. But he is good-natured."

"Ha-ha-ha!" cried Ingram. "Good-natured! Ah-ha-ha-hah! I'd take my chances with that old what-you-may-call-'im any day."

"The doge?"

"Aye!"

Ingram wiped his eyes and shook his head. "I'd sooner have my head cut off than talked off, afore God I would."

"Well, cutting's quicker, at any rate. But look. Yonder comes our reverend friend. Let's go and meet him."

Walter de Bochane, the wind riffling his light brown hair, his gnomish face crinkling with a smile of welcome, greeted his guests and said, "How fares our doughty mariner this day? Is he quite recovered?"

"Fully," replied Sinclair, with an emphasis that made Ingram laugh aloud. "God bless us, Reverend Father, but the man has more talk in him than any ten men."

"Aye," added Gunn, "and we have had more talk out o' him than we could digest between us."

The priest smiled. "You found him amiable?"

"G—Good-natured's the word," replied Ingram, and he and Sinclair both dissolved in laughter.

The mild eyes of the little cleric widened. "You are uncommonly merry, my lords. It is good to see you so."

"Ah, God help me," gasped Ingram, "but I have never met such an arrant rattling featherbrain in all my life before."

"No, Ingram," objected Sinclair, sobering a little, although a smile lingered on his face. He is not that. Talkative, yes; I gi' ye that. But the man's no fool. Far from it."

"Ye like him, then?"

"Don't you?"

"Ye–es. Yes, I do. Ha-ha! Damned if I can explain it, but yes. I do like him."

"Good. For so do I. And there's a notion in my head concerning this fellow." Sinclair nodded. "Yes, Ingram. I've a notion. But more o' that presently. We must look to the others and see how they fare. This evening we'll pay another call on this Zeno and—well, we shall see."

"Shall I come wi' ye now, Harry?" Gunn asked.

"No, sir. For you yourself would profit from more rest. I confess, coz, I was afraid for ye yesterday. I never should ha' sent ye out with Bjornsson in that boat."

Ingram grinned. "I shared that opinion, my lord, while I was in the boat. But I am hearty now and fine, save for a bit o' stiffness here and there."

"Then go lie down. Ye know I cannot function wi' a lamed right hand."

Ingram, touched by the compliment, bowed to de Bochane and Sinclair, and went off quite meekly to his bed. In truth, although he had studied to make a show of briskness that morning, he felt far from fit. His every rib was sore, and his chest felt constricted. He would never have said so, but he was glad to be excused.

Sinclair's eyes followed his kinsman as Gunn walked away. "I love that man," he said to de Bochane, "and yesterday I very nearly killed him."

"'Twas not as if you meant to, my lord. You only turned to him in a time of need, as he himself would want you to do. And he responded as he could."

"Aye, and as he always does." Sinclair shook his head. "Do I lean too heavily on him, I wonder. He has no life outside our service. No wife. No children. His whole thought seems bent on how best to serve me."

"He is your very great friend, my lord."

"God make me worthy to be his."

That evening, Sinclair, together with his brother and a rested, livelier Ingram Gunn, returned to Zeno's bedside.

"All your companions are recovering, Nicolo Zeno," Sinclair reported. "We are happy to tell you that all will soon be up and about, quite hearty."

"Ah, good. I am glad in my heart to hear it. We shall buy a mass of this good priest in thanks for our safety, eh? God and St. Mark were with us, surely."

"But I thought you Venetians could not drown," remarked Gunn.

"That is true, yes. But the priest told me how those savage people meant to deal with us, had you, my lords, not intervened." Zeno shuddered. "I think that is no death for a gentleman."

"You're right in that," cried Davey Sinclair. "To die in battle, that is glorious and fine. But to be murdered by a mob of stinking fisherfolk, Ugh! I think my ghost would walk forever were I to perish so."

Zeno crossed himself. "Let us not talk of such things."

"No, indeed," said Sinclair. "Let's talk o' living. Surely you were spared to some purpose, sir. Tell us, what is your plan now that your ship is gone?"

Zeno shrugged. "I take fortune where I find it. And we Zenos are all fortunate men. Tomorrow, the next day, who knows? I shall arrange to buy another ship and go on with the adventure."

"To see the world?"

"Yes."

"Hm-m. Tell me, sir, have ye never been to Scotland?"

"No, indeed I have not. But I have heard Scottish music in the church, and thought it delightful."

"And what of Norway? Have you been there?"

"No, my prince, I have never been to Norway. They say a lady rules there. Is that not a curious thing?"

Sinclair smiled. "Not when you know the lady. But what of Orkney? Have ye—"

Zeno shook his head.

"And the Faroes?"

"No, my prince. Forgive me, but I have not been long on my travels."

Sinclair nodded. "Well, sir, it seems to us that if you are serious in your purpose, you must sooner or later touch at these several places."

"Of a certainty, my prince. Otherwise I shall not have seen the world. And I will not, believe me, return to Venice until I have done so. You will find me resolute, for all that I am good-natured."

Ingram snorted, and Sinclair was obliged to cover a grin with his hand. "We believe you are resolute, as becomes the Lion's brother. And, to be brief, we have ourself a great liking for resolute men."

Zeno offered a fine-boned brown hand. "Great hearts speak to each other always, regardless of language or nation."

Sinclair gravely clasped the Venetian's hand. "So we have found. But tell us, Nicolo Zeno, would it be in your interest to enter our service for a time? We can promise you opportunity to see other lands, to observe other customs, to learn other tongues. And we would, of course, recompense you richly, as befits a man of your rank."

"I? In your service, my prince?"

Sinclair nodded. "To put it plainly, we have, like Venice, a watery realm. But, unlike Venice, we have no great mariners. We have a fleet, some thirteen vessels in all, but we are but indifferent seaman. If you—"

"Ah, well, my prince, if it is seamen you require, you can do no better than to employ Venetians. We are born to the life, truly. Why, my countryman, Vettor Pisani, now, when I consider how he bottled up the Genoese fleet at Chioggia—this was after he was let out of prison, of course, when the populace demanded that—"

"Yes, yes," Sinclair broke in, gnawing at his lip in amused vexation. "But we were speaking of Nicolo Zeno. Will he sail with us on a little adventure to the Faroes?"

Zeno, his dark eyes dancing with pleasure, cried, "But of course, my prince! I am indebted to you for saving me from those savages. And we Zenos are known for paying our debts. Why, one time, my brother Antonio—"

"Peace!" cried Sinclair, laughing. "Peace to Carlo, to Antonio, and to you also. God bless me, sir, but your good nature boils over and bids fair to drown us all—for a Scot will drown, if a Venetian won't. Let us unfold to you our plan."

"I am all attention, my prince," said Zeno, folding his hands in his lap and fixing his large brown eyes on Sinclair's face.

"Well, sir, what we propose is this: We will dispatch one bark to Orkney, with orders for my entire fleet to make a rendezvous with us here. In the interval, you and your companions will rest and gather your strength. Then, when our ships arrive, we will go straightway on board and make for the Faroes, which lie some two hundred miles north of here.

"There we will go ashore and let the folk see that they have now a strong lord to govern them. We must hope they will be gladder of this news than these Fer Isle folk were; but whether they be glad or no, we shall show ourselves in such strength that none will think on raising an objection."

"What sort of sailing shall we have?" Zeno inquired.

"Full hazardous. We are told the currents there run swift, and the coast very irregular. It will be no boy's play to get us safely in and out among the several isles."

Zeno's eyes flashed with pride. "I can do it, my prince. And I will do it. It will be an adventure to remember when I am very old and home again in Venice, with my grandchildren on my knees."

"Well, then," said Sinclair, getting to his feet, "we are bound for the Faroes. Providence has put you in our way, Nicolo Zeno. We do not doubt it. God grant we make the most of our good fortune."

PART IV

29

Sinclair swept through the Faroes like a westerly gale, relentless, unswerving, irresistible. Ledovo, Skuoe, Sandoe fell like ripe fruit into his gauntleted hands. Zeno and his Venetian mariners guided the fleet through treacherous shoals, around murderous rocks and through tidal rips that might well have doomed the entire army had not the brilliant navigator been with them.

The strategy was simple. Zeno would put Sinclair and his men ashore; the army would march overland; and ships and men would rendezvous on the opposite coast of a given island.

At Norderdahl, Sinclair encountered the first real resistance. An army of Faroese, led by die-hard adherents to the cause of the late lord of Skuldane, Malise Sparre, made a stand. But these were no match for the doughty Scots. Their leaders slain, the Faroemen lost what little stomach they had for the business, struck their ensigns, and laid down their arms.

Then there was great celebration in Norderdahl. Ambassadors came from throughout the isles to acknowledge Sinclair as lord and to swear their allegiance to him. Sinclair, headquartered at the hall of the best man, received these professions of homage and loyalty with princely grace. To each and all he pledged his life and honor for their safety and prosperity.

Zeno and his mariners put ashore there at Norderdahl, and great was the reception that awaited them. Sinclair assembled his entire force and, in the presence of the ambassadors, clerics and island folk, he embraced Nicolo Zeno and declared: "To this gallant captain we owe our good fortune here. His courage and his skill have been to us our greatest resource in carrying forward this work. Therefore, let all men know that we, Henry Sinclair, jarl of Orkney, do this day name Nicolo Zeno admiral of our fleet and knight of this realm."

At Sinclair's bidding, Zeno knelt to receive the accolade.

"Rise, Sir Nicolo Zeno," said Sinclair, his deep voice ringing down the length of the hall, "knight-admiral and liegeman of Orkney."

Lusty cheers rose from the throng as Zeno bent and kissed Sinclair's hands. Then Sinclair apportioned out rich purses to Zeno and his men. And he gave orders for a victory feast to which all in Norderdahl were invited.

That night, Sinclair presided over the banquet, with Zeno seated at his left, Ingram Gunn at his right. "Well, Ingram," he cried, raising his brimming cup, "is this not a happy night for us?"

"Aye," replied Ingram, grinning broadly. "I little thought we'd dragged up such a treasure from the sea when we salvaged our merry Venetian at Fer Isle."

"D'ye hear that, Sir Nicolo?" Sinclair turned and poked Zeno in the ribs. "Our cousin says you are a treasure."

Zeno half rose from his place and bowed to Gunn. "He is very kind, my prince. And you are very kind. I am overwhelmed with kindness."

"You have earned it, my friend. But stay with us and serve us as ye have these last busy weeks, and ye shall have more kindness than you can well dispose of."

Zeno's eyes sparkled in the torchlight. "My prince," he said, "may I ask one kindness more?"

"Ask."

"My prince, I have a brother—"

"Aye, Carlo the Lion. We drink his health."

"I speak of Antonio, my prince."

"Ah?"

"With your permission, I should like to send for him to join us. Like me, he has a great desire to see the world, and it would be a matter of great joy for me to have him beside me in your service."

Sinclair smiled. "And this brother, is he like you?"

"Very like, my prince."

"Then send for him, Sir Nicolo. We'll make him welcome, and that most heartily. For if one Zeno can do so much, what will not two Zenos do?"

Gunn leaned over and whispered to Sinclair. "You have a brother too, coz. Look where he leans against yonder wall, glowering like a thundercloud."

Sinclair looked to where Gunn's thumb directed. Young David Sinclair, his handsome face sullen and petulant, stood apart from the festive crowd, his arms folded on his breast, his eyes stolid and unseeing, fixed on empty nothing.

"Now what ails the fellow?" muttered Sinclair. "Ingram, go and bid him come to me."

As Sinclair watched, Ingram rose and walked down to where Davey stood, tapped him on the shoulder, and motioned for him to go up to his brother. Slowly, very slowly, Davey straightened himself and, with a studied show of indifference, sauntered the length of the hall and came at last to the seat Ingram had left vacant.

"Ye sent for me, Harry?"

"We did. Sit down."

As Davey eased into his seat, Zeno leaned across and cried, "Welcome, sir. Is this not a joyous feast?"

Davey Sinclair affected not to hear. Zeno only shrugged, but Sinclair rapped out, "Did ye no hear this gentleman speak to ye, Davey?"

"I heard something," muttered the younger man. "I did not realize he had addressed himself to me."

Sinclair's brows knit in a frown. "It would become ye, sir, to offer our friend a reply, if not an apology."

"Your friend," returned Davey, "hath had already so much from the Sinclairs that he cannot want so slight a thing as some few words from me."

Henry Sinclair's face flamed. "David," he said, his voice but little above a whisper, "smile. Smile, damn you! That's better. Now, still smiling, you will get up and go out into the antechamber. We will join you there presently. Go!"

David Sinclair, his teeth showing in a semblance of a smile, got to his feet and left the hall.

"Now, David, what's the matter?" demanded Sinclair, when they were alone.

The young man shrugged. "The matter matters little enough, plainly. I am not happy; you are. You are master here; I am not. Therefore, what can it signify that I am not happy?"

"You are my brother, sir. I would know the cause of this unhappiness."

"The cause is simple, brother. I have served you well, fought bravely, waited patiently for some recognition. And I have had only my waiting for my pains. Yet this foreigner contrives in the space of a few weeks to insinuate himself into your special favor, and you heap on him more honors and rewards than he has strength to carry." David raised his eyes to meet his brother's. "I take that ill, Harry. I do take that ill."

"I see." Sinclair nodded. "Well, Davey, I'm not a man given to explanations. I find that they take more time than I can spare, and I have yet to see where they serve any useful purpose. I will not, then, offer ye any explanation of my actions. If ye feel yourself ill used—"

"I do," broke in Davey, his voice crackling with his grievance.

"Well, then, Davey, I shall bid ye farewell and Godspeed."

"Ye can't mean it, Harry."

"Aye, I do mean it, sir. With all the goodwill in the world, I release ye from my service. We do not pull together well, Davey. I am sorry for that, heartily sorry. But I do not mean to endure being checked and baited at every turn, not even for sake o' kinship."

Sinclair's voice was mild and low, yet there was that in it to convince his brother of his brother's seriousness. Davey flared out: "So ye cast me aside, then, with no reward and regret—"

"Ah, Davey, I do regret very much that ye cannot seem to master your own impatience and have some faith in me. As to reward, well, sir, I am not aware that you have done so much more than another. But ye are a Sinclair and my brother. Ye'll not go unprovided for.

"Look ye, Davey. On our return to Kirkwall, I shall assign to ye my lands o' Newburgh and Auchdale in Aberdeenshire in return for any right ye may have through our mother to my lands in Orkney and Shetland. You will be free then to live as ye like, take service under King Robert, and make for yourself such fortune as your stength and skill can win ye.

"Is that agreeable?"

David Sinclair nodded. He could not trust himself to speak. That he had been most generously bought off, he knew. But he had been bought off. And that knowledge lodged like a bone in his throat.

"Very well, then, Davey, here's my hand on it. I wish ye joy of your possessions and a long and happy life. If ever I can be of service to you, ye have but to ask. Ye will not find me laggard in taking up my brother's cause."

David Sinclair clasped his brother's hand, turned, and fled the room.

Later that night, Sinclair imparted to Ingram the essence of his encounter with his brother.

"I am sorry to hear it, Harry," Gunn said. "I think you have done most generously by him, but this rupture is a sad thing. Could ye not ha' given him another chance? He is, after all, little more than a boy."

"He is a boy, Ingram. And I have a need for men." Sinclair raised his head and smiled. "Come, be thou my brother in his stead, and together we shall do such deeds as will win for us an honored place in the annals o' this realm."

Some days later, Sinclair and his troops, together with Zeno and his mariners, made their way back to Kirkwall in Orkney. And there Sinclair found waiting for him a handsome young Scot of some nineteen or twenty summers, but lately arrived from Longformacus in the home country.

"Well, young sir, welcome to our house," Sinclair said, on greeting his guest. "What brings ye to Orkney?"

"Ye do not know me, my lord?" A quizzical smile played over the young man's face.

"No, sir, but we trust that will be remedied presently."

"Why, my lord, I am your kinsman, Richard Sinclair."

"Jamie's son?"

"Aye."

Sinclair embraced his young relation warmly. "Afore God, lad, why did ye not say so? Richard! By the mass, ye've grown a proper man! 'Tis good to see you here, Richard. How fares your noble father?"

"Right well, my lord. He bade me tell you he thinks often of you, and that fondly."

"As we do o' him." Sinclair smiled and shook his head. "We love your father, Richard. He's as fine a knight as ever rode for Scotland. But, tell us, pray, why came you here?"

"To tell you, my lord, that Robert is dead."

"What? The king?"

"Even so, my lord."

Sinclair crossed himself. "God give him peace," he said. "He was ever gracious and kind to us Sinclairs."

"My lord, Robert's son, John, is to be crowned at Scone come 14 August. My father thought you would want to be in attendance."

"Humph. A King John." Sinclair shook his head. "'Tis not a name much loved in Scotland, Richard. We've had no luck wi' Johns ere this."

Richard smiled. "Aye, my lord. And John himself is mindful o' that, wherefore he hath declared that he will take his father's name along wi' his father's crown, and be known as Robert the Third."

"Well, God grant that Scotland's fortunes change for the better with this change o' names."

"My father says 'twill take a change o' hearts first," replied Richard. "There is such contention between this new king and his younger brother, the earl o' Fife."

"Who is in fact a Robert."

"Aye, and is in fact governor of the kingdom. He is hard and shrewd, my lord. This new Robert is far from that. And though they call him king, he will have to alter much his manner and his conduct if he would be truly king."

Sinclair rubbed his jaw. "He is not of a martial spirit, certainly. But he is a kindly, gentle man."

"My father thinks him altogether too gentle," Richard Sinclair said. "And now that he is so sickly and forever submitting to the physicians, we cannot look to him to lead us in matters of warlike enterprise. My bloody English namesake hath some several times made raids across the border into Edinburgh and Aberdeen, despite his own domestic woes. If he dared so much against the old king, what will he not venture against the old king's sickly son?"

"But surely, Richard, the nobles will rally around their new lord. They may awaken in him something of the soldier's spirit yet."

Richard shrugged. "If you and the present Douglas, perhaps, were to bide in court and be there for Robert to lean on, it might be so. But Douglas is forever fighting wi' Percy, and you are yourself so occupied with other matters that I fear none will come forth in strength to prop our poor third Robert up.

"And, so my father says, the earl o' Fife is well content that matters should stand so. He himself hath high ambition, and he is not above fomenting division and dissent even against his own brother. As to that madman Alexander, the new king's youngest brother, why, he ought not to be allowed out in the world. He is like the dog that will bite itself if it cannot find another dog to fight with."

Sinclair fixed his young kinsman with a calculating eye. "It seems to us, sir," he said, "that ye have a wealth of opinion for one so young."

Richard flushed like a maiden. "'Tis my father's notion mainly, my lord. But I do observe and I do remark."

"And very shrewdly too, no doubt. But there is danger, Richard, in a wagging tongue. For aught you know, we may ourself be allied with the earl o' Fife in league against the king."

"No, my lord," replied Richard, stoutly. "You are a Sinclair."

A warm smile lit the jarl of Orkney's face. "Why, God bless ye, Richard, and so are you. And we Sinclairs know which way our duty lies. Come, you will sail wi' us to Scotland. We'll make our oath of fealty to this new-made Robert; and then we'll show you the hospitality of our house at Rosslyn, if ye've a mind to bide wi' us awhile."

"My lord, I'd like nothing better."

Sinclair gazed steadily at this tall young kinsman, so handsome in his green jerkin and his boots of soft brown leather. He liked the youth's frank open face, the clear unwavering eyes; and he did most dearly love the boy's father. "Well," he said, at last, "we will talk more of this anon, Richard. For the moment, let it suffice that we are most heartily glad of your company. 'Twill cheer us on our long way back to Scotland to have a merry youth along to sing us all the new songs and tell us all the current scandal."

"My lord, ye must not think me a gabbling fool, fit only for idle nattering. I am a competent swordsman, I promise you, and a good rider, and—"

"And your father's son." Sinclair smiled and embraced the lad. "That is enough for us, Richard. Indeed, it is a very great deal. But, come, let us go and stir up the people, We must not delay if we are to be at Scone by mid-August."

30

King Robert, sweating profusely under the bright August sun despite the canopy above his newly anointed head, received the barons one by one, suffering them to kiss his pale, blue-veined hands in pledge of fealty.

Sinclair himself came forward, knelt, and pressed his lips to Robert's fingers. A reek of vinegar assailed his nostrils as he did so, for poor Robert's leg, long since lamed by the kick of a horse, was ever and again wrapped in a drenching, drawing vinegar poultice. It would not heal, nor could the king walk without limping, despite constant attention from his hopeful physicians.

"Ah, Baron Sinclair," purred Robert, gently urging Sinclair to rise by a slight tugging of the hands, "it is good to see you in Scotland."

" 'Tis good to be in Scotland, sire, and to pledge anew my fealty to this crown."

"Good, good," murmured Robert. "Our late father had a great affection for your family, sir. Know that his love survives in us."

Sinclair bowed gravely. " 'Tis worth more than gold to hear it, sire," he said.

The new king smiled, showing his ravaged gums and their few surviving teeth. "We cannot, God knows, offer gold, but would our love be sufficient to persuade you to stay awhile in Scotland?"

"Your Majesty, pardon me, but dear as Scotland is to me, I have yet unfinished business in the isles."

"Ah, yes. You are earl of Orkney now."

"But no less a Scot for that, sire, I do assure you."

Robert nodded. "We do not doubt it, Baron Sinclair."

"If ever Your Majesty has need of this right arm, this sword, or any other thing at my command, only ask, and you shall find me diligent and prompt in attending to whatever Your Majesty desires."

"Why, then, God bless you, baron," said the king, dismissing him. "We will remember your words in our time of need."

Sinclair bowed and withdrew, taking his place beside his cousin James in the sweltering ranks of the nobles.

"Well, coz," drawled James Sinclair, "what think ye o' the new king?"

"Why, coz, he seems a decent, kindly soul."

"Aye," said James, baron of Longformacus, with a wry twitching of his thin lips, "and I fear 'tis that will be his undoing. He's a soft man, Harry. And yon earl o' Fife, hovering there at his royal brother's back, well knows it."

Henry Sinclair squinted across the green lawn at the elegant figure of Fife, resplendent in slashed sleeves and morey hose. "I hardly know the man, Jamie, but he looks a proper fox."

"Aye, and his brother Alex is a wolf. Between 'em, yon John—or Robert, as he calls himself now—will have little joy of his crown, I warrant ye."

"Can you not rally the barons to the king's cause, Jamie?"

"Wi' what?" James Sinclair snorted. "But for Albany and some other trusty few they be a venal crew, Harry. And Fife's got to 'em. He's no a man to let the grass grow under his feet, I tell ye. Since he was named governor by Parliament, he's made it his business to sow favor here and there about the realm; and where his favor took no root, he tried fear."

"How fared his crop at Longformacus?"

"Need ye ask, coz?" James spat on the turf. "But though he could not get to me, our worthy Fife hath been main busy, and he hath managed to create division sufficient to his ends. This king'll be no happier than his father was; and as for his little son, God help him."

"You will help him too, surely."

"If I can. But I have sons o' my own to look to, Harry. Should this earl's power wax much greater, 'twill be no light matter for any man to go against him."

Sinclair nodded. "Well, coz, I pray your fears be not realized, for Scotland's sake as well as this new Robert's. But if it comes to the worst, I pray you, send for me. And whether I be in Shetland or in Orkney, I will make haste hither to ride wi' ye in this king's cause."

James Sinclair squeezed his cousin's arm. "I know ye would, Harry. And God He knows how glad I'd be to ride along o' you. But this is policy and stealth, not honest open warfare. I doubt we could find a foe to strike at did we scour the length and breadth o' Scotland. Mark me, if this king's o'erthrown, 'twill no be on the field o' battle, but in some closet behind closed doors."

"Overthrown?" Sinclair's brows shot up. " 'Tis but a day the man's been crowned, Jamie. I think ye do anticipate somewhat."

James Sinclair spat again, looked left and right, then said in a low voice, "Harry, I'd no give a farthing for the man's chances. One way or another, his brother'll undo him. And what becomes o' Scotland then, only God He knows."

"Christ, Jamie, ye're blithe today. Ye make me glad I have Orkney to go back to."

"Aye. Ye should be glad, Harry, for all that Rosslyn is so bonny. I'm no coward, as well ye know, but I wish for my sons' sake I had an Orkney of my own to send 'em to should affairs in Scotland go awry."

"You and your sons will ever find a welcome in Orkney, Jamie. And, indeed, I meant to ask ye something touching that."

"Aye?"

"This lad o' yours, Richard, that came to fetch me out o' Kirkwall, I have taken a liking to him, Jamie."

"Oh, Richard's a good fellow, Harry. A damned good fellow, even though I am his father."

"Or because you are his father," amended Sinclair, smiling. "I wonder, could ye spare him to me for a time? I think I can promise him ample opportunity to prove himself, and a fair chance of advancement."

"Why, God bless ye, coz, I'd be glad of it wi' all my heart to know my Richard was wi' you." James Sinclair laid a finger aside his long nose and winked a shrewd green eye. "Let me sound the fellow out, Harry, subtlelike, ye understand. And if it appears he'd like to go, why, I will send him along to Rosslyn where ye can make your proposals to him."

"Done and done," said Henry Sinclair, clasping his kinsman's hand. "I'll look for him at Rosslyn before the week is out."

"Now there's a pleasant picture," purred a feline voice at Sinclair's back, "a pair of cousins close as brothers, it would seem."

"Closer than some brothers in this troubled realm, I fear," replied Jarl Henry, his tone level for all that he was taken unaware by the soft approach of Alexander and the earl of Fife.

A mocking smile played about Alexander's mouth. "Abel and Cain were the very archetype of brothers, my good Rosslyn, and see how it fell out with them."

"Aye," growled Jamie, "and if poor Abel had had a Sinclair to avenge him, the coward Cain would not have escaped so lightly."

"Why, sir," Fife threw in, with a glance at Alexander for approval, "the man was marked for his villainy."

"With a device that's quartered on the arms o' certain men o' mark in Scotland, to their everlasting shame," retorted Jamie.

"Have a care, Longformacus," murmured Alexander, his low voice charged with menace. "We've something at our belt a good deal sharper than your discourteous tongue."

"Ye have that," replied Jamie, with a grim nod, "but have ye the stomach to draw it in daylight against a true Scot?"

Henry Sinclair broke in. "Peace, Jamie. And you, my lords, give over this unseemly wrangle. This is Robert's day. Surely ye would not mar it?"

Slowly, very slowly, Alexander let his gelid gaze travel from the one Sinclair to the other. "You say well, Rosslyn. This is Robert's day. We can well afford to let him have it. There will be other days."

"Robert's day will last while there's a Sinclair left in Scotland," declared Jarl Henry's cousin.

Alexander's smile was insolent. "There's one Sinclair will be away on Norway's business soon."

"My lords, peace!" Jarl Henry's voice fairly crackled for all that it was pitched too low for Robert's ear.

"For now," agreed Alexander, in a mockery of amiable acquiescence. He bowed and turned with his brother Fife to depart.

"A moment, sir," said Henry Sinclair, taking a step forward.

"Well, Rosslyn?"

" 'Tis true we'll be away north presently, but never doubt our allegiance to this king."

"Why, sir, all men know the loyalty of the Sinclairs."

"Let all men reckon with it, then. For if word comes to us of any threat to Robert's peace, we'll pack our ships with islanders and northern Scots and join forces with our kinsman here to fight in Robert's cause."

Even in his wrath, Jamie could not forbear to smile as he observed the elegant Fife slink closer to the lupine Alexander, as if he would borrow audacity from him.

"You speak plainly, Rosslyn," Alexander murmured. "We will think on what you have said."

"Do," urged Jarl Henry. "Think on it, and report it widely among the nobles of this realm. It goes against our very nature to bathe our steel in Scottish blood, but the man who turns on Robert is in our estimate no Scot."

Alexander executed an elaborate bow. "God give you good day and a safe journey, Rosslyn. And to you, Longformacus, for this instructive discourse, much thanks."

James Sinclair only sniffed and, with a smothered curse, stalked off. Alexander shrugged, smiled, bowed once more to Jarl Henry, and sauntered off with the earl of Fife close at his heels.

Henry Sinclair quickly overtook his cousin. "Jamie," he said, "do you keep Rosslyn and Orkney informed of all that happens here. Robert's safety may depend on that."

"God's wounds, coz! Ye would ha' done well to let me force yon Alexander's hand this day."

"Before the king?" Henry Sinclair shook his head in amused dismay.

"The heads o' those two plotters would make a fit gift for the occasion," Jamie said.

"Aye, and a grand present for the boy on England's throne. Christ help us, Jamie, we Scots must learn at last to give over slaughtering each other, or we shall learn to live a conquered race."

"God forbid," muttered Jamie, crossing himself.

"Amen. See ye keep close with Albany and Douglas, and be often in the king's court. I doubt not your sunny smile will serve to keep bold Alex mindful of what has passed between us here this day."

"Trust me, coz. What a man can do, I will do, and yet I see no happy reign for this new king."

Sinclair smiled. "The happiness of kings lies not within a baron's gift, I fear. But let us show at least our skill in music, and so play the stops as to mute the martial shrilling of yon Alex and his Fife."

On his return to Rosslyn, Sinclair found that Zeno had taken the place by storm. Little Willie and young Harry followed the Venetian around like a pair of adoring puppies, and young Mistress Betsy considered him her personal property and her slave. Mistress Beatrix, though yet too young to assert herself in the rivalry for Zeno's attention, so effectively insinuated herself into the Italian's graces that she could, by the mere aiming of her great eyes, command her premier place on Zeno's knee.

"Truly, husband," remarked Janet, laughing, "you have brought us a capital nurse in this bold navigator. I wonder that wee Helen does not leave off suckling and cry for Zeno also."

Sinclair smiled down on the babe at Janet's breast. "Now there is where Helen is wiser than the others," he said, tapping the infant's cheek with his finger. "Zeno's a dear man, but only a fool would leave this for that, surely."

"Ah, you talk like a man," declared Janet, tossing her head.

"I should hope so, madam. Indeed, I should." Sinclair bent and kissed his wife full on the mouth. "But ye like this Zeno, d'ye not?"

"Could anyone not like him? He is never dull, Harry. There is not a song he cannot sing, nor a tale he does not know. And withal, he is the most delightful of guests, willing always to defer, to help, to listen—"

"Listen? Zeno?" Sinclair gave a shout of laughter. "Well, to you, it may be that he listens. For myself, I never met a man who talked so much in all my life before. Ingram and I were deaf for two days after we pulled this fellow out o' the brine. Indeed, I began to think o' throwing him back in again."

"But he adores you, Harry."

"Does he so?" Sinclair looked thoughtful. "Well, I am glad o' that, Janet. The man's a treasure, I tell you. And I do not mean to let him go. We would never ha' quelled the Faroes—God's wounds! We would never ha' made it safe to shore—had it not been for the skill and courage of Nicolo Zeno. Wherefore I named him knight admiral, and wherefore I mean to study to keep him happy in my service."

Janet smiled. "But, Harry, if he wants to return to his own land sometime, which he surely will, for he hath spoken of Venice in such wise even as I have heard you speak of Rosslyn, you would not prevent his going?"

"Prevent? No, not that. But persuade, yes, and reason, and bribe if I must. We need this man, Janet. He is a sailor, by heaven. Already he has set about planning changes in the structure of my ships to make them at once swifter and more seaworthy. And sail? Why, the man could take a squadron through a maelstrom and not so much as scrape the paint. He can't be spared, Janet. Nor do I think he will want to be. He has sent for his brother, ye know."

"He told me. And if Antonio is half so pleasant company as Nicolo, we shall never be dull in Kirkwall, for all we are so far from home."

Sinclair took Janet's hand in his. "Kirkwall is home, Janet. So we must think of it now."

Janet kissed his fingers one by one. "My home is with you, my lord," she said, smiling up at him in the old way that never failed to melt him. "No more than the heart can be at home outside the body, can I be at home apart from you."

Sinclair had planned to leave soon for Kirkwall, to anticipate the autumn gales and be safely ensconced in his great hall before the rough winds blew. Yet he lingered on at Rosslyn through the sweet late summer days, telling himself that Janet would be the stronger for the delay.

Richard Sinclair arrived, all glowing and eager to be off and doing. David Sinclair departed for his new holdings in Aberdeenshire. And Ingram began to grumble and talk of visiting Caithness if Harry had no further use for him that year.

"Come, come, coz," replied Sinclair to this proposal. "We'll be embarking soon. 'Tis just that, well, who knows when we shall come again to Scotland?

"God, Ingram, I love this place. These woods, the river, yon ancient yew my grandsire planted after Longshanks's Welsh bowmen proved their weapons against so many honest Scots, those faerie towers that burn wi' magic fire whene'er a Sinclair chieftain dies. Lord, I do confess I find it very hard to leave."

"So shall we all," replied Gunn. " 'Tis not so easy as once it was to run after the hard life, the ship, the saddle, and the fray. We are both of us past forty, coz. And soon we shall be old."

"Old!" Sinclair's voice was charged with indignation. "Old, ye say? Why, damn me for a skulking Southron, I cannot trust my ears. Look at this arm! Is that the arm of an old man? Hey? Do I grow fat? Is my breathing labored? Do my hands tremble? Was it an old man scoured the Faroes? Is it an old man stands before ye now?"

"My dear Harry," protested Ingram, not a little astonished at this outburst, "I never said you were old. I said only that—"

"Never mind. No matter. I know what ye said, sir, and I deny it. Why, Ingram, I am as stout and hard as ever I was. And so are you. Look at ye! Why, there's scarce a gray hair on your head, nor a wrinkle in your face. Old!" Sinclair barked a short, sharp laugh. "You and I together, coz, we could stand up to any pair o' champions in the realm."

"To be sure," murmured Ingram, his tone placating.

"By God, we'll see soon enough how old we are, coz. Find Zeno. Tell him we sail this day week. I'll go bid Janet make ready." And as Sinclair stalked off, his back straight, his stride springy, Ingram heard him mutter again, "Old!"

On the eve of his departure, Sinclair went in and made his farewells to his mother. That lady the years had touched but lightly. A little thinner, a little faded she may have been, but Lady Isabel seemed to her son virtually unchanged. If she was less assertive, less forceful in her manner, it was only that she had found within herself something like contentment, something akin to peace. But the old fiber and the old iron still endured.

"So, my son, it is once again adieu?"

"Aye, Mother. And I am sorry to leave you." He pressed her hand softly.

"I do believe you, Harry." Lady Isabel smiled up at her stalwart son. "And I shall be very sorry to have Janet and the children gone from here."

"Nonsense," replied Sinclair, smiling in his turn. " 'Twill be a blessing to you to have the young rogues out from underfoot. Besides, John and Inge and their babes will be here still to distract you when you are dull."

Lady Isabel nodded. "John's a good son to me, Harry. And his wife is an angel, truly. I count myself blessed that they are content to bide here at Rosslyn with me."

"They are themselves blessed, as is anyone who dwells here."

"Harry—?"

"Aye, Mother?"

"About Davey. You did exactly right. Not," Lady Isabel held up her hand to forestall interruption, "not that you asked for my approbation, mind; but I want you to know that I think you did your best with him, and that you have dealt with him most generously."

"I am glad ye think so, Mother. I am sorry I could do no better."

"Well, we shall commend your brother to God's keeping, Harry. Trouble yourself no more on his account." The old woman eyed him keenly. "You do have good men about you, Harry. I am heartened by that, truly. Ingram is as trusty as your own right hand. And this Venetian, why, if he is not the very gift of providence—"

"You like him too, eh, Mother?"

"Like him? Well that's neither here nor there. But yes, I do like him. Very much. At first, I must confess it, I thought him too much the courtier—what with all his bows and flourishes. But in a little time I came to know that he did indeed respect me, and this was but his foreign way of showing it."

"Ah, he is a conqueror of ladies," said Sinclair, with a mock sigh.

"Humph. Well, no one conquers this lady, I assure you. But there's more to Zeno than bows and nosegays, Harry. I smoked that directly. You have in him another doughty ally, and you are fortunate to have him."

"So I myself believe, Mother."

"And Richard, your cousin Jamie's son!" Lady Isabel's eyes sparkled. "He puts me in mind of your father at that age, Harry. Indeed he does. He is a very proper man. I have no doubt you'll find him trusty too."

Sinclair stood and walked about the room. "Mother," he said, "when I think of all the great things that have come to me, chief among 'em all is my people—my mariners, my soldiers, and my friends. If our King Robert were half so blessed, Scotland need never fear for her borders again."

"Ah, but Robert is not Henry Sinclair, my son. There's the key to it. You are made of such stuff as attracts the strong and the true. Robert"—Lady Isabel turned up her palms in a gesture of hopelessness—"he is not of your make and mold, my son. More's the pity for Scotland."

"Well, Mother, I know ye too well to call you flatterer. So I shall take your praise for truth and pray God make it so." Sinclair bent and kissed his mother's cheek. "We are off ere sunrise tomorrow. I hope next spring to bring ye at last to Kirkwall, if God wills it. Meanwhile, do you keep well, and keep me and mine forever in your prayers."

31

Sinclair and his menage wintered over in Kirkwall, the rough gales and swirling snow keeping the household much indoors and close to the hearth. Janet was happy to have it so, and Sinclair himself found more pleasure in his situation than he would have thought likely. It was good to have a sense of home, to pass whole days in indolent ease, to lead his household to mass at St. Magnus of a Lord's Day, to hold wassail within his own stout walls, and to share with his children the Yuletide joy.

But with the coming of Candlemas, longer daylight, and the possibility of yet another spring, the castle, vast as it was, began to seem somehow shrunken, and Sinclair began to think seafaring thoughts again. March came in. And the feathered host of migratory birds came riding down the wet south winds to build again their nests in the breathless heights of the island cliffs. Sinclair felt a kindred restlessness stirring in his breast. He too would be a voyager, adventuring before this same wind over the tirelessly surging sea.

It was on Maundy Thursday—that holy day when all Christendom recalls that Passover when Christ "took the bread . . . blest it . . . and said, 'Take ye all and eat of this, for this is my body . . .' "—that young Sigurd Sigurdsson sought out Sinclair to report the arrival of a messenger from Norway.

"Send him to us," bade Sinclair.

To his pleasure, Sinclair saw Nils Eriksson, who had brought the news of Margaret's being made ruler after her son's death, accompany Sigurd into his chamber.

"Well, sir, we meet again," said Sinclair, his voice warm with welcome. "We trust you will be able to taste our hospitality this time."

"My lord," replied Eriksson, bowing low, "I am flattered to be remembered."

Sinclair smiled. "Why, sir, no one forgets the bearer of good tidings. We trust you come in that capacity again. What's the news from Norway?"

"All's well, my lord. The queen hath proved herself a most sagacious ruler and an able one. Indeed, the ambassadors from Germany call her the Lady King."

"We expected as much," murmured Sinclair. "Queen Margaret is a most uncommon lady. We are glad to know that matters go well for her. For while we doubt not that she would meet any test, we would not wish her reign troubled by those woes that too commonly afflict those whom God hath called to rule."

"Margaret hath her troubles, my lord. But none so grave as to defy resolution. Our trade is still in a state of decline; the Hansa merchants yet dominate the sea lanes; and our people are not so prosperous as in former days. The Mecklenburg pretender and his cohorts did attempt a rising, but he was thoroughly beaten and now contents himself to sulk in Stockholm with his German friends.

"Our most immediate concern now is that band of pirates who style themselves the Victuallers Brotherhood. These scavengers are under the protection of Mecklenburg, and make the cities of Rostock and Wismar their private stronghold. Their chief, a notorious brigand called Claus Stortebecker, plies up and down the length of our coast, raiding at will, and carrying off such plunder as he and his blackguard crews can lay their hands on."

Sinclair nodded. "We have heard much of these sea raiders, and knowing the sad state of Margaret's shipping, we can well imagine how vulnerable are your coastal towns to these lawless adventurers."

"My lord, there is no stopping them," Eriksson replied. "Would to God Margaret had a navy sufficient to her need."

Sinclair's eyes brightened. "Well, Nils Eriksson, perhaps we can ourself be useful. There has lately entered our service a most able Venetian mariner, and he hath shown such marvelous skill in naval matters as to make us believe ourself well able to challenge this Stortebecker and his band."

Eriksson smiled. "When that day comes, my lord, I pray you number me among your crew. But, here, my lord, I was forgetting. This letter comes to you from Margaret's hand."

Sinclair took the parchment, broke the seal and let his eye run swiftly down the lines. "Jesu!" He murmured. Then to Sigurdsson he said, "Find Sir Ingram and bid him come to me at once."

Sigurd bowed low and hurried off.

"Tell me," Sinclair said to Eriksson, "know ye the contents of this writing?"

"I do, my lord. Happily, the queen hath such confidence in me."

"You are honored," murmured Sinclair. His clear eyes took on that distant look common to him when his thoughts went ranging. Eriksson respected the silence, and so they remained, each unspeaking, until Ingram Gunn stepped into the chamber.

"Young Sigurd tells me you sent for me, my lord," said Ingram, formal in the presence of the foreigner.

"Aye. Come in, Sir Ingram. Here's our friend Eriksson come from Norway with news to start us from our winter's lethargy."

Ingram bowed to Eriksson, then said, "What news, my lord?"

"Why, sir, we must to England."

"England!" Gunn's voice rose incredulously. "Afore God, Harry, that's walking into the lion's den."

"Even so," replied Sinclair mildly. "But it is our queen who asks it; how shall we say her nay?"

"But to what purpose?"

"Why, sir, it appears that Richard's minions have agreed to lease three ships to Margaret. And we have been commissioned to go and get them, and sail them safe to Norway."

Ingram let slip a low whistle. "Jesu, Mary, coz. I had rather to Cathay than England."

Sinclair chuckled wryly. "So would we, too, my friend. We cannot think to find a courteous welcome there."

"We will be lucky an we do not find ourselves in gaol," retorted Gunn. "Or worse. We have no friends in England."

"Has any son o' Scotland? But, look you, this scrap of parchment here bears Richard's signature. It guarantees safe-conduct for ourself and a retinue of twenty-four, provided none be presently declared outlaw in England."

"Are we not all outlaws there?"

"If we are not, it is to our shame," replied Sinclair, smiling. "But at least we are not officially declared so, or were not when this was written. What say you, coz, are ye of a mind to go dodging snares wi' us in Richard's realm?"

"God bless me," murmured Gunn. "I think I shall not live to see old age. But 'twould be such sport to see a Sinclair walking freely about on that hostile, bloody ground that 'tis worth even my head to be there."

"With but two dozen men at our back, we shall walk most circumspectly," retorted Sinclair. "God help us, Ingram, but that it offers us opportunity to serve Margaret, this is a most unwelcome business."

"Who shall make up our party?"

"My lord," Eriksson broke in, "may I be counted one?"

Sinclair, who had all but forgot that the youth was in the room, looked up in amused astonishment. "So you would go with us, Nils Eriksson?"

"If you will have me, my lord, I would be most pleased to go."

Sinclair nodded. "Done. And Ingram, let us have Sigurd and my young kinsman Richard too. Zeno we must have, certainly, and his half-dozen mariners. There's the moiety soon told. Do you choose from among our men another dozen seasoned steady souls who can keep both hand and tongue in check whatever the provocation.

"That fellow Bjornsson strikes us as a man fit for this business. Be certain to include him. Indeed, it would be well to choose islanders chiefly. Let you and Richard together with ourself and Clarke suffice for the Scottish contingent. We, please God, will be able to carry ourselves wi' discretion. Any more of us, and the damned Southrons might think themselves invaded and send an army against us."

"Perhaps it would be more prudent for us not to go," suggested Ingram. "Let you charge some trusty man—Zeno, say, or Bjornsson—wi' captaining this embassy, and keep Scots wholly out of it."

"No, sir," replied Sinclair. "We do appreciate the hazard, Ingram, and we thank you for the notion. But Margaret hath asked this of us, and we are named in this safe-conduct. 'Twould go against our inclination and our very nature to bide here in Kirkwall and leave the errand to another. But if you wish to be excused—"

"Not I, my lord," declared Gunn, with some emphasis. "I could not look Janet in the face, an I let ye go off on this wi'out me."

Sinclair grinned. "So ye fear our lady wife more than ye dread the Southron foe, eh, coz? Janet will find that flattering, surely."

Ingram smiled. "Even so, my lord, I am glad 'tis you and not I must tell her of this news. She'll not, I think, take kindly to it."

Ingram proved a true prophet. For when, later that day, Sinclair was closeted with his wife and he told her he was bound for England, that gentle lady flared out at him with some heat.

"To England, Harry? No! Surely not!"

"My love, I must."

"Wherefore?"

"Because the queen bids me."

"Humph!" Janet flounced into a chair and crossed her arms over her breast in an attitude that did not speak of yielding. "This queen, it seems, sets little store by you. Or else you set too great store by her. Either way I do not like it."

"Now, Janet—"

"No, my lord, I do not like it. It is hard enough being wife to a man who is forever running in harm's way, sailing off hither and yon, warring against any number of savage foes, running up and down the world on business for another woman—"

"The queen, Janet, to whom I owe fealty by my sacred oath."

"And what d'you owe me, pray?" Janet sprang from her chair. "Harry, I am your wife and mother to your children. I have borne patiently with your ambitions and, time and again, with your long absence from our bed. I have not complained; I have never sought from you more consideration than you have cared to give. But do not ask me to sit quietly by and give my glad consent whilst you run directly into the enemy camp and risk God He knows what fate all at the whim of some distant royal lady."

Sinclair, amazed, looked at his wife. She seemed to him still the girl he had carried of from Dirleton long ago. And in truth, for all her childbearing, Janet kept her girlish figure still, and her face still bloomed with that rosy glow he'd found so endearing when he was yet a boy at Rosslyn and for the first time felt the promptings of the love that was to be. Now, in her anger, Janet looked even younger. All matronly calm had fled her face, her eyes sparkled with their old fire, and the intervening years were swept away. Why, she had been pretending all along! She had never grown older. She had been only playing at being a lady. She was still his bonny playmate, running hand in hand with him over the rolling lea.

"What are you grinning at, Harry Sinclair?" Janet demanded.

"Why, Janet Halyburton, I am only smiling at you. Come here." Sinclair held out his hands. Janet, with a great show of reluctance, drifted slowly to him, and she suffered herself to be seated on his knees.

"Now then, lass," said Sinclair, imprisoning her in his strong arms, "give over nattering and gi' us a kiss."

"No, Harry. I—" But Janet's protest was silenced by her lover's lips.

"Ah, now. That's more to my liking. Ye've a sweet mouth, Janet. Ye should not use it to abuse your loving husband, not while such kisses are to be had, surely."

"Oh, Harry," said Janet, whimpering a little. "I have been so happy with you here these last few months. I cannot bear to have you go."

"Sweetheart, I told ye long ago that the holding of these isles would often take me from ye. D'ye think me glad to go?"

"Yes!" Janet struggled in vain to free herself. He would not let her go. So she said again, "Yes. I do think you are glad. You are never really happy unless you have some business that calls you away from me. You do not love me, Harry. Truly, you do not."

"Judas!" Sinclair bolted from his chair, and Janet came near to damaging her dignity and more besides on the adamant stone floor. "Not love ye? By heaven, Janet, ye shall not say so!"

Janet, who had managed to keep her feet by dint of a step a rope dancer would envy, retorted, "I did say it. And I do say it. What good's a husband rotting in an English prison? What will become of our children then? Aye, and this child that's even now begun to grow inside me."

"Janet! Ye're no wi' child again?"

"Aye. Again. And I was glad of it, so long as I knew the child would have father and mother too. But now—now—" Here Janet gave in to tears.

Sinclair put his arms around her. "Ah, Janet, Janet, hush. Don't greet. Yer lovely eyes'll go all red. Sh-hh, sh-hh. Dinna fret yerself. There's nothing to fear, I promise ye.

"Look. I've a safe-conduct in Richard's own hand. Surely ye cannot think even a Southron king would go back on such a promise."

"It—it comes strange from you to speak of trusting Southrons," said Janet, sniffling.

"Well, as to that, I would not say I trusted 'em," said Sinclair. "But 'tis a king's word, Janet. He will not break it lightly, nor will we give him any cause to break it."

"You will go carefully?"

"Aye, sweetheart, as if we walked on plovers' eggs." Sinclair smiled and hugged his tearful wife. "And think, Janet, when I return I can tell ye of all the latest fashion, how the ladies dress their hair, and—"

"Ladies! What ladies will you be seeing, pray? I thought 'twas ships you were after."

"Why, so it is ships. But I thought ye'd be curious to hear of how the Southron women adorn themselves, and what the current laws of fashion decree for ladies of high station."

"I will thank you think on ships, husband," replied Janet. " 'Tis ill enough to have a husband subject to another woman's command, without I must bide here and think of him going up and down the streets o' London eyeing the bawds and strumpets in all their fine array."

"Madam," said Sinclair, "do you but accompany me to yonder bed, and I shall give thee that as will set your fears concerning other ladies at rest."

A gleam of mischief showed in Janet's eyes. "Why, sir, I should have thought your Lenten fasting would have left you with but little vigor for such sport."

"Thought you so?" Sinclair favored his wife with the eye of a champion challenged. He lifted her easily into his arms and carried her to the bed. "Now, madam, let us see if this endless diet of salt fish has quite unmanned me."

Later, as they lay together close in their nakedness, Janet pillowed her head upon his breast and, with a little sigh, whispered, "Harry, I do love you."

"Aye, sweetheart. 'Tis knowing that that keeps me young. For loving and being loved are all a man needs to keep the troops o' time at bay."

"Well, we are not really young anymore, Harry."

"Who says so?"

"Count the years."

"Not I."

"D'you mind so much?"

"What?"

"Getting old."

"I am not getting old. No more are you. Or did I only dream that pleasant romp wherein we were so busily engaged but a moment ago?"

Janet smiled a sleepy little smile " 'Twas pleasant, truly."

"Well then?"

Janet stifled a yawn. "Hmm. Oh. I don't know. It—it just seems that we should be more—well, settled, somehow. Truly, Harry d'you not think it is time we took to staying home, time you stayed home and left off this endless roving?"

Sinclair frowned off into the shadows stealing over the chamber floor Then he said, "We will talk of it again when I am home from England.'

32

All London seemed aswarm with life that sweet May morning as Sinclair and his party came riding into the city. People of every station and all descriptions bustled about the narrow streets, bent on business of every kind imaginable. Mendicant friars, whores, hawkers of wares of all kinds, 'prentice boys, messengers, beggars and gentry, soldiers and sailors, nobles on horse, and peasants on foot all vied for passage up and down the clogged arteries of the ancient town.

"Santa Maria!" cried Zeno, as he jogged along at Sinclair's elbow, "the whole world has come to London."

"Aye, it would seem so," replied Sinclair, reining in abruptly to avoid trampling a baker's boy who chose that precise moment to risk his life and his burden of fresh loaves by darting across the cobbled street. " 'Tis well we have the hospitality of the Gray Friars, for I confess I do not know how we would find lodging in this hive."

"Have we much farther to go, my prince?" Zeno inquired.

"Some three short miles, more or less. But if we can make no better progress than this, we may count ourselves in luck to reach the abbey in time for our dinner."

It was, as Sinclair had feared, a slow and exasperating passage. But he and his men at last threaded their way the length of High Street, and found the going easier on the last mile of their journey. Toward noon, they raised the abbey tower, and on the very stroke of twelve, they drew up at the porter's gate.

There a grizzled, stubble-bearded lay brother bade them welcome, summoned the hostler to see to the horses and, with many a bow and beaming gap-toothed smile, led Sinclair and his company in to meet the abbot.

That worthy, who might well have been brother to Friar Tuck, was even then on his way to the refectory when Brother Porter and his charges caught up with him. "Oh, my lord of Orkney," rumbled the abbot, rubbing his hands as if nothing could have given him greater satisfaction than this ill-timed arrival, "welcome, welcome. You and your men are only just in time to partake of our simple fare."

Sinclair bowed. "We trust, Reverend Father, that we do not inconvenience you."

"No, no. Not at all, my lord," replied the abbot, with a wave of his plump hand. "Brother Porter here will just run along and stir up Brother Cook to lay on more food. You and your chief men must sit at my table. For the rest, they may disperse themselves among the brethren, provided they do not tempt them from our rule by offering to share the meat upon their platters."

"We shall so caution them, my lord abbot," said Sinclair, smiling. "We would not have our men be an occasion of sin to yours."

"Ha-ha!" cried the abbot. " 'Tis well said, my lord. Yet I daresay these monkish rogues o' mine know more o' sin than even these lusty men o' thine. A convent's as full of temptations as a court. You would marvel, truly, at the energy the Devil displays in his attempts to upset the order of our lives."

"He is busy everywhere, surely," remarked Sinclair, "but I think nowhere so busy as here in England."

"Spoken like a true Scot!" replied the abbot, chortling. "This must indeed seem alien ground to you."

" 'Tis not a place we'd come to by choice, my lord abbot—meaning no discourtesy to you, of course."

"Of course, of course. Never think it. I am myself by birth an honest Irishman, and while I have been long in England I have managed to control my enthusiasm for the people and the place. But, come, my lord, introduce me to your men, and then let us for God's love go in and dine, for I am growing faint with hunger."

"Why, sir, this is my kinsman, Richard Sinclair, son of the baron of Longformacus; this gentleman is Sir Nicolo Zeno, late of Venice and now admiral of our fleet; Sir Ingram Gunn, our cousin and our good right hand; Sir Nils Eriksson, knight of Norway; my squire, John Clarke. These others are stout islanders from Shetland and Orkney, and mariners who came with Sir Nicolo on his travels to this part o' the world."

"Welcome! Welcome all!" cried the abbot, nodding and waving his hands. "Sir Nicolo, I pray you sit by me at table. We'll talk of Petrarch over the roast meat and Dante over the wine."

Zeno's face lighted up with a radiant smile. "Ah, Reverend Father, you are plainly a man after my own heart. Do you know: *'Pace tranquilla senza affanno—'* "

" *'Simile a quella ch'e nel ciel eterna,'* " quoth the abbot, " *'move da lor inamorato riso.'* "

Zeno clapped hands in delight.

"Ah, 'tis lovely, lovely," said the abbot, with a sigh, leading the way to the refectory. "There is nothing like it ever come from the clerks of this realm, surely. But, be seated, my friends, pray. Fall to. Let us console our bellies with good meat, and afterward our souls with poesy."

The hospitality of the friars proved a great comfort to Sinclair during his brief stay on what was to him uncongenial ground. The abbot and his brethren stinted nothing in seeing to the wants of their guests. And Sinclair, for his part, was content to keep close to the abbey and leave to Zeno the overseeing of the last details of arming Margaret's ships. He found peace within those gray walls, and for the first time in many years, he found himself at leisure, with time to read, to think, to reflect on what had been and plan for what might be.

He found good company in the abbot when he tired of his own society. But, more often than not, Sinclair was satisfied to move to the pace of the liturgical day, and to take his pleasure in books or in solitary walks about the well-kept grounds.

Zeno was in his element. Scarcely a day passed that he did not return with a fresh cargo of gossip from the town, made all the more pungent for his exuberant delight in being the bearer of news.

English women, he declared, were surely among the most beautiful anywhere. Their grace, their style, their elegant manner of dress—was there anything to rival it on earth? "But, my prince," he reported, shaking his head sadly, "their faces are so shaven and plucked as to make them look like so many eggs. In truth, they have no brows! Their foreheads rise like marble domes, and even the backs of their so lovely necks are quite innocent of hair."

"If you do truly love us, Sir Nicolo, say nothing of this to Lady Janet on our return to Kirkwall, or she'll not rest till her own fair face is every bit as eggish."

"Never fear, my prince. When your lovely lady inquires of me concerning the fashion here, I will so contrast the English women with the ladies of Scotland as to make the former seem like ill-made poppets, the latter like creatures from the realm of Faerie."

"Trust you," murmured Sinclair, smiling. "But tell me, are we nearly ready to be off? Poor Ingram counts himself a prisoner here, and we ourself are full eager to put to sea. For all the kindness of our holy host, we are in England, and England is rather more distant from heaven than any Christian soul would care to be."

Zeno flashed his beautiful white teeth in a wide smile. "My prince,

I cannot in prudence debate the point, but surely this green and lovely place hath something of Eden in it this fair evening."

" 'Tis fair enough," allowed Sinclair, surveying the broad sweep of rolling green lawn, the greener still for the silvery shower of that afternoon, "but 'tis home to a cruel and warlike race that time out o' mind hath troubled the peace of my own dear native land."

Zeno shrugged. "War is the natural conditon of man, my prince. But be of cheerful heart. The English workmen show uncommon skill, and they are quick to learn. Inside the week, we shall be ready to sail."

"Good. Let nothing hinder you. You will find us ready to depart the very moment you pronounce the work complete."

There came, however, an unlooked-for delay. For on a warm and drowsy afternoon, while Sinclair, Ingram, Richard, and the abbot were walking together in the orchard, there appeared quite suddenly before them a veritable peacock of a fellow, his hair elaborately pressed and curled, his cote hardie of figured Sicilian silk, his tights parti-colored, his shoes of red-and-white checked leather with toes so long and pointed as to make of mere walking a feat of no small skill.

"By Peter!" murmured Richard Sinclair. "Now there's a pretty man."

"God's truth," growled Ingram. "Mine eyes are dazzled. This is the very flower o' Southron manhood, surely."

The splendid vision drew near and, with many a swirling flourish, inquired, "Your pardons, sirs, but can you tell me where I might find the earl of Orkney?"

"Would to God ye could find him in Orkney," replied Sinclair, sniffing at the cloud of scent surrounding the apparition. "But, as it happens, 'tis he that stands before ye."

"My lord," the dandy said, his voice conveying prayerful awe as he executed yet another bow, so low and so profound as to bring his nose within an inch of grazing the greensward.

Sinclair barely nodded. "Whose man are you? And wherefore have you come?"

"My lord," replied the fellow, with still more obsequious capering, "I am attached to the household of the great Lancaster."

"What? John o' Gaunt?"

"Indeed, my lord, I have that honor. And I—"

"In God's name, man, no more bowing, pray! You make us dizzy."

"My lord is pleased to be witty."

"Why, as to your lord, we can say little beyond that he hath shown some understanding of what it means to be a Scot. As to this lord, we mean not to be playful, sir. We do assure you that these courtly whirlings and twirlings are to us obnoxious. So state your business plainly and with less ado, and we shall be forever grateful."

"As you please, my lord," said the fellow, stiffly. "I came only out of good nature and a kindly concern for one of your company—a chevalier, he styles himself, one Nicolo Zeno."

"Zeno? What's the matter?"

"Why, my lord, there was some matter 'twixt him and a cutpurse—"

"Is Zeno hurt?"

"But slightly, my lord. He bade me most especially to assure you that 'tis no grave matter."

"Where is he? How did ye leave him?"

"I left him talking, my lord, and that volubly. He lies in a house over Aldgate. 'Tis not so far from here. If you like, I'll gladly guide you there."

Sinclair turned to his young kinsman. "Richard, our horses. Yes, Ingram's too. We will ride with this gentleman at once."

In a matter of minutes, the two Sinclairs and Gunn were trotting briskly along behind their courtly guide. Their progress through the town was somewhat eased by the very sultriness of the day. Few were abroad that afternoon, and it was not long before the riders found themselves in Cheap Street; then it was on to Leadenhall, where the great Maypole had not yet been taken down, but towered in its tattered finery above even the tallest building in the row.

"There is the gate," cried their guide. " 'Tis that house, just above the arches, where your friend lies."

"Sir," said Sinclair, gravely, "we are much indebted to you. We confess we did mistake you for something less than what ye are. But you have, by this service, shown us our grave error. If ever we can be of service to you—"

"No, my lord," broke in the courtier, "do not think of it. 'Tis I who am honored to have been of some use to you. And now, adieu. God grant that all will be well with your friend. Farewell."

With that, the fellow turned his horse's head and dashed away.

"Richard, remind me now and again of that man, whenever you hear me pass judgment on a fellow creature. I took him for a fool and worse, yet he hath done me this service, waived our thanks, and is gone before we so much as learned his name."

"Aye, and remind me, too," said Ingram Gunn.

"Kinsmen, I will," replied Richard, smiling. "But ye must do as much for me, for I did wholly share your first opinion of the man."

"Well," said Sinclair, dismounting, "let us go and see to this mad admiral of ours. We pray God he is in no serious way. He is not a man lightly to be spared."

Sinclair led the way up the stairs to the door of the solid stone two-story structure. Before his fist hit the panel, however, the door swung wide to reveal a portly man of middle height, hazel-eyed and ruddy cheeked, with a forked beard but lightly touched with gray. He was garbed like any prosperous burgher, and around his neck was hung a golden chain of no mean worth.

At the sight of his visitors, he bobbed a quick little bow and, in a cheerful voice, inquired, "Are you the lord of Orkney?"

"We are," Sinclair replied. "We were told our friend lies wounded here."

"Come in, come in, my prince," called a merry voice from within. And the stout little householder stood aside to admit the Sinclairs and Gunn.

Immediately on entering, Sinclair spied Zeno. He sat propped up in a chair, several pillows at his back. His shirt was off, and a white linen cloth bound roung his left shoulder made stark contrast with his olive skin. Sinclair hurried to him. "My friend," he said, his voice charged with anxiety, "how goes it with you?"

"Very well, my prince. That spawn of the gutter only scratched me. Had I my wits about me, I would have drawn my sword before approaching him, but I was so angered by the flagrant way the fellow went about his work that I only flung myself upon him and beat him with my fists." Zeno shook his head. "What a country! In Venice, the thieves will at least wait till darkness drapes the veil of decency over their deeds. Why, I remember a time when my brother and I were—"

"Yes, yes. We are sure you do," broke in Sinclair. "But softly, my friend, softly. Ye must not tax your strength. Tell us, how did all this happen? And how came ye here?"

"Ah, is this not a charming house?" Zeno smiled. "What a view from those windows! You can look over the whole city from the west wall there, and from the east, you can see—"

"We can see that we will not ever get a direct answer to our question," interrupted Sinclair, with some asperity. "You, sir, perhaps you will enlighten us?"

The stout burgher, his eyes twinkling with repressed laughter, bowed and said, "I shall try, my lord. This gentleman interrupted a fellow who was intent on relieving me of the considerable weight of gold coin I was carrying. That rogue took the interruption ill, and was so ungracious as to pink your friend with the point of his dirk.

"I then brought my rescuer here, and here you find him quite of a piece and not in the least cast down by this unpleasantness."

Sinclair smiled. "That's plainly told, sir, and plainly seen. We are in your debt."

"No, my lord. 'Tis I who am in debt. This good Venetian spared me a deal of awkward explanations and, what may be worth more, my life."

"Charming! Is he not charming?" cried Zeno, to no one in particular.

"Aye," said Sinclair, dryly. "And you, my friend, are plainly charmed, or else you would even now lie bleeding to death in a London street."

"Pah!" cried Zeno. "The fellow was not up to his work. When he saw the color of my blood, he paled like a moonstruck maiden, clapped his dirty hand over his mouth, and turned and fled like Judas from the temple."

"I do regret, Sir Nicolo, that we could not show you one of our more accomplished rogues," said his host, ironically. "Another time, perhaps. I would not have you leave England with so unfavorable an impression of the quality of our criminals."

"Ha-ha!" Zeno slapped his thigh. "This man, my prince, is he not a jewel among men? Such wit, such spirit! He is charming, charming."

"So you have said," murmured Sinclair. Then he addressed himself to the householder. "Who are you, sir?"

"A servant of the crown," the man replied. "I am comptroller of the Customs and Subsidy of Wools, Skins, and Hides in the Port of London. In short, my lord, I am a wool counter."

"Wool counter!" cried Zeno. "My prince, this man is a poet. Truly. And he hath been sometimes a soldier, and hath gone several times ambassador to Italy and France. Wool counter indeed! Why, he is surely the most learned man in London. Look at his books, my prince. Have you ever seen so many in one house before?"

Sinclair's gaze swept the room. It was, as Zeno said, well filled with books. And if it was not altogether free of dust and spiders' webs, yet it was a very comfortable scholar's chamber, such as might suit any man of letters.

"It seems, sir, that you do give but a very modest account of yourself."

"Why, no, my lord, for I do not count it a mean thing to be wool counter in London. It is the king's business I do, and thereby do I earn for myself a decent livelihood and buy time o' nights to spend among my books."

"Well said, sir, truly. And while we will say nothing of your king or of this kingdom, yet will we acknowledge ourself your debtor for thus tending to our impulsive friend.

"Come, sir, you know our name; what are you called?"

The comptroller's full lips curved into a smile. "My wife calls me one thing, my friends another, my foes another still. But my honest father was pleased to name me Geoffrey, and Geoffrey Chaucer is the name I have carried with me through nearly fifty years on earth."

"Well, Geoffrey Chaucer," said Sinclair, offering his hand, "we are very glad that our friend has saved your gold, and very grateful that you have saved our friend. Should you ever find yourself in Scotland or even in the isles of our domain, do but identify yourself as Geoffrey Chaucer, friend of the Sinclairs, and all doors will open to you."

"My lord, you are very kind," replied Chaucer, with a bow. "If there can be friendship between England and Scotland, let it begin with us here today and flower into fraternal love between the peoples of both realms."

"Sir, we could wish nothing fairer. And though we must presently betake ourself from England, yet will we remember your courtesy and therefore think more kindly of your land hereafter.

"Sir Nicolo, are ye fit to travel?"

"My prince, I am fit for anything," declared Zeno, rising nimbly from his chair. "But surely you will not leave without hearing Master Geoffrey read some of his verses? I tell you, they are fine, my prince. Fine and quite unexpectedly so, for this gentleman indites in the English tongue."

"In the English?" Sinclair's eyes mirrored astonishment.

" 'Tis a whim of mine," said Chaucer, his smile diffident, even apologetic. "But as this gentleman's illustrious countryman, Dante Alighieri, dared to write in the vulgar tongue of his land, so have I ventured to put my poor rhymes in the language of this place."

"Well, Richard," said Sinclair, availing himself of a chair, "and you, Ingram, be seated and let us hear this new thing."

"I am all attention, coz," murmured Gunn, gazing on their host with mild curiosity.

Chaucer, his hands folded on his paunch, smiled benignly on his guests. "How this conceit came into my brain, I know not. But it did occur to me that, as love is the subject of my story, and as St. Valentine is the patron of lovers, it would be fitting to make St. Valentine's Day the setting, as it were, for my story. As ye know, folk long have held that 'tis on this day that all birds of the air choose their mates. So in my poem I have a poor wight wander into a fair garden where all the birds are gathered, and here he listens as the various fowls discourse on the nature of love. There are eagles, ravens, merlins, turtles, geese, ducks, and birds of every kind assembled in what I choose to call in English, 'The Parlement of Foules.' "

"A clever notion," murmured Sinclair, politely, affecting not to see humorous astonishment in his younger kinsman's face. "Read on, Master Geoffrey, pray."

"As the whole is mortal long and your time, my lord, is short, I will but excerpt some lines sufficient to acquaint you with the nature of the work." Chaucer cleared his throat and began:

A garden saw I, ful of blosmy bowes,
Upon a rever, in a grene mede,
Ther as that swetnesse evermore ynow is,
With floures whyte, blew, yelowe, and rede;
And colde welle-stremes, nothing dede,
That swommen ful of smale fisshes lighte,
With finnes rede and scales silver-brighte.

On every bough the briddes herde I singe,
With voys of aungel in hir armonye,
Som beseyd hem hir briddes forth to bringe;
The litel conyes to hir pley gunne hye,
And further al aboute I gan espye

The dredful roo, the buk, the hert and hinde,
Squerels, and bestes smale of gentil kinde.

"It sounds a very fair garden indeed," remarked Ingram Gunn.
"A perfect garden," amended Richard, "such as fowls would choose
for their mating."
Zeno leaned over and said to Sinclair, "Is this not fine, my prince?"
But Sinclair said only, "We want to hear the fowls discourse."
Chaucer nodded, and shuffling his manuscript, he took up his rhymes
farther on:

Nay, God forbede a lover shulde chaunge!
The turtel seyde, and wex for shame al reed;
Thogh that his lady evermore be straunge,
Yet let him serve hir ever, til he be deed;
For sothe, I preyse noght the gooses reed;
For thogh she deyed, I wolde non other make,
I wol ben hires, til that the deth me take.

"Why, well said, turtle," said Sinclair, smiling. " 'Tis a most courtly
and most faithful bird."
Chaucer smiled at this pleasantry. "I find you are not in accord with
our next feathered philosopher. Listen:

Wel bourded! quod the doke, by my hat!
That men shulde alwey loven, causeles,
Who can a reson finde or wit in that?
Daunceth he mury that is mirtheless?
Who shulde recche of that is reccheles?
Ye, quek! yit quod the doke, ful wel and faire,
Ther been mo sterres, God wot, than a paire!"

" 'Quek!' " echoed Ingram Gunn, laughing aloud. "By Peter, the duck
is in the right of it."
"For shame, coz," cried Sinclair. "The honest turtle's the fowl for me.
Yon duck's as false as any fowl can be."
"A rhyme, a rhyme!" cried Zeno, applauding. "Hear that, Master Geof-
frey. My prince is now become a poet, too."
Chaucer smiled. "He hath a proper poet's view of the matter, cer-
tainly. And the tercelet is of one mind with him."
Chaucer read some several verses more, then quite suddenly broke
off and laid his manuscript aside.
Sinclair, caught unaware, leaped to fill the abrupt silence and, more

loudly than was his wont, he declared, "Most unusual, sir, we do confess it. One does not expect to hear the serviceable language of the street employed in the making of verses. We are amazed to find it works so handily."

"Aye," said Richard Sinclair, following his kinsman's lead, " 'tis a new thing surely, and a very nice conceit too, I may say. I very much liked the duck. I agree with Sir Ingram that he sees the matter more plainly than either turtle or falcon."

"But none can love the cuckoo, hey?" Sinclair threw back his head and laughed.

Chaucer's hazel eyes gleamed with sympathetic mirth. "I am glad my poor lines amused you, my lord," he said, with a slight bow.

"Indeed they did, sir. We confess 'twas something strange to our ear at first, but the conceit is good, very good."

" 'Tis better than good," averred Zeno. "My English is very little, to be sure. But no ear could miss the meter, and only a fool could miss the wit. He says here as much about parliaments as about love. I like it hugely."

"You are very kind, Sir Nicolo," murmured Chaucer. "My debts to your Petrarch and your Dante are indeed great. Your approbation eases my mind somewhat concerning them."

"I should have thought your debt was to the French," Zeno remarked.

Chaucer smiled. "You have a keen ear, sir. Yes, I am indebted there also. But my hope is to work my way through to a truly English line. It goes very slowly with me. Too slow. But I have a new conceit forming in my brain, a series of tales in verse told by various folk who find themselves together for a time as they go a pilgrimage to Canterbury. If time is spared to me, I hope to do something wholly English with that. I have got so far as my prologue, and—"

"We would delight in hearing it, Geoffrey Chaucer," said Sinclair, getting to his feet. "But it grows late, and we must get our friend back to the abbey and have his hurt seen to."

"Of course, my lord." Chaucer was now all solicitude. "Forgive me if I have detained you overlong."

"Not at all," replied Sinclair, graciously. "We are most grateful to you, not only for the help you gave our friend, but for your very entertaining verses."

In a flurry of thanks and adieus, the Sinclairs, Zeno, and Gunn took their leave of the poet-comptroller and made their way at an easy pace back to their convent lodging.

"Is not this Geoffrey a most amiable man?" Zeno remarked, as he rode behind his chief.

"Most amiable," agreed Sinclair. "But I am very glad you got no worse hurt in saving his purse for him."

"Pah! 'Twas worth the scratch and more to hear his curious verses."

"Was it so?" Sinclair sniffed skeptically. "Well, my friend, we can be glad that this Geoffrey hath the wool counting to line his pockets with. For as a poet—" The lord of Orkney shook his head.

"You know something of the art, my prince?" Zeno's tone was light, but ever so slightly challenging.

"Why, as much as another man, certainly." Sinclair favored Zeno with an odd questioning glance. "We know enough, Sir Nicolo, to see the folly in trying to bend English into verse. And as to ducks and pilgrims, well, there's no harm in it, and no doubt it serves to keep the man from worse mischief in his idle hours. But your friend Geoffrey had better stick to his countinghouse. We can only hope he proves a better comptroller than he is a poet, else he will lose his seal of office and die a pauper."

33

Hardly had Sinclair and his party returned to Kirkwall, when he announced his plan to sail immediately on to Norway to deliver Margaret's ships. Janet, now far along in her pregnancy, strove valiantly within herself to put down contention and complaint. She knew he would, must go. But it went hard with her to have him forever roving.

"Dear heart," said Sinclair, his voice gentle and low, "I shall not be long away. Let me but turn over these vessels to our friends in Norway and I will hie me straightway home to wait the coming of this child."

But there was another arrival of consequence, even before Sinclair set sail for Bergen. Toward sunset of a day in early August, a galley put in to Sinclair's bay, a boat was lowered, and there came ashore a gentleman most elegantly arrayed. He wore a bright voluminous houppelande, high-collared, with long sleeves, the skirt open from the knees down to reveal hose striped red and yellow. Tippets of silk hung from the sleeves of his cote hardie, and on his head he wore a chaperon in the English mode. He wore his sword in a baldric from which his daggers also hung, and his fingers were bright with the sparkle of many rings.

Richard Sinclair was first to espy this splendid vision, and he lost no time in alerting the house. Sinclair, Ingram Gunn, and Nicolo Zeno hurried with Richard to behold the glorious stranger.

"Afore God," murmured Sinclair, " 'tis such a flower as never bloomed so far north before."

" 'Tis either a great man or a tailor," ventured Gunn. "None other could appear in these parts turned out so fine."

Zeno laughed aloud. " 'Tis no tailor, my friends, nor a great man either. But it is a great man's brother, which is very much the same thing." And he ran off down the beach crying, "Antonio! Antonio! Over here!"

Sinclair turned to Ingram, grinning broadly. "Well, coz," he said, "here comes another Zeno."

"Aye. An he talks like his brother, we are done for."

"An he sails like his brother, we are twice blessed."

The brothers Zeno came hurrying up to Sinclair. "My prince," panted Sir Nicolo, "here is my brother Antonio come from Venice to join your service."

Antonio swept his chaperon from his dark curls and executed a most profound bow. "My prince," said he, in Latin, "I am penetrated with delight; nay, ravished to my soul, to meet at last the illustrious sovereign of these so beautiful isles. Command me, my prince. Antonio Zeno is at your service."

"Well, sir," replied Sinclair, a warm smile lighting his stern countenance, "we are very glad to see you. Your brother has given us such an account of you as to make you more than welcome."

"Ah, so gracious! My prince quite overwhelms me with his courtesy. My brother hath in his letters said you were the very peak of gentleness. 'Tis plain he spoke the truth; no more, no less."

"Your brother is an eloquent man," Sinclair remarked.

"Ah, that comes of being born in Venice, my prince. We Venetians are all of us quite, quite eloquent. Our hearts are very near our lips; 'tis how we are made, my prince. We are poets, all of us."

"We do believe you, sir."

"And now, my prince, you have two Zenos at your command. I know I speak for Nicolo as well as for myself when I say, Ask of us what you will. You will find us ever ready and studious to serve."

"Well, sir, there is a thing we would ask—"

"Ask, my prince. Only ask."

"Hem—where did you, ah, acquire those clothes?"

Antonio Zeno surveyed himself with evident pleasure. "Are they not fine, my prince? Indeed, I feel myself quite princely in them. Our ship, you see, was obliged to stop at London—"

"Ah," said Sinclair, his tone dry as the sand they stood on, "that makes all plain."

"But ye would not call him plain, my lord," Ingram ventured.

"Nay, coz, for that would be plainly false." Sinclair chuckled. "Come, my friends. Let us go in and present this new Zeno to our household. They will be as dazzled as we are, and as glad to see him."

Antonio Zeno was soon proved his brother's equal for charm, enthusiasm, and loquacity. Talk bubbled up out of the man irrepressibly.

Together, he and Nicolo were quite capable of drowning the entire castle in words. But, to Sinclair's pleasure, Antonio was as much the man of action as his brother had proved to be, and when Sinclair broached the subject of sailing to Bergen, Antonio was eager to go along. "For," he said, "I am never really content on land, my prince. Oh, no. I am most happy when I can feel the roll of a good ship under my feet and hear the crack of the sails as the wind fills them with its mighty breath. I care not whether we sail to Norway or to hell, so long as we are sailing."

Sinclair put Antonio in command of one of his own barks, serving as escort; and, midway through August, he set out with Margaret's ships and the main part of his own fleet for Bergen. The weather held for their voyage. The days were long, hazy, and hot—weather breeders, the Shetlander Bjornsson called them—and the convoy made a slow but pleasant passage over the calm sea.

At Bergen, Sinclair and his men found cordial welcome. The English ships drew swarms of folk down to the quay, and all marveled at the trig lines and the menacing bombards. Hale old Ogmund Finnsson, Margaret's wise friend and counselor, declared the vessels to be "the salvation of our coastal towns."

Sinclair was glad of the old man's satisfaction. He bore a great affection for Finnsson, and was ever mindful of his own debt to the aged courtier.

Finnsson told him that Margaret had ordered the hospitality of the castle for Sinclair and his men, and that she had asked most particularly that Sinclair make himself available for an interview at her earliest opportunity.

So it was that, on the second day following his arrival, Sinclair was ushered in to the queen's chamber, where he found Margaret quite alone, seated at a writing table, lost in thought over the documents before her.

Sinclair smiled an inward, rueful smile as he felt again the old familiar stirring of the heart, rather like the throbbing of a wound long healed. Older she may have been, but only the more appealing for her seeming vulnerability under the weight of her greater burden. Had she, he wondered, ever guessed, ever sensed or suspected the turmoil she had wrought in the mind and heart of her premier noble?

Margaret, as if only now aware of his presence, rose to greet him. Sinclair strode forward, knelt, and kissed the white fingers. As he rose, he could not forbear to scan the pale aristocratic face before him. Margaret was lovely still, but there was no mistaking that time, grief, and the cares of state had done their work. Tiny lines showed at the corners of the heavy-lidded eyes, and the fair brow was showing the beginnings of furrows that would be. Margaret looked tired, and her voice, when she bade him welcome, lacked something of its former vibrance.

"We are very glad to see you again, Jarl Sinclair," she said. "Ogmund

Finnsson tells us that our ships are all that we had hoped they would be."

"Indeed, Your Majesty, they are fine. My good friend Zeno had charge of the arming of them, and I am confident that they will give a good account of themselves in Your Majesty's service."

"How fares it with you, my friend?" Margaret's smile, though wan, was genuine. "You appear to be every bit as hearty as when last we saw you."

"I am well, thank you, madam. The isles seem to be in good order, and my loyal Venetian has so masterfully undertaken the managing of my fleet that I count my ships quite the equal of any naval force in this part of the world."

"We have heard much of your Venetian and his brother these two days past," said Margaret. "They are the talk of Bergen."

Sinclair smiled. "They are the talkers of Bergen too, I have no doubt. But it would be easy to mistake them on that account. For all their courtly ways and windy speech, they are most capable navigators and deeply learned in the ways of the sea and ships."

"We hope to talk with them before you leave," Margaret said. "We are much interested in the state of things in Italy, and would be pleased to learn from them how matters stand at Rome."

"They will be delighted to meet with Your Majesty, I can promise you. As to talk," Sinclair laughed, "well, Your Majesty will discover that these Zenos are charged with more words than they can conveniently dispose of."

"How are your family?" inquired Margaret, smiling.

"All thriving, Your Majesty. The children—" Sinclair broke off abruptly, seeing the pain in Margaret's eyes as she thought of her own lost son.

With a visible effort, the queen gathered her inner forces and said, "How many small Sinclairs are there now, my friend?"

"Five, Your Majesty. And shortly we shall have another, God willing."

"God willing," echoed the queen, softly, her gaze turning to some remote horizon within. Then she smiled and said, quite briskly, "Well ours is an enormous family now, including the peoples of Norway, Denmark, and Sweden. You may tell your lady wife she is fortunate in having so few to manage."

Sinclair chuckled. "I assure you, Your Majesty, you would think that few a legion were you ever to be closed up with them on a wet day in Kirkwall. But they are dear—"

"Your Majesty!"

Sinclair and Margaret turned to see Nils Eriksson standing breathless in the doorway.

"What means this intrusion, sir?" demanded the queen.

"Your Majesty, my lord, pardon me. But word has come of a fleet—pirates, Your Majesty—on a course for the Shetlands."

"Jesu, Mary! Who told you of this?" asked Sinclair.

"A German merchant, my lord, but just arrived in port. He swears he barely escaped the rogues himself in the evening's fog, and believes they forebore pursuit only because they mean to raid the isles."

"Jarl Sinclair," said the queen, "stand not on ceremony. You have pressing business. Go to it, with our blessing."

"Your Majesty, farewell. Pray God uphold our cause."

Within the hour, Sinclair had rallied his men on the quay and told them the news.

"Huzza!" cried little John Clarke, tossing his arms in the air and capering like a schoolboy. "A fight, by God!"

"Aye, we can promise ye that, my friend," said Sinclair, grimly. "On board, on board, all of ye. May God send us a wind as will carry us quickly to the foe."

"Amen!" cried Nicolo Zeno, and he clapped his brother on the shoulder. "Did I not promise you great times, Antonio?"

The younger Zeno laughed gaily. "You have kept your promise, brother. Let us show our prince what a pair of Zenos can do."

God sent a wind. Or else the Devil did. For not a day out of port had Sinclair's vessels sailed when the hitherto brazen sky turned on a sudden dark, sullen, ominous. As the first drops fell, the wind rose, lashing the slate-gray sea to roiling foam. Lightning streaked down the murky sky, and almost before the mariners could leap to the lines, their ships were tossing like chips in a maelstrom.

"Now Christ and St. Katherine defend us!" cried Sinclair, "Get the sails down, damn it. Sir Nicolo! Direct the crew!"

Zeno, although he could not hear his orders, was doing his frantic best to save the ship. Screeching at the top of his voice, he ranted, railed, cursed and cajoled as the mariners, in dire peril of their lives, scrambled to haul the canvas down.

"Unlucky, unlucky," muttered Sinclair, as he watched his sails being rent to tatters by the fierce and sharp-fanged wind. The heroic effort of the crew seemed to him pitiful, hopeless. And even as he watched, one man went down hard; then another, and another. He let go his own hold on the rail and lunged into the midst of the struggling men. He managed somehow to clutch the ankles of one fallen mariner even as another went sliding headlong to his death in the frenzied sea.

"Below!" Sinclair roared. "Get below! Save yourselves!"

Few could hear him, but once those few began inching their way to the ladder, the others followed. Sinclair bent and shouted into the ear of the man he held. "Can ye move on your own, man?"

The seaman, his face white with terror, shook his head.

"Come on, then." Sinclair got one of the man's arms around his neck and he crawled with him to the hatchway. Great waves sloshed over them, threatening to sweep them both into eternity, but Sinclair dug in and all but clawed his way across the heaving deck. Friendly hands reached out at the last; strong arms relieved him of his burden; and a cheerful voice cried out, "Well done, coz! Now come in out o' the wet."

Sinclair, his sides heaving, his breath whistling in his nostrils, could only just manage a grin. Ingram, a dark welt showing on his forehead where a splintering spar had caught him a glancing blow, took hold of his kinsman's arm and hauled him through the hatch.

"By God, Harry," cried Gunn, "what would ye not give to be away home in Rosslyn now?"

Sinclair leaned heavily on his friend's shoulder while he struggled to get his breath. Then he gasped, "If—if ever—we see—the blessed place again—I–I'll go down on my knees—and kiss the very earth."

"Well, earth's the right place to be buried, at any rate," returned Ingram, dourly. "Though I don't know but what I might kiss it myself, could I ever set foot on any ground again."

"How—how fare the other ships?"

"Christ, Harry, I've been that busy I've had no time to look."

Sinclair could not help himself. He began to shout with laughter. And a strange sound it was in that place, in that situation. But there was a power in it, a power to put back heart and nerve so nearly lost up there on the pitching deck. The mariners cowering there in the close and stinking hold heard their lord's laughter ring loud and strong through the fetid gloom, and their own laughter welled up in their throats and spilled out in echo of Sinclair's.

"Aye," cried Sinclair, "that's my bonny lads! We'll ask no quarter, not even from yon hurricane. We've a stout ship and a stouter crew, with the finest admiral that ever sailed. We've never lied to ye, men. We'll not lie to ye now. Sir Nicolo's a master mariner if ever there was one, and he will see us through."

In the cheering that attended his bold words, Sinclair heard an ironic voice at his shoulder. "You do me too much honor, my prince. I am overwhelmed."

"We'll all be overwhelmed in another minute," muttered Sinclair. "Have we anything like a chance?"

"I could say better had we a priest among us, my prince."

"How so?"

"Why, those who were shriven would have a chance of heaven. For the rest," Zeno shrugged eloquently, "there is no chance outside Christ's mercy."

"Would to God it were not so dark," growled Sinclair. "We have no way of knowing how it fares with the others."

"What is there to know, my prince? We are all of us riding in our coffins. Night is coming on. If this storm doth not abate, and that shortly, the morning will find none of us alive."

"Sir Nicolo, we must pray. Bid the men all to beseech our Lord and His saints to spare us. Let no man leave off praying while this tempest rages."

Zeno laughed. "Our blessed Savior will be pleased to hear from this lot. It hath been so long since last He heard from most of them, He no doubt thought them long since dead and burning."

"Well, then, my friend, let us hope that our Lord will be so pleased that He will incline to spare us yet awhile. Go and bid the fellows pray."

34

If any slept through that long and dreadful night, it must have been an uncommonly devout and trusting soul. For the rest, bruised, drenched, sick, and thoroughly afraid, there was nothing for it but to try to secure a hold on something and hang on—despite the stench, despite the groans, despite one's own hurts and one's own guts heaving.

Sinclair somehow kept moving among the men, touching a shoulder here, a hand there, speaking some word to hearten and sustain. The swinging lantern gave but a feeble light, and the wild pitch and roll of the frail bark made Sinclair's going difficult in the extreme. More than once he went crashing against the oaken walls; and once, as he reached out to save himself, the man's whole weight came down on his left hand, his wrist bent back, and a searing, sickening pain shot the whole length of his arm. How he kept from crying out, he could not tell. But he knew he must not. His eyes teared, and he felt his knees buckle under him, but he would not, could not go down.

"How goes it, Richard?" he said, recognizing his young kinsman in the wavering yellow light.

Richard Sinclair looked up at his father's cousin with earnest eyes. "How does it go with you, my lord?"

Sinclair essayed a sickly smile. "There have been better nights, Richard, but few spent in better company."

"Does Sir Nicolo offer any hope?"

"Ah, God bless ye, boy, Zeno's all right. He will sail us through this—aye, and worse, too, if need be. Tell me, are ye afraid, Richard?"

"Aye, a little."

"Good. I've no use for a man who does not know fear. It's how he deals wi' his fear that tells me the kind o' man he is."

"Are you afraid, my lord?"

"An I were not I'd be a by-Our-Lady lunatic." Sinclair managed a laugh in spite of his pain. "Many a stout man here's beshit himself tonight, I warrant ye. Aye, and no disgrace in that either. Ye cannot judge a man's heart by his bowels."

Richard began to giggle. "N–nor his bladder neither, I hope."

"Ha-ha! What's a little more wet in this place, hey? Ah, Richard, Richard, ye're your father's son and no mistake. He'd be main proud o' ye."

In the last long watch of that night of terror, Zeno found his way to Sinclair. "My prince," he said, "the wind's abating."

"Now God and St. Katherine be praised," murmured Sinclair. "We thought the ship was pitching less, but did fear to trust to our landsman's judgment."

" 'Tis no mistake, my prince. The storm is moving off. God is surely with us."

"Men!" cried Sinclair, in a voice that rang through the reeking hold. "Take heart! The gale's a-dying! Sir Nicolo says the storm's nigh over."

A feeble cheer went up and died raggedly away.

"Now hear me. We've some hours yet afore the first light. And what we shall have to deal with then, no man can say. So rest, we charge you. Sleep if ye can. But each man o' ye, before he shuts his eyes, will say his thanks to God and the Virgin for sparing us this night."

Sinclair bade Zeno come with him, and he led the way to the cramped cabin aft. "My friend," he said, when they were out of earshot, "you have once more proved your worth. We are more than ever in your debt."

Zeno, his eyes dark-ringed and reddened, his ringlets straggling every way, his clothes ruined with their salt drenching, massaged his aching temples and said, "Dawn will show us how much or how little we have to be thankful for, my prince. If we have lost no ships this night, then you may proclaim to the world that miracles happen still."

Sinclair nodded, his face grim and gray. "In truth, my friend, we were so glad at being spared ourself that we had almost forgot our comrades. And they had no Sir Nicolo to steer them through this horrible night."

"One other ship had a Zeno, for what that may be worth, my prince. In this circumstance, 'tis luck more than skill that brings a vessel through."

"Whether 'tis skill or luck or both, we are alive. Let that content us for this hour at least. D'ye think ye could sleep?"

"On a pile of anchor chains, verily."

"Then avail yourself of this cabin and take what rest ye can. Come morning, we'll have work aplenty." As he was speaking, Sinclair was caught off balance by an unexpected roll and, seeking to catch himself, unthinkingly reached for a brace with his left hand. "Christ's wounds!"

"My prince, what's the matter?" Zeno, weary as he was, leaped to Sinclair's side.

"Ah, God, 'tis my wrist, Sir Nicolo. It's gone and broke itself, seems likely. By Corpus, but it hurts."

"Let me fetch old Matteo, my armorer. He's a gift for setting bones."

"Fetch him, then," said Sinclair, his face gone fish-belly white. "But see you blab nothing o' this to the men. They must not think us more injured than we are."

In a trice, Zeno returned with the grizzled Matteo. The latter had but little English, but even that little he did not need. When Sinclair held out his arm, the old mariner, with a gentleness that belied the horn and callous of his hands, explored the hurt with light, deft fingers. He turned to Zeno and nodded. The bone was broken.

Matteo beckoned Sinclair to the cot and motioned him to seat himself on the deck with arm outstretched on the coarse blanket. With an apologetic look in his warm hound's eyes, Matteo nodded encouragement to his patient; then, with a merciful swiftness, he snapped the bone into its proper place and, with a bit of lath for a splint, he bound up the break full snugly with strips of unbleached linen.

Sinclair, his white face clammy with cold sweat, did not attempt to rise at once. But he did force himself to extend his right hand to Matteo. "Tell him," he said to Zeno, "tell him he has our thanks and—here, take the dagger from my belt and give it to him. Tell him it is a gift from the lord of Orkney to a good and faithful friend."

Zeno translated for Matteo, and the old armorer, his face aglow with pride and embarrassment, stepped forward and, bowing low, kissed Sinclair's right hand. Then, at a sign from Zeno, he backed his way out of the cabin and returned to his mates.

"Your friend works swiftly," Sinclair muttered. "He seems an able man."

"And so he is, my prince. Most able. But here, let me assist you into the bed."

Sinclair made a feeble protest, but Zeno affected not to hear and, quite tenderly, tucked his prince in. Then he himself lay down on the bare boards and, for an hour, slept.

With the first light, Zeno dragged himself up on deck; and Sinclair, who had slept not at all for the pain in his arm, came with him. Two, three, four more or less whole ships they saw, spread wide over the glassy sea. And four were nowhere to be seen.

"Now Jesu help us," groaned Sinclair. "Have we lost so much?"

"Jesu be thanked that we have saved so much, my prince. A storm like that—" Zeno shrugged. "We could all be feeding the little fishes now. Besides, who knows? The others may turn up. The sea is very wide, my prince, and the storm was very strong."

"God grant ye are right, my friend. But here is my kinsman. Sir Ingram, what news?"

Gunn, looking much the worse for the night's adventure, came weaving up to the poop. "Christ, Harry," he muttered, looking dazedly at their sister ships, "where are the others?"

"We do not know, coz. Sir Nicolo thinks some may have been blown over the horizon and will yet come limping in to a rendezvous. But we cannot blink it; some must surely have gone down."

Gunn rubbed his forehead, then pinched the bridge of his nose, as if he would by this means clear his brain. Then he said, "Our own seams have opened, Harry. We're taking water."

"How bad?"

Gunn shrugged. "The joiner says there's nowt to fear. He has every available man armed with mallet and chisel and caulking away. 'Twould do your heart good to see John Clarke sweating down there. He's mad clean through at having to take orders from a Venetian, but I told him that if he meant ever to romp with his Kit again, he'd better close his mouth and ply his mallet."

"Well said," said Sinclair. "And Richard?"

"He's tapping to. They all are. It's—Harry, your arm! Are ye hurt?"

"Not so much. My by-Our-Lady wrist's snapped, is all. Matteo set the bone for me, and—look! Nicolo! Is that not a sail?"

The three men leaned over the rail, straining their eyes against the hazy sunlight. A speck, something, appeared to be moving toward them, growing larger as it came. At last Zeno cried, "It is, my prince. 'Tis one of our own!"

"Now God be thanked," murmured Sinclair. "Sir Nicolo, signal the others. We will ride here at anchor till midday in hopes some others of our missing friends appear. If they show not by then, we'll risk no more to these weakened walls of oak, but set our course for Bres in the Shetlands. There we will take stock of our situation and determine our future course.

"One thing is sure: If those pirates were caught out in this as we were, our isles are safe from them today."

An hour passed; another. The straggler bark moved in, nearer and nearer to the other survivors. From those mariners on deck, there came a welcoming cheer as the prodigal came in. And Zeno, who all the morning had run hither and yon about his own ship, directing the work and setting things right, now came to the rail and stood alongside his lord. Silently, Sinclair and Zeno watched until the men aboard the straggler could be distinctly seen. Then Zeno, tears streaming down his face, whispered, " 'Tis he. My brother." Then he waved his arm and shouted lustily, "Antonio! Antonio!"

From across the calm waters there came an answering halloa, and a figure on the forward deck was seen to wave.

"Deo gratias," Zeno all but sobbed. "Deo gratias."

And Sinclair, heartsick and ashamed at the sudden realization that he had not given a thought to the weary Nicolo's private fears, had to turn away.

Slowly the morning passed. Zeno, having seen his brother alive and apparently unhurt, went cheerfully about the ship overseeing such repairs as could be improvised. Somehow the men managed to piece together a sail. And, with the seams well caulked and the cordage unsnarled as best it could be, Sinclair's ship was ready once more to run—or at least limp—before the wind.

At noon, Zeno went to Sinclair where he stood still gazing out to sea, scanning the glinting gray-green expanse for a sight of what he was destined not to see. "My prince," said Zeno, softly. " 'Tis noon."

Sinclair squinted up at the sun, then looked at Zeno and read the truth in those dark eyes. He crossed himself and murmured, *"Requiescant in pace."*

"Amen," Zeno said. "Shall I give the order to sail, my prince?"

Sinclair looked at Zeno. The Venetian's face was drawn, pallid, mirroring the exhaustion brought on by frantic labors, fear, and lack of sleep. The man's right eyelid was twitching spasmodically, and his hands trembled even in repose. He looked thoroughly done up. And yet, something of that nervous energy still shone in the tired eyes, lent still some strength to the hoarse and breaking voice.

"Give the order, Sir Nicolo," said Sinclair, his own voice hollow, lifeless. "We must make land. Then we shall rest."

Sympathy shone in Zeno's eyes. For all his own weariness, he knew something of the heavier burden borne by his chief, and he was sorry that he himself could not shoulder more. He pressed Sinclair's hand and said, "All will be well, my prince."

"God grant it."

Zeno turned then and rasped out the order. Sinclair heard the creaking of the blocks as the halyards were hauled through, heard the snap of the bellying patched canvas, and felt the ship spring to life beneath his feet. But there was for him no joy in it. Their bold venture had ended in ruin and death. He could not respond to the sweet breeze and blown spray. A piece of him lay forever buried with his lost ships and his lost men in the cold depths of the eternal sea.

When the surviving fleet made anchor at Bres, Sinclair ordered all ashore; and the men, grateful for the solid earth under their shoes, disposed themselves about the sun-warmed sands and heard their lord unfold his plan.

"My friends," Sinclair began, "know that you have by your courage and your skill won forever a secure and lofty place in our grateful heart. You are such men as kings would yearn to lead, and we count ourself favored of God to have you in our service.

"For our brothers that were lost, we can do no more than mourn and pray. But we will make most generous provision for their widows and their children, and while we live we shall not cease to honor and bless the memory of the fathers, husbands, friends who sailed with us on this enterprise."

Sinclair paused for a moment and scanned the faces around him—young Richard; the Zenos; John Clarke, lying prone upon his belly with his ageless cherub's face cupped in his hands; Ingram, on his feet, as if in defiance of his own body's demand for rest; Bjornsson the Shetlander; Matteo, the armorer; and all the bonny Scots, islanders, and Venetians that were left of Sinclair's band. The island lord's heart yearned over these hardy men, and felt again the old wonder that these should so freely follow him.

"We are grievously hurt by this misadventure," Sinclair resumed. "Our fleet, which is our bulwark 'gainst the invaders and our chiefest strength next only to yourselves, is so reduced and so crippled that we have now no choice but to begin immediately rebuilding.

"Yet, because we believe that what those pirates once attempted they will attempt again, we dare not leave these islands undefended. Our stronghold at Kirkwall is our assurance of safety for the Orkneys, but these Shetlands lie open and vulnerable to any bold enough to sail against them. It is our purpose, therefore, to fortify this place, to erect here a stout defense with men and bombards sufficient to ward off any attempt on these our lands.

"Our friend, Sir Nicolo, we will ask to oversee the building of the fort, and we will spare to his use the moiety of our fleet's bombards."

"My prince!" Nicolo Zeno stepped forward.

"Sir Nicolo?"

"My prince, you know that I would gladly undertake any task you see fit to assign to me. But you will need me to guide the remnant of your fleet safely back to Kirkwall."

"Ye forget, my friend, we have another Zeno."

At this, a chuckle rippled through the ranks of the weary men. Sinclair himself smiled, then he said, "Sir Nicolo, we would have you take up this work. You have more knowledge of armament than any other here. Moreover, it concerns us greatly that you have been put to such exertion these last days. Do you but bide here and see the work done. We promise you that you shall have more seamanlike occupation once we have rebuilt our fleet."

"My prince, I will do as you ask."

"Good, then. Tell off such numbers of men as you will require, and take for your own purpose whichever bark you deem to be most sea worthy.

"For the rest, we shall—with Messer Antonio's help—make for Kirk wall, and thence to my lands in Scotland, where we shall make repairs and build such new vessels as are required to replace those that we have lost.

"When winter is past, and we are again strong in ships and in our own sore-tried spirits, we will make here a rendezvous to take up again the work we must perforce leave now unfinished.

"For this night, we will ask our kinsman Richard to go on ahead and inform the best men of our presence here. We will quarter on the folk and recruit our strength for the work ahead. If need be, we will tarry here a day, or even two or three. For we are ourself main weary, and we are mindful of your own sore need of rest.

"Richard, go now and summon the best men. And you, my good friends, summon up your courage to endure this unhappy while. Be not dismayed, though God He knows we have good reason. Yet we will be strong again, and we will yet know happy times.

"And we shall yet have some good work to do."

35

The sight of the crippled fleet laboring into the bay brought Kirkwall folk of all degrees down to the beach in wonder and dismay. These were a people wise in the ways of the sea and ships, and there was among them a common uneasiness at the slow, erratic approach of the battered vessels. And the disparity of numbers, between ships that had set out and ships that were now returning, did not go unremarked.

"God grant no eager fool go running off to Janet now," muttered Sinclair, as he stood with Ingram watching the landscape sharpen in color and detail as their bark neared shore. "She is too near her time for to have such news brought in all hot and smoking in the mouth of some Job's comforter."

"Maybe curiosity will detain the bearers of ill tidings," Ingram said.

Sinclair's lips curled in a wry smile. "What, and lose the chance of being first? Coz, you know not the ways of the newsmongers. Look! God damn the luck! See yon long-shanked fellow legging it for the castle? In another minute the whole house will be roused, and Janet and the children will be greeting and wailing as though the Day o' Judgment were at hand."

"Ye could not hope to keep it from 'em, coz."

"Wherefore d'ye think we touched here ere going on to Scotland? But I had hoped to tell my own story in my own way." Sinclair smote his thigh with the flat of his hand. Then he said, "Look you, Ingram. When we make the beach, I'd have ye talk wi' the people. I'll say summat

272

touching the events of the past few days, then tell 'em that you will sketch in the fine points.

"Convey our sympathy to the widowed and orphaned, and assure 'em of our purpose toward them. Ye may tell 'em we'll have masses sung for all the dead, and that we ourself will see to the maintenance of every family as has lost a husband or a father. You know what to say."

"Aye. But, pardon me, coz, I think it's you must say it."

Sinclair turned to his kinsman with a questioning glance. "Do ye?"

"Aye. Look you, Harry. These people are your family too. God He knows Janet will be sore troubled, but she must realize ye have a father's duty to these folk. And, if you will suffer me to play the wise gray counselor, coz, I think it's you must talk to 'em, not I."

Sinclair gazed long into his friend's eyes. Then he said, "Thank you, Ingram. I will."

When the pulling boats grated in through the shallows and nosed up onto the beach, the Orkney folk milled about wide-eyed and murmuring. But Sinclair took a stand in the prow of his boat and, raising his uninjured arm, silenced his people and said, "My friends, we have, as ye see, encountered some misfortune. A storm caught us off the Shetlands and robbed us of both ships and men."

At this, a great buzzing ran through the throng.

"Pax!" cried Ingram. "Let your lord be heard!"

"It grieves us to report that some brave Kirkwall men were lost. But we will not delay in naming them, for we would not have ye kept on tenterhooks. Sir Ingram, read the roster."

Gunn, in a loud clear voice, read off the names of the dead, his reading punctuated by shrieks and cries at every name. And every cry tore like hot pincers at Sinclair's already ragged nerves. He did not flinch, turned only a little paler, though inwardly he ached for the wrenching of his heart.

And even when he saw Janet and his children drawing near, for the news had indeed run on before him to his hall, his gaze wavered not, nor did he utter a word until the doleful litany was done.

Then he said, "My dear people, ye will not find us wanting in your hour of most need. We have ordered that masses be sung for our lost friends, and we will not fail in our fatherly duty to each household that finds itself bereft. These brave men perished in our cause, and we are mindful of our duty to those they leave behind."

"God bless Jarl Sinclair!" cried a woman in the crowd. And others echoed her cry.

Sinclair winced as if he had been struck, and his eyes stung with tears he could not shed. "God bless all of you," he managed to say. "We—we ask that you keep us in your prayers as we do you in ours.

"Our kinsman, Sir Ingram, will see to the needs of the bereaved families. He has full authority in this, to be as it were our very hand in distributing such monies as are needful to maintain each household until the eldest son is grown and ready to play a man's part. If the sons prove worthy of their fathers, they shall not want for employment while a Sinclair rules in Orkney."

Sinclair turned to Ingram. "I can say no more. Busy yourself among them; take down the numbers and condition of each family and see to it that none is in present want. As for the future, well, we can only see to it that none loses more than has been lost already."

"I'll see to it," Ingram said. Then he called to the people, "Make way for Jarl Sinclair! Make way!"

Sinclair passed among the folk, looking neither to left nor right, for he had no need of their sympathy and could not trust himself to show his own for them.

When he reached the spot where Janet stood, their children clustered around her, he halted and said, " 'Twas not fit ye should run down to the beach, sweetheart."

Janet, her face white and strained, her great eyes dark with anxiety and grief, had not expected this. Stung by her husband's words, she said, "Is this your greeting to me, then?"

"When we are alone within our walls, then will I greet ye as I meant to," replied Sinclair, mildly, his good hand straying to Beatrix's sunny curls. "Unhappily, it seems someone could not bear to keep ye waiting for news I meant to bring to you myself; and, unhappily, ye could not keep within to spare yourself this—this misery."

"I am your wife, Harry," Janet whispered.

"Aye, and I thank God for it. But I had rather ye did not run out among the folk all distressed at the first hint o' trouble."

"Pardon me, my lord. If being Lady Sinclair means I am to forgo my woman's nature and deny my woman's heart, then it had been better for me to wed with one of the common men."

"Too late," replied Sinclair, ironically. "There be a deal fewer men to choose from now. Come, Janet, no more o' this. Let us go into our own house. I am weary and sore and of no mind to talk now."

Nor did he talk again with Janet until afternoon of the next day. His tired body demanded sleep, and it could not be denied. Late that following morning, Sinclair woke, aching in every muscle. But after a hot bath and a good bit of beef washed down with brown ale, he began to feel somewhat recovered. He met with Ingram briefly to learn how the folk had received him and what provision would be required; then, satisfied that what could be done had been done, he sent for Janet to join him in his chamber.

"My dear," he said, rising as Janet entered, "how glad I am to see ye."

"You were not so glad this time yesterday," remarked Janet, her voice cool and distant.

Sinclair's own voice sharpened. "We can, if ye choose, fence wi' each other over this. For my part, I lack stomach for it. My concern was that ye be not frightened or disturbed."

"Your concern is to your credit, my lord. But I think I could credit it the more had you not gone off on such a risky business—"

"It was my business, Janet."

"Not so! 'Twas hers." Spots of color showed in the pale cheeks.

"Margaret's?"

"Aye, if you are pleased to call her Margaret. Why should you be at her beck and call, pray? You have matters enough to attend to here and in Scotland without abandoning your family at the whim of this—this foreign woman."

"She is the queen, Janet. I hold these lands in fealty to her."

"And what of your fealty to me?"

"Do ye ever doubt it?"

"Yes! Yes, I do." Janet's tiny fists clenched and her eyes darted fire. "Look at me—fat, ugly, old; fit only for getting children on. And in a little while I shall not be fit for even that. Why should you stay here with me? What man would not go off right eagerly to serve another woman, particularly so handsome a one as—"

"Woman!" roared Sinclair, "Hold your tongue!"

Janet, stunned, stared wide-eyed at her husband.

"Now, then, madam," said Sinclair, his voice glacial, "I'll thank ye to mind your house and leave the minding o' this earldom to me. I believe I know my several duties, and I believe I do as well as any man in my effort to fulfill them all.

"Margaret is my liege here, even as Robert's my liege in Scotland. You, lady, are my wife, whether here or in Scotland or any other where. And I do love you, honor my vows, and keep faithful.

"Ye're neither old nor ugly. As to that other matter, 'twill resolve itself in due course.

"Finally, as to my choice of biding or going, I have none. God He knows how often I dream o' Rosslyn. And He knows too how it would please me to have whole days and weeks together to spend with you and with our children. But I am not one o' those who can ask others to take my risks for me while I toast my backside by the fire safe at home.

"I mean to hand on this title and these isles secure and strong. My sons shall have the possessing of them in leisure and at peace, or so I pray, and to that end I labor. If this causes you some pain, I am main sorry for it. But know that it pains me also.

"Even so, I'll do what must be done. I cannot change, Janet. Not at this late hour. I must do as I see fit, according to the light God gives me." Sinclair's face softened, and he held out his uninjured hand to Janet. "Never doubt I love ye, lass. Come, gi' us a kiss and let's be friends again."

Janet took his hand in both of hers and pressed it to her cheek. "My love," she murmured, "pardon me. I—I am grown so whimsical of late that I scarce know my own mind. But when I heard the ships were lost, my heart went cold, and I feared—oh, I feared so that you were lost with them. And I could not bear that. Truly, I could not."

"God bless you, sweetheart," Sinclair said, holding her close and stroking her soft hair. "Had I the ordering o' this world, I'd make it law that those who love should die together. I would not go first and leave ye to weep for me, yet I would not for anything in heaven or on earth have ye go before me."

"Ah, talk no more of dying, love." Janet leaned her head upon his breast. "Please God, we shall yet have time together."

"I am certain of it," Sinclair said, and he bent his head and kissed her. "But when that time will be, I cannot say. I must to Scotland, ye know that."

"Aye." Janet nodded. "And I know I must not try to persuade you to send Ingram or Antonio Zeno in your stead."

"Thank ye for that, Janet. 'Tis painful enough to have to absent myself again so soon without having to be harsh with ye on that account." Sinclair encircled his wife's waist with his right arm and walked with her about the room. "It is very important that these men see me as a sharer in the common weal and woe. I cannot in conscience bid them sail into danger, nor can I ask them to mend what's broken, if I will not myself be one with them. I think it is important too that they all understand that we are not undone by this misfortune; that my purpose is not altered; no, nor my courage either. By the Mass, we'll have our men proud to follow us, or we will yield the coronet to another."

"Were I a man, I should be very proud to follow you, Harry."

Sinclair grinned. "Were ye a man and in your condition, ye'd confound the faculty at Paris."

"Do not mock me, sir," said Janet, primly. "I meant to pay you a compliment."

"And I am grateful for it. I want to be a good master, Janet, a true chief, and an honest lord."

"Are you not these things already?"

Sinclair shook his head. "I do not know. I'm as full o' flaws as any other man, I suppose. I know I am often impatient, angry, too proud by far, and very much inclined to put ambition ahead o' Christian duty." He forced a little laugh. "I fear I shall be a long, long while in purgatory ere all my faults are burnt away."

"Not so! You are a good man, Harry; a very good man, generous, patient, and kind. When the time comes, thy soul shall fly straightway to heaven and Christ shall give thee angel ships to sail across a sea of stars."

Sinclair laughed and embraced his wife. "That will do fine till thou'rt come, lass. Then will I be content to give over roving and sit beside ye, forever young under trees forever green, talking our eternity away under smiling cloudless skies."

"Then I shall die quite happy," Janet said.

"When the time comes. Meanwhile, live, I pray you. And bear this child. Think on me while I'm away, and know that however glad I shall be to be again at Rosslyn, I cannot be happy apart from you."

But, despite his very real reluctance to be off, Sinclair hastened the preparations for his departure. September was far gone, and soon it would be cold. He would not delay an hour longer than necessary.

Antonio Zeno and Ingram bore the main burden of Sinclair's impatience, but they had the willing hands and loyal hearts of their surviving shipmates to aid them. All, it seemed, were anxious to set the fleet right again and to prove themselves undaunted by their earlier misfortune.

With cordage and sails replaced and hulls well mended, stores of food and water were got in. By 27 September all was ready.

"We sail tomorrow, then," Sinclair said, when Ingram reported the preparations done. "God, it will be good to be going south again."

Ingram smiled. "After this week's work, I am glad to be going anywhere."

Sinclair eyed his cousin. "You are weary?"

"Harry, this is no boy's body anymore," replied Ingram, with a rueful rubbing of his neck. "Ye drove us main hard, coz. And I for one am heartily glad the work is done."

"An I did not need ye, Ingram, I'd bid ye stay in Kirkwall."

"What? And miss my chance to see Scotland again? Not if ye love me, Harry. Do not think it."

Sinclair grinned. "I meant only to show some tender feeling for old bones, coz."

"A bit late for that, thank ye. No, Harry. I've helped to bake this cake. I mean to have the eating of it, too."

Sinclair took Ingram by the arm and walked with him along the windswept beach. "Ingram, Ingram, I cannot imagine going anywhere without ye. But, in truth, I am concerned that ye not overtax your strength. These last days have been arduous ones for you and for us all. And if I thought ye'd truly rest here, I would forgo my own desire and order ye to remain."

"Christ's wounds, coz! 'Tis Janet who's with child, not I. Would ye coddle me like a wee puling babe?"

"No, sir," replied Sinclair, with some warmth. "But I would have ye strong and hearty against our next adventure off these coasts. Wherefore d'ye think I bade Sir Nicolo remain in Shetland, hey? D'ye think I would not have him wi' us in Rosslyn if I could? God He knows Antonio's a great man to have about a ship, but Sir Nicolo's a master."

"Why did ye leave him, Harry?"

"Because the man was used up, coz. He was that worn out that I feared for his health. And ye know that if he were here, nothing would keep him from overseeing all of this business, even to the last plank and the last peg. He'd be no good to me dead in Scotland, Ingram. I need him alive and well, and so I gave him charge over Bres. We can find him there when we need him."

Gunn shook his head. "Ye're a provident man, Harry. I do confess your calculations outrun me by many a league."

"Why, there's nothing wonderful in it, coz. Sir Nicolo's an important man. I value him. Even if I did not like him—which, as ye know, I do, and that hugely—I need him. And I also need a fort at Bres. The work will keep him occupied; he will not feel that he has been invalided out of my service; and when we return, why, he shall be well and fit to sail once more."

"God willing," murmured Gunn. "But how is it that ye suffered me to come on to Kirkwall and endure all this labor afore ye came to think on my well-being, hey?"

"Because, sir, I thought a Highland Scot tougher than a Venetian." Mischief shone in Sinclair's eyes. "But now that I have considered the matter ripely, methinks ye should bide here after all. There will be a deal o' work about the castle, what with a new baby and all. Perhaps I can apprentice ye to the midwife. 'Tis a high calling, and one that may earn your bread for ye when your frail health fails."

Ingram glowered at his friend. "In another minute, my lord, I may forget myself and challenge ye to wrestle me right here on the beach. We'll see then who's hale and who is not."

"Alas, coz!" replied Sinclair, sweetly. "I wish I could oblige ye, but—" And here he waved his wrapped wrist before Ingram's eyes.

"We are both old cripples, the pair of us," growled Ingram. "So we'll go on to Scotland as best we can, holding each other up along the way."

36

To be at Rosslyn again was for Sinclair a quiet, holy joy. Tears started in his eyes as he and his band clattered onto the bridge that spanned the Esk, and saw the towers of Rosslyn rise against a backdrop of yellow autumn leaves. He could not help it. He gave spur to his horse and outdistanced his followers by full fifty yards and more.

First to greet him was his brother John. Evidently well content in his marriage, John Sinclair had grown a bit stouter since last his brother had seen him—a bit stouter, a bit grayer, but still fit and ready to ride to the hunt, or to romp with his boys or to answer a call to arms if need be.

"God bless me, Johnny," cried Sinclair, swinging down from his mount. "God bless me, but it's good to see ye."

Sir John embraced his brother. "Ye've been long away, Harry."

"Aye, and will be away again soon, God willing."

"What? So eager to be off?"

"No, sir. Far from that. But we've had a run o' bad luck, Johnny. I mean to get things right again, and that quickly. How fares our mother? And Inge and the children?"

"Well, all well, God be thanked."

"And Davey?"

"We seldom see him, Harry. He seems content to stay in Aberdeen."

"Ah." Sinclair's eyes clouded, remembering. Then his face brightened.

"Why stand we here nattering like a pair o' old crones? Here's Ingram, come with our kinsman Richard and the brother of Nicolo Zeno."

"Welcome! Welcome all!" cried John Sinclair. "Ingram, I am very glad to see you. And Richard! Ye've grown a man, truly. I'd not like to wrestle with ye now, my lad. I fear I'd take a drubbing for my pains."

"And you, sir, are most heartily welcome." He shook Antonio Zeno's hand. "I have met your brother, and I admire him extravagantly."

"Then, Sir John, I hope this brother finds favor with you also," murmured Antonio, bowing.

"Never doubt it, my friend. You and I are blessed in our brothers, and we shall be ourselves as brothers for our brothers' sakes."

Antonio beamed. "Charming! You Sinclairs are surely the very flower of courtesy and politesse."

"Come, all of ye, into the house. I'll have your horses seen to directly." John Sinclair, arm in arm with Antonio Zeno, led the way into the great hall.

There, Lady Isabel came forward to embrace her firstborn and to weep on his neck for joy. "Harry, Harry, I am so glad to have you home again."

Sinclair kissed her and said, "Mother, it is good to be here. And that good is all the greater for seeing you so well."

The old woman's eyes sparkled. "I am never ill, my son. God is good. But tell me, How are Janet and the children?"

"Well, Mother, thank you. By now there is another child, very likely. 'Tis well we built so grand at Kirkwall, else I'd be hard put to house them all."

"Will you be here long, Harry?"

Sinclair shrugged. "That will depend on how the work goes. We've got ships to build and ships to mend. For myself, I mean to stay only until we've two or three barks seaworthy. Then I must off to Orkney. But Ingram will remain behind with Antonio to see the work completed.

"Indeed, we'd not have come so far south at all had we not so thoroughly cleared our Caithness lands in building our fleet in the first place. At two planks to a tree, I fear our forests will suffer much ere we're full strength at sea again."

"Well, we shall make the most of the time you are here," said Lady Isabel, with a resigned little sigh. "But it does seem hard at my age to see so little of my son."

Sinclair grinned. "You and Janet have a common complaint. But, look you, Mother, when Ingram's work is done, why d'ye not come with him back to Kirkwall? 'Twill be spring by then, and the isles will be at their lovely best. Ye should see the place, Mother, and we meant to have ye there long since."

"D'you mean it, Harry?"

"Aye, an ye feel fit to travel."

Lady Isabel's face was radiant. "I shall feel fit, never fear. Oh, Harry, how pleased I am! But Janet—"

"Will be delighted to see you. Indeed, Mother, she was most insistent that I not forget to bid you come. And it will go hard wi' me should ye fail us in the spring."

Weeks passed in a swirl of strenuous endeavor. Each morning found Sinclair up betimes and out to oversee the felling and hauling of the oaks that would provide the timbers for his fleet. On the coast, Zeno drove himself and his shipwrights relentlessly; and Ingram was everywhere, urging the men to make haste against the coming cold and shorter days that would limit the hours of work.

On All Hallow's Eve, Zeno sent word to Sinclair that three barks were now fully repaired and ready to take to sea. Reluctantly then, Sinclair made ready to leave his beloved Rosslyn. "I have to go, Johnny," he said. "I like not to leave Janet this long alone; moreover, I think it unwise to be long away from the isles. My people are loyal enough, I have no doubt, but how they would conduct themselves should the pirates attempt our coast again, I cannot say."

" 'Tis no easy thing to rule, hey, Harry?"

"I never looked for ease, John. But I will be very glad to have my fleet whole and afloat again. We are vulnerable out there, like a flock of chickens for any passing hawk to prey on. A bare isle's no place for strategy. Ye must stand and fight, or be pushed off into the sea. Wi'out good ships to guard our coasts," Sinclair shook his head, "an invader could roll over us like a carter's dray."

"Well, go an ye must. But come home again soon, Harry. God grant we may yet have time to sit and talk easy."

Sinclair smiled wryly. "I think I was never meant to have that, Johnny."

"Alas for Scotland that ye are not master here instead o' Robert, then. He means to take his ease, come what may."

"He is idle, then?"

"Always. And yet the man's surrounded by plots and counterplots, and who can say when Richard will try our borders again? We are almost as vulnerable here as your folk in the isles. Why, man, the king's own brothers are leagued against him. If he cannot keep order in his own house, what will he do if Scotland's threatened from without?"

Sinclair frowned. "Is it the earl o' Fife?"

"Him chiefly. But Strathearn and Athol, the old king's sons by our great-aunt, are no more friends to this king than is his brother Fife. And Alexander, him they call the Wolf o' Badenoch, is no tame wolf, I assure ye. None o' these would mourn for this present Robert, and any one o' them is capable o' regicide and worse."

"Ye think it might come to that?"

John Sinclair shrugged his heavy shoulders. "I do not say it will, but I think 'tis but their fear o' Jamie and yourself that holds the wolves at bay. Robert can count himself blessed if he but die in his bed."

"Methinks I'll pay a call at court ere I set sail for Kirkwall," Sinclair said. "I pity Robert if I do not love him. And it may give him some small comfort to see one loyal baron at least."

"Do see him, Harry. And give him assurance that the Rosslyn men are true."

On the chill gray morning of All Souls', Sinclair set out for the coast to keep a rendezvous with Richard and the mariners who would sail with him to Orkney. John Clarke rode with him and together they made a rapid journey to the court at Edinburgh. There they were received warmly and, after a very little delay, Sinclair was ushered in to Robert's presence.

The king looked far from well. He sat with his lame leg upon a stool, his head propped by a frail translucent hand. A network of tiny lines was etched about his eyes, and his color was sickly gray. Yet the smile, revealing poor blackened stumps of teeth, was warm and kind.

"My dear Orkney," wheezed the king, "we are delighted to see you in Scotland once more."

" 'Tis a delight to be here, my liege. Would it were possible for me to bide here and yet rule the isles. Then would I be a happy man."

Robert pressed trembling fingers to his temples. "Happy? Ah, who is happy in this life?"

"I had hoped to find you so, my lord."

Robert's mouth stretched in a soundless little laugh. "So much for hopes, my friend. But come, take a little wine with us and tell us how matters fare with you."

The goblets were brought, and as king and noble sipped together, Sinclair recounted his latest adventures.

"Ah, the active life!" Robert nodded approvingly. "Would to God we ourself were fit to be out and doing. But we are as ye see us. 'Tis our sons will have to take up the work when we are gone. Fine lads, fine lads! My Davey's already a noble horseman, and wee John bids fair to grow as stout 's his brother.

"Yon Davey'll make a strong king, Orkney, a strong one and a bold one, if only we can contrive to hold the throne secure till he's of an age to grace it."

"Anything we Sinclairs can do, my lord—"

"Aye, aye! We know that, and we are heartened for knowing it, my friend. We may yet have occasion to call on your good offices."

"Your Majesty has but to ask."

The king's eyes grew watery, and he was obliged to pinch the bridge of his nose to stem the flow. "It's my sons, d'ye see, Orkney. 'Tis they who must be protected from—from wicked men."

"The young princes are assured of a haven at Rosslyn or at Kirkwall, my lord. This do I pledge, and in this will instruct all of my house—that should Your Majesty ever desire it, his sons shall find hospitality and safety with any named Sinclair."

Robert pressed Sinclair's hand. "God bless ye, God bless ye for a loyal noble Scot! Leave me now, Orkney, pray, but take a king's blessing with ye. Know that ye stand chiefest in our love, that our poor prayers attend ye in all ye do."

Sinclair bowed out of the chamber and, with a strangely burdened heart, rode with Clarke down to the coast where they embarked next day for Orkney.

At Kirkwall, Sinclair found all flourishing. And not the least thriving of the lot was a lusty boy child whom they had christened amid much pomp at the church of St. Magnus. This son they called John, for his uncle, his father's brother.

"Ah, lass," declared Sinclair to Janet, when they lay abed the evening of John's baptismal day, "ye've given me another fine son. It makes me feel quite young to hear a baby crying about the place again."

"You are young, Harry, and trim and hard and fine as ever you were."

"But something wrinkled."

"Pah! Your face is handsomer than when you were first my husband," Janet said, tracing the lines with a little finger. "Ye have still all your lovely hair, and ye've no belly at all."

Janet laid a cool hand on her husband's bare flesh. "I thought you beautiful when first I ever saw ye, Harry," she said. "And I find ye fairer now than I did then."

"Hey, lady, have a care," said Sinclair, laughing. "Ye've only just delivered yourself of one bairn. Such talk as this can only lead to the getting of another."

Janet pressed her still lovely nakedness against him. "Wherefore should you concern yourself, my lord? 'Tis I must bear the burden."

"I shall burden ye directly," murmured Sinclair, taking her in his arms and kissing her soft mouth. "Nay, never mind the rushlight, sweetheart. Mine eyes are glad for looking on ye. Let them have their joy."

Sinclair kept close to Kirkwall that winter, content to spend long hours with his family and his few books. He expected that, with the spring, his ships would come, and then it would be time to consider adventuring to sea once more. Till then, well, it was good, very good, to be indolent the while.

But ere his fleet came up from the south, a lone bark came down from the north and put in at Sinclair's bay. John Clarke brought word of it, and Sinclair himself came down to the shingle to watch the mariners row in.

"Why, 'tis one of ours, surely," he remarked to his squire. "Come from Shetland, or I do mistake myself. And look, there's Sir Nicolo seated in the stern. Why comes he here, I wonder."

Clarke replied, "Look, my lord, how they all but carry Sir Nicolo from the boat. He's either hurt or ill, surely."

"God forbid," muttered Sinclair. "Come, let us go to him."

Sir Nicolo, supported on either side by a stout mariner, tried to smile in greeting to his prince. But the result was a pitiful grimace, reflecting weariness and pain.

"My friend," Sinclair said, his concern evident in his voice, "how is it with you?"

Zeno shook his head. "Not well, my prince." The words wheezed from him, and they were followed by a hard, rattling cough that seemed to well up from the depths of his lungs. "Jesu, Maria! It—it hurts me to cough."

"You men, carry Sir Nicolo up to the hall. John Clarke, run on ahead and order a bed prepared. Bid the cook make a hot broth, buckets of it! And stir up one of the kitchen boys and charge him to run and fetch the leech. Go!"

"My prince—"

"No, Sir Nicolo. We'll talk presently. For now, suffer yourself to be silent and save your breath. You have taken a heavy cold from the sound of you, and can spare no wind for words."

Sir Nicolo was borne off to the castle. There he was put to bed and, thanks to a spiced posset of hot milk curdled with wine, fell soon into a heavy slumber.

But the leech looked grave. In answer to Sinclair's anxious inquiry, he would only venture that Zeno's lungs were full and that he was hot with fever. "I have seen many such cases, my lord," said the leech, "and some have mended, and some have not. He hath been in this state no little while, and the voyage here in this rough weather did him no good, surely."

Sinclair groaned aloud. Then he said, "Make his comfort your chiefest care, my friend. Heal him if you can. We will stint you nothing for your service to this man."

The leech bowed. "I know my lord to be most openhanded and generous," he said. "But if money could buy health, the rich would never die. Prayers more than potions are needed in this case. I think my lord's gold would be better spent on masses than on medicine."

"You are an honest leech," Sinclair said. "And for that we thank you. Well, he shall have masses, too; but you do what you can for him also. He is as dear to us as any brother, and we cannot bear to lose him."

It was not until the next day that Sinclair found Zeno able to talk, and then it was with difficulty. The sick man, his ordinarily dark complexion faded to a ghastly pallor, labored for every breath. Yet he wanted to talk, needed to talk; nor would he let Sinclair leave him till his narrative was told.

He had grown bored at Bres; the sea beckoned. And hearing from the fisherfolk wonderful tales of Greenland, he resolved to sail thither and explore for himself.

"I came to the coast, my prince, and found there a church and a monastery of Dominicans hard by a hill that spouted fire, like the mountain in Naples.

"I stayed a good while with the friars, and talked Latin with them. They are ingenious men, my prince. They contrive to heat their halls and prepare their food by means of a hot boiling spring that bubbles up into their very kitchen. They even bake their bread in brass pots which they lower into this same spring."

"Would to God we had such a spring here in Kirkwall," said Sinclair, smiling. "We'd build our castle around it and keep warm all winter through."

Zeno coughed, spat, and wiped his lips. "The winters in Greenland are far worse, my prince. 'Tis cold three quarters of the year. Yet these friars contrive to maintain small covered gardens, warmed and watered by this wonderful spring; and thus they have year round a supply of fruits and herbs of various kinds; wherefore the people of the place believe the holy men to be gods, and do them great homage and bring them many gifts."

"What is the condition of the folk?"

"Rude and savage, my prince. They have few arts, save only the hunter's and the fisher's. The harbor there never freezes because of that same hot spring, so birds and fish are drawn there in great numbers. The folk give over most of their time to catching them." Zeno paused and sipped at his bowl of steaming broth. Then he said, "They also trade in summer with mariners come from the many isles thereabout, and from Trondheim and Norway. The friars do much trading, exchanging dried fish and animal skins for wood and cloth and such comforts as their rule allows."

"Aye," said Sinclair, "wood would be main precious, surely. We would ourself be glad of a ready supply. We must now depend on Rosslyn's forest for our fleet, and that is neither so vast nor so convenient as we would wish."

Zeno grinned weakly. "We should perhaps build as the Greenland folk do, my prince."

"And how is that?"

"Why, they make wonderful little boats in the shape of a weaver's shuttle. They frame them from the bones of a strange fish, a huge creature, tusked and leathery, that is common to those waters. And with the skin of that same fish, they cover the frame, stitching it most cleverly with many doubles so as to make the whole craft impervious to water.

"I have seen them venture out into the wildest seas in these little boats, and yet come to no harm."

Sinclair smiled. " 'Twould require the bones and skins of many such fish to build on a scale sufficient to our need, I fear. We need forests, my friends, not fish."

"Well," said Zeno, with a tired sigh, "I am glad to have seen the place, but I fear I shall pay dearly for it. If I could but go home to Venice, I think I should get well."

"You will get well," Sinclair said, wiping the sweat from his friend's waxen face.

"And if I do, may I have leave to go home? I have a wife and children, my prince. I would see them again before I die."

"No more talk, now," Sinclair said, getting to his feet. "Sleep. Get well. And then we'll speak o' Venice."

Tears formed in Zeno's eyes. "I think I will never see her again," he said.

"Nonsense," said Sinclair, with a heartiness he was far from feeling. "You are feeling a little low this evening, but by tomorrow, why, you will be sitting up and chattering away like any magpie. Rest, now. Sleep is the great healer of all human hurts. Ye'll see. Tomorrow will find ye quite changed for the better."

As Sinclair made to leave, Zeno called to him. "My prince?"

"Sir Nicolo?"

"I have never thanked you for all your favors."

"You have more than thanked me, my friend. You have served me bravely and well."

Zeno gazed at Sinclair with his wide dark eyes, a faint smile tugging at the corners of his bloodless lips. "I love you, my prince," he said.

Later, and often, Sinclair was to wish that he had said what was in his heart to say to his brave chevalier. As it was, he only growled, "Sleep now," and he quit the chamber.

And when they told him next morning that Zeno was dead, Sinclair would not believe them. He went himself to his friend's bedside and saw with his own eyes that quick, light, nervous body lying cold, composed, and at last at rest. He knelt then beside the bed and whispered, "Now, God, receive a noble soul."

And he buried his face in his hands and wept.

37

With the coming of spring, Ingram Gunn returned to Kirkwall with a fleet, and with Lady Isabel and Antonio Zeno.

The latter, when he learned of his brother's death, was like a man distracted. He ran weeping through Sinclair's hall, demanding to see the prince. "Where is he?" he cried at the top of his voice. "Where is this lord who let my brother die? Prince! Prince, come forward and answer for my brother. Damn you, come out to me!"

Sinclair, who had just concluded an interview with an emissary from Margaret's court, stepped out into the corridor as Antonio raged past his door.

"Messer Antonio!"

Zeno turned, his face contorted with grief, his eyes blazing. "You!" he hissed. "There you are."

"Friend, what means this outcry?"

Zeno approached. "My brother is dead."

"We know that. We followed his bier not a month ago, and a piece of ourself lies buried with him there in the cathedral."

Tears coursed down the Venetian's face. "Why was I not told? Eh? Why did you not send for me? Or was it that, as my brother could be of no more use to you, you wished only to have him quickly in the ground and out of your thoughts?"

Sinclair's face went hard and cold. His eyes narrowed and his jaws set like a sprung trap. "Messer Antonio," he said, his voice brittle as skim ice, "step in out of the corridor, pray. We will not play at fishwives with ye. Go in!"

Nothing cowed, but aware of the proprieties, Zeno went stiffly in before Sinclair.

"Now, sir," said Sinclair, leaning against the door and folding his arms across his chest, "we will overlook what was said just now, for we know something of grief and what it can do to reason.

"Thy brother died. I wept for him. I grieve for him yet, and ever shall. That your grief's the greater, I'll not gainsay. You are his brother. But never doubt we loved him, too."

Antonio, calmer but not yet ready to let go his anger, said, "If you loved him, why sent you not for me, his brother, so that he might have seen at least one face from home before he quit this life?"

"My friend, there was no time. He arrived here one day, and was gone the next. And even if I had sent word to Rosslyn, your brother would have been interred before you came." Sinclair crossed the room and laid his hand on Zeno's arm. "Reason with me, Messer Antonio. How could I know your brother was ill until he came here. Once he was here, our only thought was for his welfare. Any message we might have sent could as easily have passed you on the sea. There was no knowing when you and Ingram would return, or if indeed you were already on your way.

"God He knows we would have spared ye this. We would have had ye at least prepared to hear this news. But, as it is, we can only offer our sympathy and ask your pardon for any offense we may have given.

"Believe it, Messer Antonio, because we loved your brother we also love you. Ye cannot think we would willingly give you pain, add to your pain in such an hour. Can ye believe that we would?"

Zeno raised his tear-stained face and met Sinclair's clear gaze. Then he said, "No, my prince, I cannot believe it of you."

"Then, sir, tell me we are yet friends."

Zeno took Sinclair's proffered hand. "My prince, forgive me. My excess of sorrow, it—it quite unbalanced me."

Sinclair nodded. "We have ourself gone about like one benumbed these several weeks. Your brother—" Sinclair shook his head. "I find it very hard, Messer Antonio, very hard to bear.

"But come," he said, smiling, "you are here, and it is good to see you even in so sorry a time as this. Only ask of us what ye will, and ye shall have it. No one named Zeno can ask aught of Orkney and be denied."

"My prince, I ask only your leave to go home."

Sinclair nodded. "Yes, yes. Of course that is what ye would wish. And we would not thwart ye in this or in anything. But we had hoped—No, no. You are right. We shall miss you, Antonio. With your brother gone, and now you—" Sinclair shrugged. "Well, we shall have to trust that

our mariners have profited something from their association with real
seamen. But we shall not henceforth sail so boldly, with no Zeno to
command our fleet."

"To command the fleet?"

"Aye, 'twas our thought. You are the only man fit to wear your
brother's honors. But, there. We'll talk no more of it. Perhaps one o'
the Shetland men—"

"Bah! Farmers and fishermen! There's not the stuff of a true admiral
in the whole lot."

Sinclair's smile was rueful. "We fear ye are in the right, my friend.
But someone must lead the fleet, or else we shall have to build more
forts and content ourself with trying to protect what we have in that
way."

"A plague on forts!" cried Zeno. "Oh, they are good enough for
keeping soldiers and women out of harm's way. But a fleet's the thing
for an adventurous man, a man of spirit and high ambition. You cannot
fight pirates from a fort. You cannot extend your realm from a fort. Nor
can you serve the so gracious lady king of Norway from a fort.

"No, no, my prince. It is ships, ships! Without them, your realm will
shrink to a few barren isles. Your power will diminish, and those bold
rovers of the sea will plunder at will along your coasts. You need your
ships."

"We need an admiral."

Zeno gnawed at his lip a moment, then smiled up at Sinclair and said,
"I think my brother would have wanted me to succeed him."

"We are sure of it."

"Well, then, I will. For a time. But permit me to speak plainly, my
prince. I mean to return to Venice one day and assume the support
and protection of my brother's family."

"Indeed, Sir Antonio, that shall be as you yourself decide. For the
present, we shall announce to our people that you are now knight-
admiral in your brother's stead, and we shall entrust to you the whole
responsibility for our fleet."

"My prince, I am ready for any enterprise."

Sinclair nodded. "We are confident of that, Sir Antonio. And, indeed,
we have at hand some business that concerns you. We were only
moments ago in conference with a messenger from Norway. The Pope
at Rome, it seems, wishes to effect a transfer of bishops. Henry of
Orkney's to go to Greenland, and John of Greenland's to come here.
Rome has sought Margaret's aid in this, and she hath turned to us.

"If you, as admiral, will undertake this venture, we will send word
to Margaret that her appeal was not in vain."

Zeno bowed. "My prince, I am glad of the work. We will lay in our
stores and prepare to sail at Bishop Henry's convenience."

Sinclair smiled. "God bless ye, Sir Antonio," he said. "So long as we have your skill to call on, we can maintain dominion over our seagirt realm. Aye, and extend it, too. But we will talk more o' that anon. For now, ye have our grateful thanks and our prayers for a safe journey."

Within the week, Sir Antonio set sail for Greenland with his episcopal passenger.

Life at Kirkwall took on an unwonted serenity, and never had his island stronghold seemed more fair to Sinclair that it did in that spring of 1395. The sun shone warm on his castle walls; his fleet, but for the barks Zeno required, bobbed smartly on the bright blue waters of the bay; the air was full of birdsong and the scent of heather; and life seemed to Sinclair never sweeter, never so dear.

He missed Nicolo Zeno often, but it was less painful to him now with Ingram back again. Nor did he allow himself unhealthy, morbid grief. A man is born; a man dies. That is common to all. What occurs between that birth and that death is all that signifies. Nicolo Zeno had lived his life. The man who can say as much has nothing to complain of.

For himself, at fifty, he was pleased if not content. He would never be content; he knew that, accepted it, and was not troubled by it. Long ago he had made a conscious choice, had weighed occasional bursts of happiness against the steady, slow smoldering warmth of contentment, elected the former, and lightly let the latter go.

There was much good in his life just now. Janet seemed happy. His children showed such promise as to assure him of heirs worthy of his name and station. He had his friends around him; the isles were peaceful; all was well.

Yet, almost as if he dreaded contentment's overtaking him in spite of his resolve, Sinclair began to chafe under the yoke of idleness.

"Plague take it, Ingram," he said to his friend, as they strolled together one fair evening along the shingle, "I should have gone to Greenland myself."

"To see the monastery poor Nicolo told of?"

"To see whatever's to be seen; to be doing something. Here it is nothing but settling quarrels over land boundaries, and occasionally visiting judgment on some poor wretch who's misbehaved himself. 'Tis a life for an old man, coz; 'tis not enough for me."

They walked along in silence for a time, drinking in the beauty of the night. Then Ingram said, "Will ye never be happy, Harry?"

Sinclair linked arms with his friend. "Aye. In heaven, I trust. And even before then, if I get some good work to do. Look yonder, Ingram. That whole vast expanse o' sea is as yet unmastered and untamed. Ships of many nations ply her waters; pirates and smugglers dart about on her broad bosom, unchecked and undismayed. And here we sit, satisfied to keep our little lands intact, hoping to go unmolested by those brigands of the deep."

"If you can do so much, coz, ye will have done more than any governor before ye."

" 'Tis not enough, my friend. It hath come to my mind that if we but built a larger fleet, well armed and well manned, we could effectively control this North Sea. And we should, for our own sake and for Norway's."

" 'Tis a modest ambition," observed Ingram, smiling.

"No, sir, do not play wi' me. I am in deadly earnest. Why should the German merchants be let to make these waters their private domain? Why, man, they all but own the whole commerce of these parts. And as to those pirates, are we to submit to their bullying? Think what might have befallen in the Shetlands had not that dreadful storm blown in to spoil their pretty plan.

"No, my friend, I think it ill becomes me to lie low in Orkney in hopes that we may be left in peace. That may be poor Robert's way in Scotland; 'tis not our purpose here."

Ingram rolled his eyes to heaven. "God help us," he said. "Just when I began to believe I had been spared to a safe old age to die in comfort in my bed, ye begin to talk o' more adventuring. Consider these gray hairs, kinsman, pray, and leave something for your sons to do hereafter."

"Why, Ingram, if ye feel that way, we can arrange for ye to bide at Rosslyn to oversee the building o' more ships. My brother John will be glad to provide ye wi' such comfort as your aging bones require, and ye may live out your days at his fireside, a-dandling his little ones on your knees."

Gunn stopped dead in his tracks. "Oh, no, Harry. Ye think to cozen me, but I know ye of old, my friend. I'll no be gulled into foolhardiness by such tricks as that."

"What tricks? Ingram, I do confess—"

"Ye should confess yourself to be a sly and tricksy rogue. Ye think that by painting me old and useless, I'll counter by insisting ye let me sail wi' ye. In another minute, ye'd have me begging for permission to be drowned in full armor. Hah!"

"Ye do me grave injustice, coz," murmured Sinclair. " 'Twas yourself expressed the wish to die comfortably in bed. I only—"

"Ye know I did not mean it, and yet ye play as if ye thought I did so ye can tease me into changing my mind."

"Ye did not mean it?"

"No, I did not. And well ye know it, too."

"Good!" cried Sinclair, thwacking Ingram on the back. "Then ye'll sail wi' me again! Ah, 'twill be like old times, Ingram. Ye'll see. Why, we have only begun to live, man. There's a whole wide ocean out there for us to master. And we'll do it too. By God, we will."

Poor Ingram, thoroughly confused between what he had meant to say and what he had said, saw only that Sinclair had got round him, and that he was not likely after all to die comfortably in his bed.

"When Zeno returns," Sinclair went on, "we'll put our heads together, we three, and we'll map out our campaign. I tell ye, Ingram, we mean to see our pennant fly in every port on the North Sea. Aye, and we'll drown our share o' pirates, too, and make those Germans let go their iron hold on trade."

"Ye'll need a deal more than a dozen barks for that, coz," murmured Gunn. "There'll be not an oak left standing in Rosslyn ere ye're done."

Sinclair frowned. "Aye, there's the curse of it, Ingram. Would to God these isles bore forests. 'Tis a poor joke to give a man an ocean realm and no timber. But while there stands a tree in Scotland we'll not despair, hey? We'll have our ships, my friend. And we'll do great deeds together. God send Antonio home soon, is all my prayer now. God bless me, Ingram, but I am eager to begin."

Sir Antonio did return as summer faded from the land. And Sinclair, full of his own dreams, lost no time in broaching his thoughts to Zeno. Together with Ingram Gunn and young Richard Sinclair, the Lord of Orkney and his admiral sat late over the wine, talking of what would be.

"My prince," remarked Zeno, tracing with his finger the circle left by his goblet on the oaken board, "this ambition is as vast almost as the sea itself. And that charms me. We Venetians love a bold plan, a grand design. For in attempting great things, some things are inevitably accomplished, and so the world progresses as time moves on.

"The problem, the chief problem, it seems to me, is that of timber. And it may be I have happened on a solution.

"Whilst lying over in the Faroes to wait out a sudden gale, I met a man, a fisherman he was, who told me a curious tale."

"All fishermen have their curious tales," remarked Ingram, smiling.

"As do some fish," Richard chimed in.

"Even so," said Sinclair, "we should like to hear this one. Go on, Sir Antonio, pray."

"Well, my prince, this fellow was, some six-and-twenty years ago, out at sea in a company of four fishing boats. A tremendous storm arose and swept the boats before it, helpless, for many days westward over the sea. The fate of the other boats I do not know, but this man's vessel was dashed ashore at a great island which the inhabitants call Estotiland.

"He and his five companions were taken by the people to a fair and populous city to stand before the king of that place. None there spoke the language of the fishermen. It happened that there was one there, another castaway, who knew the language of the fishermen, and he interpreted in Latin between them and the King.

"It was this king's wish that these fishermen bide in his country, and in no position to debate the matter, they did remain there for some five years. They learned the language and became well acquainted with the character of the place."

"How did he describe it?" Sinclair asked, helping Zeno to the wine.

"Why, my prince, he said that this Estotiland is but a little smaller than Iceland, that it is a rich country abounding in good things. It is more fertile than Iceland, being watered by four rivers that rise in a very high mountain in the interior."

"And what of the people?"

"Ah, he says they are very intelligent, possessing all the arts like ourselves. He believes that in past times they had intercourse with our people, for he saw Latin books there, which they do not understand."

"I thought ye said the fishermen talked Latin with the king," objected Gunn.

"No, no, Sir Ingram. Another castaway, from God He knows where, he talked their language with the fishermen and talked Latin to the king. But, they do have their own language and letters."

"Well, this is interesting, to be sure," acknowledged Sinclair, draining off his cup. "But I have yet to see how it relates to our scheme."

"I am coming to that, my prince."

"Ye need not hurry yourself on my account," murmured Ingram, stifling a yawn and winking at Richard.

"Have patience, Sir Ingram," said Antonio, mildly. "All shall be made plain in due course. Now, then. This fisherman told me that to the south of Estotiland lies a great and populous country, rich in gold and covered with great forests."

"Forests?" Sinclair sat up, attentive.

Zeno nodded. "Yes, my prince, vast tracts of woods. The people there have many walled towns and villages, and they make small boats and sail them. But they have not the lodestone, nor do they know north by the compass. The fishermen were for this reason held in high esteem in that land, though they were common enough fishermen so far as I can tell."

"Aye, when it comes to being common, give me an honest fisherman every time," remarked Ingram.

Zeno went serenely on. "The king himself sent the fishermen farther southward still, in boats that he provided, to a country they call Drogio. But they encountered rough weather, which drove them onto the land, and there they encountered something rougher. Savages!" Zeno's eyes glistened and his voice went low. "The fishermen were taken captive and, alas, most of them were eaten by their captors."

"Good God!" Sinclair exclaimed. "Cannibals!"

"Even so," said Zeno, enjoying the sensation his narrative had created.

"How is it, Sir Antonio," inquired Ingram, "how is it that your man escaped his fellows' fate?"

"He was too hardened a sinner," ventured Richard Sinclair. "They could not chew the fellow."

Even Sinclair grinned at that, and Zeno was himself obliged to laugh.

"Ah, you make a jest, young sir! Charming! But, in truth, this man and one or two others saved their lives by trading off a secret."

"A secret?" Sinclair's brows shot up.

Zeno smiled. "Yes, my prince. You see, these are a very rude and uncultivated people. Indeed, they go about naked, and lack the wit to clothe themselves with the skins of beasts they take in hunting. They suffer terribly from the cold."

"So the fisherman taught them weaving," hazarded Ingram Gunn.

"No, sir. But they taught them the use of nets for taking fish."

"Wonderful," murmured Sinclair.

"So I thought, my prince. But this new thing caused trouble among the inhabitants."

"How so?"

"Well, they are a very warlike people. They have no kind of metal, but they make lances and bows of wood which, when they are not using them for hunting, they turn upon each other. They have laws and chieftains, but different in different tribes. And when a neighboring chief learned that our fisherman's captors had a new way of taking fish taught them by these strangers, he straightway made war on the captors and, because he was the more powerful, succeeded in capturing the captives."

"God bless me," said Ingram, reaching for the wine.

"Amen," said Antonio Zeno, with all goodwill. "Now it happened that our fisherman had a great desire to return to his home."

"I should think he would," said Richard.

"Yes. He was a long time in those parts, and he had quite thoroughly tried the hospitality of the place. But his companions despaired of fleeing, and had not the courage to go with him. So he bade them farewell and made his escape through the woods in the direction of Drogio.

"Happily for him, the great chief of those who dwelt in that forest received him kindly, for he was the sworn enemy to the neighboring chieftain, and he gave him a kind of safe-conduct from tribe to tribe until he came at last to Drogio."

"Whew!" Sinclair shook his head. "The fellow lacks nothing for courage, truly. To go off alone and on foot through a country peopled by savages is not a thing your ordinary fisherman would do. No, nor your ordinary knight either, when it comes to that."

"In truth, my prince, this fisherman is a most extraordinary man. He found a cordial welcome in Drogio, where, by great good luck, he learned that mariners from Estotiland were there en route to the Faroes. He sought passage with them; and they, as none of them knew the language of the Faroes, were very glad to have him along as their interpreter. He traded in their company to such good effect that he became quite rich, and was able to fit out a vessel of his own and return to the Faroes where he lives quite well."

Sinclair shook his head again. " 'Tis a marvelous tale ye tell us, Sir Antonio. D'ye think it is a true one?"

Zeno nodded. "I do, my prince. Wherefore should the fellow lie to me?"

"A man may not tell the truth and yet not lie, Sir Antonio, from a desire to entertain, perhaps, or to impress a stranger with exaggerated narratives that, though founded in truth, stray from it in the telling." Sinclair rubbed the tip of his nose with the flat of his hand. "Forests, eh?"

"Vast forests, my prince. And plentiful fisheries and much game."

"And cannibals," threw in Ingram. "Do not forget the cannibals."

"Damn!" cried Sinclair, rising in his place. "Damn, but ye have piqued my interest, Sir Antonio. Indeed ye have. Why, if even half o' what this fisherman told is true, we would have abundant timber for our fleet, a new source for fish to trade, and furs. And we could encourage some of our own folk to settle there—"

"Among cannibals?" cried Ingram.

"We would tend to the cannibals, my friend, and teach them to love salt fish." Sinclair nodded. "Aye, we could do it. With forts there and here, and with our fleet between, we would indeed be masters o' this sea.

"By God, Sir Antonio, we must interview this fisherman o' yours, and that directly."

"So you shall, my prince." Zeno rose also. "For I took it upon myself to invite him here to Kirkwall. He should arrive within the week."

38

Bjorn Eyvindson carried himself with the natural dignity of those who have endured great hardships. He was a compact ready-looking man, nearer to sixty than fifty. His sun-browned face was seamed and crinkled like an old glove, but his eyes retained something of their youthful light. He spoke softly when he spoke at all, and his speech was colored by accents alien to his native place. There was about the man an air of reserve not commonly found in the hale company of those that follow the sea; but there was no mistaking his inherent intelligence, and if his speech lacked polish, yet there was no doubting the sincerity of this quiet, hardy adventurer.

"Pray, be seated, Bjorn Eyvindson," said Sinclair, graciously. "We have a great curiosity to hear your story. Sir Antonio has told us the substance of it, but our friends here and ourself would be pleased to hear whatever you may have to add."

"What has he told ye, my lord?" asked Eyvindson, seating himself next to Richard Sinclair.

"Why, that ye were for some dozen years a traveler in a strange land peopled by savages, that you ingratiated yourself with the chieftains by teaching them the art of taking fish with nets, and that you eventually effected your escape to friendlier parts, whence ye made your way home."

Eyvindson nodded. "That is my story, my lord."

An awkward silence hung in the air. Clearly, the old mariner was not one to abuse the ears of his host with an excess of words.

"Hem!" rasped Ingram Gunn. "Sir Antonio tells us that some o' your companions were eaten by these savages."

"Aye," said Eyvindson.

"Were ye not afraid?" Gunn inquired.

"Often."

Silence gathered in again. Then Sinclair ventured, "Sir Antonio tells us ye have since prospered and live quite comfortably at home."

"Aye, my lord."

"Then ye go no more to sea?"

"No, my lord. God be thanked."

"And did ye never feel a desire to return to those distant lands?"

Eyvindson shook his head. "I'm not a man as tempts fate, my Lord."

"Hum. These savages. Think you that they would be sufficient in arms and numbers to resist a company of armed men?"

Eyvindson plucked at his gray tuft of beard. "Their weapons be poor things, my lord. Armor'd be proof against them, I think. If a party was to move in strength among 'em, they'd have scant trouble."

"And you speak the language of this Estotiland and also the language of those wild, uncultured parts?"

"Aye, my lord."

"Bjorn Eyvindson," said Sinclair, rising and pacing before the hearth, "let us impart to you something of our mind concerning this far land.

"We have, as ye might expect, a most pressing need for timber. Our fleet is our chief weapon and our chief security. But without forests to supply us with wood for building and repair, we are severely straitened. We have, 'tis true, goodly stands o' trees at our barony in Scotland. But 'tis neither expedient nor to our purpose to be forever dividing our time and our energies 'twixt here and there. Had we sufficient tracts of timber in these northern parts, we could the more effectively exert our lawful rule over these isles and this sea. D'ye smoke our intent?"

"Aye, my lord. Ye would sail westward."

"Indeed we would. In truth, my friend, our heart lightened when Sir Antonio told us of your adventure, for it seemed to us as if providence had brought to our hand the very means we sought for strengthening at once our fleet and our government.

"In time, wi' God's help, we might extend our rule even to those distant western lands, build towns there and develop the fisheries, improve the lot of the inhabitants, and provide opportunity for our own people to better themselves as settlers in those parts."

Eyvindson nodded. "There be riches there, surely, in timber and fish and furs. The savages told me that much farther south there are other tribes that have both silver and gold and do work it handsomely."

"What is the condition o' those tribes?"

"My lord, they say that the climate there is gentle, that culture is far advanced. The people build on the grand scale and have a passion for ornament. But also they worship idols and make human sacrifice to them."

"Jesu!" muttered Gunn. "Are they all so bloody-minded?"

"Some o' the forest folk were very gracious, sir, according to their light. And at Drogio I was treated very well."

"It sounds a chancy business to me," averred Gunn. "I'd no be eager to try my luck in lands where such a thirst for blood abounds."

"Nor would I, sir," said Eyvindson, with a grim smile. "God brought me out of it once. I'd think myself a fool to test Him by going there again."

Sinclair frowned. "But ye would go in a company of armed men?"

"For what purpose, my lord?"

"Ye'd be well paid."

"I am not in want, my lord," Eyvindson replied.

"And if we command ye to go?"

Eyvindson got to his feet and looked directly into Sinclair's eyes. "You are lord of these isles, sir. I know that. And I know that ye have both the right and the might to make men do your bidding. But I have heard it said ye've a heart like other men. I trust ye would not press this burden on an old man's shoulders."

Sinclair bit his lip in vexation. Then he managed a smile and said, "My friend, fear us not. We have no love of might for might's sake. We mean to rule as befits a Christian lord.

"But ye must see, surely, how pressing is our need. And, plainly, you alone can help us. Ye know where these lands lie; ye know the language of the several tribes. Without your help, we shall be asking our people to run far graver risk. For, depend upon it, Bjorn Eyvindson, with ye or without ye, we mean to sail thither."

The old fisherman tugged at his beard. "My lord," he said, "I be a simple plain-spoken man, wi' little understanding o' the ways o' jarls and such. But I know something o' the ways o' men, and as a jarl's a man, it may be said that I see some glimpses of the sort o' being you are."

Sinclair smiled. "Speak away, friend Eyvindson, and let no marks of rank deter ye. We love a man as says his mind plainly."

"Well, then, my lord, it seems to me that had you been born a common man like me, we might have been fishermen together, and been friends. For ye appear to be the sort o' man a body could throw in with and sail along of in all weathers."

"Thank you, Bjorn Eyvindson," said Sinclair, gravely.

"But, as it is, you are a lord. And a lord must put all manner o' things ahead o' fellow feeling and kindness. As I sees it, ye're situated thus: ye wants the lands to the west, and ye needs a man as has been there to guide ye.

"The man as has been there, which is me, has no stomach for going again. Your own heart goes against making the man go, but as ye are a lord, ye must put your need ahead o' your heart.

"Is that not the way of it?"

"You have summed up the matter very neatly," said Sinclair. "And how is it to be resolved?"

"Well, my lord, I am a man as sets great store by common sense. I believe I'd be a fool to go. And I am too old and too proud to play the fool. So I will not offer to go. If you, being a lord, tell me I must go, then I will go and be counted obedient. But I'll not be counted a fool."

Sinclair rubbed his forehead. "We take your meaning, friend," he said. "The burden of folly must rest wi' me."

"Aye."

"Well then, so be it. Bjorn Eyvindson, as jarl of Orkney and your sovereign lord, we command that ye lead us to the western lands. For the present, you will bide here at Kirkwall and use your time to instruct our friend Sir Antonio in the languages of those parts, for he is uncommon quick to learn new tongues. We will see ye comfortably lodged and well cared for. And when we are ready to embark, you shall sail with us and be our guide and our interpreter."

Eyvindson nodded. "As ye say, my lord."

Sinclair bade John Clarke see to Eyvindson's comfort, then he said to the old fisherman, "We thank you, Bjorn Eyvindson."

"No thanks are owing, my lord," Eyvindson said, fixing Sinclair with clear unflinching eyes. "Ye've given an order and I must obey, is all."

Sinclair could feel the back of his neck go hot. There was no insolence in this old man, but there was something—something that said plainly whose man he was. Vexation vied with grudging respect for Sinclair's mind toward Eyvindson. But policy it was that won out.

He said, "Even so, my friend, we acknowledge our debt to you. Ask for whatever is needful to make your stay pleasant. We'll stint ye nothing. Go now, with this man. We will speak with you more anon."

"Whew!" breathed Ingram Gunn, when Eyvindson and Clarke had gone. "He's a tough old fellow and no mistake."

"Aye," growled Sinclair. "He does not extend himself in matters o' courtesy."

"Well, coz, courtesy demands much. But does it ask a man who has escaped great danger to return to it willingly in his old age?"

Sinclair eyed his kinsman with a cool and thoughtful look. "Ye need not go, Sir Ingram, if this journey seems too fraught wi' perils."

"Now, dammit, Harry!" Ingram's eyes blazed and color mottled his cheeks. "I never said I wouldn't go."

"We know that, sir."

"Christ's bones, man!" Ingram smote his palm with his fist. "I hate it when ye come the lofty lord wi' me. By the mass, I do."

"Sir Ingram!"

"Nah, nah, Harry. No 'Sir Ingram' wi' me. We've come a long way together, you and I, and it'll no go down—"

Sinclair turned to the others. "Richard, Sir Antonio, leave us, pray."

Zeno and the young Sinclair bowed and departed, then Sinclair turned back to the wrathful Gunn and said, "Ye owe me an apology, I think."

"Apology be damned," retorted Ingram. "What d'ye owe me? Ye're angry because yon sailorman put the burden where it belongs, and so ye take your anger out on me. Well, I'll no bear it, Harry. I will not. I deserve better from you. God He knows I do. And He knows too that 'tis no friend's part to rate me like a scullion that's spilled the soup before Zeno there and young Richard."

"Ye think me unjust?"

"Unjust? No. Ye're no unjust, Harry. Ye're ungrateful. Ye ask one man to sail into hell, and because he does not kiss your hands and thank ye for it, ye turn on your friend, the best friend ye have in all the world, and shame him before—before some others."

Sinclair stared at his friend for some moments, then he said, "Ingram, we are old friends and kinsmen too. If ye feel I have been ungrateful, I am sorry for it. But kinsman or no, I am sovereign here." His voice rose and took on force. "And I will not be spoken to by anyone as you just now spoke to me, also before Richard and Sir Antonio."

Gunn nodded. He could not trust himself to speak for the pain and anger in his heart.

"Now then," continued Sinclair, more softly, "we are both of us hot and wrathful. For my part, I would rather break my good right arm than break the bond between us. So, as a friend and for friendship's sake, I pray you, let us leave this quarrel in this chamber. Let's part now, you and I, for some hours. When we meet again, we will talk more of this voyage, and of that only."

"Very well," said Ingram, stiffly.

"And Ingram?"

"Aye?"

"Have no concern for this Bjorn Eyvindson. He will do his duty, and he will be well rewarded for his pains."

Gunn nodded. "I never doubted your generosity, my lord," he said. And he bowed and left Sinclair alone.

Sinclair stood looking after his departing friend. Then he heaved a great sigh and, looking to heaven, said, "Lord, Thou knowest I never meant to wound my friend. But the work is there to do. And I must see it done."

Ingram Gunn, meantime, his ordinarily genial face like a thundercloud, went storming down the corridor, his heart overflowing at his lips in pungent phrases. "Cannibals, by Christ! The by-Our-Lady stubborn stiff-necked—ah! Lady Janet! God gi' ye good day, you and the children."

The sudden appearance of Janet, with small John and Helen in tow, caused Ingram to veer sharply from his course and to put on a smile that might have deceived a blind man, but no other.

"Good morrow, Sir Ingram," said Janet, very sweetly. "You seem to be in a merry humor today."

"Oh, yes. Ha-ha. I am always wonderfully lighthearted." A green-apple look gave Ingram's smile the lie. "It comes from having a good digestion, so the physicians say."

Janet laughed. "I would say, sir, from the look of you, that you have swallowed something that defies even your digestion."

"In truth I have not swallowed it, for it sticks in my throat and it will not go down."

Something in Gunn's tone let Janet know that this was no light matter. She bade the children run and play, then turned to her husband's friend and said, "Now, Ingram, what's the matter?"

And he told her.

That evening, when Sinclair retired with Janet to their chamber, he found himself in troubled waters.

"My lord," said Janet, unfastening the cincture of her gown, "you seem uncommonly low-spirited tonight."

"Do I, Janet?" Sinclair, sitting on the edge of their bed to ease off his shoes, looked up at her inquiringly.

"Indeed you do. Is anything amiss?"

"No," said Sinclair, slowly. "Not as I know of."

"Oh. I thought perhaps there was something you wanted to tell me." Janet doffed her gown and, on naked feet, came and stood before her husband.

Sinclair shook his head. "There's nothing, love. But I thank ye for your concern."

"That man who was here today, the one I saw walking with John Clarke, he brought you no bad tidings, I trust."

"No, no. He's only an old mariner come from the Faroes to see me."

"On what account, pray?"

Sinclair shrugged. "He has some story of being a castaway in a strange land far to the west. Sir Antonio met him while he was on that errand for the Pope, and he thought I should hear the man's story."

"You found it—interesting?"

"Aye, somewhat."

Janet seated herself beside her husband and took his hand in hers. "Harry, look at me."

"With pleasure, lady," said Sinclair, smiling, and making as if to kiss her.

But Janet avoided his lips and said, "Harry, you are planning to leave me again."

"Well, Janet, I—"

"You are, are you not? You mean to sail off to God He knows where and once more leave me to cry my heart out and worry myself into white hairs while you play the bold young knight a-questing."

"Now, Janet, I—"

"Harry, when will you be satisfied? You have the isles; you have this castle; you have the children—and me, such as I am now that I am no longer young."

"Janet, Janet, ye always will be young. Ye cannot—"

"Do not tell me what I cannot, my lord. I will tell you. I cannot bear to have you go off again, not now, not at this time o' life." Janet let go his hand and doubled her own small hands into fists. "Are ye determined to have me a widow, Harry? Is that your wish for me?"

"No, o' course not. But—"

"Well, I have been more widow than wife since first you won your precious claim to Orkney. And now—now when we are settled, when I had hoped we might grow old together in peace and content, you break my hopes and my heart by plotting still another venture to carry you off from me."

Janet began to sob. " 'Tis not just, Harry, 'tis not fair, and 'tis not kind. God He knows I have tried to be a good wife to you, to be submissive, meek and longsuffering, to bear your children and warm your bed, and ask no other reward than to be allowed to live with you."

Sinclair put his arms around her. "Ye've been a good wife, Janet; a splendid wife. No man could want a better. And I love ye still wi' all my heart."

"That you do not!" Janet cried, breaking out of the circle of his arms and flying to a far corner of the room. "You do not love me, Harry. An ye say that ye do, ye lie in your throat."

"Now by Christ, woman, that will do," roared Sinclair, rising up in dignity and wrath. "I say I love ye and I do not lie."

"If ye loved me ye'd no leave me; not now, not when we've both grown old."

"Old?" The word fell in a whisper from Sinclair's lips. His brows knit, and he stared at Janet with unbelieving eyes. "Old, d'ye say?"

"Yes, old! Look at me, Harry. Look at the gray coming in my hair, the lines in my face. I'm not a girl anymore, Harry. I am six times a mother. Our eldest son's of an age to marry. Aye, and Willie, too. And Betsy."

"Betsy?" Sinclair looked incredulous. "Ye talk foolishness, woman. She's but a baby."

"Oh, indeed? When have ye looked at her, Harry? When have you really seen her or any of us? You are blind, I tell you. We are all growing older, and so are you. And what's to become of me with you dead and the children all gone off? What comfort shall I have then? And what hope?"

"Now, now, now," protested Sinclair, going to her and taking her hands in his. "Easy, lass, easy. I'm no dead yet. And the children are all around us still. I think ye go a bit previous wi' your grieving, Janet. I grant ye, I'm no stripling. But I am sound and hearty and likely to live a long while yet."

"For what? To be eaten by savages?"

Sinclair clapped a hand to his forehead. "Eaten by savages—ah, now, God damn it, now it comes. Ye've talked wi' Ingram."

"I'll neither admit it nor deny it," Janet said, with a haughty toss of her head. "I have talked with many this day. But this I know. I may be only a silly woman, with no rights and no voice, but I have my legs, thank God. And if you go yourself on this foolhardy voyage, I will use my legs to walk away out o' this and find a refuge for myself and for the little ones in convent or castle away to the south among my own people."

"Mind your vows, woman! I'll brook no such rebellious talk from you."

"Will you not, then?" Janet's eyes blazed fury. "Very well. I'll talk no more. I have said my say."

Sinclair felt an overwhelming urge to lay hands on this new Janet and beat her soundly. Instead, he fell back on his dignity. "Madam," he said, going back to the bed and retrieving his shoes, "there can be no use in talking more o' this. It may be that I am old, as ye are pleased to say. Certain it is that I am too old to be thus baited and bullied by a tyrant in petticoats.

"God gi' ye good night. We old folk need our sleep, and 'tis plain I shall get none of it here." And he left the chamber.

Janet, her breast filling with inexpressible anger and hurt, flung herself on the bed and found relief in tears.

39

The atmosphere at Kirkwall was charged with tension. Sinclair and Janet, although they did not take up again the subject of their debate, were merely civil. Relations between Sinclair and Ingram Gunn were carefully ordered, constrained, and cool. Bjorn Eyvindson haunted the place like a bad conscience, and even Zeno could be heard muttering to himself as he bustled about the work of readying the fleet for the long voyage westward.

"Now God deliver us from mean-spirited folk," Zeno remarked to young Richard Sinclair, one cloudy afternoon in late October as they trudged together up from the beach. "You northern people are too full of spleen for my liking."

"Are we so?" Richard smiled at the volatile Latin.

"Indeed, sir. Consider this Faroes fisherman, Eyvindson. He glooms about like a ghost, and like a ghost speaks only when he is spoken to. No doubt he is a very good man in his way, and under his tutelage I am making fair progress in those jawbreaking languages of the western savages. But you cannot talk with the man. 'Tis like trying to converse with yonder rocks."

"He is not a merry fellow, I grant ye," allowed Richard.

"And what is worse, his sour face and unrelenting gloom begins to disaffect the men."

"Does he talk against this westward voyage, Sir Antonio?"

"Why, no, my friend, he talks hardly at all. But the men," he shrugged, "they have heard things—whispers of cannibals and monsters and the like. They have sometimes questioned this melancholy fellow and were, I think, shaken more by what he did not say than by anything he said.

"He has a way, this Eyvindson, of intimating that he could, if he would, say much, and that he chooses not to."

Richard Sinclair smiled. "It is a fashion I have observed in others, folk who would have their hearers think them privy to grave and weighty matters beyond the grasp of common minds. It is a harmless vanity."

Zeno pulled a long face. "It may not be harmless to our business, sir. For if the shipmen let these baneful fancies take hold in their imagining, they may well refuse to sail."

"So bad as that?"

Zeno nodded. "But yesterday I came upon a group of idle fellows talking, and when they marked my near approach, they straightway left off and made a sudden show of busyness."

"Men will talk, Sir Antonio."

"Yes, sir, but what do they talk of? I took it on myself to corner the youngest lad among them, and by some artful questioning I learned that all their discourse was of serpents, storms, and those sea hags some call mermaids, whose singing hath such glamour as to lure unlucky mariners to their doom."

"Tales to fright the children with," said Richard, laughing.

Zeno shrugged. "I have been myself a great voyager, my friend, and have yet to see such things. They may exist. The sea is so wide, and so deep, that it may harbor any manner of being. For my part, I give no credence to such tales, but these men believe, and their belief may so unman them as to spoil our hopes for this adventure."

Richard Sinclair's fair brows knit in a frown. "Ye might do well to talk to them."

"And they would do well to listen. But I think they will not listen to me. They are good men but, like most islanders, they are slow to trust a stranger. If your noble uncle or else Sir Ingram were to talk to them, they would surely listen. But I," Zeno shook his head, "I am a Venetian. I could not be more foreign to these folk than if I had come down from the moon."

"Why not speak with my uncle, then?"

Zeno's look was eloquent. "Would you? No, sir, I thought not. We all walk wide of Jarl Henry these days.

"And Sir Ingram, a dear delightful man, truly, and commonly quick and keen, now goes about frowning and close-mouthed, as grim almost as old Eyvindson. 'Tis as if he nurses some private hurt and will not suffer anyone to say a cheerful word in his presence for fear of forgetting what it is that gnaws him."

"Why, sir, I believe he and my uncle have quarreled; there's the why of it."

"Quarrels, poof! In Venice we quarrel all the time. It is our favorite sport. But we do not go around looking like a thundercloud for six, eight, ten days together. No! We fight. We get it all out in the open. We thrust and parry for a bit, scratch each other here and there, let a little overheated blood flow, and poof! It is over, and we get on about our business."

Richard shook his head. "I do not think Sir Ingram would ever challenge our worthy lord, nor do I believe the challenge would be taken up if it were offered."

Zeno sniffed. "No. Those two would rather go along like this for God knows how long, cold and brooding and scarcely speaking. I tell you, my friend, it damps my spirits, truly. 'Twould be better for us all if they would draw swords at once and play the leech, one to the other."

"Ye may be in the right, Sir Antonio. I know only that this place is under a cloud just now. And I wish to God it were not so."

One of many who shared Richard Sinclair's wish was Lady Isabel, who had come to Kirkwall that past spring. She had been happy at her son's great hall, delighting in the newness of the place and in the daily company of her grandchildren. But now a chill, not of October's making, had settled on the place, and Lady Isabel grieved silently for her daughter-in-law and her son. It seemed to her that they had everything to make them happy. And what in her eyes was more, they had each other. Yet they seemed now as distant from each other as Rosslyn from Kirkwall.

For a time, Lady Isabel held back, forbore to mediate, resisted every impulse to lance the festering hurt. But finally, after yet another gloomy meal where even the youngest children maintained a strained and watchful silence, she sought out her son and broached the awkward matter to him.

"Good evening, Mother," said Sinclair, getting to his feet and laying aside his book.

"I hope I do not intrude, Harry," said Lady Isabel, smiling.

"Not at all. Be seated, pray. I am very glad of company."

Lady Isabel eased her slight frame gracefully into the chair opposite her son. "I love these quiet nights," she said. "There is such peace here, peace as deep almost as the sea that surrounds us on this little plot of earth."

"Aye, Mother, it is peaceful."

"Too peaceful for you, my son?"

Sinclair flashed his mother a questioning look, then smiled and said, "A little idleness goes a long way with me, Mother. In truth, I have scant stomach for it."

"Dear Harry," Lady Isabel smiled fondly at him, "yours was ever a restless spirit, I fear. But soon or late there comes a day when the heart craves rest, craves it and needs it and must have it or break."

"Then that will be a time to rest."

The two were silent for a moment. Then Lady Isabel, seemingly absorbed in plucking at a thread in her sleeve, ventured, "Harry, I promised myself long ere I came here that I would not on any account permit myself to play the meddling old woman."

"A worthy vow, madam, and one that you have kept."

"Till now."

"Oh?"

"My dear Harry, I am neither blind nor insensate. The joy has gone from this place, and there is now within these walls such a current of malaise as to be almost palpable."

"If you are uncomfortable, Mother, I am sorry."

"Now, Harry, do not go all haughty and stiff with me." Lady Isabel rose and went to where he sat and stood smiling down at him. "We have known each other a goodly while, my son. And I have watched you grow from infancy to prime manhood. There is little about you that I do not know, and less than little that I do not admire and love. But I do confess that when you take on that flinty look of affronted majesty, then I wish you were a little boy again that I might box your ears and make you mend your ways."

Sinclair had to grin. "Mother, I thank God that my people cannot hear ye now. What would they think to hear their chief thus rated?"

"And what, pray, d'you suppose they think when they see you glooming and glowering about like a bear with a sore paw?"

Sinclair's eyes widened. "Does it matter what they think?"

"A question for a question: Does it matter what they think, what your nearest friends think, what Janet and the children think?"

"That is three questions, and the answer to them all is—yes."

"Well then?"

"Well then?"

"Oh, Harry, you do vex me." Lady Isabel rose abruptly, turned away, and took a stand by the chair she had lately occupied. "You say that these things matter, yet you play with me when I bring them up to you."

"Mother, I am sorry." Sinclair rose and went to her, taking her hands in his. "It does matter very much. And I am sorry that—that this house has grown so cold of late. But either I am master here or I am master nowhere."

"Does anyone doubt that you are master here?"

"They would have cause to doubt, if I let my actions be ruled by woman's whim." Sinclair grew agitated, and he took to pacing up and down. "Look you, Mother. There is a great opportunity just within my grasp. Off to the west lie lands as yet unspoiled, virtually untouched, and rich in timber, fish, and furs. Could I but establish my rule there, then could I control these seas, and then would Orkney rank with any other sovereign power in this part o' the world. Am I to deny myself, my people, and my heirs all this because Janet would not have me go?"

Lady Isabel shook her head. "Oh, Harry, and to think how you charged me with my own ambition when I was so bent on forwarding your claim to Orkney. Who is ambitious now?"

"I am, madam, I freely own it. I mean to see my line so firmly based and so widely known as to assure a century of Sinclairs their future in this realm. We will be a power, Mother, and we will grow great."

"I do believe it, my son. But can you not achieve all this without you run yourself into the very mouth of danger?"

"Mother, I would not ask another man to do what I would not."

Lady Isabel scanned her son's face with keen and searching eyes. "I think your men know that, Harry. What is more, pardon me, I think you seek this adventure for its own sake. You do not have to go, you want to go. And it is this difference, I do believe, that goes to Janet's heart."

Slowly, Sinclair's features relaxed into a smile. "Yea, Mother, I want to go."

Lady Isabel clapped her small white hands. "There speaks my honest Harry," she crowed. "It is the doing of the thing, is it not? To be going again, to be doing again, to be taking the risk and daring the wind and waves. 'Tis that that lures you every bit as much as the prize."

"Mother, can ye blame me?" Sinclair's eyes shone with a brilliance his mother had not seen there for many a day. "What's a man for if not for deeds, hey?"

His mother smiled. "I do not blame you, Harry. Indeed, I love that spirit in you. But there is this to consider. If you go sailing off on every errand of this realm, who is to maintain peace here? And think, too, if you were to perish in this adventure? Is your son ready now to rule in your stead? Would the Sinclair hold on Orkney end with you? What becomes then of your century of Sinclairs?"

"Why, young Harry is a very promising youth. He—"

"He is just that. Promising. I think, Harry, that for his sake you would not want to have your honors fall to him ere he is strong enough to bear their weight. Think of England, Harry. Think of the woes that country has known, and all because the crown came too soon to Richard's head. Is that what you want for your son?"

Sinclair frowned, and he rubbed the back of his neck as if it pained him. "Well, Mother, if it comes to that, surely Johnny could serve as regent here."

"Your brother is in many ways an admirable man, Harry. But he is no ruler, nor has he any training for it." Lady Isabel smiled. "Dear John! He is so—so settled. 'Tis hard for me to realize that you are the elder brother."

"Talk to Janet. She thinks me in my dotage."

"Nonsense. She loves you, is all. And she fears that harm might come to you if you undertake this business for yourself."

"I know that she loves me, Mother. And I love her. But this is my work to do."

"Not so!" Lady Isabel lifted her head higher. "Those who rule must entrust to others much of the business of their realm. This is how the work of any kingdom gets done. You have at your command most excellent able men. They live only to serve you. Let them serve. Give them their rightful chance to prove what manner of men they be.

"Oh, Harry, let go. Let go a little. Bide here and govern. Train up your sons against the day when you can rule no longer. And leave this other matter in the hands of those whose concerns are neither so weighty nor so wide."

Sinclair shook his head. "Mother, Mother, ye are forceful as ever in debate."

"You do see the right of it?"

Sinclair smiled. "I see that you are a meddling old woman after all. But never mind. I'll think on what ye have said. It may be you are in the right."

"Oh, Harry, I am sure of it. Do you not see—?"

"Mother," said Sinclair, gently taking his mother's arm and guiding her to the door, "enough. I'll think on it, I promise you. Do not ask for more."

Later, much later that same night, a solitary figure went stealing softly down the stairs that led to the great hall. All was still. The whole house slept. But Henry Sinclair could not sleep. And so he stood now before the dying fire, looking up at the great sword that hung above the gaping hearth, his thoughts straying to Rosslyn and its lore of bold Sinclairs long dead. Their deeds lived on, like the great yew his grandsire'd set beside the rushing river, still green, still growing, as much a part of Rosslyn as the very stones of those stout walls.

Long he stood there, long enough to travel in his thoughts across the miles and years between himself and old Sir William, friend to the Bruce.

God, he thought, I want this work. It galls me to yield it up to others. Or what's the use in being lord if I am to bide here like poor Robert in Scotland, and leave to others the work that should be mine? I am not Robert! Am not an idle, sickly, aged man. My arms are strong; my body sound; my heart hungry for adventure.

And yet, and yet—I have a duty to these folk. "Duty!" There is the word that beaches me.

A sardonic smile crossed Sinclair's face. He was, he knew, gaffed and landed. If he would have his people dutiful, he must above all honor duty. And he would.

Next day, he summoned Zeno to his chamber, and with him Ingram Gunn and Richard Sinclair.

"My friends," he said, "it has come home to us that we may not follow our heart's desire in this business we have undertaken. For reasons of policy, we have concluded that our place is here in Orkney."

Ingram made as if to speak, but Sinclair forestalled him. "Peace, friend Ingram. Let me have done with this.

"It goes against our nature and our inclination to absent ourself from this enterprise, but we too have sometimes to bend our will like any other man, and accept what we do not relish for our portion.

"Therefore, we appoint our worthy admiral, Sir Antonio, to command the western expedition. He shall be as ourself in the conduct of this business, and shall have full authority to act and direct the forwarding of all things needful to its execution.

"Sir Antonio, d'ye accept this commission?"

Zeno, his dark eyes shining with delight, rushed forward to kiss Sinclair's hands. "My prince," he cried, "most willingly! Your faith in me will not be disappointed."

"We do not doubt you, sir," murmured Sinclair. Then he turned to his young kinsman and said, "Richard, we know something of your mind concerning this adventure, and we will not disappoint you. You shall go as captain of our men-at-arms."

Richard, his cheeks flushed with pride, bowed to his father's cousin and said, "I will do all faithfully, my lord."

"And I, my lord?" asked Ingram Gunn.

Sinclair smiled. "Well, sir, we find ourself of two minds concerning you—"

"But of one heart, I trust."

"Aye, and that wholeheartedly, I promise ye." Sinclair's face, as much as his words, told his friend that all was well again between them. "Let us walk out together, you and I, and talk of this further beyond earshot of these younger bloods.

"Sir Antonio, Richard, God gi' ye good day. Let your work go forward with all speed, and see that you keep us current on all things pertaining to it."

With that, Sinclair quit the room with Gunn, leaving Richard at the mercy of the jubilant and loquacious Venetian.

"Tell me, coz," said Ingram, as he and Sinclair paced along the corridor, "does Janet know of your decision?"

"Aye. I told her of it this morning, early."

"I am glad."

"So is Janet." Sinclair's grin was rueful. "It seems that I can please my friends only by doing that which most displeases me."

"Then God grant ye friends worthy o' the cost."

Sinclair pressed his kinsman's hand. "He has, Ingram. He has. But, tell me. What am I to do wi' you?"

"Ye have only to ask—"

"I know that," broke in Sinclair. "I know that if I know anything. But what is your wish in this, to go or stay?"

Ingram shrugged. "Where can I be of most use, Harry?"

"Christ, man, will ye no say ye'd rather bide along o' me?"

To Ingram's astonishment, he saw tears brimming in Sinclair's eyes. "Why—why, o' course I had rather, Harry. Jesu, we ha' been so long together that it goes against the grain for me to think on sailing off wi'out ye. But I thought—"

"Ah, have done wi' thinking, will ye?" Sinclair's voice was gruff. "An it be no hardship for ye, I'd take it kindly if ye'd stay."

There were tears in Gunn's own eyes as he and Sinclair clasped hands.

40

Harmony reigned now at Kirkwall, and through the long winter and well into May, the whole isle bustled with preparations for the grand voyage. Zeno was in his glory, like a man who'd found his true calling. He was everywhere at once, bullying, cajoling, praying, and cursing with all the fervor of his passionate soul. And at his elbow everywhere went the pale ghost that was Bjorn Eyvindson.

Zeno had hoped to sail in mid-June, and there seemed no reason why this could not be. The fleet stood ready to brave the sea in new canvas and fresh paint. The holds were crammed with stores sufficient to maintain the crews and the two hundred men-at-arms that would sail with them. Short of loading on the great barrels of drinking water, little else remained to be done.

But, toward the end of the first week of June, Bjorn Eyvindson fell ill. He had no cough, no sign of fever, but the man went down like a tired horse, and nothing that the leech could do would make him rise again. He lingered, the old Faroese, till past the time Zeno had planned to sail, and when it became plain that the man was dying, Zeno went to Sinclair and begged leave to depart.

"June is nearly gone, my prince," he said. "We have above a thousand miles to go, and we dare not lose the fine weather by delaying longer. This poor old fisherman is bound to die. He cannot last the week. Let us be off on our voyage and leave him to his own. Since we must go it alone in any event, there is nothing to be gained by our staying."

Sinclair shook his head. "No, Sir Antonio," he said. "Should the man recover, he is to go with you. If he does not, then we shall send for some one or two of his fellows who have been so far as Estotiland, and persuade them to sail with you."

"But, my prince, the delay! We cannot—"

"You will have to endure it, my friend," replied Sinclair. "We value you too highly, not to speak of our fleet, to let you depart without some semblance of a guide."

"Guide!" Zeno all but spat the word. "My prince, I can sail anywhere between heaven and hell. And I have enough of the language now to enable me to discourse with the peoples of those lands. What reason have we to wait?"

"Sir Antonio, we do not like this delay anymore than you do. Nor do we like having our judgments questioned. But consider. Here is an old man whom we have all but forced into our service. His illness may be feigned or fancied, in which case your departure would bring about a most miraculous recovery, a recovery that would leave us in an uncommonly awkward position concerning a man we have no wish to harm.

"If, on the other hand, Eyvindson is indeed dying, then our sense of justice dictates that we not speed his death by a departure that plainly tells him we have given him up to God. And our sense of prudence tells us that there is too much to lose in this enterprise to send you forth without the aid of some one or two mariners who have sailed that way ere now.

"There are two hundred men and more risking the hazards of this journey. And half my fleet. And my admiral." Sinclair smiled and clapped Zeno on the shoulder. "Trust us, sir. We value your life more, it seems, than you do yourself. Leave it in our keeping, then, and know we mean to keep it safe."

"There is another side to this, my prince," Sir Antonio said. "I may have been at fault in not coming forward with this sooner, but formerly there was no prudent time to lay it before you, and latterly, when you so kindly charged me with this business, I thought it less than honorable to look to you for help in a matter that was plainly mine to grapple with."

Sinclair grinned. "You are a windy, politic fellow, sir. I well know that my late splenetic humor cleared a path for me more readily than could a dozen brawny fellows armed with axes. But, come, sir. What's the matter?"

"Why, my prince, it is the men. There is a fear grown up amongst them, a fear fed by this Eyvindson, that we are bent on sailing into perils of such magnitude that none shall see his home and hearth again."

"What perils?"

"Why, the usual mariner's stuff, my prince—sea monsters, cannibals, whirlstreams, and whatever other nightmare thing that shipmen talk of over their frothy cannikins."

"And now that Eyvindson lies ill?"

"It only serves to stoke their fear," Zeno said. "One part of them will swear the man feigns illness to escape the terrors they must face. The other faction full as loudly swears the man is truly sick and like to die for very dread of those same horrors that unite the warring parties in their fear."

Sinclair nodded, his face sober. "Well, sir, it must be dealt with. These are good men, and nothing lacking in their loyalty. If we were to speak to them—"

"My prince, pardon me, but that is exactly what I wish you would not do. If I am to command them, I cannot begin by turning to your high authority at this first contretemps. For, consider, when we are well out to sea, to whose authority shall I turn then if troubles come?"

Sinclair laughed. "God's only, I suppose. Well, sir, do as you think best. If my pleasure or my purse can serve, you have my leave to wave either one or both before them."

Zeno bowed. "Thanks, my lord. I will speak to the men this very evening, and see what a Venetian hand can do to stiffen the resolve of these hardy northern folk."

Sinclair and Zeno parted then, Jarl Henry to matters that waited on his attention within, Sir Antonio to the busy harbor where the work of preparation pressed on to completion.

In the long twilight of that evening, as Jarl Henry drowsed over the inky columns of his daybook, his indifferent attention was broken by a diplomatic cough at the open portal of his chamber. He looked up, blinked twice, pinched the bridge of his aristocratic nose, and looked again. There in the doorway was framed a figure so splendidly arrayed as to quite ravish the noble Scot's strained eyes.

"Sir Antonio," he murmured, "is it you?"

The trig, compact Venetian, a vision in white silk slashed with crimson, floated in on slippered feet, wrapped in a cloud of musky scent. From a shapely head of artful curls he swept a cap of crimson velvet graced with a snowy plume from some unlucky bird that never knew those windswept northern isles, and executed a leg-extending bow that brought his nose within a hand's breadth of the rush-strewn flagstone floor. "My prince," he said, regaining his pikestaff posture, "God give you good even."

"What's this, what's this?" cried Sinclair, barking a half laugh and rising from his seat. "Ye've no forgot your marriage vow and gone a-poaching among the lasses hereabout, I hope."

Zeno's beautiful teeth flashed in a good-humored smile. "No, my prince; for, with all respect to the beauties of this place, I have seen nothing here to rival that which waits for me at home."

"Then why this splendor, sir? We have not seen you so tricked out since your arrival. Indeed, so accustomed are we to seeing you about in rusty stuff we'd quite forgot your—hem—enthusiasm for fine feathers."

"Why, my lord, a man of fashion will dress to the occasion. Silks and velvets are nothing to the purpose when a man's business is with ships and lading."

"And this evening?" Sinclair's pale brows arched like drawn bows.

"Ah, this evening we make merry with our men. For, acting on my lord's suggestion, I told the mariners we'd broach a cask or two and hold, as it were, a midsummer's wassail on the beach this night."

Sinclair chuckled. "You scheming fox!"

Zeno bowed again. "My lord is full of compliments."

"And full o' doubts and questions. What purpose, pray, impels you to go among such rude and hardy folk clad like a peacock courtier? 'Twill be a marvel, sir, if they do not take you up bodily and hurl you into the sea."

Zeno sniffed delicately at the nosegay clutched in his gloved left hand. "My prince, if you are at liberty to saunter down to the harbor some little while hence, you may perchance see something instructive."

Sinclair nodded. "We will."

"Only come not forward, my lord, I pray. Content your noble self with hanging back, and be as it were an auditor in the Venetian school of political philosophy."

"We take your meaning, Sir Antonio. We will be as a ghostly presence there, neither felt nor heard nor seen."

"Much thanks, my lord," said Zeno. He bowed his adieu and departed in a perfumed mist.

"Now God and St. Katherine bless me," muttered Sinclair. "Ingram and Richard must be witnesses to this. Our trusty admiral means to teach us how to manage craft of another kind."

Sinclair summoned his lieutenants, and full secretly they made their way to a slight rise that overlooked the beach. There they dropped prone upon the thin dry grass and peered out through the wispy screening growth to watch the unfolding of the play.

Some two hundred hardy mariners milled about on the sand, laughing and talking loudly as they drained off their cannikins. Zeno, as he moved among the men, was all but invisible to the secret watchers. Only his elegant plume revealed his whereabouts, so effectively was his small form dwarfed by the men in his command.

Ingram Gunn, extricating a pebble that was digging into his belly, grunted windily. "Blood and wounds," he growled, "how is a body to see anything in that throng o' bodies?"

"Patience, good cousin," counseled Jarl Henry. "Our trusty Zeno knows what he's about, even if we do not. And unless—ah, see there! The admiral boards his ship."

"An unfinished ship," remarked Richard, squinting in the light that glinted off the wavelets in the bay.

"Why, sir, yon small Zeno's a barely finished man," said Sir Ingram, chuckling low in his throat. "He swarms the scaffolding like a by-Our-Lady ape."

"Say rather a Jack o' Naples," amended Richard.

"Venice, Venice," murmured Sinclair. "But, *pax*, friends; he's gained the deck."

"And has not spilled a drop, the thrifty man."

"True for you, coz," Sinclair replied. "See how his goblet winks in this lingering light. But, *pax*, I pray ye. The admiral calls for silence, and we must defer to him in this."

The gabble of rough voices from below died away, and the high clear voice of Sir Antonio came readily to his hidden audience on the soft evening air.

"My gentle friends," cried Zeno, raising his cup, "let us pledge the health of our most excellent prince, Jarl Henry!"

"Jarl Henry!" roared tenscore lusty men.

"That was shrewd," murmured Sir Ingram.

"And timely," Richard Sinclair added, smiling broadly.

"Hush, now!" ordered Jarl Henry, digging his young nephew hard in the ribs. "Sir Antonio's courtesy is a model I would set for you to emulate, ye rogues."

"And his costume too?" asked Sir Ingram. "Devil have me if I have ever seen such pretty clothes before."

" 'Tis a pretty man that wears 'em, coz," replied Sinclair. "Let us hear him."

"My good friends," Zeno continued, "this is a happy day. Jarl Henry himself bade me broach a goodly cask or two, so pleased he is with these your labors."

"God bless Jarl Henry!" cried a great brawny islander, waving his arm and christening those around him with a great sloshing of ale. "Aye, and Sir Antonio too."

The cry was taken up full-heartedly.

"Thanks, good friends," Zeno cried, "for myself and for Jarl Henry, thanks. It is right you should ask God to bless him who thinks so carefully and well of you. And when you hear how carefully and how well, I do not doubt but what you will cry again, and louder still, 'God bless him!'

"For, friends, this Jarl Henry, a true knight and a great prince, has even amid all the cares of this his realm taken your cares upon himself, has heard your unspoken cries, has had compassion on your fears, and in the exercise of stewardship has reckoned his account to find himself so deeply in your debt as to quite exhaust the coffers of his bounty."

Zeno paused for breath as a confused murmur, accompanied by a great scratching and wagging of heads, swept through the ranks of men.

"What did he say?" demanded Ingram Gunn. "What did he say?"

"God bless us, coz," replied Sinclair; "it wants a readier wit than ours to fathom it."

"He calls you debtor, uncle," said Sir Richard. "That much is plain."

"Aye," growled Jarl Henry, "and we have told Sir Antonio he might draw upon our purse in this. Pray God he draws not with both hands."

But Zeno soon put Sinclair's mind at ease.

"Hear me," he cried, and the questioning mariners fell silent. "Jarl Henry is that pleased with the work you have accomplished here, and so mindful of the terrors of this projected voyage, that he has bid me tell you he holds you all excused. You need not go this perilous journey."

"Before God—!" Sinclair very nearly gained his feet before Sir Ingram tugged him down again.

"Patience, coz," said Ingram sweetly. "Where is your faith in Zeno now?"

"But, God's bones, coz, what folly is this?" Sinclair's breath came hard and a decided flush crimsoned his cheek. "We never said such; we never did. What is this silk-and-satin popinjay about?"

Jarl Henry's confusion was widely shared among the mariners, as was evident in the welter of voices and wildly expressive gesticulation breaking out on the beach. Then a stentorian voice rang out: "Sir Antonio! Sir Antonio, a word!"

"Who is it speaks?" cried the little Venetian, peering into the throng.

"Kristofersson, Sir Antonio. Jan Kristofersson, shipman come lately from Stronsay."

As the men grew nearly silent, Zeno bade the mariner speak.

"Sir," Kristofersson said, "how does it happen we are excused?"

"Why, Jan Kristofersson, because my lord has heard that many souls among you fear to go. This dread of monsters and cannibals, of strange peoples in strange lands, is a very prudent caution." Zeno wagged his head emphatically. "Moreover, there are the women and children to think of."

Rumbling assent swelled to a chorus of support.

Zeno waved for silence and pressed. "So tender is Jarl Henry's feeling in this, that he would have no man sail against his will."

"Would I not, then?" muttered the hidden Sinclair, as his name was roundly cheered once more.

"Then does Jarl Henry mean to give up this plan of his, after all this work of preparation?" Kristofersson demanded, when the cheering stilled.

"By no means," Zeno replied. "Ours is a thrifty prince. He will not see your labor wasted."

"Then who sails in our stead?"

Zeno chuckled at Jan Kristofersson's question, and rubbed his silk-and-satin sides in evident delight. "There, my friend, is the question.

For while you island folk are very excellent folk for preparation, it requires another breed of men to dare the unknown terrors of the sea."

"I smoke him; I smoke him, the rogue!" Jarl Henry was hard put to keep his voice low as he clutched the arms of his kinsmen. "Observe and learn; here is a master at his work."

A great shaggy bear of a fellow at Kristofersson's shoulder raised his voice above the mutter of the crowd. "Here now, Sir Antonio, do you mean to call us cowards?"

The man's question provoked a prolonged growl of anger from his mates, but Zeno smiled as innocently and as cheerfully as ever. "Why, no, friend, none calls you coward; certainly I do not call you coward. I do but commend your careful caution—and Jarl Henry's kindness.

"You have done your work well; you have earned the praise and the just reward of your most generous prince. What you have done, no men could have done better—nay, not so well. Jarl Henry says so, and I say it too. Indeed, for myself, were I at some future time planning such an enterprise, I would send straightway to these very isles to recruit such men as you to oversee my preparations."

Zeno's smile was beatific. It might have melted glaciers. "Ah, my friends," he said, extending his arms as if he would embrace them all, "when it comes to preparations for great deeds, commend me the prudent islander."

It was a sorely puzzled throng that received this seeming compliment. But the puzzle was soon solved as Zeno, with a fencing master's skill, thrust his point home.

"And when the preparations are done—and done so carefully—I will know where to look for reckless men to brave the hazards of the journey. I'll look to Venice!"

Two hundred voices echoed the word: "Venice?" And Jarl Henry later swore he'd felt the ground beneath him tremble at the explosion of outraged dignity welling up from the wounded hearts of his stout mariners.

" 'Fore God, coz," cried Sir Ingram, "this is near a riot. Will ye no go down there and save yon Zeno's skin?"

"An I did that, coz, the man would never thank me. No. We must leave—Look! Young Kristofersson scales the scaffolding. If he lays a hand on Sir Antonio, his life is forfeit!" Sinclair scrambled to his feet, his face pale, anxious, strained.

"He means no harm, I think, uncle," young Richard Sinclair said. "See? He calls for quiet. He means to speak."

Kristofersson, towering above the little admiral, held out stout arms until the angry buzzing stilled. His massive chest was heaving, and his voice, when he ventured to speak, cracked with scarce-contained emotion.

"Men of the isles," he croaked, "hear me! I am Kristofersson. You know me for a peaceful, willing man and an able shipman."

"Aye!" cried some dozen loyal mates.

"And ye know me for no coward."

A dozen more gave their assent.

"I take it hard, I think it hard that, after all our labor, some scurvy foreign crew—your pardon, Sir Antonio," Kristofersson nodded to Zeno, who only smiled in simple-minded benignancy, "—some scurvy foreign crew should man our ships and have for themselves such prizes as may be wrung from this adventure.

"I ask ye, is this just?"

"No!" thundered from throats two hundred strong.

"Ye say true," asserted Kristofersson. " 'Tis not just, and 'tis not Christian. And were Jarl Henry here, I'd say it to his teeth. I would!"

"Now, I call that bold," murmured Ingram Gunn.

"The very peak of daring," Richard agreed.

Jarl Henry laughed. "God help us, there speaks a lusty mariner. The man that dares me to my teeth is not a man to fear mere hags and monsters."

"For my own part," Kristofersson cried, "and meaning no offense to Sir Antonio here, I'd sooner see these goodly ships put to the torch than see them manned by any but an island crew."

Shout after lusty shout applauded this plain speaking, and it was many long minutes ere Zeno could, with some show of reluctance, publicly confess his folly insomuch as even thinking of recruiting among his countrymen. When he had done, peace and good brown ale reigned supreme on the edge of Kirkwall harbor. It was certain now that none but an island man would hoist a sail or pull an oar in the service of Jarl Henry.

But for all of Zeno's politic art, fortune smiled not on his cause.

June faded into July. Still Eyvindson lingered, barely conscious but alive on his bed of pain. Zeno pressed home his plea, but Sinclair was adamant. There would be no going without Eyvindson or some acceptable substitute. To cover the eventuality, Sinclair went so far as to dispatch a bark to the Faroes with instructions to recruit any who claimed to have sailed to Estotiland. But the bark returned without having found a single doughty mariner who had sailed so far. Nor was Zeno able to satisfy Jarl Sinclair that he had drawn from Eyvindson all the information he needed to chart a course to Estotiland.

With August's passing Zeno's hopes died, and, ere the month was out, so did Bjorn Eyvindson. The only one to weep at the old man's death was Antonio Zeno, and his were tears of rage and frustration.

Sinclair would not hear of daring the autumn gales, and Zeno himself could not mount a serious argument, but it went against his very soul to be thus thwarted. There was nothing for it now but to endure another winter of waiting ere the great adventure could begin.

It would be for Zeno a long and weary time.

41

Snow lay deep in the lanes and on the lea. Christmas had come and gone, and a new year had dawned in Kirkwall. At Sinclair's stronghold there was much feasting and deep drinking to while away the long dark days. It was a cold time but a good time, a time to hug the hearth and rejoice in the warmth of kinship and friendship, a time to be glad of home and homely things.

Jarl Sinclair was himself very near to that contentment he had long ago foresworn. Peace reigned in his hall. His children, strong sons and fair daughters, were growing up around him like tall pines and pliant willows in that wintry barren land. Old friends were by him, and his lady wife, still blooming and as ever fair, seemed to him dearer even than when they were first plighted. He began to feel himself kin to the patriarchs of old, his battles won, his wanderings past, with nothing for it now but to go gracefully down to a good old age in the security and comfort of those stout walls.

Very nearly he accepted this, and was almost glad. There were, he reasoned, far worse fates. He had had a good life, a full life, with honors and achievements aplenty. No illness plagued him, no old wounds flared to spoil his comfort or trouble his hours of rest. He was, for a man past fifty, remarkably fit. Indeed, there was little in his carriage or his aspect to denote the accumulated years. Some strands of silver shone in his reddish hair, a few lines lent added dignity to that stern, strong face. But he was as ever erect and heavy-muscled, and his step was as ever light. His eyes were the eyes of a young man still, and his heart the heart of a youth.

There were days, days when the wind was soft and the brief winter sun shone with unwonted brightness, when Sinclair would wander to the armory and look with longing on his idle tools and suits of war—the basinet helmet, his camail and surcoat, his pommel sword, his shield—and he would feel again the old hunger and the old longing to be once more a voyager-warrior lord. Dear Christ! 'Twould be as sweet as life itself once more to go ranging at the head of a goodly band, to fare hard and dare all in some quest worthy of his powers.

But Sinclair spoke of this to no one. He would ride out the yearning in stoic silence, bidding his heart to still its clamor, bidding his soul to fold its wings and rest.

And when the mood was lifted and his spirit calm once more, he would fling himself into the swarming domesticity of his hall and preside with a cheerful countenance over the little celebrations and the minor feasts that served to brighten the round of common days.

So it was that, on the eve of Ash Wednesday and the start of Lent, Sinclair held forth at the head of the vast oak table in the great hall while ale and meat went around in rich abundance in the company of those he loved. Lady Isabel was there, and Janet and the younger children—for young Harry and Willie, together with Betsy and Beatrix, were sojourning with their uncle, Sir John, at Rosslyn. Also in attendance at Kirkwall were Zeno and Ingram Gunn; John Clarke and Richard Sinclair; the priest, de Bochane, come over from Shetland with Sigurd Sigurdsson, Herdis Thorvaldsdatter's son; and also certain mariners, men-at-arms, and best men from many isles.

The great hall rang with song and laughter; many a flagon was drained that night, and the great ox that was so long a-roasting on the capacious hearth below was reduced to a pile of bones ere the feast was done. One guest and another rose and slipped away as the long night wore on. At last there remained only Sinclair, his wife, his mother, Zeno, Richard, and Sir Ingram Gunn, seated around the table, replete, drowsy, but unwilling to go just yet to bed.

"God ha' mercy," groaned Ingram, loosening his belt. "I have eaten and drunk enough this night to sustain me clear to Easter morn."

Sinclair laughed. "Well done, old glutton. The dreary fast before us should hold no terrors for thee."

"I will remind our friend of his words in a day or two, my prince," Antonio Zeno said. "We will see then how manfully he sits to his lentils and salt fish."

Young Richard pulled a wry face. "Afore God, Sir Antonio, do not talk of it. I know I shall dream of this late ox full forty nights together."

"Richard, Richard," admonished Lady Isabel, with a gentle smile, "make not a god of thy belly, but think on the eternal merit of a little present suffering."

"Aye, lady," grunted the young captain, "I'll not gainsay the wisdom o' that. But God He knows how frail's the soul in a contest with the gut."

"Then we shall set a guard about kitchen and larder," Sinclair said. "We would not have so dear a kinsman fall from grace over a slice o' beef or a scrap o' mutton."

"And who will watch the watchers, pray?" inquired Lady Janet. "For I know a certain noble lord, who shall be nameless, that once in Lent grew so surfeited with turbot, tench, and herring that he made a midnight foray on the larder of a castle some distance to the south of here, and—"

"Pax, pax!" cried Sinclair, laughing. "Tell no tales!"

"Nay," protested Richard, "let the lady speak, for I am but a poor weak wayward Christian as needs example to light my way."

"Well, sir," said Janet, flashing a roguish look at her lord, "it happened that this certain nameless noble was so far gone from the path of right conduct that he even ventured to climb up on a barrel to reach down a flitch o' bacon hanging from a rafter."

Ingram shook his head in mock sorrow. "Lady, ye harrow our very souls with this sad parable."

"Wait, pray, till you have heard the sorry ending. It seems that greedy wretch managed somehow to miss his footing, and bacon, barrel, and baron all came crashing to the floor with such a clatter as roused the cook and full half the household. These came running to the larder and found there the fallen sinner supine amid the ruins."

"What mortification!" cried Zeno.

"What slander!" cried Sinclair, wiping his eyes and shaking his head. "Janet, Janet, I cannot thank ye for this revelation. What will our friends think o' me now?"

"Why, sir," volunteered Sir Ingram, " 'tis heartening, truly, to know that retribution falls equally on sinners of every degree. Indeed, thy lady wife hath done a service to us all, and hath given us a most instructive sermon to start us on this Lent."

"Humph! An it serves to keep you out o' the larder, coz, 'tis words worth more than gold." Sinclair shook his head. "It seems hard, truly, that once a fault has been confessed and the sinner shriven, his fall from grace should be raised again to discomfit his repentant soul."

"Be not cast down, my son," said Lady Isabel. "Soon or late our faults will find us out. But others may profit from our past sins; count it therefore a happy fault that wards off another from like falling."

Richard Sinclair grinned. "Aye, madam. For my part, I mean never to fall so far. I'll shun barrels and favor ladders, and will thereby ascend to heaven at last."

Sinclair sniffed. "We counted ourself nearer heaven at Rosslyn than at any other place. It wanted only a little bacon to make our Eden complete."

"What serpent and what Eve deceived thee, my prince?" inquired Zeno. "Is it for this high-hanging fruit of the sty that you were driven out of paradise to winter here on this windswept northern isle?"

"No, sir," retorted Sinclair. "There was no serpent in it, nor no Lady Eve, only a gnawing in our gut that drove us to indiscretion. But, much as we value this jewel among isles, ye say rightly when ye call Rosslyn paradise. 'Tis a rare day we do not think with love and longing on our castle there."

"Ah, God, coz, it is a fair spot," said Ingram. "Even a Caithness man will allow it. We had happy hours there, you and I."

Sinclair nodded. "Often, before sleep, we wander there in our imagining and see ourself a lad again, chaffing old Duncan or riding at the quintain under the shrewd and watchful eye o' dear old Knox. God bless him.

"D'ye mind the time that Malise Sparre distracted my horse and near brought me to disaster?"

"I remember the drubbing that earned him," replied Ingram, grinning. "Ye were marvelous wroth that day, coz. I'd not ha' stood in Sparre's shoes for all the gold in England."

"He was an odious fellow even then," murmured Sinclair. "Had he been able to mend his ways, he might be living yet."

"He was warned off, coz. 'Tis no one's fault but his that he heeded not the warning."

"What warning's that, coz?"

"Why, old Meg, the witch woman, d'ye no remember? She proved a true prophet in Sparre's case at any rate, for he told me himself—that day so long ago when you and Janet and I rode wi' Sparre down to the glen for to have our futures told—he told me she had prophesied he'd reach for what was not his and so come to grief." Gunn shook his head. "Old Meg! Odd. I have not thought o' her once in all the years since then. But now that I do think on it—by God, Harry! The woman was a witch! She did tell us true!"

"About Sparre, it may be she—"

"But look!" Gunn's voice grew agitated, loud. "Did she no tell Janet she would marry the lord of an ocean realm?"

"Aye. She did," said Janet, wonderingly. "She did say so, Harry. And she said I'd bear six children, too!"

Sinclair's face drained of its ruddy hue. "'Knight and more than knight,'" he muttered, "'baron and more than baron; liegeman of a pair o' crowns.'

"Jesu, Mary! She did see it! That poor crazy old body surely had the sight. She foretold all o' this. Good God!"

"I remember it," said Lady Isabel. "I remember it as if 'twere yesterday. You came into my chamber and you told me you had been to see Meg o' the Glen. You told me she said you were to follow the sword."

"Aye, Mother. And 'twas then ye showed me Sigurd's sword that hangs yonder, and ye told me for the first time of my claim to Orkney." A strange light shone in Sinclair's eyes. "The thing's beyond doubt, and yet—can such things be? Can a poor daft old crone truly have seen what was to be?"

"Saul went by night to the witch at Endor," Ingram said. "That's set down in the Bible, Harry. Mayhap our Meg was an hundred times great-grandchild to that same Bible witch."

Sinclair rose from the table. "My friends, pardon me. I—'tis close and smoky here, I must get a breath of air."

And without troubling to don his cloak against the cold, Sinclair hurried out into the crackling starlit night.

The wind was blowing in from the west, catching up the powdery snow and sending it swirling over the treeless open land. The sea ran high, renewing under cover of darkness its relentless assault on the land. The hiss of the wind at play, the surge of the waves against the rocks, the crunch of his own footfall—these were the only sounds that came to Sinclair's ear. His cheeks stung to the lash of the blown snow, and his lungs burned with every inhalation of chilled salt air. The glittering chips of silver that were the stars, flung wide in a charcoal sky, were to his tearing eyes mere smears of dancing light.

This talk of Rosslyn and of the old woman's prophecy had strangely stirred the man's heart. And it had wakened a long dormant memory, reviving it with startling clarity in his mind. Meg's voice sounded in his brain, and her words came out at his own mouth:

" 'West, west, west. A fair wind is at your back. Before you I see a wild and rugged coast, all grown over with great stands of trees.

" 'Strange men . . . their faces like earth and dead leaves, surround you. Above you, a great bird circles and soars . . . a sheaf of arrows in his claws.' "

"Harry?"

Sinclair wheeled about. "Janet? Janet, it is cold, lass. Ye should not be out here in this blast."

"I—I fetched your cloak."

"God bless ye. I did not feel the cold till now." Sinclair threw his fur-lined cloak about his shoulders. "Let us get in out o' this."

"No. Wait." Janet moved closer, sheltering in the ward of Sinclair's bulk. "Hold me, love. Please."

Sinclair wrapped his arms around her, enclosing her under his cloak. "Now let the wind blow, sweetheart. We'll weather it in this fashion and keep forever warm."

Janet looked up at her husband, her tears glistening in the cold starlight. "Yet not forever, is it, Harry? No—" Her small hand pressed against his mouth. "Do not speak just now. Let me say this, though it cleave my very heart. For if ye speak, I'll weaken, I know it, and I will never be strong enough to say it again.

"Harry, I love you. I love you for trying to be what ye could not be, for my sake only. Ye did try. But," Janet shook her head. "It is not in you to bide while others go. I—I do not know if old Meg is at the root of this. But I know she told the truth in all else. And it may be I fly in the face of destiny in trying to hold you here. I'll try no more, Harry. What must be, will be. God He knows I am too frail a body to stand alone against the fates."

Janet lay her head on Sinclair's breast and, her voice straining against the sobs that welled up in her own breast, said, "Sail away west, my only love. Go if ye must. But, oh, my lord and my life, come home again to me."

Part V

42

With the coming of March and the returning birds, Sinclair's fleet sailed out from Kirkwall on a westward course. Hearts heavy at parting lifted with the brisk wind and the clean slash of prows through the light chop of the sparkling sea. Ingram Gunn, standing aft with his noble kinsman, declared, "By the mass, Harry, this is well begun! Was there ever a fairer day for setting out on such a venture?"

Sinclair smiled. "Ye're not sorry ye came, then?"

"Man, I could not bide if you were bound to go. Ye know it. But this day's an omen, surely. Our business cannot help but prosper under such bonny skies as these."

"Would ye could persuade our worthy admiral o' that. He goes about as dour as a December day."

"Ah, well, Harry, he feels himself disappointed. He thought to lead this expedition, but now ye're here he's no the chief, and the notion was that dear to him." Ingram winked. "He'll come around to his old self again, coz. Zeno's not one to stay low for long."

"God grant ye are right, Ingram. It troubles me to see the man downcast. We had warm words but yesterday when he talked again o' going away home to Venice."

"Ye cannot blame him, Harry. He has been long away."

"Aye. But I could no more go this journey wi'out Zeno than I could go wi'out ships. And he knows it."

"And so he applied the lever, hey?" Ingram grinned. "Ye cannot fault his strategy in that."

"No, nor do I fault the man for anything. He is disappointed. I know something o' that. And I know too he must hunger for home like any other man. But he chose an awkward time to fret me with it. This voyage has been too long in the planning to have it nearly die in the borning."

"Ah, Zeno's as curious to see the western lands as you are, coz. He had to rant and blow a bit for his pride's sake, but he'd no more have gone to Venice now than I'd ha' gone to England. He is too much the adventurer to let slip a chance like this."

Sinclair grinned. "I counted on that, Ingram. I counted on that all along."

The fleet made for the main island of Shetland, where the men alternately rested and laid in fresh stores. Then, on 1 April, they hoisted their sails to catch a favoring wind and headed out into the open sea. A fair sight they made, the dozen barks together, their white sails like the wings of doves under a blue sky above a blue sea.

"God is surely with us, Sir Antonio," remarked Sinclair, catching up with his admiral in a rare idle moment. "The wind blows straight from heaven to make our passage easy."

Zeno frowned. "It may be from heaven, as you say, my prince. But I like not the look of the sea this day. See the white showing, like manes of mermen's steeds?"

Sinclair, glad that Zeno had dropped something of his recent stiffness and reserve, said lightly, "Ah, well, my friend, there is no sea you cannot steer us through."

"I am an excellent navigator, my prince. That is true. But not even my great brother Carlo could answer for the fate of a ship in a gale."

"Come, my friend. D'ye think we have forgot how ye brought us through that tempest off the Shetlands?"

"God brought us through, my prince, not Zeno. And as it was, we lost three barks and any number of good men." Zeno scanned the seemingly innocent sky and shook his head dubiously. "There is a storm coming, and no mistake. With your permission, my prince, I would signal my captains to haul in their sails."

"Haul in—?" Sinclair stared at the Venetian in amazement. "My friend, look how the sun smiles down upon us; see how our bonny ships run before the wind. Ye cannot mean to lose the advantage o' this day?"

"With your permission, my prince," repeated Zeno, and there was that in his tone that could not be misread.

Sinclair pursed his lips and blew out a great gusty sigh. Then he nodded and said, "Sir Antonio, you are my admiral. An we did not leave this to your judgment, we'd throw our own judgment into question. Do as ye think fit."

Zeno smiled. "My prince, you have just saved yourself a deal of canvas and one admiral. With God's help, it may be I can save your fleet."

As the afternoon wore on, Sinclair was tempted to question and to doubt. But well before the sun had set, the wind rose and took on a blustering tone. The blue sky turned to a deeper hue, and that darker blue deepened to a smudgy charcoal gray. White caps danced on the slate-colored sea, and the first fat drops plopped and splattered on the oaken deck.

Sinclair, drawing his cloak more snugly about him, stared anxiously through the gathering gloom at the masts of his clustering flock. Almighty God, he thought, are we to live this horror once again?

"Coz! Harry!"

Sinclair turned to see Ingram approaching. The wind, whining now and playing on the rigging like a madman with a harp, caught Ingram's words and blew them back in his throat. He lurched closer and, cupping his hands to his mouth, cried, "Zeno says we must go below!"

Sinclair nodded. He caught hold of Ingram's arm, and together they leaned into the wind and weaved drunkenly to the hatchway. Sinclair bid Gunn go first, but in his following he was thrown off balance by a sudden veering of the ship, and he slammed into Ingram with such force as to send them both crashing to the deck below.

"Jesu, Harry," said Gunn, looking up at Sinclair who had fallen virtually astride him, "if ye were in such a mortal hurry to come down yon ladder, I'd ha' gladly stood aside and let ye go first."

Sinclair, laughing, scrambled to his feet and offered Ingram his hand. "For this courtesy our thanks, gentle coz. No doubt ye spared me a bruising by thus carpeting the deck."

"Aye, and took a royal purple lump or two for myself, I warrant ye," growled Gunn. "Damn ships anyway, Harry. And damn me for a fool for ever setting foot in one again."

"From the look o' things, coz, ye'd best give over cursing and try what prayers can do."

And pray they did, mariners and men-at-arms, servants and masters too. But for eight terrible days and nights together, the tempest raged unabated. Many a stout heart quailed, and many a strong man wept in mortal dread. Zeno and Sinclair between them strove heroically to manage ship and men, to hold oak planking and terror-stricken minds intact. Day after day, the howling wind and the churning sea drove the ships on; and day after day, Sinclair tried to hearten his men with the thought that "tomorrow, surely, the storm must pass."

But it did not, not until so many tomorrows had piled on as quite to bury courage, hope, and faith, until Sinclair himself had no more words to give, until Zeno was near the point of exhaustion, until the men had fallen into a nerveless stupor that bordered on a kind of living death.

So it was that, on the morning of the ninth day, when Zeno, his face white and strained, his eyes fever-bright, croaked out the news that the storm indeed had blown itself out, no one cheered, no man smiled, no one so much as stirred.

"My prince," rasped Zeno, hoarsely, hanging heavily on Sinclair's shoulder, "we must get them up and out into the air."

Sinclair's mouth worked, but no words came. So he shook his head and staggered to where the nearest man, a Shetland mariner, sat slumped in a pool of his own vomit. With an herculean effort, Sinclair reached down and seized the fellow's shirt with both hands and hauled him to his feet. Zeno, seeing Sinclair's intent, came to his aid. Together they dragged the man up the ladder, leaving a bit of skin from his shins on every step, and none too tenderly let him fall to the deck.

Sinclair's sides heaved from this sudden exertion, but as he gulped in great breaths of morning air, he could feel life returning to his weary frame. "Come," he husked. "Let's get the rest."

Zeno shook his head. "My prince, if we try to lug them all, we will ourselves drop dead before we are half done."

"We cannot let them rot there," Sinclair said. "For their own sake, we have to get them up and out."

Zeno nodded. Then, on a sudden, he whipped out his dagger and cut a length of rope. "I will drive them out, my prince."

Sinclair winced. Then he said, "God help me, Sir Antonio, I see no other way."

Down they stumbled into the hold once more. And Sinclair, with tears in his eyes and rage burning in his breast—rage at this circumstance, rage at his ill luck, and rage at what he was doing—joined Zeno in slapping, cuffing, kicking, cursing, driving the benumbed and all but helpless men up the ladder and out onto the open deck. And when he came to where Ingram lay, white faced and staring, his cheek stained with his own bile, Sinclair's rage exploded in his throat and near to strangled him.

Sobbing and cursing, he seized his beloved kinsman by the hair and slapped him hard across the face. "Get up, damn ye! Get up! Get up, get up, get up!"

Ingram's head fell forward on his breast, and Sinclair, weeping, slumped to the deck with Ingram cradled in his arms.

So Zeno found them, and he gently bade Sinclair rise. Together, the brave admiral and his heartbroken lord half dragged, half carried the unconscious Ingram up into the mocking sunlight. They bore him aft and set him gently down. Zeno, panting, straightened his cruelly aching back and looked across at Sinclair. "Be of good cheer, my prince. He will soon be well."

Sinclair, his stubbled face creased with pain and grief, nodded. "It may be so," he muttered. "It may be so. But I think I can never pardon myself for bringing him to this."

When the men of Sinclair's bark had regained something of their former strength, Zeno posted several of the hardiest about the ship to spy out stragglers from the fleet. There were dismally few. Of the dozen that had sailed from Kirkwall, but seven remained. Of these, but five were yet seaworthy.

Zeno and Sinclair held a council with the captains of the surviving ships. It was agreed to shift men and such stores as could be salvaged from the two crippled vessels and distribute them among the five sound barks.

At Zeno's direction, whatever was intact by way of sail, rigging, precious spikes and nails, and some sound lumber was also saved. And he himself recovered the lodestones, floating needles, astrolabes, by which a man could measure the sun's height, and the sun-shadow boards—wooden disks marked with concentric circles that, when floated in a basin of water held level at midday, revealed within a degree or so the latitude. They would remain in the area for another day, in hopes that one or more of the missing would turn up. Then they would meet again to determine their course of action.

It was a long, full day.

The transfer of stores and men taxed the already strained nerves and sinews of the adventurers, and ere nightfall more than one man had dropped from sheer fatigue. At sundown, Sinclair commanded a full ration of meat and ale for all hands, then he bade his captains order their men to rest.

The several captains, together with Zeno, Ingram, and Richard Sinclair, gathered around their lord on the poop of his bark. A weary crew they were, haggard, hollow-eyed, sick at heart and aching in every muscle. Sinclair's own sore heart brimmed with compassion for them all.

"My friends," he said, his voice unsteady and low, "it appears that we have once again led ye into peril. And once again we have suffered a most grievous loss of stout ships and stouter men.

"We had thought this business would bring us gain and glory. It has brought us only pain and sorrow. 'Tis God's will, ye may say; and we will not gainsay ye. But it goes hard, mortal hard wi' us to play the sage philosopher over another body's bones.

"Yet," Sinclair heaved a deep sigh, "here we are, spared for God He knows what purpose, alive and afloat, with full half an ocean between us and our homes.

"Our brave admiral tells us he cannot guess how far westward we have come. But that we have come west there can be no doubting. This same tempest that has left us bereft of ships and friends hath surely sped us far along the way we meant to come.

"Sir Antonio advises that we cannot be many days off from that land we sought. And having come so far, it is our purpose to go farther and to accomplish that for which we have already paid so dear." Sinclair's reddened eyes scanned the faces about him. "We know what ye have suffered; we know the condition o' the men. And because we would deal wi' ye justly and wi' mercy, as becomes a Christian lord, we have asked ye here to learn if any man among ye is of a mind to turn back now and sail for Orkney. Speak your minds freely, pray. We count it no fault in any man who desires to turn back."

Bjornsson the Shetlander, who had captained one of the crippled barks, stepped forward. "My lord," he said, "as one o' those most hurt in consequence o' this wicked tempest, I venture to speak first."

"Speak away, my friend."

"Well, my lord," said Bjornsson, scratching at the silver stubble on his chin, "I cannot speak for the men-at-arms, they being landsmen and of another, different breed. But a mariner knows that danger's the portion of any as takes to the sea. I doubt that any Shetland man is ready to go back. For myself, I mean to go wi' ye. My bark's ruined, true; but ye have in me stout arms and a willin' heart—or ye will have so soon as I am rested."

"Thank ye, friend Bjornsson," said Sinclair, gravely. "The loss o' the ship's no fault o' thine. We are heartily glad we did not lose you with it."

"My lord!" Richard Sinclair spoke up.

"Aye?"

"My Lord, 'tis true, as Bjornsson says, the men-at-arms are of a different breed. But never doubt our fealty or our courage. We came on purpose to sail west wi' ye, and so we mean to do. God He knows we have no love of tempests, nor for stewing in our own puke eight whole days together in a stinking hold. But let your admiral only set us safely down on solid ground again, and we will prove ourselves worthy men."

Sinclair, with a faint smile, said, "We do not doubt ye, Richard. Wherefore we chose ye for this task.

"But, Sir Antonio, what say you? Are we fit, d'ye think, to go forward with this business?"

Zeno shrugged. " 'Tis a matter of the spirit, my prince. The barks left to us are sound enough. If the men are of one mind with their captains, I see no cause for abandoning this scheme."

"And what of your own mind, Sir Antonio?"

Zeno grinned. "My prince, I am a Zeno, and a Zeno does not turn back."

"Sir Ingram, how say you?"

Ingram Gunn, who had been leaning heavily the while against the rail, roused himself with an effort and stood erect. "Christ, Harry, an I was ninny enough to come away wi' ye, I am surely fool enough to go on."

Sinclair himself, weary and heartsick as he was, joined in the general shout of laughter that greeted Ingram Gunn's reply. Then he said, "God send us such fools always when great work's to be done.

"My friends, get ye to your rest. God send ye healthful slumber; God send us all a better day."

43

Before noon of the following day, mariners and men-at-arms alike thrilled to the cry of "Land!" from the lookout. Due west and dead ahead lay what appeared to be an island of considerable size, hilly and well forested, with an excellent harbor that seemed to offer a placid welcome to the little fleet.

"By the mass, Sir Antonio," Sinclair exulted, "this looks to be a very fair discovery indeed."

"It appears that we are ourselves discovered, my prince. Look!" And even as Zeno pointed, Sinclair saw the vanguard of hundreds of men, armed with bows, emerging on the run from the shelter of the trees.

"These be no naked savages," Sinclair muttered.

"Not naked, certainly, yet they appear to be sufficiently savage to my taste," Zeno replied. "Do you intend to parley with them, my prince?"

Sinclair frowned. "We cannot ask our poor lads to walk into that mob. And God He knows we are in no condition to do battle if battle's offered. It—look! They are launching a boat! Bid the lookout beckon them to us, Sir Antonio. We are surely equal to dealing with those few, at any rate."

As the islanders' boat drew near, Richard Sinclair and Sir Ingram came up to where Sinclair was standing on the poop.

"They seem indifferent glad to see us, coz," remarked Ingram, eyeing the approaching emissaries with no little suspicion. "I cannot make out the meaning o' that shouting, but I doubt they are bidding us welcome to their shores."

Sinclair nodded. "No doubt ye're in the right of it, Ingram." He turned to his younger kinsman. "Richard, disperse some dozen of your men about the ship and bid them keep watchful. They are not to draw except on word from us. Make that plain, we charge ye."

"I understand, my lord," said Richard, and he hurried off.

Zeno now bid his mariners let down the rope ladder, and in a moment a dark-haired, blue-eyed man clad in a belted tunic clambered over the rail. Nine more came after him, all armed with knives only. There were no smiles on those faces, as ten pairs of eyes flicked right and left, taking in every aspect of ship and crew.

"Speak to them, Sir Antonio, pray," Sinclair commanded.

Zeno tried. He tried the language of Estotiland and the several tribal tongues he had learned from Eyvindson. But there was no light of recognition in the islanders' eyes, and no response save for a subdued muttering among themselves.

Zeno turned to Sinclair and shrugged. "Either my accent is at fault, my prince, or these men know nothing of the languages Eyvindson taught me."

"Swounds!" Sinclair clapped his hands in exasperation.

At the sudden sound, one of the islanders made as if to unsheath his dagger. Bjornsson the Shetlander, seeing him, cried out impulsively in his own native dialect, "Hold! Leave that sticker in its housing!"

To his astonishment, the man replied in the Shetland tongue, "Peace, friend. We are too few to give thee cause for alarm."

Sinclair wheeled around. "Bjornsson! D'you know what yon fellow said?"

"Aye, my lord," replied the mariner, wonder in his tone. "The man spoke in my own tongue."

"Come forward, man. Ask him what place this is."

Bjornsson addressed the islander and put Sinclair's question to him. Then he translated for Sinclair. "He says, my lord, the place is called Icaria. He was a castaway here in his youth and has remained since then."

Sinclair nodded. "Tell him we come in peace. We intend no harm, but wish only to go ashore to replenish our stores of water and wood."

Bjornsson relayed the message, then turned to Sinclair and said, "He tells me these are a fierce folk whose forebears came from Ireland long ago. They admit no strangers here, and will not suffer us to set foot on their land."

"Jesu, Mary," growled Sinclair. "God bless all courteous island folk. Well, ask him if we may trespass on the ocean for a little time at least—out o' bowshot. No! Do not say that. Ask, rather, if there is not a sheltered harbor nearby where we may at least rest ourselves and make ready to sail still farther west."

Bjornsson bespoke the man, then told Sinclair, "He says there is a fair harbor on the eastern side, but he bids ye not tarry, for yon bowmen on the beach are of a hostile mind."

Sinclair sniffed loudly. "If we were not grievously short o' men and main weary wi' battling wind and sea, we'd gladly offer to go ashore and instruct these worthy folk in courtesy." He turned away in disgust, calling over his shoulder to Bjornsson, "Ye may bid 'em all go to hell, if they know what that is. Aye, and a swift journey to 'em, too."

Bjornsson communicated the essence of Sinclair's speech, and saw the surly ambassadors over the side and into their boat.

"What now, my prince?" asked Zeno, as the islanders pulled away.

"Hoist the sail, Sir Antonio. Make for the eastern side. It may be we can avail ourselves of wood and water there before yon merry archers can foot it thither."

The captains of the other barks, taking their cue from Zeno, ran up their canvas and, flocking after their leader, made a half circle around to the eastern shore. There, as the islanders had said, they found a harbor, broad, deep, and sheltered from the prevailing wind. Sinclair now ordered Richard to lead a party ashore to gather wood and to fill their casks with fresh water.

Richard, taking with him three boats and a dozen men in each, ordered the casks on board and made rapidly for the cove. Sinclair, watching anxiously from the rail, bade Zeno leave the sail up and stand ready for a hasty departure. It was prudently thought of.

For scarcely had Richard's men begun to disperse on the beach when a chorus of wild, blood-chilling yells split the air, and a horde of islanders came swarming down to the strand. As Sinclair watched in helpless horror, Richard's men dropped their casks and ran for the boats in a veritable rain of arrows. One man went down, and another, and another. They did not rise again.

Valiantly, Richard's men strained at their boats, pushing off into the shallows, and still the arrows flew, some finding their mark in human flesh, more slicing through the calm surface of the water.

"Christ and St. Katherine!" roared Sinclair. "Pull away, damn it! Pull away!"

"Shall I charge the bombards, my prince?" cried Zeno.

"No time! Sail in as close as ye dare and pick up the men. Oh, Christ! There's Richard down!"

The young captain, having urged his men on board, was in the act of climbing into the last boat when an arrow took him in the shoulder and sent him splashing headlong into the shallow water. Two men, courting death for themselves, leaped from the boat and managed to haul Richard up and over the gunwale. They scrambled in after him, and their mates pulled away with a strength inspired by sheer terror.

"If Richard's killed, by Christ, we'll drop the business now and come west again only to lay waste this cursed land," Sinclair vowed. Then he cried, "Send Matteo to me! The armorer, Matteo!"

The old Venetian, hearing his name on the lord of Orkney's lips, came hurrying aft.

"Sir Antonio, tell this man to stand by to tend the wounded," Sinclair commanded.

As the boats came alongside, strong hands reached down to pull the oarsmen in. Sinclair shouldered his way through to where Richard lay, his blood staining the planks. The young captain tried to smile up at his chief. "I—I fear we brought ye back no stores, my lord," he said.

Sinclair knelt beside him. "Are ye bad hurt, Richard?"

Richard shook his head. "It burns like hot coals, but I think I am not dead yet."

Sinclair beckoned to Matteo. The old armorer deftly cut away Richard's shirt and examined the wound. Then he looked up at Sinclair and nodded encouragingly.

"Thank God," murmured Sinclair. Then he said to Richard, "Ye'll be all right now. Matteo's as good as any leech."

Richard, tears in his eyes, said, "We—we left some good men behind us, my lord."

Sinclair squeezed his kinsman's hand. " 'Tis no fault o' thine, Richard. We should never ha' sent ye ashore. Rest easy, now, and get well. We need ye strong and fit."

Zeno approached. "My prince, where will you have us go?"

"Circle the island, Sir Antonio. Bid the lookouts keep sharp eye on the land. Our stores are perilously low. If we see any opportunity to try again, we'll land in force and in full armor to take on the water and wood we need."

Zeno seemed to hesitate, then he shrugged and ordered the steersman clear the harbor and head north. And as the bark sailed forth, Sinclair, wrath boiling in his soul, stood looking back to the beach where lay a half-dozen goodly men-at-arms who would rise to fight no more.

After sailing up the coast and around the northern cape, Zeno now found himself navigating through treacherous shoals. At no point along their way had they been able to attempt a landing. The islanders, as if they had smoked Sinclair's intent, followed the progress of his fleet. At no time could the mariners look shoreward without spying those who spied on them. Now, with hostile inhabitants on the land and an equally menacing shoaly bottom under them, the adventurers were in a fair way to lose their ships, their lives, or both together.

But Zeno was in his element. Delicately, deliberately, he threaded his way through the shallows, seemingly serene but never for a moment relaxing his vigilance.

"By Peter, coz, I think the man enjoys this," Ingram Gunn declared.

Sinclair nodded. "Never doubt it, Ingram. For my part, I'd trade the Shetlands—aye, and the Faroes to boot—to be safe in Kirkwall now.

But our worthy admiral could not be happier. He is proving himself to himself once more. And to us."

"He has nothing to prove to me," said Ingram, licking his salt-caked lips. "Let him but get us safely out o' this, and he may call his famous brother a ploughman for all o' me. I'd no gainsay him were he to call himself the greatest admiral since Noah."

Sinclair, tense as he was, had to chuckle. "No doubt he'll be inclined to brag and blow a bit, but he is welcome to it. This is no kind o' sailing for me. 'Twould be as easy to walk on eggs wi'out cracking 'em. I tell ye, Ingram, it makes me sweat."

"Aye, and yon fellows on the shore add nothing to my comfort." Ingram spat into the sea. "They'd sweat us, more than likely, could they but lay hands on us."

Sinclair glanced to the beach and scowled blackly. "Whoreson butchers! I mean to return one day and pay 'em out in kind."

Ingram shook his head. "Ye'd have me in a quandary, then, Harry. After that plaguey storm, I vowed I'd never go to sea again. But if ye promised me a crack at those gentlefolk, I do not see how I could keep my vow."

In all, the expedition lost ten days in circling the island and picking their way through the shoals. When Zeno had at last got them safely through and had led the fleet out into open water once more, Sinclair abandoned further thought of replenishing his supplies in that hostile land.

"We must sail on," he said to Zeno. "We'll not risk another life in this quarter. Yonder isle may as well be desert for all we'll have from it."

Zeno nodded. "We've a favoring wind, my prince, and we have struck a spell of fair weather. We can do no better than to run before the wind and hope we strike a more congenial coast presently."

"It had better be soon," muttered Sinclair. "These men have suffered much as it is, without our having to go on short rations and scant water."

"Then we'll keep sailing west?"

"Aye. And, Sir Antonio—"

"Yes, my prince?" Zeno turned and looked at Sinclair with an oddly pert inquiring eye.

Sinclair grinned. "Sir Antonio, you are surely the greatest by-Our-Lady mariner that ever came out o' Venice."

Zeno's smile was beautiful to see. "I think you may be right, my prince. But we must never tell by brother Carlo so."

Sinclair laughed aloud. "God love ye, man, ye never disappoint me. Go! Lead your fleet, and carry us safe to some happy isle where we may find refreshment and rest."

For a week the fleet kept on its westward way, with clear skies above and a running sea below. The mariners sang at their work, and the spirits of the adventurers rose as they widened the miles between themselves and the island of Icaria. To Sinclair's relief, the wounded were all mending. No fever or infection overtook them; and, under Matteo's tender care, most were already up and about and talking of the quantities of blood they'd spill if ever Sinclair would lead them in strength to Icaria again.

Richard Sinclair talked little. He seemed subdued, older, more thoughtful. His kinsman's hearty greeting and his evident joy when the young captain first appeared on deck elicited only a wan smile in reply. At first, Sinclair was inclined to ascribe this change in Richard to the effect of his hurt. But when, after a week had passed with no sign of his brightening, Sinclair made a point of drawing him aside to talk.

"Richard, have I told ye how glad I am to see ye well again?"

"Not more than twice a day, my lord," replied Richard, with but the ghost of a smile.

"You are feeling better, are ye not?"

"Aye. The wound's near closed. Old Matteo can set up for a surgeon anytime he's of a mind to quit the sea."

Sinclair nodded. "I mind the time he set this wrist for me. No man could ha' done it neater. But come, Richard, if ye are healing, how is it ye go about so dark and dour. 'Tis not like ye, lad. Is aught amiss?"

Richard shook his head. "I am well, my lord, truly. But, God help me, I cannot sleep o' nights for thinking on the men we left back there on the beach. I—I do not mean to trouble you with it, my lord. Perhaps I am grown squeamish, I do not know. I have thought—I think I should be replaced as captain."

There was anguish in the younger Sinclair's voice and in his eyes. The look he turned on his noble kinsman went to the older man's heart.

"So that's the way of it, then?" Sinclair's voice was neutral, calm.

Richard nodded. "I—I see their faces nights," he said.

"Hum." Sinclair bit his lip and scratched his head. "And ye think ye would do well to yield your place?"

"I think I must, my lord. It would not do to have a womanish captain when there's soldierly work to be done."

"No, no. Indeed it would not. Ye may be in the right of it, Richard. Ye may be." Sinclair slipped a fatherly arm about the younger man's shoulder. "I shouldn't wonder but what I may yield my own place presently."

"You?" Richard's eyes widened. "But ye cannot. You are—"

"Well, now, ye cannot know how it is wi' me, Richard. But I'm of a mind to tell ye, now that you have opened up the matter, so to speak." Sinclair gazed steadily into Richard's eyes. "I see faces too, Richard. I see my old friend Hafthorsson, that broke his neck in trying to get my castle built. I see the men that went down off the Shetlands, and those that were lost in the tempest that overtook us on this journey and even those I led and lost in battle against the Southrons long ago. Aye, and I see those that you see, too."

Sinclair shook his head. "There's been a deal o' dying under me, Richard. There's been days when I wondered, truly, if I was not under a curse."

"No!" Richard's whole protest was all in the one word.

"Aye, but I have thought it, Richard. And now that ye've turned my mind on it, I wonder if it is not time I set aside ambition and risked no more the lives of others to further my own cause."

"But you are a sovereign lord, even as a king in your own realm."

"And you, Richard, are a captain of men-at-arms." Sinclair paused to let his point go home. Then he said, "Richard, if ye did not grieve for those that are lost, I would myself relieve ye of your duty. But, lad, when a man takes up the sword, he knows that he or another must die of it. The men ye lead know it; they that died knew it. I do not say that makes it any easier; I do not even say that makes it right. But so long as men make war there will be captains, and there will be corpses. And captains must sometimes lead men into such hazards as may make corpses of 'em all.

"We did not fashion this world, Richard. But we were born into it, and we must live in it as best we can. We have been blessed more than most. We have lands and a people to govern, and a rich inheritance to make secure, to enlarge if we can, and to pass on intact to our sons. That is the task that has fallen to us, and we mean to carry it out as best we can."

Sinclair shook his head. "God He knows we have stumbled sometimes. He knows we have done such things as we will forever wish undone. But we have stuck to the task. D'ye understand?"

Richard nodded.

"Now your task is to captain my men-at-arms. Ye may err, ye may go grandly. Ye may do both, one time and another. And some o' the men must die, and some will live. God alone He knows why. You yourself may fall wi' them, or ye may go on and live to a good old age in comfort on thy father's lands at home. However it may fall out, ye have your task, Richard. As your father's cousin, as your lord, and as your friend, I'd have ye stick to it if ye can."

"As you will stick to yours?"

"Aye."

Richard nodded. "Well, then, I will. But I think I shall never forget those men."

"Remember them always, Richard. Pray for their souls. Have masses sung for 'em. But do your task."

The wind shifted now to the southwest, and the sea churned roughly. Zeno altered his course to run before the wind, and for upward of a fortnight the fleet continued on this way. Then, some three weeks and more out of the treacherous shoals off Icaria, the wanderers spied a great land mass that seemed to be growing up before them on the horizon.

"Well, my prince, there is land," said Zeno cheerily. "But what manner of land it is, or what kind of folk inhabit it, is any man's guess."

"Jesu, Sir Antonio, will ye look at yonder mountain?" Sinclair pointed to the towering hill that dominated the skyline.

"Indeed, my prince, I cannot help but see it. But is that not—? Yes! 'Tis smoke, my prince! There is smoke going up from the mountain!"

"Then the place must be inhabited."

"Of a certainty."

Sinclair rubbed his jaw. "God bless me, Sir Antonio, I know not what to think. After that last encounter, I confess I've little stomach for going blithely ashore. And yet, the men's bellies will be growling presently if we do not lay in fresh stores."

"The sea is running high, my prince. If we do not soon choose a course, we will run on past the place. There seems a goodly harbor yonder. Shall I put in?"

Sinclair hesitated, then he said, "Aye. Put in. We'll show ourselves in the harbor and see if any come down to greet us as they did at Icaria. If we are opposed in any strength here, then God help us, for I know not how much longer our stores can last."

Almost simultaneously with Sinclair's decision, the wind suddenly died down. The waters calmed, and the fleet slipped easily into the harbor. There, in the shadow of the smoking mountain, the voyagers flocked to the rails to scan the beach, watching, waiting for any sign of human life.

None showed. There were only the wheeling, soaring birds overhead, their cries echoing from the surrounding hills. No other sound disturbed the perfect calm, save for the lapping of the wavelets and the faint sighing of the dying breeze.

44

For an hour, two hours, Sinclair's men held back, waiting, sharing their lord's reluctance to run headlong into the kind of reception that had lately befallen them. Still, nothing in the shape of a man appeared.

"My prince, but for yonder plume of smoke, I'd say this land's without a people," Zeno declared.

"Aye," said Sinclair, nodding. "If there be any here, they must have seen our sails by this time. Either that, or they are lying in wait to surprise us so soon as we touch land."

Richard Sinclair approached. "My lord, shall we dispatch a boat?"

Sinclair tugged at his ear and whistled tunelessly. Then he said, "We will all go, Richard. We cannot ask a few to risk that which befell us at Icaria. We will ourself go in the first boat, for if there is trouble this time we mean to take the brunt of it ourself.

"Sir Antonio, give the signal. Let us get the boats over and make for shore."

Over the calm waters of the inlet, the broad-beamed boats skimmed lightly as swans. The wind was down, all was still. But oarsmen and passengers alike did not cease to scan with wary eyes every bush, every rock, every tree thick enough to afford concealment.

"There is lovely cover for an ambush here," muttered Sinclair to Zeno, who was seated with him in the bow.

"In truth, my prince, I'd not give a groat for our chances if there be

345

any savages waiting. These men are hungry and full weary. They would be hard put to defend themselves in any contest, but a surprise attack would be the end of us."

"Well, if it must come, let it come with ourself in the vanguard. Perchance some of those in the other boats can contrive to make their escape."

The rowers in Sinclair's boat gave a last strong pull, then shipped their oars and let their craft ride in to a grinding halt. Nothing. Sinclair got cautiously to his feet, half expecting an arrow to come flying from behind the rocks or one of the pines that stood watch along that coast. Still nothing.

"Now God bless us," Sinclair said, leaping lightly out of the boat, "it seems we have this pretty place all to ourselves."

He turned and waved the other boats in. The men needed no urging. Full eagerly they tumbled from the boats and collapsed gratefully on the shining sand. Then was there a general doffing of helmets and mail, and a few more lively or more fastidious souls stripped naked and went running into the water to wash away the grime and stench of their long confinement at sea.

Sinclair smiled as he watched his weary followers take their ease. They had come a long way together, through terror and grave dangers. Not for the first time did he count himself blessed in the courage and fealty of this band.

A shout from young Sigurd, Hafthorsson's son, broke in on Sinclair's musing. He turned and saw the golden-haired Shetlander emerging with cupped hands from the shade of a clump of birch.

"What have ye found, lad?" Sinclair cried.

"Eggs, my lord," replied Sigurd, running up with his precious burden. "Look! Fresh birds' eggs!"

At this news, the whole party dashed into the trees and commenced to plunder the nests. The woods rang with shouts and laughter as the famished voyagers slaked hunger and thirst with the tiny delicacies.

"By Peter," declared Ingram Gunn, wiping his lips, " 'tis as good as a feast. I never thought to take so much pleasure from a fistful o' wee eggs. God, but they are good."

Sinclair grinned. "After weeks o' salt meat, salt fish, and precious little water, I could as easily eat a serpent raw. But look ye, Ingram, there is such a plenty o' birds and fish hereabout, why d'ye not organize a hunt? Let's us this night at least have ourselves a glorious banquet."

"Done!" cried Ingram, cheerily. In a matter of minutes he organized parties of fishers and fowlers, and soon the two bands were scouring shore and shallows with bow and spear and net.

Others, under Sigurd's direction, gathered firewood, while Richard led yet another party in quest of fresh water.

Before sunset, smoke stood up from a dozen fires on the beach, and the grateful smell of cookery filled the sweet air. One of the few remaining barrels of ale was brought in from the fleet, and for the next hour and more gorging was the business that occupied them all.

"Ah, my prince," said Zeno, sighing contentedly as he tossed away the clean-picked carcass of a plump wood pigeon, "this bounty comes to hand in good season. I cannot say when I have sat to my dinner with more gusto."

"Will ye no try this bit o' fish, Sir Antonio?"

Zeno shook his head reluctantly. "My mouth wants it, my prince, but my belly, alas, can hold no more."

Ingram put out his hand. "I believe I can just manage it, Harry, an I put my mind to it."

"Take it and welcome, coz," said Sinclair, laughing. " 'Twould make a sick man well just to watch you eat."

"It hath the contrary effect on me," growled Richard, shaking his head. "I wish, Sir Ingram, that ye would not face me whilst ye gobble yon poor flounder. Afore God, I cannot bear to watch ye."

Ingram grinned. "Your delicacy does ye great credit, Richard. An I had not wi' my own eyes seen ye devour a dozen speckled eggs wi'out benefit o' cooking, I'd take ye for one of those airy poets that live on nectar and dew."

Richard groaned and rubbed his belly. "Do not remind me of it, pray. There's such a griping in my guts—oh, Jesu!" He scrambled to his feet and dashed for the brush, pursued by shouts of laughter.

"Ha-ha!" cried Ingram Gunn, wiping his eyes. "Our young captain's took wi' the flux, belike. Ha-ha-ha! Oh, eggs make a proper purge, right enough. We must tell this to old Matteo against a time he must treat us for binding."

Sinclair grinned. "From the numbers that are even now making for the trees, coz, it appears we shall so richly manure this land as to raise up a second forest full equal to the one at our backs."

"A pity 'tis not oaks and hardwoods," murmured Zeno. "Yonder firs are of scant use in building ships."

"Aye," Sinclair agreed. "But, in truth, we have no cause to murmur, my friend. 'Twas a fair wind that blew us to this place o' plenty. Our stores were that low, we feared—ah, but here our gallant captain comes. Hey, Richard! How fares it wi' you?"

Richard, decidedly pale and rueful, seated himself gingerly beside his chief. "I believe I am quite hollow," he growled. "My poor hind smarts and my knees are gone all watery. For some days past I wondered if I would ever shit again. Back there, I wondered if I would ever stop."

Ingram shouted with laughter. "Ye had a social time of it, I warrant. Full half the men are groaning in the shade o' yonder trees."

"Praise God the wind is right at any rate," murmured Sinclair.

Richard chuckled weakly. "Another wind is rising at our backs, my lord. Such a deal o' farting I never heard in all my life before. 'Tis like the siege of a city back there. An all those bombards were charged wi' shot, yon forest would be leveled in an hour."

Ingram, quaking with mirth, rolled over on the sand. "Ah-ha-ha-hah! Whew! What delicate lads these are! Poor tender creatures! I swear, Harry, we shall have to forbid 'em men's rations lest they—lest they—" On a sudden, Ingram broke off. His face went dead white, and beads of sweat glistened on his brow.

"Coz, what ails ye?" Sinclair inquired.

But Ingram did not linger to reply. He struggled to his feet and, clutching his middle, scurried off to the sanctuary of the forest.

"So much for men's rations," said Richard, when he could get breath enough to speak again. "Let us hope yon Gunn's not so overcharged as to burst when he fires. I mean to have some sport with him over this."

Sinclair shook his head and dashed the tears from his cheeks. "We must allow he deserves it," he said. "But go easy with him, Richard, pray. There's naught ye can say that will match the instructive circumstance wherein he finds himself at this moment."

Sinclair and his men camped that soft warm night on the beach under a sky full of stars. They broke their fast next morning on the cold fragments of the past day's feasting, then Sinclair summoned Richard, Zeno, and the chastened Ingram to a council.

They walked a little way down the strand and took their ease amid a heap of boulders. The sea was calm that bright June morning, the light breeze barely rippled the waters of the harbor. Birds were everywhere busy, building, mating, gathering food for their insatiable young. Now and again a silver-sided fish broke the mirrored surface of the shallows with a soft splash, as if indifferent to the purpose of the voracious wheeling gulls.

"God bless us," murmured Sinclair, gazing out over the perfect seascape, "is this not a lovely land?"

"In truth, my prince, I have never seen a fairer," replied Zeno, his own voice for once subdued. " 'Tis as if we were come to a new world, as yet unspoiled by war and trade and the thousand businesses of men."

"What day is this?" Sinclair asked.

" 'Tis Sunday, my lord," Richard Sinclair said, "Trinity Sunday, in the church calendar."

Sinclair nodded. "Then," he said, "we christen this place Cape Trin, in the name o' the Father, and of the Son, and of the Holy Ghost."

Reflexively, the others crossed themselves, and Ingram said, "Amen."

"My friends," said Sinclair, leaning his broad back against a sunwarmed boulder, "whether or not this is the place Eyvindson told of, we cannot say. Yet, plainly, we have come upon such a coast as we have dreamed of. It remains now to discover what lies inland, and whether there is here land enough and timber enough to suit our purpose.

"Richard, are ye feeling fit for some business of consequence?"

The younger Sinclair's face brightened. "Aye, my lord. My wound troubles me not at all now, and I would be main glad o' something to do."

Sinclair nodded, smiling his approbation. "Well, then, as the day's so fine, and ye are feeling so fit, we charge ye with exploring inland to discover what ye can of the character and resources of this place."

Richard ginned broadly. "I am the man for it, my lord."

"We do not doubt it," Sinclair said. "We'd have ye make for yonder mountain, Richard, and learn the source o' that smoke. It may be that there lies a village or a city there, and who can say what manner o' folk they may be? We'd have ye take an hundred o' the men, well armed and in full armor, against the possibility of a hostile encounter."

"Aye, my lord."

"Now, Richard, we would caution ye against seeking a fight. Ye'll have an hundred men, 'tis true, and good men, surely. But we are none of us so strong as when we left Kirkwall, and we would not have them tried beyond their powers. If battle offers, shun it. Understand?"

"I do, my lord. We will avoid it if we can."

"Good, then. Ye need not overburden the men wi' rations and water, for this is plainly a bountiful land, and we would not tax their weary sinews wi' more than the weight o' their own arms."

" 'Tis well thought of, my lord. I make no doubt we'll find sufficient game and water and eggs—"

Ingram groaned aloud, bringing a mischievous grin to Sinclair's lips.

"Ye'd better leave off your litany o' victuals, Richard, lest our poor kinsman be taken with a griping o' the bowel."

"In truth, he doth look wonderfully green," Richard remarked. "Would ye no like to go lie down awhile, Sir Ingram, till the fit is past?"

Ingram scowled at the young captain. "A man as'll mock another's pain had best beware o' the day when the sick man's well again."

Sinclair chuckled. "Pax, friends. We'll talk no more o' eggs this morning. Richard, assemble your men and bid them make ready for the march. We will bide here upon this pleasant beach against your return."

Richard nodded and hurried away.

"There goes a very worthy young man," Zeno remarked. "He has the spirit of a Venetian."

"And the humor of a Saracen," said Ingram, laughing in spite of himself.

"Humph! He was too easy with ye by half, Ingram. Ye gave him materials sufficient to construct a gibbet, and he made only a schoolboy's catapult of them."

"Yet David slew Goliath wi' a paltry pebble, coz. And yon Richard's aim was very near the mark."

Within the hour Richard's troops, their helmets gleaming in the clear midmorning light, stood armed and ready on the beach. Sinclair stood before them, arms akimbo, respect and admiration shining in his eyes.

"My friends," he said, "we bid ye go full warily. Make of your eyes most diligent clerks; note everything. See ye do not set too brisk a pace, for ye may not remark much if ye move along too rapidly. Godspeed. We'll keep ye in our heart and in our prayers till ye return. Farewell."

He stepped to one side, with Ingram, Zeno, and the mariners at his back, as Richard Sinclair led the troop away. Those remaining on the beach watched till the last glint of the last helmet disappeared in the pines; then, with strangely heavy hearts, they turned away and settled in to wait out the time till their friends should be back with them once more.

45

For all that it was so pleasant to be idle on the beach, watching summer advance upon the land, Sinclair could not be easy in his mind. He found himself time and again turning his gaze inland, scanning the line of dark old trees in hopes of catching a glimpse of burnished steel through the porous wall of green.

On the evening of the third day after Richard's departure, Sinclair ordered that a watch be kept all through the hours of darkness, and that a great fire be maintained as a beacon to guide the explorers in. But the fourth day came and went, and the fifth and the sixth and the seventh in dull procession, without a sign of Richard and his men.

"Christ, Harry, but they've been long away," said Ingram Gunn, as he walked with Sinclair along the strand.

"Aye." Sinclair's face was grim. "If we have sent them to their doom, then there is no penance rigorous enough to atone for this great folly."

"Perchance the land is wider than we thought, coz. And ye did bid Richard go easy."

"But, Christ's bones, Ingram, we never meant for him to be gone so long." Sinclair shook his head. "If he is not back in three days' time, I will myself take a score of able men and go out on his track."

"Count me among 'em, Harry, pray."

Sinclair looked at Ingram. "I'd no deny ye, coz," he said, "but in truth ye would do better to bide here and rest. I may be a most indifferent friend, slow to heed and slower still to thank, but I have not been

352

SWORD OF THE NORTH

altogether blind, my old friend. The least exertion seems to leave ye scant o' breath. D'ye think I did not remark how spent ye were after our fowling foray two days since?"

"Ah, God, Harry, ye'd have made a marvelous by-Our-Lady nurse." Gunn forced a laugh. "Ye fret worse than a hen when the hawk's about. But I'm too old a body to be took in under your wing. There's naught amiss wi' me that a little sleep can't mend. In three days' time, ye'll find me fit for anything."

"God grant ye're right, Ingram." Sinclair placed his hand on his kinsman's shoulder. "If you go down sick, I'll lose whatever joy I'd hoped to have o' this adventure."

"Wait three days, coz, then ye may worry yourself to your heart's content for all o' me. Only wait three days."

But on the afternoon of the next day, the waiting was over. Zeno, busying himself aboard his bark with overseeing the replacement of some lines, happened to glance shoreward in time to see Richard Sinclair, at the head of his band, emerging from the shade of the stand of evergreens.

At Zeno's glad cry, a general shout went up, and Sinclair, who had been scouring his sword against his own planned foray after Richard, let the weapon fall and went running up the beach to embrace his youthful kinsman.

"Richard, Richard," he cried, "afore God it's good to see ye. We had about decided to lead a party out in search of you."

Richard, his handsome face shining with the joy of achievement, returned his lord's embrace right fervently. "Had ye so little faith in me, my lord?"

"Nay, Richard, 'twas not lack o' faith, but the long weary time o' waiting that put me in mind of going after you. But come, lad, you and your fellows must be in need o' rest. Get ye down to the tents and we'll break out ale and victuals for ye, that ye may bait before ye tell us all ye have discovered."

"Oh, God, I am too full o' talk to leave any room for food, my lord. But give me some ale to wet my throat and I will tell ye of the most glorious land ever I set foot on."

The men-at-arms were soon divested of helmets and mail, and they sprawled about the sand at their ease, quaffing the last of Sinclair's ale, as Zeno, Ingram, Sinclair and the mariners all gathered round to hear Richard's account of his journey.

"Our going was easy enough," he said, "for there is little undergrowth in that virgin forest. Indeed, it was like nothing so much as strolling the aisles of some grand cathedral.

"We found abundant stands o' hardwood, my lord. There is timber here sufficient to build an hundred fleets."

Sinclair and Zeno exchanged significant looks, then Sinclair asked, "How did ye fare for victuals, Richard?"

"Very well, my lord. Birds and game abound here, and we had no difficulty in supplying our wants. Moreover, we came upon any number o' springs of sweet fresh water wherewith to quench our thirst. The land here is well watered and, I believe, very rich. A man might supplement his fishing and hunting with such crops as suit his palate."

"Did ye find no people, Richard?" asked Ingram Gunn.

"I am coming to that, Sir Ingram. All in due course." Richard smiled and drained off his ale. "Yonder mountain is a curious thing, truly. That smoke ye see is of no man's making. It comes from a great fire inside the mountain itself, and how long it has been burning or how long it will burn, none can say.

"And from this mountain runs a spring that appears to issue a substance like pitch, black and oily, as it bubbles down to the sea."

"Jesu," murmured Sinclair, crossing himself. " 'Tis like St. Katherine's well near Rosslyn! We mean to see that for ourself. It may be an omen of a happy kind."

"Well, my lord, it led us to a large river that flows into a very fair and sheltered harbor, so ye may be in the right of it. From all that I could see, certainly, this is a rich and fertile land. The people—"

"Hah!" cried Ingram. "There are people then!"

"Aye, Sir Ingram. We came upon a goodly number o' them dwelling in caves hard by yonder mountain."

"What is their condition?" asked Sinclair. "Did they show a hostile intent? Seemed they likely to resent our presence here? Have they towns or—?"

Richard held up a forestalling hand. "Slowly, slowly, my lord, pray. They have no towns that I could see. They are apparently content to take such shelter as they can find in the hollows and crannies that God or nature hath provided.

"They made no sign of hostility; indeed, they seemed a timid folk, small in stature, and inclined more to flee than fight."

"Said they anything at all to you that you could comprehend?" asked Zeno, his dark eyes bright with interest.

"They said little, and I comprehended less, save when they pointed to the object named. They are shy, wild things, Sir Antonio, and it was not easy to find one who would stand still long enough for anything like an attempt at conversation."

"These do not sound like the folk Eyvindson described," Zeno said. "Those were a stout and warlike people; these, it seems, are quite otherwise. Tell me, sir, can you recall anything of their words at all?"

Richard scratched his head and grinned. "I recall their word for woman."

A general shout of laughter went up at that, and Ingram cried, "Well done, Richard!"

But Zeno hissed for silence. "What is it, pray?"

"Well it sounds like *a bit*. And the river they called *seboo*, I think. Or was that the spring? No, no. That had a longer name. Indeed, they have the most wonderfully long names for things that 'twould all but break a man's jaw to say 'em if he could remember 'em.

"Their greeting is something like *kwaa*, or so I remember it. And *boosool*, they also said in such a manner as to make me think it must be akin to our 'good morrow.'

"The mountain they call *kumdunk*, or something very like it, and a dagger they call *wokun*. They were much taken with our swords, I can tell ye. And when I pulled off my helmet, they started like frightened children." Richard laughed, then to Zeno he said, "I am sorry, Sir Antonio, that I can recall no more of their language. I heard a deal of it, but for the most part their meaning escaped me."

Zeno frowned. "I recognize none of the words you have told me. It must be we come to some place other than any that Eyvindson told of. In truth, my prince, I know not what to make of this."

"Do ye not, Sir Antonio?" Sinclair smiled. "Whether 'tis Eyvindson's land or no matters little. What matters is that we find ourselves in a place rich in timber, fish, and game, with good harbors and fertile soil. The inhabitants are clearly of a pacific mind, and if we cannot now talk easily with them, yet we need not fear them nor waste our energies in building fortifications and laying plans for battle and siege. Indeed, there is no city to lay siege to."

Sinclair got to his feet. "Richard," he said, "ye have done well. For this ye shall be knighted with all due ceremony so soon as we are once again in Kirkwall. For this present, kneel and we'll confer the accolade here on this wild, unspoiled coast."

The young captain went down on one knee before his lord and received the slight weight of the sword upon his shoulder.

"Rise, Sir Richard Sinclair, knight of Orkney." Sinclair's smile was warm as he offered his hand to his young kinsman. "You and your men have earned our lasting gratitude. Never was our trust more securely placed.

"Take your rest now, and be easy. On the morrow we will meet in council to determine our future course."

That evening, Richard and his men were very much the center of attention as the mariners plied them with questions about their exploration. Interest in the inhabitants ran high, and many a sly wink and ribald jest went around concerning the native women. Richard protested that neither he nor his men had trifled with the shy, wild beings, but his auditors chose not to believe—or to seem not to believe—his assertions of innocence.

Sinclair's squire, John Clarke, was noisiest in his expressions of doubt. "Ye cannot mean, Sir Richard, that after a month o' fasting ye did not help yourself to one o' yon lasses?"

Richard shook his head, smiling. "I know 'tis hard for an old rooster like you to credit it, John Clarke, but there was no fornicating done."

"Fornicating!" Clarke spat in the sand. "Why, God bless ye, Sir Richard, there be no sin in it if these be not Christian folk. Or if there is, 'tis but a very little sin at best."

"What chop logic's this, John Clarke?" Sinclair inquired, looking askance at his squire.

"Why, my Lord, 'tis plain as a pikestaff. If a creature be not baptized, that creature is in a state o' nature, so to speak, and is no more accountable for faults than a dog or a horse."

"That is an interesting and most convenient notion, my friend." drawled Sinclair, "but it overlooks the accountability o' the other creature, whom we take to be a lickerish Scottish squire who was duly christened and who, God help him, must one day answer for all his naughtiness."

"I think God judges soldiers differently from the way He judges common folk," declared Clarke, huffily. "When a man lives a life o' perils and hardships, none can begrudge him a bit o' sport when he finds it."

Zeno chuckled. "I think, my prince, you must convert these people to our faith if only to protect them from your squire."

Sinclair shook his head. "That work we leave to others," he said. "But you, John Clarke, see ye conduct yourself with all discretion. We would not take it kindly were we obliged to make war on these folk because you provoked some goodman's wrath. The horns o' the cuckold have caused more blood to flow than ever the horn o' Roland did."

Richard Sinclair and his men went early to their rest that night under a canopy bright with stars. The mariners soon followed, and presently the whole encampment slept, lulled by the wavelets that kissed the pebbled shore.

Night deepened. The soft warm breeze from off the sea sighed in the branches of the sentinel pines. An owl took up her sad lament, and soon the forest echoed with the cries of her feathered kind that joined in her doleful keening.

In the camp, a lone figure stirred, rose, and walked down to the water's edge. Long he stood, looking out over the starlit sea. Then, availing himself of a natural seat among the stones heaped upon the shore, he wrapped his cloak about him and settled in to watch the stars retreat before the advancing eastern light.

Sinclair was still at his lonely post when the brightening dawn called the others from their rest.

46

In the forenoon, Sinclair called Zeno, Richard, Ingram, and the several captains of his fleet to a council. When all were seated comfortably on the ground, Sinclair unfolded his plan.

"My friends," he said, "we slept little last night for thinking on the advantage that has fallen to us here. From what we ourself have seen, and from what Sir Richard hath told us, 'tis plain that we have here the answers to many questions that have troubled our mind of late.

"We have no doubt that, with these rich resources, we can maintain and enlarge not only our fleet but our very realm. Moreover, we can find here such materials for trade as will enable us to develop that foundation of commerce on which all great powers stand. In league wi' Norway, Denmark, and Sweden, we can launch such a fleet and undertake such a thriving trade as to crowd the Hansa merchants clean off the sea.

"And, we believe, this land is bountiful enough to support whole towns of Orkney folk who may seek to better their lot by settling here and taking up the work of developing the resources of this place.

"From what Sir Richard tells us of the inhabitants, we need look for no difficulty from that quarter. So long as we move discreetly among them and in nowise interfere with their pursuits, we should be able to forward our business here in undisturbed tranquility.

"We count it, therefore, God's providence that led us here, and we mean to claim this land for Orkney, for ourself, and for our heirs, to the advantage of our whole people. This will we communicate to Queen

Margaret on our return to Kirkwall, and we will seek to assure her of our unchanging fealty even as we seek to extend our sway over these western lands."

"When will ye be returning to Kirkwall, my lord?" asked Ingram Gunn.

Sinclair smiled at his kinsman. "Why, Sir Ingram, not today, surely. Nor tomorrow. Indeed, now that we have come to it, let us unfold to you our whole thought concerning that.

"It seems to us prudent to let no delay come between us and our purpose. For who can say what ships and what men might not arrive on this coast in the interval? The sea is wide, my friends, but it is not without limits. The same winds that blew us here could as well blow some foreign adventurers to this selfsame spot. And they, as well as we, can surely see the richness of the place. If we do not at once establish our claim, and that forcibly, what is to prevent another from usurping us and seizing that which God hath dropped even in our lap?

"No, sir, we mean not to lose all this before we have even secured it. Therefore, it is our intent to bide here for some considerable time, to build a settlement, however small, and to gain thereby a solid footing on this ground that will be as our warrant to hold it fast for Orkney."

A murmur went up among the men, and the several captains huddled in whispered debate around Antonio Zeno.

A frown creased Sinclair's face, and he said, "If there be some question, we should like to hear it."

Zeno got to his feet and stepped forward a pace. "My prince," he said, "I pray you, think not that any here is of a mind contrary to your own. You know us all to be loyal men, proud to be in your service and grateful for thine openhanded bounty."

Sinclair nodded. "We know that, Sir Antonio. And we trust ye know that ye may speak freely before us, so great is the favor ye have found wi' us."

Zeno bowed. "You are ever courteous, my prince. Well, then, I will speak freely. This plan of thine comes as something unexpected. For my own part, I will gladly follow where you lead. But you should know, my prince, that there are many among the men who think longingly on going home. The hazards of this enterprise have, as you know, taken their toll—not only of lives and ships, but of nerve and sinew as well.

"In my own mind, I am persuaded that these men have proved altogether admirable. They have endured great hardship and great terror with uncommon courage and longsuffering."

"We'll not gainsay it, Sir Antonio. These are a gallant breed."

"And yet, my prince, even the most gallant grows at last weary, comes finally to a point where thoughts of home crowd out all other thoughts, and so succumbs to the hungers of the heart. I think, my prince, your plan will fill many a heart with dismay. Loyal as they are, the men hope and expect to be soon bound for home."

Sinclair rubbed the back of his neck and pursed his lips in a soundless whistle. "So," he said, "ye think they'd no be willing to bide here for a time?"

Zeno shook his head. "I venture to say not one in five would be of a mind to stay, my prince."

"We could wish we had known which way their thoughts were tending," Sinclair muttered.

"Had I known where your own thoughts tended, my prince, I would have reported this to you ere now. But, as it is—"

"Aye, aye. 'Tis no fault o' thine, Sir Antonio. But you, Sir Richard, have ye heard like talk from among the men-at-arms?"

Richard got to his feet. "I have, my lord."

Sinclair nodded. "Well, then, there is nothing for it but to lay the matter before them all and to sound them out as to whether there be any of a mind to stay. For look you, lord or no lord, we have ourself been so tempered by time and events as to leave us wi' little appetite for leading folk where they would not be led. Summon the men, and let us learn their mind in this."

As soon as the mariners and men-at-arms were all drawn together before him, Sinclair mounted a boulder and broached his plan to them. Hardly had he said his say when a great uneasiness ran through the ranks, and a considerable buzzing rose on the sweet June breeze.

Sinclair called for silence. "My friends," he said, "let us be heard out. It has come to our ears that some among you are of no mind to delay your return to Orkney. And, truly, your faces tell me more than words that this report's no baseless rumor.

"We are of no mind to hold any here against his will, for we know something of your longing, and we know too what manner o' hardships ye have endured till now.

" 'Tis neither to our purpose nor our inclination to plead, to hold out promises of rich rewards, or to seek other means of enticing ye to stay. We will say only that here is good rich land, peaceful and ripe with promise. Those who stay can look for the first fruits of this enterprise and be, as it were, the chief men of this our western outpost. Beyond that, we can offer nothing more than labor, loneliness, and our thanks.

"If ye choose to go, 'twill be no mark against ye. That we assure ye wi'out reservation. We had rather bide here wi' a willing few than keep ye all here against the inclination of your own will." Sinclair's gaze swept the ranks before him. Then he said, "Freely choose, we charge ye, and fear nothing. Let all who would leave for home stand over to our left; those who would stay, move right."

For a moment, the men stood fast, looking to one another as if for guidance. Then, slowly, the cluster dissolved, and when the separate groups were formed, there stood but a score of men on Sinclair's right.

"Jesu, Harry," murmured Ingram Gunn, "our bold admiral did not overstate the case."

Sinclair nodded, a rueful smile on his lips. "And what of you, Ingram?" he said, softly, "Will ye stay or go?"

"As you choose, coz, so will I."

Sinclair squeezed his kinsman's arm. " 'Tis as good as an army at my back," he said. Then he addressed the men.

"We thank you for this honest answer," he said, "and for much else besides. Ye may go back to your tents wi' light hearts, my friends. We will make plans for your immediate departure, and will bid ye Godspeed wi' all good will. For, know this. Ye have earned our abiding love, and not even so wide a sea as lies 'twixt here and Orkney can sunder the bond between us. Go now. We will report to ye presently our plan for your leavetaking."

"God save Jarl Sinclair!" cried a mariner on his left. And all the men, right and left, echoed the cry.

Sinclair, with a wave of his hand, turned away, taking with him Ingram, Richard, and Zeno. He led them to higher ground, then halted and stood looking back at the camp, profound disappointment in his eyes.

"My prince," ventured Antonio Zeno, "I am sorry for this turn of events. I hope you do not count it disloyal in the men."

"No, sir. We said what was in our heart to say, and we would not take back a word of it. We do not blame the men, my friend. Not many would choose to winter in this wilderness, not for glory or for gold."

"But you mean to stay, my prince?"

"Aye, Sir Antonio, we do. We intend to establish our claim here, and if we cannot build a town and fortify this coast, yet we can discover the full extent o' the wealth o' this place and enlist the Queen o' Norway's aid in securing it for our common good. What may be in years to come, no man can say. But surely, soon or late, some enterprising people must come here, found cities, and raise up a strong and thriving settlement.

"We had hoped to build here some dozen houses, and thereby to strengthen our hold on this rich land. Failing that, we can at least give some months to taking stock o' the resources and to building friendship with the inhabitants against a time when we can return in numbers sufficient to establish our own people here."

"Richard, are ye sure these cave-dwelling folk are as timid as ye told us?" Ingram Gunn inquired.

"Aye, Sir Ingram. They remind me of nothing so much as deer, for they are even as shy and as quick to run."

"God grant ye are right," muttered Ingram, "for we shall be woefully outnumbered."

"So were we, even at a hundred strong," Richard said, "and no one so much as frowned at us. We've nothing to fear from them, I promise ye."

" 'Tis a pity theirs is not one of the languages Eyvindson taught me," Zeno said. "I would be the more useful for that. As it is—"

"As it is," broke in Sinclair, "ye'll no be staying with us, Sir Antonio."

"My prince?" Zeno seemed not to understand.

"We said ye'll no be staying, my friend. There's above an hundred men yonder who dream of going safely home to the isles. And there is one man best able to bring them there."

"Not I, my prince! You surely cannot mean to—"

"Yes, sir." The set of Sinclair's jaw bespoke his determination. "For, look you, we mean to deal justly wi' those brave men. They came wi' us through many a hazard, saw ships and comrades lost, and came very near to death themselves, one way and another, in serving us. We'll no send 'em back out on yonder sea wi'out a master mariner to guide 'em. Our conscience is burdened sufficiently wi' blood. We do not mean to load it further."

"My prince," said Zeno, with an effort at restraint that cost him much, "I know you to be the most just and honorable of lords; but think, I pray you, on what you ask of me. There was a time when I had hoped to lead this expedition. That, for one reason or another, was not to be. But you had me come anyway, and that I gladly did. And, despite the horrors of that dreadful tempest, I have contrived to bring you to this place.

"Now, when there is adventure to be had, strange people to observe, and God knows what wonders to be seen, you bid me turn about like a ferry pilot and go back the way I came.

"If that is to be the extent of my part in this, then I would have done better to return to Venice when my poor Nicolo died. Indeed, I should have done so."

Sinclair felt compassion for the offended Zeno. He could see that the man was deeply moved and almost in tears. He placed a hand on the gallant admiral's shoulder and said, "My dear friend, if we did not think ye the finest navigator that ever sailed, we would not place so grave a burden on ye. 'Tis no light thing to get those men safe back to Kirkwall. But it is a matter very near our heart that they do return safely, for they have earned that much at least."

"I think not," said Zeno, stiffly. "They would not stay with you."

"But they did come so far. Come, Sir Antonio, let us not debate before our friends. And above all, let us not part—as part we surely must—in anything but love and friendship. D'ye think we would not have ye stay, for your own sake, for friendship, as well as for to bring us out o' this when the time comes?

"Man, we loved your brother. And that same love we bear you in full measure. Do not believe even for a moment that we send ye away gladly or with a whole heart. But we have a duty to those men, and 'tis through you and you only that our duty may be done."

The tears came now, rolling in great pearls down Zeno's olive cheeks. "My prince," he said, "pardon me, but this goes very hard, very hard. You have your duty to those men, you say. And I have a duty to you. My one wish is that I be found always dutiful. If you command me to go, it is my duty to go. But there is that within me bids me stay and be ready to bring you safely home to your so dear family and your people when it shall please you to quit this place.

"Those men," Zeno shrugged, "they are very good men, to be sure. But you are a prince and father to a whole realm. If you be lost, then an entire people are bereft of a wise and generous ruler whose like they cannot hope to find again."

Zeno went down on one knee and seized Sinclair's hand. "Consider, my prince, I beg you. Think what a loss you may risk for many times the number of men you would have me carry away."

Sinclair drew Zeno to his feet. "My worthy, worthy friend," he said, "God bless ye. We—our thanks are hardly adequate to this great testimony of the love ye bear us. But as ye love us, tempt us no further from our purpose, pray."

Zeno swallowed hard, raised his tearful eyes to his lord and said, "I will trouble you with no further pleading, my prince. But give the order, and it shall be done as you command."

"Thank you, Sir Antonio," Sinclair said, his own eyes wet. "This obedience has cost ye dearly, we know. And we are grateful, as we will attempt to prove on our return.

"Your task, then, is to lay in such stores as ye can gather hereabout, then take the barks and the men and set your course for Orkney. Once there, ye will report all that has happened, and ye will tell Lady Janet that we mean to be wi' her again ere another summer's past."

"You do not mean for me to take all the barks, my prince?"

"Aye. Leave us the boats, for we shall need them to explore this coast. And we will keep such rigging, lodestones, sun-shadow boards, and the like as were salvaged from the ships we lost. What ironmongery and sound boards as ye can prudently spare us, we'll also take. For the rest, we will look to these forests to provide. We'll build ourselves a bark here in due course, and in that will we few make our way home when the time comes."

"And who—who will be your navigator, pray?"

"Bjornsson. He stood with those that chose to stay, and he is an able mariner, ye'll grant him that. We have no doubt he can get us back, though not so handily as you."

"He is a fair sailor," allowed Zeno, grudgingly. Then he heaved a great sigh. "There are a hundred arguments against this policy, my prince. But I have said I would obey. And I will. But once you are back in Kirkwall, then I intend to take my leave of you and go home at last to my dear Venice."

"Of course, my friend. We will talk o' that again when we are once more together in my hall. Go now. Begin the preparations for your departure. This lovely weather promises a fair voyage; it would not do to lose it."

Ingram, Richard, and Sinclair stood and watched as the downcast Venetian slowly retraced his steps to the beach.

"There goes an excellent man, Harry," Ingram said.

"Aye," said Sinclair, his tone leaden and low. "I love the fellow, Ingram. It as as hard almost to let him go as it was to bury his brother. These partings come no easier wi' the years, I promise ye."

But part they did. Three days sufficed for laying in water and wood and stores of fish and fowl. And at dawn of the fourth day, Zeno caught the outgoing tide and led the fleet out into the open sea.

Sinclair, though he had steeled himself for this moment, wept openly as Zeno embraced him. "God be wi' ye, Sir Antonio," he whispered. "Get the men safe home."

Zeno could not speak. He only nodded, then turned and all but ran down to the waiting boat that would carry him to his bark.

As the fleet pulled away, a cheer went up from the departing men. But those on shore could only wave a heavyhearted mute farewell. They stood and watched until the last white sail disappeared around Cape Trin; then, with one accord, all eyes turned to Sinclair as if seeking from him some assurance that they had not been fools to stay.

But he said only, "Arm yourselves, and take such things as ye deem needful. Sir Richard, you will lead us now to meet wi' the inhabitants o' this place."

47

D'ye know, Harry," remarked Ingram Gunn, as he walked along beside Sinclair, following Richard through the forest, "I never felt so alone in all my life before."

"We are not many," Sinclair acknowledged, ducking his head to avoid a low-hanging limb. "I will confess to you, Ingram, as I watched the fleet sail off 'twas all I could do to keep from plunging into the water and swimming after them."

Ingram chuckled. "I am glad to hear it, coz. I had begun to think I was the only one."

Richard Sinclair set a quick pace, and long before sundown, the little band was many miles inland. They camped that night in the cover of the towering pines, making a very good supper on the plump breasts of trusting doves that learned too late of the coming of the hunter among them.

A night's rest on the soft forest floor restored tired limbs and flagging spirits. The depression that had set in with Zeno's departure seemed to lift in the soothing forest shade, and a kind of holiday mood displaced the gloom. As Richard had told them, the way was easy, and the bold wanderers trooped along like schoolboys playing truant on an early summer's day.

"Heigh-ho!" cried John Clarke, skipping two steps for every one his fellows took. " 'Tis good to be stretching the old legs again after so long a while at sea."

Bjornsson smiled down on the little squire. "Spoken like a true landsman," he said. "As for me, I have not walked so far in my whole life before. My feet must think it strange to be treading on anything but oak planking."

"I like a good walk myself," chimed in young Sigurd Sigurdsson. "It gets a man's juices flowing and gives him a hearty appetite."

"Humph! Ye need no help with your appetite so far as I can see," Clarke said.

"There's more o' me than there is o' you," replied Sigurd, grinning. "It follows then that I must eat more to keep me fit."

"You may be fit," Clarke retorted, "but your clothes'll be sore stretched to fit ye, if ye continue to devour four whole doves at a sitting."

"You should follow my example, John Clarke. Who knows? Ye may yet achieve a grown man's stature. If ye do, ye're welcome to my castoff clothes to cover your lengthened frame."

Thus bantering and laughing, the men marched along. They made their nooning by a sparkling brook, and took an hour's rest under the trees.

"This time tomorrow should find us at the smoking mountain," Richard told them. "Then will we try the hospitality of these wild folk."

Sinclair nodded. "We bid ye all go peacefully among 'em. We have no cause to look for trouble. Provoke none, we charge ye, or be ready to answer to us for the consequences."

"But if they mistake our peaceful intent, my lord," John Clarke inquired, "what then?"

Sinclair's smile was grim and fraught with meaning. "Why, then, John Clarke, ye had best invoke the angels and commend your soul to God."

Richard's estimate proved sound. Toward noon of the following day, the men found themselves at the foot of the great hill. A pungent odor filled the air, and a taste of sulfur was on every tongue.

" 'Tis Satan's chimney," Clarke declared, gawking up at the smoking summit. "My friends, we are standing on the very roof o' hell."

"God grant the roof's a sound one, then," muttered Sigurd. " 'Twould be a most untimely fall were we to drop through into the pit."

"Yonder's the oily spring I spoke of," said Richard to his lord. "See where it bubbles up out o' the mount?"

Sinclair crossed himself. "God and St. Katherine," he murmured, gazing down at the black ooze that stained the surface of the swirling waters, "grant that this may be a happy omen for us."

"My lord," whispered Richard, "make no sudden move, I pray, but let your eyes travel up the side o' the mount. Our coming's been remarked."

Casually, Sinclair allowed his gaze to wander upward. Then, with a sharp intake of breath, he saw a single, all but naked figure crouched before a hollow in the rocks. With an effort, he made himself look away. "Is that one o' them?" he muttered.

"Aye," Richard replied. "He may be one they told off for sentry duty. I'll hail the fellow and see if he will come down to us."

The young captain raised a hand in greeting and called out to the man above, *"Boosool!"*

The native straightened up and scurried behind a sheltering stone. Then very slowly, very cautiously, he peered over it at the men below.

"Boosool!" cried Richard Sinclair again, waking the echo in the rocks with his cry. *"Kwaa!"*

"God bless me," muttered John Clarke. "I never thought to hear such sounds coming from the mouth of a Scot!"

"Let's hope yon naked fellow knows what Sir Richard's saying," Sigurd said.

"Well, he can hear him that's certain," Clarke replied, "him and his neighbors too, no doubt. This heathenish halloaing'll bring 'em all down on our necks presently."

"By God, John Clarke, ye're in the right of it. Look! The whole by-Our-Lady mount's alive with 'em!"

Even as Sigurd pointed, Clarke saw scores of brown faces appear at the mouths of any number of caves that honeycombed the hill.

"Jesu," the squire muttered, crossing himself. "Now we are for it."

But Richard advanced a little way up the slope, and beckoning with his arm, he called again, *"Boosool!"*

Here and there, a squat muscular figure ventured from the hollows. One, a little taller than the rest, clad like his fellows in only a breech-clout, but wearing a necklace of bright beads, was seen to confer with some two or three. He pointed to the men at the base of the hill, then signed to the others to follow him as he led them down the hillside.

"Well, at least they come unarmed, my lord," said Richard. "Let us hope they show themselves friendly as they did before."

The brown men descended on naked feet to a point some ten or twelve yards from where Sinclair stood. There they paused, hesitant, seemingly uncertain as to how near they should come.

" 'Faces like earth and old leaves,' " Sinclair murmured.

"Eh, my lord?"

" 'Tis nothing, Richard. Nothing. D'ye think it prudent to approach 'em?

"Not in numbers, surely, But the pair of us might, I think, go to them without inspiring fear."

Sinclair motioned for his men to stand fast. Then he and Richard walked slowly up to the wary natives. They seemed to Sinclair to be poised for flight, their watchful eyes noting every movement he and Richard made.

"It might be well for us to smile, my lord," Richard said.

"God bless me, I fear to show my teeth lest they think I mean to bite them," Sinclair replied. "They are trembling, Richard, or my eyes deceive me."

"Softly, softly, my lord. We must seem wondrous strange to them." Richard placed his hand on Sinclair's arm. "We had best stop here, I think."

The two Scots halted, not two yards from the small cave-dwellers. Richard raised his right hand and said gently, *"Kwaa."*

The natives turned to one another and chattered among themselves. Then the man in the necklace came forward one pace and said, *"Boosool, Nedap."*

"What means this *'Nedap'?"* Sinclair whispered.

Richard shrugged. "I know not, my lord. But let me try to inform this man of who it is ye are, for he seems to be their lord or chief, and it is fitting that he be first to know ye."

Richard pointed to Sinclair, and with particular emphasis announced, "Jarl Sinclair." This he repeated several times, making a stabbing notion at Sinclair's chest with his forefinger.

A frown creased the native chief's face at first, then understanding dawned in his beautiful dark eyes. "Glooscap!" he said, also pointing at Sinclair.

Richard shook his head. "Jarl Sinclair," he repeated.

The chief smiled and, again pointing to Sinclair, said, "Glooscap."

"God bless me," muttered Richard. "I cannot tell if he is trying to say your name or if he is calling you something else, my lord. But 'tis plain he is naming ye."

The chief turned to his men, spoke briefly to them, then pointed once again to Sinclair and said, "Glooscap."

His men nodded and, almost as one, also pointed to Sinclair and repeated the name their chief had told them.

The chief turned to the strangers, pointed to his own bronzed breast, and said, "Kobet."

"Plainly, he names himself," Sinclair said. Then to the chief he nodded and said, "Kobet."

Delight shone in the chief's face. He touched himself again and said, "Kobet." Then he pointed to Sinclair and said, "Glooscap."

"Fair enough," murmured Sinclair. And to the chief's evident satisfaction, Sinclair pointed to himself and said, "I am Glooscap."

After some muttered debate, the natives now dispatched one of their number to summon the entire tribe. Inside the next quarter hour, Sinclair and his men found themselves seated on the ground within a circle of curious onlookers, all very anxious, it seemed, to have a close look at these fair-skinned visitors. As Sinclair attempted, with signs and rude pictures scratched in the dirt with a stick, to communicate who he was and where he and his men had come from, he felt a frustration not unmixed with occasional flashes of light. It was soon evident that these folk recognized him for a chief in his own right, and that they were much impressed by his armor and his sword. But they were most enchanted by the pictures he made on the ground. When he drew a rough sketch of his bark, or of his castle in Kirkwall, or of a crown to indicate his allegiance to Margaret and Robert, there was much crowding in to look and much discussion as to what this all might mean.

"Christ's wounds, Ingram," Sinclair growled, tossing his stick away, "I can no more tell if they understand me than I can fly to the top o' yonder mountain."

"Well, Harry, ye're keeping 'em marvelously entertained at any rate. I think they'll no be inclined to eat us so long as ye keep on with drawing your pictures."

"These are no man-eaters, Ingram. That much I'll venture. Indeed, they seem a very decent, courteous people. But would to God I could understand their tongue."

"If ye could make them understand 'tis past time for dinner, I'd be main grateful."

Sinclair grinned. "Now that I can do, and wi'out pictures, I warrant ye." He got to his feet and called out, "Kobet!"

The sturdy chief, on hearing his name from the stranger's lips, smiled broadly and also stood.

"Kobet," said Sinclair, going through an elaborate pantomime of eating and rubbing his belly, "Glooscap is hungry."

Kobet understood at once. *"Sumades,"* he said.

"No, dammit. Hungry," Sinclair said, trying not to laugh. "Hungry."

"Sumades," Kobet repeated, and he signaled to one of the old women. She clapped her hands, and a flock of her sisters departed with her up the slope with many a giggling backward glance at the strange pale giants below.

"Coz, I do not know if those lasses be his scullery maids or what," said Ingram, grinning. "But if they do not come down wi' a side o' beef or a haunch o' mutton, ye'd better go back to drawing pictures or we'll all starve."

But Kobet had understood. And soon the women returned, bearing artfully woven baskets well filled with fresh fish and meat. A lovely maid, dressed in a short frock of deerskin, whom Kobet addressed as Miledow, stepped forward with a show of modesty worthy of any holy nun and knelt to make a small fire by dint of twirling sticks.

"By Corpus," exclaimed Bjornsson, "that's marvelous, that is!"

"Aye, she's a toothsome bit," John Clarke declared, with a nudge to the Shetlander's ribs.

"I was not speakin' o' the lassie," Bjornsson protested.

"Then ye're even hungrier than I," said Clarke, laughing.

Kobet, smiling, pointed to the fire and said, *"Booktaoo."*

"Booktaoo," repeated Sinclair. *"Booktaoo,* fire. There, by God, we've begun to learn something. They call a fire *booktaoo."*

As preparations progressed, and through the course of their meal, the adventurers began to acquire the rudiments of a vocabulary. *Pulesk,* they discovered, tasted as good whether one called them that or pigeons; meat is still meat, though it was called *weoos* there; and water, even if a man chooses to call it samoogwon, is still as grateful to a parched and dusty tongue. And when a man belches, smiles, rubs his belly, and says, *"Keloolk!"* it needs no interpreter to explain that he had enjoyed his dinner.

"By Peter," said Ingram Gunn, sighing happily and wiping the grease from his lips on the back of his hand, "this is as good as a Highland welcome, Harry. These folk know something o' hospitality."

"Aye, coz. Yon Kobet's as much a gentleman here in his own land as any we could name among old neighbors. Thanks be to God we did not come blundering in wi' sword in hand and conquest in our hearts. These may not be a Christian folk, Ingram, but we know Christians, you and I, who'd be none so quick to deal thus fairly wi' a stranger."

48

Sinclair and his men now found themselves so warmly befriended and so idyllically situated that loneliness and past fears were all but forgot. Here were food and water in ample supply, hospitality from natives and nature alike, and the promise of as sweet a summer as any man could wish for.

Ambitious to thoroughly acquaint himself with the land, Sinclair contented himself with establishing a temporary campsite at the base of the smoking mountain. Here his men pitched their tents, and here they bided for some days to rest and ready themselves to go exploring.

Sinclair used this time largely in efforts to communicate with Kobet, and he succeeded to the extent that the native chief assigned to him as a guide Kekwaju, a handsome youth of not more than twenty, lithe, strong, and keen of eye.

Kekwaju proved keen of intellect too, for he readily grasped the jarl of Orkney's purpose, and he himself won from Kobet permission to recruit six sturdy fellows together with their canoes to carry the explorers along the rivers that watered this land.

"I do marvel, Harry," said Ingram, "at how well ye manage to make yourself understood wi'out their language."

"So do I, coz," said Sinclair, shaking his head. "But it seems that when the need is great enough, a man can put his thoughts over somehow. Yon Kekwaju is no fool, nor indeed is Kobet. Sometimes they seem even to anticipate my thought before I can contrive to frame it in signs or pictures."

"God grant we encounter no sudden difficulty on our travels,' said Ingram, grinning. "We'd be sore put to make a picture or to gesture a cry for succor. An I were being pursued by a bear or a wolf, I'd feel somewhat more hopeful could I bellow out and be understood."

Sinclair eyed his friend thoughtfully. "Ingram, it has been on my mind that ye should not go wi' us on this journey. We'll no doubt have hard going, with God He knows what hazards along the way. And though I have no doubt ye would endure it for my sake, I'd as lief have ye bide here, partly to recover your strength, and partly as hostage to Kobet that he may have no doubt of our purpose to return wi' his men."

Ingram tugged at his ear. "Well, Harry, I would not like to think o myself as an old invalid, but I must allow my joints groan at the prospec o' stumbling about the wilderness day after day."

Sinclair had not expected this. Indeed, he had readied himself to simulate anger, to shout down Ingram's objections at being left behind Concern clouded his eyes as he studied his kinsman's face. "Are ye feeling unwell, Ingram?"

"No-o, not unwell. But I do feel tired, Harry." Ingram pulled a wry face. "It galls me to acknowledge it, but this body's no as tough as it once was."

"D'ye want Matteo to—?"

"No, no. Afore God, Harry, I want no dosing with simples and such. And I would take it kindly if ye said nothing o' this to the others. Tell 'em ye leave me hostage, if ye like. But, as ye love me, never let on that Ingram Gunn is feeling the weight of his years."

Sinclair clasped his cousin's hand. "Fear me not," he said. "I only pray some weeks of idleness will set ye right again."

"Christ, I will be idle enough, wi' none but yon strange folk for company."

Sinclair grinned. "Ye'll have at least one Scot biding wi' ye. We've told Richard he's to remain here, too."

"Richard?"

"Aye. He is wonderfully quick at grasping the language o' these folk. It suits my purpose to have him master it entirely. When we come again in numbers to build a city here, Richard would make a most excellent governor. Did he have the language, 'twould serve him well in serving us.

"Moreover, I am anxious that young Sigurd have this chance to prove what he can do, acting as captain in Richard's stead."

Ingram nodded. "Sigurd's a promising fellow, Harry. I do not doubt he'll prove an uncommonly able man."

"If something of his father survives in him, he will. That's certain." Sinclair clapped his old comrade on the shoulder. "Be easy here, Ingram. We will be some weeks away; how many, I cannot guess. On our return, we'll ready ourselves to winter over and commence the building of our bark. For I mean to sail for Orkney when spring returns."

"That will be a glad day, Harry," Ingram said. "My eyes are hungry for the sight o' home."

Before the week was out, Sinclair and his party, together with their guides, set out from the smoking mountain, leaving Richard and Ingram to pass the long summer days as best they could among an alien people in an alien land.

Richard spent his daylight hours sharing the life of the tribe, fishing, gathering herbs and berries, venturing out on brief fowling forays, and absorbing all that he could of the lore and language of his hosts. He was much in the company of Kobet, for the chief greatly admired this tall stranger who took such pains to learn the names of all common things. But another friend he found gave Ingram some uneasiness and disturbed somewhat the pleasure he took in the long, idle summer days.

One bright morning, as Ingram and Richard lolled in the shade of a butternut tree, they spied the lovely Miledow approaching the slope of the mountain, a birchen bucket of water in either hand.

"That's one bonny woman," Ingram drawled, plucking up a blade of grass and biting down on its juicy stem.

"Aye," said Richard, getting to his feet, "and too delicate for such a heavy burden.

"Miledow," he called. *"Choogoonaan. Kescook."* ("It is heavy. Hand it to me.")

Ingram watched, grinning, as the tall young Scot relieved the maiden of the buckets.

"Welaalin," Miledow said, her voice soft as the morning air. ("I am obliged to you.")

"Tame aleen?" Richard asked. ("Where are you going?")

Miledow pointed to the hill. *"Elumea,"* she said. ("I go home.")

"Wijaadenech," said Richard, smiling down into the dark doe eyes. ("Let us go together.")

Ingram saw them no more that day. And for many days thereafter he saw but little of the young captain. When he did see him, he was more often than not with Miledow.

"God's nails!" muttered Ingram to himself. "A lark's a lark, but if yon Kobet gets wind o' this, our young suitor's summer play may end in grave trouble for the lot of us."

He agonized over the matter for some days, reluctant to speak to Richard in a way that might not be welcomed or appreciated. Richard gave him no help. When they were together, the younger man not once mentioned the maiden, and all Ingram's attempts at roundabout hinting went serenely unremarked.

Then it happened that Ingram and Kobet himself, together with some four or five men of the tribe, were fishing in a nearby stream for trout one perfect July morning when they spied Richard and Miledow all unaware embracing in the shadow of the pines.

Kobet nudged Ingram and cried, *"Ankaptaan!"* Which, though Ingram did not know it, meant only, "There they are!" But there was no misunderstanding the guttural laughter and knowing looks that went around, and Ingram, satisfied that Kobet knew and did not disapprove of this dalliance, resumed his fishing with an easier mind and a lighter heart.

Richard was, after all, a grown man, so Ingram reasoned. It was not up to him to admonish the younger man, nor had he any stomach for meddling. He had himself loved in his day, and who was he to cavil at Richard's choice? Harry brought them here. Let Harry deal with it on his return.

That return was long in coming. July and August—*Upskooe-goos* and *Kesagawe-goos* the natives called them, meaning the month when the sea fowl shed their feathers and the month when the young birds are full-fledged—had faded into the pale gold of September, or *Majowtoowe-goos,* the running month, and still Sinclair had not returned. Ingram's concern mounted with the close of each succeeding day, but Richard reassured him, repeating Kobet's own oft-repeated expressions of confidence in the safety of the explorers.

"He says it is a wide land, Sir Ingram, with many lakes and many isles. And he says that Kekwaju is a master of the ways of the wild."

"That's as may be," said Ingram, grumpily. "But Harry isn't, nor any o' the men. What if they got separated? Or what if bears attacked 'em while they slept? Where's your famous Kek-what-you-may-call-him then, hey?"

"Sir Ingram, I love our kinsman, too. But I'm no going to make myself sick wi' worrying about him."

"That's plain enough," said Ingram, dourly. "Leave the fretting to me, whilst you go frisking about wi' yon Mildew or however ye call her."

"The lady's name is Miledow," said Richard Sinclair, ice edging his tone. "It means hummingbird. And I'll thank ye to speak o' her respectfully."

"Aye, aye," said Ingram, "wi' all respect, to be sure. And it is a very pretty name for a very pretty lady. Go along, go along. Do not let my concern for Harry spoil your play."

But it was Ingram who was at play when, in the forenoon of a mid-September day, Kekwaju led the wanderers into the clearing at the base of the smoking mountain. To while away the long days, Ingram had fashioned neatly worked pine sticks to make up a game of jackstraws. Kobet and his men had been quick to learn the game, and very slow to tire of it sufficiently to allow the children of the tribe a chance to learn to play.

So it happened that, as Sinclair came out of the forest, he found Ingram seated on the ground surrounded by small raven-haired boys and girls who were struggling equally with the pale man's peculiar language and the tricky ways of the jack.

"Nah, nah!" Ingram was saying. "It moved, ye little pagan—Mikchik or Chick-chick or whatever ye're called. Look here! Ye must go ever so gingerly, d'ye see, so as not to disturb the heap. Like so."

"Well done, sir!" cried a hearty voice at his shoulder, and Ingram turned to see Harry Sinclair grinning down at him.

"Harry!" He leaped up and embraced his cousin in a hearty bear hug. "By the mass, Harry, but it's good to see ye! Are ye well? Is everyone back safe? Did ye encounter any o' them man-eaters?"

"*Pax, pax!*" cried Sinclair, laughing. "We are all well, thanks be to God, and we had a most instructive time of it. But do not let me interfere wi' your game—"

"Pah! 'Tis only something I did to pass the long days and keep my mind occupied. I tell ye, Harry, yon Kobet and his men are daft about jackstraws. For a time there, I had begun to think I'd done a dreadful thing in teaching 'em the game. They'd no hunt nor fish nor do anything but sit about the whole blessed day and toss the silly sticks."

Sinclair threw back his head and laughed. "And how did ye finally cure 'em of it, coz?"

Ingram rubbed the tip of his nose with the flat of his hand, grinned, and said, "I sat down and carved me a pair o' dice."

"Ha-ha-ha! Ye did not! Oh, Ingram, Ingram, I love ye for a provident man."

"Not so provident, Harry," Ingram spat in the dust. "That damned Kobet won near all my silver, and when my luck finally turned, he tried to pay me off wi' some trifling damned seashells."

Sinclair wiped his eyes, shook his head, and gasping, he declared, "My dear old friend, there never was such a comical fellow as you are."

"I'd no call it comical to be cleaned out of all my silver," Ingram growled. Then he grinned and said, "But it is funny, come to think of it. Perchance ye'd care to dish the dice wi' Kobet yourself, Harry?"

"Not I. No, sir, I know that foxy look o' thine. Ye hope to see Kobet serve me as he served you." Sinclair poked Ingram in the ribs. "Ye'll no catch me wi' bait o' that sort, my friend.

"Besides, what I want now is a bite to eat and a little rest. We have come a long rough way, Ingram, and ha' seen such grand country as will take me weeks to tell ye of. After I have—" Sinclair broke off and looked about. "But where's Richard? Nothing's amiss with him, surely?"

Ingram scratched his chin. "Well, there is and there isn't. But here is Kobet come to bid ye good morrow."

The chief advanced with stately mein and said, "*Kwaa,* Glooscap."

"*Kwaa,* Kobet," replied Sinclair, gravely. "*Welain?*" ("Are ye well?")

"*Aa welae*" ("Yes, I am well"), replied the chief.

"*Weledasse, nigumaach*" ("I am glad, my friend").

The basic courtesies thus observed, Kobet now ordered meat and drink for the explorers, and Sinclair, his men and their guides, seated themselves on the ground and fell to with a good will.

"Christ, Harry," muttered Ingram, "you and Kobet were nattering away like old cronies. Ye seem to have learned a deal o' the language while ye were away."

"I had to, Ingram," said Sinclair, wiping his mouth on the back of his hand. "I cannot speak it easily, like French or Latin, but I have enough words to say good morrow or to ask for another portion o' fish. Necessity's a most excellent schoolmaster. And, indeed, that excellent Kekwaju and his fellows were more than patient wi' my halting efforts to frame the words they know so well. These are a kindly people, Ingram. Wandering with them these past weeks has only served to increase my admiration of them. I have no doubt that, wi' a little effort, we could soon teach 'em all our arts and make 'em in every way fit to feel at home in Scotland or any other Christian realm."

"Ye may be right, Harry, but they would have to leave those damnable reeky tubes o' theirs at home or they'd find no welcome anywhere."

Sinclair laughed. "The *tumakun?*"

"Aye, that thing they crumble up dried herbs in and set afire so as to drink in the smoke." Ingram shook his head. "I confess I tried it, partly out o' courtesy and partly from curiosity. And when I had done puking, I was green and shaky for a week after."

Sinclair slapped his knee and laughed. "You too? By God, Ingram, I ventured to try the thing one night when we were camped on a lovely island some fifty miles from here. I near to strangled on it, then doubled over and spilled my supper on the ground. I think ye can be sure the *tumakun* will never be the fashion among Christian folk, my friend. The world would drown in vomit if it were."

"What o' the country, Harry? Did it meet your hopes?"

"In every way, my friend. Once we have an hour to ourselves, I will impart to ye all that we discovered. You and Richard— Now, dammit, I had forgot. Ye started to tell me why he was not here, and then Kobet had this feast laid on and the dear man slipped my mind completely. Where is he, coz?"

Ingram pointed with his thumb. "Yonder he comes, Harry, wi' his bonny sweetheart, Lady Miledow."

Sinclair's gaze followed the line of Ingram's gesture, and he saw Richard, hand in hand with the beautiful brown maiden, sauntering slowly toward them over the sunburnt grass.

"So that's the way of it with him," he murmured. "God bless me, Ingram, I never thought o' that."

Ingram sniffed. "He's thought o' precious little else the whole time ye were away."

"Kobet knows o' this?"

"Knows of it and has given his blessing, or whatever it is their chieftains give when they approve o' this kind o' lollygagging."

"Jesu, Maria," said Sinclair softly. "I hope—well, we must go carefully in this, Ingram. It is a Sinclair we have to deal with, and a Sinclair's a wonderfully proud and touchy thing."

Ingram eyed his kinsman oddly. "Ye've noticed that?" he said.

49

Autumn now splashed the land with colors. Mornings were crisp; the nights very nearly cold. Kobet and his people began to think of withdrawing to the shelter of the forest, and Sinclair turned his thoughts on selecting a site for wintering over.

He settled at last on the top of a rugged promontory commanding a sweeping view of the ocean. The animals, he reasoned, would seek high ground in the time of snows, and hunting would be more fruitful in this location. There were, moreover, fine stands of hardwood trees that would provide him with the materials needed to construct that bark which was to bear him and his men back to Kirkwall when spring came in.

The native folk were busy now, building their rude rustic houses in the forest and laying in stores for winter. The women hurried to complete the making of shirts and leggings of deerskin and cloaks and coverlets of fur. The men were daily occupied with preparations for the great October hunt, and the whole settlement bustled with activity.

" 'Tis good to know that these folk do not attempt to get through the winter half naked and living in yonder caves," Sinclair remarked, as he stood with Richard, Ingram, and Bjornsson watching an arrow maker ply his craft. "The people Eyvindson told of were not so prudent, as I remember."

"Aye," Richard said. "Not only are these people provident, but Kobet has even offered to have houses built for us—*wigwams,* they call 'em—so we can keep tolerably warm ourselves."

"They are cunning builders," said Bjornsson. "I looked over one o' them wee houses myself just yesterday, and they are wonderfully snug."

"They will need to be," growled Ingram. "Did ye feel the frost in the air this morning? For my part, I'd like stone walls around me and a hearth wide enough to lead a mounted troop through."

Richard grinned. "Kobet thinks we are strange and wasteful in our use o' fire. He says we build great blazing piles that only burn themselves out before morning, whereas they keep a small fire going all the night through."

"That comes o' living in those little *wigwams*," ventured Bjornsson. "There's precious little room to heat, and so a small fire does 'em very well."

Sinclair nodded. "We would do well to learn from these folk," he said. "They have a goodly store o' practical knowledge that can help us in outlasting the winter here."

"It might be prudent, my lord, to persuade some one or two of 'em to bide with us," Richard said. "No doubt they could gi' us much good counsel in housewifery that would lessen the hardship of a winter in the wild."

Sinclair eyed his young kinsman shrewdly. "There's merit in what ye say, Sir Richard. Let me think on it. We will talk more of it presently."

Sinclair and his men joined in the great hunt, traveling with Kobet's men in their frail canoes to a great island well populated with deer and smaller game. There the strangers matched skills with the natives in a spirit of boyish competition. Nor did they fare badly. Ingram brought down a fine fat buck, the largest taken by any of the party, and Sinclair himself won general acclaim by bringing down four deer in a single day.

"We can never match these folk for tracking," allowed Richard Sinclair, as they rested one sunny noon in a ferny glade, "but our bows at least are better."

"And our shooting," Ingram added, "although I'd never say as much to yon Kobet."

"Kobet's well aware of it, Sir Ingram," Richard said. "D'ye know they speak of our noble Jarl Sinclair as a wonder-worker or a god?"

Ingram grinned. "Ye'd better no tell Harry, or he'll be looking to have the title made hereditary. Ha-ha!"

Richard had to laugh himself at this irreverence. "But, in truth, Ingram, from what I can piece out of their talk, the ruling of 'em is his for the taking."

"He'll take it right enough. And a good thing too. For now he can leave Orkney to young Harry, Rosslyn to Willie, and these western lands to John. 'Twill save a deal o' quarreling in after years."

Richard smiled. "Ye're a farsighted man, Sir Ingram. D'ye always scent trouble at such a distance?"

Ingram looked at Richard with an appraising eye. "Sir Richard, some-times I do. And as a friend, and as a man who has seen something o' life and the ways o' this world, I—well, I would urge ye go carefully where this pretty Lady Miledow's concerned."

Richard's face took on a masklike coldness. "Have a care, sir," he said. " 'Tis not to my liking to have the lady's name bruited about so lightly."

"Dammit, Richard, I mean no disrespect to your lady, nor to yourself. In truth, I think her uncommon lovely, and ye know, surely, of my regard for you." Ingram took up a brown leaf and crumpled it in his fingers. "But, well, I fear it, Richard. I fear it may give ye more pain than ye had bargained for."

Richard got to his feet. "Sir Ingram, did I doubt your intentions, I'd think myself obliged to challenge ye. But I cannot believe ye mean other than kindly."

"I thank ye for your faith, at least," murmured Gunn, leaning back against the great oak that shaded them.

"Now," Richard continued, "I pray ye take my intentions fairly, too. In the first place, I love Miledow. In the second place, I mean to be wed with her. And, finally, I count it nothing what other men may think.

"You have forgot, perchance, what it is like to love, Sir Ingram. Aye, and our noble lord also. But I do love, and that wholeheartedly. I'll let no graybeard's cold and gloomy counsel dissuade me from following my heart."

"Well, damn you for an impertinent puppy!" Ingram got to his feet, his eyes flashing with something of their old fire. Richard, startled, actually flinched.

" 'You have forgot what it is like to love, Sir Ingram,' " mimicked the older knight. "Why, ye mincing, mewling, miniature Sinclair, have I not loved the same woman for up'ards o' thirty years? Loved without hope, without her so much as even guessing that I loved. By Peter, I know more o' loving than—Jesu, mercy!"

Ingram clutched at his breast and slumped to the ground, his mouth open, his eyes starting from their sockets.

"Ingram!" Richard rushed to the fallen man, knelt, and cradled his head in his arms. "Ingram, for God's sake, what ails thee?"

The young knight fumbled to loosen the lacings at Ingram's throat. Ingram, gasping for breath, tried to say his thanks.

"Hush, man, don't speak. Let me gi' ye some water." Richard produced a flagon and moistened Ingram's lips.

"Jesu," muttered Gunn, weakly, "I thought my time had come. 'Tis passing off, now. Here, help me to sit up, lad. Thank'ee. Whew!"

Richard, having propped the older man against the tree trunk, now studied him with anxious eyes. Sweat beaded Ingram's face. His chest labored with irregular heavy breathing, and his strong hands twitched uncontrollably.

"I'll go and fetch our noble kinsman," Richard said.

"No!" Gunn's voice crackled with alarm, and he groped for Richard's hand, caught it, and held it fast. "If ye ever loved me, Richard, say nothing o' this to Harry."

"But Christ, Ingram, ye're fearfully sick. He must know of it."

"No. Please. Richard, I am no good at begging favor, but I am begging now." Ingram, his face deathly pale, licked his lips and squeezed Richard's hand hard. "This—this thing's come over me once or twice ere now. It—it will be gone off presently. I'd no have Harry troubled wi' it. He's got so much to think of, so much to do. Leave it be, Richard, I beg ye. Leave it be."

The young captain hesitated, swayed by the earnest pleading in Gunn's eyes.

"Look ye," Gunn went on, "I—I never meant to speak so harshly as I did just now. I have always loved ye, Richard. I meant no harm."

"I know that," Richard said, touching Ingram's clammy cheek. "Ye're a bonny, bonny knight, Sir Ingram, and a true friend to my lord. Ye spoke for him when ye railed at me. I—I do not know if ye're in the right o' this or no. But I cannot doubt the love that prompted ye to speak."

"God bless ye, Richard," said Ingram, smiling. "If ye truly love this lass, do as ye will. Ye'll get no more sermons from me. I lack both wind and wisdom for it. Only keep mum about this—this passing illness, pray, and it shall be as if we had never quarreled."

Richard nodded. "As ye wish, Sir Ingram. It may be I do wrong in keeping silent, but, God help me, I hardly know what's right anymore."

Ingram winked and placed a finger to his lips. "Gi' your conscience a rest, lad. This old body's tough enough to last a good while yet."

The burden of Ingram's secret weighed heavily on Richard Sinclair. And though he went about with seeming cheerfulness, yet his eyes often and again were drawn to the older knight, watching for some sign of another seizure. But Ingram, whether he was truly recovered or not, made a brave show of youthful energy, and even sallied forth on the last day of the hunt to bring in on his own shoulders an unlucky doe that he had brought down with a single well-aimed arrow.

With the return of the hunters came the time of the great feast which, Richard explained, was a yearly celebration among these folk. The forest rang with song and laughter, and the strangers shared wholeheartedly in all the festive doings.

"Afore God," murmured Sinclair, as he sat with his men in the great circle around the fire, "these fellows can foot it right nobly. Look how yon Kekwaju leaps and prances. He is a bonny dancer and no mistake."

"Humph," grunted Ingram, his cheeks well stuffed with venison, "my Highland neighbors could teach 'em something about dancing, I warrant ye."

"Gi' us a dance, then, Sir Ingram," piped John Clarke, helping himself to another handful of roast meat.

"Aye," echoed Bjornsson, "show us how it's done, Sir Ingram."

Sinclair grinned. "Ye're caught now, coz. Ye must either step out or give over grousing."

Ingram got to his feet, wiping his hands on a bunch of dried grass. "Gi' us room," he said, "and I'll show these folk what a light-foot Scot can do."

"Sir Ingram!" Richard Sinclair rose in his place. "Pray, have a care. Ye must not—"

Ingram turned a wrathful gaze on the young captain. "What must I not, Sir Richard?"

Richard, reading the warning in Ingram's voice, smiled weakly. "Ye must not let the honor o' Scotland be put to blush by yon heavy-footed fellows."

Ingram laughed. "Strike up a song, my lads. I'll no disgrace ye."

Then, to the wide-eyed wonder of the forest folk, Ingram Gunn leaped into the circle of firelight and set to capering madly in a wild Highland fling.

"Jesu, Mary!" cried Sinclair, clapping his hands, "See how my brave Ingram goes!"

"Yon Kekwaju's gone green wi' envy," declared Clarke. "And Kobet's struck wi' wonder."

For fully five minutes Ingram whirled and leaped in sprightly Highland fashion, while his audience cheered him on. And when he had spun to a stop, a broad grin lighted his flushed face. Kobet himself came forward, and taking the beads from around his own thick, muscular neck, he presented them to Ingram Gunn.

Ingram, returning to his mates amid ringing plaudits, grinned at Richard and said, "What think ye of your sick man now?"

Their autumn celebration over, Kobet and his people now left their summer caves and removed to the forest to pass the winter in the close comfort of their wigwams.

Sinclair, after a lengthy parley with Kobet, reported to his men that Kekwaju, along with Baktusum-ook, Team, and Kaktoogwak, together with their women, would winter with them in their high camp.

"This is good news, coz," Ingram said. "We shall be the better for having those stout men with us."

"'Twas Richard put me in mind of it," Sinclair said. "And it was well thought of."

"My Lord," said Richard, "I would like a private word with you touching this matter."

"Walk out wi' me, then, Sir Richard, and ye may unburden yourself as we go along."

Together, the two Sinclairs strolled toward the forest edge, savoring the winy air and the tang of woodsmoke drifting up from Kobet's encampment.

"Well, Richard, and what is on your mind?"

"My lord, what of Miledow?"

Sinclair stopped, turned, and faced the young knight squarely. "What of her, Richard?"

"My lord, I'll no be mealy-mouthed about it. I love her. And I am of no mind to spend the winter apart from her."

Sinclair nodded. "We appreciate your forthrightness in this, Richard. Nor are we unmindful that ye have come to care for this lady. Indeed, she is everything that is lovely, and we can understand how little ye would relish separation."

Sinclair rubbed the back of his neck and squinted up at the sullen sky. Then he said, "Richard, we have been slow to speak to ye concerning all o' this. Ye're a grown man, wi' your own mind and your own heart to heed and follow. For our part, we have burdens enough to carry wi'out we take on the unwelcome and unappointed task o' chaperon.

"But ye must know, surely that this—this matter can come to nothing. Wait. Hear me out." Sinclair placed a kindly hand on the younger man's shoulder. "We'll no ask how far the business hath progressed. But we must remind ye that, soon or late, ye must part from her."

"Why?"

Sinclair shook his head. "Richard, Richard, ye cannot be that blind. What would ye do? Take that child o' the forest back to Longformacus and set her up as Lady Sinclair? She could not bear it. 'Twould be as another world to her, peopled by alien folk wi' alien manners, alien speech and alien ways. 'Twould be caging a wild bird, Richard. And that bird would soon cease to sing, would pine and likely die so far from her native haunts. If ye truly love her, ye could not bring her to that."

Richard scuffed at the sod underfoot with the toe of his shoe, then he raised his head and said, "I could bide here."

"Could ye?" Sinclair's smile was kind, but his tone incredulous. "Think, Richard. Could ye live out your years in this wild when beyond the sea ye have waiting for ye lands, a title, honors, friends? I know, I know. Just now, ye truly believe it; ye believe ye could count it all as so much dross alongside such a love. But, trust me, in time ye'd come to regret it. Ye'd find yourself hungering for home so that ye'd think ye'd die of it. And how is your lady then, hey?"

"My lord, I do not mean to appear ungrateful for your counsel or your kindness. But that I love Miledow is all my thought. That she loves me is all my joy. Ye cannot ask me to give her up. For that is something I cannot do."

Sinclair nodded. "God bless ye, Richard. 'Tis a bonny, bonny thing to love and be loved. Old as I am, I have never lost the wonder of it. I—Jesu, I have no wish to play the croaking prophet o' doom in this, but I do not see how I can counsel other than I have.

"Wi' spring, we mean to sail away. And when if ever we shall return, only God He knows. But you must come wi' us when we go, Richard. That is unalterable as Holy Writ. I cannot face your father wi'out I bring ye whole and well out o' this with me."

"Even against my will?"

"Even so." Sinclair smiled. "Ye're a Sinclair, that I know. And I know how adamant a Sinclair can be. But, Richard, I am a Sinclair too. Clash wi' me, and ye'll find yourself out-Sinclaired at every turn, I promise ye."

Richard grinned. "My lord, I do believe ye."

"Ha-ha! Ah, Richard, I love ye as my own son. And because I love ye, I will risk something to tell ye where my thoughts are tending. It hath seemed to me that this land is all that I had hoped to find, that one day we shall build here a thriving city, and we shall need a trusty man to govern in fealty to Orkney.

"Ye've shown yourself your father's son, and in all ways worthy to be called a Sinclair. In some future time, if all goes as we have dreamed it, we may very likely approach ye wi' proposals concerning the governance of this place."

"My lord, I—I have never had higher praise. It comes most—" Richard broke off suddenly, his eyes wide and shining. "But if I am to return to govern here, then Miledow and I could be together always. My lord, if that could be, why, I would count myself richer than if I come into possession of all my father's vast estates."

Sinclair smiled. "Ah, God," he said, shaking his head, "I hope I have not put down false hopes for ye to build on. This is all 'if' and 'perchance' and 'as it may be,' Richard. I cannot promise anything."

"Aye, my lord. I know that. But there is hope."

"There is always that." Sinclair put his arm around his young kinsman's shoulders. "Look ye, Richard, ye must gi' us your word ye'll go back wi' us to Orkney in the spring. And for that word, ye may have ours that ye can bring Miledow into our camp to make a spring o' this winter that is now nearly on us."

Richard's smile was almost painfully joyous. "Ye have my word, and here's my hand on it, my lord. Wi' all my heart, I thank ye. If I have your consent I'll run now and find Miledow and bring her to my wigwam."

"Aye, go, lad. God gi' ye joy of it."

Sinclair stood and watched as Richard loped away. Then he shook his head and muttered, "God grant your present joy make up for future sorrow, Richard. I fear ye lie open to most mortal grievous hurt."

50

Richard's winter idyll was in marked contrast with the cruel cold that gripped the land. With November, the first snow fell, and from then on, the relentless, unremitting chill held fast. Only the mighty sea itself seemed able to withstand the deathlike spell that lay over woodland and shore. At the base of the promontory where Sinclair's forces perched, great rushing tides, tides that would send waves churning in at awesome height and speed, kept the harbor free of ice all winter long.

Bjornsson, charged with overseeing the construction of the ship, was in his element, and he meant to build grandly.

"I've found a master oak, a windfall, well seasoned, as will serve us for a keel," he told Jarl Henry, "And another as fine, but so shaped by wind and weather as to make a noble prow. There's God's own plenty of pine hereabout for masts and thwarts. We could not be happier situated for our task than this.

"Look, my lord," he said, sketching his plan with his shipman's dirk on a patch of bare ground, "I see her as a decked ship, wi' two masts, and lofty castles fore and aft. We'll use thick planking, as for a ship o' war. She'll no fly so fast before the wind as some, but she'll stand up to any amount o' punishment."

Sinclair, on one knee beside Bjornsson, smiled his approval. "She'll bear us safely home to Kirkwall, I make no doubt, and will be a fine addition to our fleet. Get on with the work, friend Bjornsson. You'll have the steering of her, so we trust ye to build most shrewdly."

Under Bjornsson's direction, the whole force—mariners and men-at-arms alike—worked through the brief daylight hours, sweating in the frigid air as they felled trees, shaved planks, and framed the ship that would carry them home. The old Shetlander had no need to drive the men; they were glad of the activity and more than glad of the thought that spring would find them bound away to be once more with friends and dear ones sorely missed.

But if the short days were filled with work, the long nights lent themselves to sociability and good feeding on plain fare.

More often than not natives would gather in Sinclair's wigwam, built larger than the rest as befitting his stature as chief, and huddle about the fire while songs and stories and the dice went around.

Kekwaju and his friends proved great storytellers, and Richard, an apt interpreter, retold their tales of spirits, wizards, talking beasts, and malevolent giants to the delight of Sinclair and his men. John Clarke became a great favorite with the native folk, for he had himself a fund of tales and songs that Richard would translate into the language of the forest people. On one cold gusty night, Richard found himself moderating a warm debate.

Team, one of the men with Kekwaju, delivered himself of the opinion that Jack was a great fool to trade off his mother's cow for a handful of beans when he might have butchered the cow and had thereby much weeos to eat.

Richard communicated this thought to Clarke, who countered by saying that Team was taking the short view, that later events proved Jack to be wise beyond his years.

But Team could not get beyond the initial folly. Meat is meat, and beans are beans, and only a fool would take beans for meat.

Clarke turned red and waxed choleric, and ventured some opinions concerning Team's intelligence. These Richard let go unreported.

"Christ," growled Clarke, in a manner that won for him the sobriquet *Mooinaweesit* ("He Talks Bear Talk"), "yon Team's got no more sense than the giant had. It stands to reason, don't it, that Jack was no fool? Here he was as poor as any beggar, and he ended up rich and comfortable all his days. If that's the fate o' fools, then God ha' mercy on all wise men."

How long the debate might have raged, or how it might have ended had not Sigurd wisely brought out the jackstraws, none could say. But Richard, relieved of his role as mediator, slipped very gladly from the company and returned to his own wigwam to lie with Miledow in love and warmth till morning called him out to work on the ship once more.

Richard alone of all Sinclair's band felt no joy in the progress of the builders, felt no delight in the perceptible lengthening of the days. Spring would hold no pleasures for him this year, only parting, pain, and the prospect of separation, perhaps forever, from the woman he loved.

February—or *Abungunajit* ("snow blinder"), as Kobet's people called it—went out in a raging blizzard that buried the peninsula in deep wet drifts. But the brighter sun of mid-March loosened winter's hold upon the land, and Richard, with a heavy heart, noticed patches of earth appearing in the wake of the retreating snow.

Time's pulse quickened in his ear, and the young Scot felt a new urgency in his loving, coupled with a profound sadness that dimmed even those peaks of glad abandon when Miledow turned to him in the hushes and snow-cloaked darkness of those last late winter nights.

As if by unspoken contract, neither Richard nor Miledow talked of his imminent leavetaking. But it was always there, looming above their bed of furs, overshadowing their lovemaking, diminishing the painful sweetness of their dwindling days.

With April's first morning the builders' work was done, the bark was launched, and the cheers of Sinclair's men echoed and reechoed from the rocks at the sight of their ship bobbing gently in the bay. That night, Richard went sadly to his beloved and lay with her wakeful all the night long.

"My love, my love," he whispered to her in her own tongue, "I cannot bear this parting. My heart hurts. I think it must break if I go."

Miledow cradled his head in her arms, feeling the splash of his hot tears on her naked breast. "You will go," she murmured, rocking gently back and forth. "You will go far across the wide waters to Glooscap's country. You will never come back to Miledow. In time, you will forget—"

"Say not so," protested Richard. "All my life, and with my dying eyes, I will see no face but yours before me."

Miledow shook her head. "It cannot be so. Time and the many miles will come between us, my white-skinned lover. The sea is so wide and the years are so long. Glooscap the Mighty will take you far from me. He will not bring you back again."

"I will come back, my only love." Richard kissed her and crushed her to his breast. "Only wait for me. Wait for me."

Miledow caressed the young knight's face and looked up earnestly into his unhappy eyes. "Always I will be here. And always I will look to the sea for your returning, even though the voice of my heart whispers that you will never come again. For me, there will be no more joy in the warmth of summer, no more delight in seeing the birds return. Flowers will bloom again beside the forest pools. They will not bloom for me.

"The rains of many springs, the snows of many winters can never quench the fires you kindled in my breast. I am your woman. I will watch for you, wait for you, hunger for you until I am one with the dust beneath our feet."

Tears coursed down Richard's face. "By the God of my people," he whispered, "I will love no other so long as I shall live."

Sinclair now set the time of departure, calculating to sweep out into the open sea on the powerful rush of the ebbing tide. But first there must be a formal leavetaking, with a feast for Kobet and his people, for these had proved kind neighbors and most genial hosts, and Sinclair was not one to let the amenities pass unobserved.

On a bright April morning, then, he invited Kobet and his chief men to come to the bay to see for themselves the product of the winter's labors. Kobet, knowing Sinclair's men had been about the work of building a vessel, looked about him, thinking to spy a large canoe. But when he discerned the bark, he cried out, *"Munegoo!"* ("An island").

Sinclair, puzzled at first, broke into a grin of understanding. The bark was like no vessel these folk had ever seen. With its masts like two trees rising from a mass some forty feet in length, Sinclair's ship was to Kobet's eyes indeed a new-formed island that had magically appeared where no isle had been before.

"Let us take our friends for a turn about the harbor," Sinclair said, and Bjornsson and his crew readily obliged.

Great was the wonder of the forest folk as the mariners hoisted the sails, and the island now began to move. Excitement, not unmixed with fear, brought words of awe and admiration to Kobet's lips. As for the rest, they could only cling to the rail and stare in wide-eyed amazement as the coastline sped by.

"Kobet says ye have tamed a whale to carry ye on his back," Richard reported to his lord. "Now they are certain you are a god."

Sinclair laughed aloud. "If my fortunes fail in Scotland and the isles, then I can always find a welcome here. A god! Ha-ha! Old Friar Donal, may he rest in peace, how he would splutter to hear it! And what would the unlamented Bishop William say?"

When their guests were again on land, Sinclair's men laid on a great feast, with such an abundance of fresh meat and fish that none could fail to come away well satisfied. And when the feasting was done, Sinclair, with Richard as his interpreter, rose to address Kobet and his people:

"My friends," he said, "we go now to our lands over the sea. We will never forget your kindness and your many favors to the strangers in your land.

"One day, it may be, some of our people will come again to live among you. For ourself, we do not believe we shall see you any more." At this, a loud cry went up from the people, and Richard, to his dismay, saw Miledow cover her face with her hands.

Sinclair held up his hand for quiet, and when all were still, he resumed, "If we do not come again, yet will you live on in our heart as noble friends and generous benefactors. We will never, never forget you.

"Sometime, surely, priests will come from my land to these shores, and they will teach you of the great lord, Jesus, Son of the only God Hear them, we beseech you, for they are bearers of good tidings.

"But the sun is moving ever west, and soon the great tide will run to the sea. We must go, with sadness and with thanks. May the God of my people watch over you; may He bless you and keep you in health and joy. Farewell, my brothers. Farewell."

Sinclair embraced Kobet then, and said some few private words to him in parting. Then he ordered his men to the boats and bid them hasten to catch the tide.

Miledow, on seeing Richard step into Sinclair's boat, cried out, *"Aagei! Kesalk ak boosit! Nap! Nap!"*("Alas, I love him, and he sails away! I am dead! I am dead!")

Two of Kobet's men held her back, for she seemed bent on plunging into the water after her love. And Richard, seeing her weeping, struggling in the fast grip of the men, rose in his place as if he would leap from the boat and swim to shore.

"Richard! Sit down, sir!" Sinclair's voice cracked like a whip.

Richard turned, uncertain as to whether he must now defy this lord he had served so loyally. But Sinclair gave him no time to consider the thing. "Richard, will ye disgrace yourself before the men?"

Like one stricken in body and mind, Richard groped for his place in the stern and sank slowly down, his eyes fixed on the still writhing, weeping Miledow, her cries ringing in his ears, piercing his very soul. And as he watched, the girl suddenly tore loose from her captors and broke for the forest like a frightened doe. None followed her. She was quickly lost to view amid the greening trees.

Kobet and his people clustered even to the water's edge, calling out their farewells to the great lord, Glooscap, and his men. They saw the god-man cliḿ aboard his floating island, heard the singing of his men as they raised their white sails, and watched as the sudden swift surge of the tide carried the bark out of the harbor and onto the heaving bosom of the bay.

"Nu mo jag," the mariners chanted in the old Icelandic tongue, as they hauled away. *"Nu mo deg."* ("Now must I. Now must you.") It was a great satisfaction to the stout Bjornsson to feel his ship respond to the rhythmic effort of her singing crew.

But one man did not sing, did not cheer, did not lend a hand on the lines. Richard Sinclair, his head bowed on his knees, sat alone and apart in the stern, weeping unashamed.

Sinclair, looking back to the receding coast, caught a flash of movement from the corner of his eye. Looking up, he could just distinguish a slight figure poised on the very brow of that promontory where he had lately camped. And even as he looked, before he could start or speak, he saw the tiny figure launch out into the air and go hurtling down the breathless height to watery depths below. A silvery splash, then—nothing. The eternal waters closed the wound the fall had made, and on they rolled as they ever had and ever would.

Sinclair never spoke to Richard of Miledow again. If, in after whiles, the young knight talked of her to him, Sinclair would say only, "I know ye loved her, lad; I'm sure she loves ye still."

But for the Sinclairs, the one with the burden of his love, the other with that of his secret, the voyagers were as joyful a crew as ever put to sea. Bjornsson could talk of nothing but how well his bark behaved; Ingram of nothing but seeing Caithness again; Sigurd of Shetland; John Clarke of the wenches he meant to tumble; and each man of the thing nearest his own heart. Richard Sinclair spoke scarcely at all.

"Christ, Harry, but the lad's hard hit," Ingram murmured, as he and Sinclair stood aft of a fair morning, staring down at the foaming wake.

"Richard?"

"Aye"

Sinclair nodded. "His heart's nigh to breaking, Ingram. And my own heart aches for him. But he can bear this, and he must, himself alone. There's naught that you nor I nor any other man can say or do to help him. We must leave him to himself and pray he heals quickly."

"D'ye think ye may send him back there one day, Harry? To govern, I mean?" Ingram's kind eyes revealed his hope. "It might be that if he were to go back—"

"Ingram, if he were to go back, it might kill him." Sinclair shook his head. "No, my old friend, Richard will not go back to that place, not in my service, at any rate. If there's hope for him, it lies in Scotland."

"But, coz, I know ye love the lad. Wherefore—?"

And Sinclair told what he had seen.

"Jesu, Mary!" Ingram crossed himself. "Ah, God, Harry, the poor wild thing!"

"Aye. Christ have mercy on her. And on Richard. I could not tell him, coz. Ye can see that."

Ingram nodded. "We must let him keep what he has of her, Harry. God give him joy of his memories."

Bjornsson brought the bark across the bay and out onto the open sea. There a contrary wind blew up out of the northeast, and all the Shetlander's skill could not prevail against it.

"Now God damn the luck," the old man growled. "Here we are, bound away for home at last, and the plaguey wind turns against us."

Sinclair lent what encouragement he could. "Not all the Zenos in Venice could sail better, friend Bjornsson. If the wind go contrary, what can a man do but trim his sails and run before it till God in His good pleasure turns the wind around again?"

But God, evidently, was pleased with the wind as it was. And so for some days the bark was driven on a southerly course till, to Sinclair's amazed delight, they found themselves entering on the waters of a great bay. And spreading all before them lay a rocky coast, forested down to the water's edge.

"Now where under heaven are we?" Sinclair murmured, gazing in awe at the prospect before him.

"God He knows," said Bjornsson, anger and disgust mingling in his voice. "But 'tis not Kirkwall, and that is where I meant to take us."

"Will ye no look at those trees?" Sinclair shook his head in wonder. "Whatever land this is, we mean to have a look at it ere the wind comes round again to favor us. Make for land, pray. We will camp on this coast tonight."

51

Sunlight and birdsong called the voyagers from their rest. A glorious morning, green and gold, poured out over the rugged coast, sending forth a call to new beginnings and a new day in a land that lay as if new-minted from the stamp of Him that coined the planets and the stars.

"Jesu," murmured Sinclair, reverently, as he surveyed the scene spread out before him, "have we found paradise?"

"It is a fair land, truly, coz," said Ingram Gunn, his own voice hushed as if he stood in the nave of some great cathedral. "Can this be that Drogio Eyvindson told of?"

Sinclair shook his head. "No, sir. We have, by my reckoning, come so far south as to miss Estotiland and Drogio entirely."

"Where are we, then?"

Sinclair shrugged. "Kobet called his country Megumaage. Had we not come so far over open sea, I could be persuaded that this is but an extension of his land. But, as it is, I can believe only that we have come upon a country Eyvindson never knew."

" 'Tis so perfect," Ingram said, "I could be persuaded that no man ever set foot here till this very day. Even in Kobet's land, wild as it was, ye could see smoke curling up from the wigwams and breathe in the stench that is common wherever men abide. Here, it seems a sin so much as to piss, so pure it all appears, and so unspoiled."

Bjornsson came up, tugging his forelock. "Jarl Sinclair," he said, "the

390

wind yet blows contrary. Would ye have us board ship and try to beat our way back to our course?"

Sinclair shook his head. "As the wind conspires against our going, let us venture a little way inland, even to the crown of yonder hill, that we may overlook this ground and appraise its worth to Orkney."

"Ye do not mean to bide here long, my lord?"

Sinclair smiled. "Be easy, my friend," he said. "We know the men are yearning for home. We will not try their loyalty further by asking them to endure a long delay."

"God bless ye for that, my lord. Having come through the winter alive, we would be tempting fate, as ye might say, to tarry here over-long."

"We have a home too, friend Bjornsson, and a family that we love and long to see. But a few days here will cost us nothing, and will serve to sweeten our homecoming joy.

"Do you summon the mariners, and bid Sir Richard assemble his men, that we may make our purpose plain to them and assure 'em of our firm intent to be soon gone away."

When the men were gathered around him, Sinclair divulged his plan. "And," he said, concluding, "we promise ye that we will not linger here above a week. We know where your hearts are tending, as is our own heart also. But share this last adventure wi' us, wi' all the good will ye can muster, and I warrant ye our good friend Bjornsson will then carry us full swiftly over the sea to Kirkwall.

"Now, then. It seems to us prudent to leave here wi' the ship her stout captain and his crew. We know not if this place be inhabited, or what manner of folk may be dwelling hereabout. But, surely, it is the wiser course to have our ship well guarded. Lose that, and we lose our hope of summering in the isles.

"For the rest, we mean to lead ye overland to the top of yonder hill. It cannot be above two days distant, and it should afford us a vantage point from which to survey this country for some miles in all directions. That done, we will straightway descend and retrace our steps to this spot, from whence we will at once set sail for home.

"As 'tis yet well short o' noon, let the men-at-arms put on their armor and make ready. We march within the hour."

Those who would be going with Sinclair now bustled about, donning helmets and mail.

"God, but it's a grand morning for a stroll through the woodland," said Ingram to Richard Sinclair, attempting to kindle a smile in that young man's melancholy face.

But Richard said only, " 'Tis all one wi' me."

"Ah, come, lad. Who can be low on such a morning? Christ, my very blood is singing wi' the joy of it. An I were so young as you, I think I could run the whole way."

Richard managed a faint smile. "As could I, Sir Ingram, but there is
a lump o' lead within my breast that weights me down and slows my
step to creeping."

Ingram's kind eyes warmed with compassion. "God love ye, Richard,
I know ye are sadly burdened. But be o' good courage. If ye have not
your love beside ye, ye have at least this good fellowship and this good
work in the service o' the best o' lords. 'Tis not everything, I grant ye.
But many a man would be glad to have so much."

Richard, tapping his helmet down securely, replied, "I thank ye, Sir
Ingram, for your kind intent. I'll do my best to wear a pleasant face as
we swing along together. I do not mean for my private grief to mar the
joy o' this adventure."

"Well said, Richard. If ye can but pretend a joy ye do not feel, ye
may soon feel a joy that's not pretended."

Richard grinned. "I'll be some miles unraveling the sense o' that, I'll
wager. But you can explain it as we walk along."

Sinclair now said his farewells to Bjornsson and the mariners; and
with a wave of his arm, he summoned those who were bound away
with him through the wilderness. "Sir Richard," he said, "take the lead.
Sir Ingram and I will be at your back; the others to follow in good
order. Set us a lively pace, we charge ye, for we mean to see tomorrow's
sunset from the crown of yonder hill."

Richard nodded and stepped off briskly to a rhythm he alone could
hear. Sinclair and Gunn, Sigurd, Clarke, and the rest fell in behind the
young captain and followed him into the warm, breathless hush of the
forest.

At hour-long intervals, the marchers would stop and rest. During the
third such halt, Ingram, his helmet in his hands, his back leaning against
the trunk of a black walnut tree, declared, "We stop too often, Harry.
At this rate, we'll never reach that hill by tomorrow evening."

Sinclair, blotting the sweat from his brow, grinned and said, "Better
we get there later than not at all. This body's glad o' the rest, I'll no
deny it, and these bones right glad o' the chance to lie down."

"Pah! That comes o' lazing about all winter. Ye've gone soft, Harry.
Time was we'd range the woods all day wi'out so much as nooning. I
never knew ye to crave a respite then."

Sinclair laughed aloud. "What? Have ye become a boy again, so impatient of getting to where ye're going that ye begrudge each little stop
along the way?"

Ingram's smile was wicked. "I'll gladly slow my pace to yours, for
friendship's sake and out o' kindness for old bones. If ye can no endure
the rigors of the forced march, Harry, I'll no be—"

"Now hell and damnation, ye old braggart!" Sinclair donned his helmet and got to his feet. "Old bones, is it? Slow your pace to mine, hey?

"Richard!"

"My lord?"

"Lead us out now. We'll not halt again till sundown, understand?"

"Aye, my lord."

"Every man up! On your feet! You, John Clarke, strap on your sword, man, and gather up your gear." Sinclair, hands on hips, surveyed his little band. Then, satisfied that all were ready, he signaled Richard to step out. "And lively, mind, unless ye want to have us treading on your heels."

Richard, a grin playing about his lips, nodded and swung out, setting a hard, quick pace through the quiet aisles of the virgin forest. Mile on mile they marched, not laughing now, nor bantering, but only striding along like men pursued. Shoulder to shoulder, Ingram and Sinclair kept pace, each in his own mind determined not to yield to the weight of his armor, the oppressive warmth, or the protests of limbs and lungs.

The air, as they moved deeper into the forest, grew heavy and close. No wind stirred. Clouds of small insects swarmed before the faces of the men, assaulting eyes and nostrils with maddening persistence. Throats ached with thirst, and trickles of sweat snaked down backs and sides.

"Jesu," wheezed John Clarke, flapping his hand at the gnats that danced before his face, "this is turning into a by-Our-Lady footrace."

Sigurd, beside him, licked his dusty lips and said, "Save your wind to cool your porridge, friend. I can spare none o' mine to chat wi' you."

Behind him, Clarke could hear men stumble where no obstacle was. Ahead, he could see Sinclair and Ingram, their helmets catching an occasional flash of sunlight as it filtered down through the dense foliage, going grimly along in tandem, like a team hitched to the chariot of time—a team that could not, would not go down till time itself should halt and cry out for a rest.

Sinclair, steaming in the oven of his armor, began to question his own sanity. What boy play was this, in God's name? Here he was, of an age when most men took their exercise in going from bed to table, charging along at this killing pace, and all because his silly pride would not let pass a gibe from Ingram Gunn.

And Ingram, for his part, had long since begun to feel profound regret for having set this play a-going. He shook his head and grinned at his own folly.

Sinclair, seeing that grin, mistook it altogether. He set his lips the tighter and doggedly marched on. Almighty God! Had Ingram gone mad? Or had he indeed grown young again? To grin like that when surely his legs must be as knotted and his feet as sore as Sinclair's own! Why, the man was past bearing, truly.

An hour and five miles more, and now the breath began to whistle in Sinclair's dry, dust-coated nostrils. Sweat ran into his eyes and stung unmercifully. His shoulders ached, and he felt as if there were an arrow lodged between them. Another quarter hour of this and, pride or no pride, he would have to yield. 'Twould be gall and wormwood to his very soul, but God, how good it would be to—

"Halt!" cried Richard Sinclair, holding up his hand.

So sudden was the cry, and so mechanical had his marching become, that Henry's legs kept moving until he actually collided with his young kinsman. "Pardon," he croaked. "We—we could not help it."

"Wherefore have we halted?" rasped Ingram, staring at Richard with glazed eyes.

Richard's lips worked a bit before the word would come. Then he said, "I make it near to sundown, though 'tis mortal hard to tell in this dense shade. Jarl Sinclair bade me lead ye on till then. I think 'tis time we made our camp and supped."

No one gainsaid him. Few had breath sufficient, and none was of a mind to disagree.

The men took their simple meal in silence, and early sought out such comfort as the forest floor could offer aching bones. Night settled over the woodland. The marchers slept like the dead.

It was well after dawn before the first man crawled stiffly from his earthen couch. And Sinclair and Ingram were the last to rise. The lord of Orkney eyed his loyal kinsman ruefully and slowly shook his head.

"Afore God, coz," he said, "that was a merry game ye set us to. My whole frame cried out in protest when first I tried to get up on my legs this morning."

Ingram, massaging his lower back with both hands, grinned wryly. "I'll concede myself a fool for starting it, if you'll concede yourself the same for playing along."

"Done and done," said Sinclair, grinning in his turn and offering his hand. He turned to his captain then and said, "Sir Richard, we've no doubt ye'll lead us to the hill this very day, but do so leisurely, we pray."

"Very leisurely, my lord," Richard said. "For if ye mean to go faster than a snail's pace, ye must look elsewhere for a man to lead ye."

"Is this rebellion, Richard?" asked Sinclair, amused.

"Aye, my lord. For my feet are in revolt against my will, nor will they foot it as I will, but do drag themselves along like laggard 'prentice boys to Monday morning's labors."

A frugal breakfast and an unhurried start made stiffened limbs somewhat more limber. Richard observed the hourly halts with all the single-minded devotion of a beadsman fingering his paternosters, and so in easy stages the marchers covered the few remaining miles. They made their nooning in the shadow of the hill, and shortly after noon they were standing at its base.

"God bless me," said Sinclair, staring up in awe, " 'tis a goodly climb we have before us."

Ingram grinned, mischief in his eyes. " 'Twill serve to work the stiff-ness out," he said.

"Nay," protested Sinclair, laughing, "bait me no more. We'll take this slowly, coz, or not at all."

"I plead the latter cause," declared John Clarke. "There's naught hereabout I care to see so much as to make me want to clamber up so mortal high."

"Well, John Clarke, ye can bide here if ye like. And so may any of like mind," said Sinclair. "Is there any other who does not choose to go? None? Well, Clarke, take your ease, then. We will wake ye on our return."

"Ye cannot mean to leave me here alone, my lord?" Clarke looked about uneasily. "There may be wild beasts or wilder folk lurking nearby."

Sinclair chuckled. "Then I fear ye must struggle along up wi' the rest of us, John Clarke, for no one else cares to remain below. "

"Lead on, my lord," said Clarke, glumly. "I will follow."

The way before them was marked by a narrow trail, as if worn there by frequent passage. But no sign did they see, none had they seen, of human habitation. Whatever folk had made this path were now nowhere about. But that human feet had made it, Sinclair doubted not.

"Well, but where are they then, my lord?" asked Richard.

"Richard, I do not know. It could be a plague has carried 'em off. Or it may be they have, like Kobet's folk, summer dwellings nearer the sea. For my part, I am content to go our way unmolested. The way is hard enough wi'out we meet with any who might make us feel unwelcome."

Upward they toiled, the trees thinning out, the sun pouring down hotter and brighter as they neared the summit. Richard still led, with Sinclair at his back and Ingram close behind.

"We—we are nearly there, my lord," puffed Richard, pulling himself a step farther along with the help of a low-hanging limb.

"Don't try to— Ugh! Ingram, dammit, mind where ye're walking! Ye near upended me." Sinclair, bumped from behind, narrowly escaped a fall. He turned to remonstrate with his cousin and saw that Ingram had himself gone down.

"Ha-ha! Old Timbertoes!" Sinclair cried. And he bent to help Ingram to his feet. But the hand he gripped responded not to his touch. The finger did not move at all. "Ingram!"

As his men clustered around, Sinclair went down on one knee beside his friend and, with a mighty effort, turned him over on his back. Ingram's eyes stared up unseeing, his face contorted almost beyond all likeness to the face that Sinclair loved.

Sinclair's fingers tore at the lacings and fumbled to touch his kins-man's breast under the coat of heavy mail. Nothing. That heart so freely given to the service of his lord and friend was now forever stilled.

Slowly, Sinclair raised his head, his face a mask of horror and disbelief. His eyes darted from man to man, as if he sought among them some one man with power to restore life to his fallen friend. Then this lord over the destinies of so many men bowed his head, and for the one man he loved most among them all he offered up the tribute of his tears.

When he had recovered himself sufficiently, Sinclair dispatched Richard and Sigurd to the beach to summon the mariners. The others he commanded to bear Ingram's body back down the hill and to prepare for him a grave under a granite outcropping that would forever shield this gallant knight from summer's rains and winter's snows.

For two days and two nights, Sinclair and his men kept watch beside the grave. On the morning of the third day, Sigurd and Richard returned with Bjornsson and his crew.

Sinclair ordered old Matteo, the Venetian armorer, to take his tools and work as best he could an effigy in the stone that would forever guard the body of his friend. Matteo, working with hammer and spike, punched out the figure of a knight in surcoat and basinet. Then he borrowed Richard's sword, laid it on the stone to determine its length, and tapped out its outline in the hard, resisting rock.

"We will have his shield, Matteo," Sinclair said, "bearing his arms so that in future time anyone passing this spot will know a Gunn lies here."

Sinclair traced in the dust the triangular outline of a shield and drew therein the crescent, mullet, and buckle of the Gunns. And these, as well as he could with his blunted spike, Matteo translated into stone.

Sinclair laid his hand on the shoulder of the sweating armorer. "Well done, my friend," he said. "Now make a line across the blade o' the sword, as if 'twere broken, to signify a warrior's death."

That done, Sinclair, his helmet in the crook of his arm, a soft breeze riffling his graying locks, turned and addressed the men.

"My friends, this loss goes deep. Our heart is rent by a blow so swift and cruel and all unlooked for that it can never be healed and whole again. This—dear, beloved, gallant friend was more than a friend to us. In all things, he was as our other self, privy to our most secret thought, wise in counsel, faithful in all things.

"God hath been ever liberal and openhanded wi' us, and we have received from His unfailing bounty gifts, honors, and riches far beyond the common lot of men. But nothing—nothing that He ever gave was half so great or half so dear as the friendship of this good, brave, honest knight."

Sinclair paused, fighting back the sob that welled up in his throat. He shook his head, raised his eyes, and said, "So now we give back to God this friend He gave to us.

"Lord Christ, receive the soul o' Thy servant, Ingram Gunn. Let not his human frailties weigh heavily against him in Thy judgment. Be merciful unto him, we pray, and grant him a place of honor in the company o' Thy saints."

Sinclair knelt then beside the grave and, making the sign of the cross above it, murmured, "Ingram, Ingram, my dear good friend, farewell."

Pale and controlled now, Sinclair got to his feet and donned his helmet. "Sir Richard," he said, "lead us back to the coast. We will leave straightway for home."

Full thirty days and more Bjornsson steered eastward under friendly skies over a running sea. And as they neared the coast of Kirkwall, the eager men massed forward, each hoping to be first to catch a glimpse of home.

But Sinclair, wrapped in his cloak against the brisk wind and the blown spray, stood alone in the stern, looking back at the far horizon to the west.

"Land! Land, by God!" someone—Sigurd?—shouted. And a lusty loud huzza went up from a score of throats.

A faint smile tugged at the corners of Sinclair's mouth. He turned slowly and went forward to join the men.

Reunion with Janet was painfully sweet. And when Sinclair told her of Ingram's death, they wept together for their lost kinsman and friend.

"Harry, he loved you so."

"Janet, he loved you."

Janet smiled then through her tears. "And yet he never once by word or look revealed the burden on his heart."

Sinclair grimaced in pain. "That heart was nearest mine save yours alone, Janet. In truth, I think that half my own heart lies buried in that distant land with him."

"We will have masses sung for him, and—oh, Jesu, Mary! Harry! Is not old Meg's prophecy fulfilled? Did she not speak of Ingram's finding such a grave?"

"Aye, she did, Janet. She had the sight, there's no denying, but whether from God or Lucifer I would not care to wager. I wonder—" Sinclair shook his head and made as if to smile the thought away. But Janet would have none of it.

She clutched at his arm and said, "Do you not wonder, husband, do you not fear what it was she saw for you?"

Sinclair laughed. "Why, insofar as it was good, and insofar as it hath proved true, I do not fear it, Janet."

"It would be strange indeed, sir, were you to fear what has already come to pass," retorted Janet, her pursed lips showing her disapproval of her lord's lame attempt at wit. "But did she not say you would die by the sword?"

"Something like," said Sinclair, smiling and drawing Janet to his breast. "But my roving's done, my battles are all over. I mean to bide here with you, my old love, and assign to others the labor of bringing out the wealth of the western lands."

Janet snuggled close. "D'you mean it, Harry? Truly?"

"Aye, lass." Sinclair stroked his lady's soft, still blooming cheek. "I'm past fifty and ready for the chimney corner now. You and I will grow old together and leave to our sons the work we have begun."

But old Meg proved the better prophet at the last.

In August of 1400, two years after Sinclair's return to Orkney, England's fourth Henry invaded Scotland. Even as his army reached Edinburgh, his fleet sailed north to the Orkneys and launched lightning raids on several of the isles, looting and burning in the timeless fashion of Southron troops.

Sinclair, at the first alarm, dispatched Janet and the younger children to the relative safety of Rosslyn. "No tears now, lass. Do you give greeting to my brother and to Lady Isabel, and keep a smiling face before the children. I greatly doubt that Henry's forces will find their way to Rosslyn, and should they try our mettle here at Kirkwall, surely these walls are proof against their bolts and bombards."

Janet clung to her husband. "Send for me so soon as danger's past."

"Aye, and we'll call our Harry and our Willie home from Norway, too, and keep late summer festival in joy and peace, my old love. Get ye gone, now; God keep ye. Our trust is in these massy walls."

Had Sinclair but kept within the walls! But when the watchers on his ramparts roused the hall with word of British sail in Scapa Flow, not two miles from the beach at Kirkwall, Jarl Henry, his burnished armor gleaming in the summer sun, rode out at the head of his men to repel the invader, and to meet that soldier's doom old Meg had prophesied for him so long ago.

That night, as the first pale stars were gleaming over Rosslyn's lofty towers, a little page came scampering all breathless into the great hall where Janet and Lady Isabel sat to their supper with Sir John Sinclair.

"Sir John! Sir John!"

"What's amiss, lad?" the knight demanded, starting up from his chair. "Are the Southrons come?"

"Nay, Sir John, the towers—the towers are all ablaze with light, as if the castle were on fire. An yet there is no fire anywhere."

"Christ help!" murmured Sir John, crossing himself. "It is the ancient omen. A Sinclair chief is dead."

Before the first snow fell at Rosslyn, Henry Sinclair's body was borne in armor to rest uncoffined in the ranks of his noble forebears. Lady

Janet, escorted by Willie and young Harry—now lord of Orkney in his
father's stead—followed her husband's body dry-eyed and in stoic calm.
Her tears had all been shed that night the towers flamed.

> Seemed all on fire that chapel proud
> > Where Roslin's chiefs uncoffined lie,
> Each baron for a sable shroud
> > Sheathed in his iron panoply.
>
> Seem'd all on fire within, around,
> > Deep sacristy and altar's pale,
> Shone every pillar foliage bound,
> > And glimmer'd all the dead men's mail.
>
> Blaz'd battlement and pinnet high,
> > Blaz'd every rose-carved buttress fair—
> So still they blaze when fate is nigh
> > The lordly line of high St. Clair.

                                               Sir Walter Scott

L'envoi

Deep in the western wilds, around a small fire that served to hold
the shadows at bay, men, their faces the color of earth and old leaves,
gathered to listen to the teller of tales:

> ... Glooscap
> Invited all to a parting banquet
> By the great Lake Minas shore
> On the silver water's edge.
> And when the feast was over,
> Entered his great canoe
> And sailed away over the water,
> And the shining waves of Minas;
> And they looked in silence at him
> Until they could see him no more.
> Yet, after they ceased to behold him
> They still heard his voice in song,
> The wonderful voice of the master.
> But the sounds grew fainter and fainter,
> And softer in the distance,
> Till at last they died away.

A white moon rose over the western waters, lending its pale light to the hunter and the hunted in the fields of night. Away to the south, that same moon shone, its beams filtering down through the summer canopy of a great forest to splash coldly on a massive slab of stone. Around the rock, wild blackberry tendrils curled; and the tall grasses, helmeted like sentinels, kept their silent watch.

But the subtle, slow invading moss had already penetrated this ineffectual picket, and was even now encroaching on the crudely outlined figure of an armored knight that hands long dead had hammered into the living stone.